A Home at Honeysuckle Farm

CHRISTIE BARLOW

A division of HarperCollins Publishers
www.harpercollins.co.uk

Harper*Impulse* an imprint of
HarperCollins*Publishers*
The News Building
1 London Bridge Street
London SE1 9GF

www.harpercollins.co.uk

This paperback edition 2018

2

First published in Great Britain in ebook format by
HarperCollins*Publishers* 2018

A catalogue record for this book
is available from the British Library

ISBN: 9780008240929

This novel is entirely a work of fiction.
The names, characters and incidents portrayed in it are
the work of the author's imagination. Any resemblance to
actual persons, living or dead, events or localities is
entirely coincidental.

Typeset in Birka by Palimpsest Book Production Ltd,
Falkirk, Stirlingshire

Printed and bound by CPI Group (UK) Ltd, Croydon, CR0 4YY

Christie Barlow is the bestselling author of *A Year in the Life of a Playground Mother*, *The Misadventures of a Playground Mother*, *Kitty's Countryside Dream*, *Lizzie's Christmas Escape*, *Evie's Year of Taking Chances* and *The Cosy Canal Boat Dream*. She lives in Staffordshire with her four kids, horses, chickens and a mad cocker spaniel.

Her writing career came as somewhat of a surprise when she decided to write a book to teach her children a valuable life lesson and show them that they are capable of achieving their dreams. The book she wrote to prove a point went on to become a #1 bestseller in the UK, USA and Australia.

Christie is an ambassador for the @ZuriProject, which raises money and awareness for communities in Uganda. She is also Literary Editor for www.mamalifemagazine.co.uk, bringing you all the latest news and reviews from the book world.

She loves to hear from her readers and you can get in touch via her website, Twitter and Facebook page.

🐦 @ChristieJBarlow
📘 ChristieJBarlow
www.christiebarlow.com

Also by Christie Barlow

A Year in the Life of a Playground Mother
The Misadventures of a Playground Mother
Kitty's Countryside Dream
Lizzie's Christmas Escape
Evie's Year of Taking Chances
The Cosy Canal Boat Dream

For Sharon Pillinger,
Whose tireless cheering and continuous
excitement for my books has never
gone unnoticed.
Thank-you.
Love AB x

Prologue

At ten years of age, Brook Bridge village was all I'd ever known. Nestled right in the heart of the countryside on the outskirts of Staffordshire, it was a quaint little village that radiated olde-worlde charm with its narrow streets and timber-framed properties, many of which boasted thatched roofs. It was a close-knit community where everyone was friendly and people looked out for each other. I loved everything about living there.

The summer months were always the busiest, when visitors would flock to admire the old, striking Tudor buildings and explore the nooks and crannies of the shabby-chic shops and historic pubs that lined the cobblestoned high street.

I'd look forward to Sunday mornings, my favourite time of the week, when I'd stroll with Grandie over the arched stone bridge which led us to a quaint courtyard that was a magnet for painters and photographers. On the corner we'd relax outside The Old Tea Shop, hugging our hot chocolate and treating ourselves to one of Mrs Jones' scrumptious cakes that were truly delicious.

I lived with my mum on the fringes of the village at Honeysuckle Farm, in the annexe which was attached to Grandie's three-storey rustic brick farmhouse. I'd felt safe ambling about the barns, riding my bike over the uneven grass and splashing about in the stream. The countryside surrounding the house stretched for miles and in the quilted fields of golden and green squares knitted together by the hedgerows grew potatoes and root vegetables for all those delicious autumn stews that Mum would rustle up. And not forgetting the abundance of fresh eggs laid by the chickens which roamed freely around the farm. It was simply the best place to live.

Beyond the corncribs there was a rickety old wooden bridge that arched over the trickling stream with its rust-coloured willow bushes growing on the banks; this was my favourite spot. I'd sit on the huge grey rock at the foot of the maple tree and watch Billy, the chestnut Welsh cob, graze in the field.

I'd just broken up for summer, the long school holidays stretched out before me, and I was happily waiting for my friend Grace to come over for a play day. As I jumped and splashed through the shallow waters of the stream in my Wellington boots, I didn't have a care in the world.

Little did I know that my life was about to drastically change ...

* * *

Happily skipping back towards the farmhouse, with the promise of buttery scrambled eggs on homemade granary bread, I flung open the door to the porch that housed an array of boots, coats and umbrellas. Kicking off my muddy wellies outside the back door, I felt slight disappointment that there were no delicious aromas wafting from the kitchen. Marley was curled up in his basket at the foot of the Aga, but the sleepy spaniel never even attempted to open his eyes when I walked into the room.

It was at that moment that I heard raised voices coming from the living room. Barely daring to breathe, I tiptoed down the hallway, my eyes falling towards the gap in the living-room door.

Grandie was standing at the far end of the room, his hands resting on the mantelpiece of the huge stone fireplace, his head bent low. Mum was sitting on the edge of the coffee table, her eyes firmly fixed on the floor.

He let out a long shuddering breath and turned back towards Mum, who shifted her gaze towards him.

'Jesus Christ, Rose,' he shouted at her, 'when the hell were you going to tell me?'

Mum was now physically shaking but she didn't answer him.

I'd no idea what was happening or what Mum was supposed to have done, but a feeling of trepidation rushed through my body. An eerie atmosphere swathed me, one I'd never felt before, cocooned in my perfect idyll.

Rooted to the spot, I waited anxiously to see what would happen next.

As Grandie's voice continued to boom I felt scared, my heart hammering against my chest. I'd never heard Grandie shout before, and I'd never heard him and Mum argue. I didn't like it, I didn't like it one little bit.

'Everything I've done for you, and this is how you repay me.' Grandie's face was flushed.

Mum hung her head once more, unable to look him in the eye.

'I thought I'd brought you up better than this. How could you betray me like this? Have you no shame?' He snorted with disgust. 'Get out of my sight, I never want to see you again.' His face was thunderous, his eyes dark.

Those words jolted Mum.

I held my breath, not daring to move.

'W-w-what do you mean?' Mum stuttered, her cool façade now slipping and tears beginning to stream down her face.

'Exactly that, get out of my sight,' his voice boomed again, causing her to spring to her feet.

'Are you serious?' This time her eyebrows shot up and she dared to hold his gaze.

'Deadly serious.'

The words hung in the air.

'Right then, in that case I'll go and you'll be sorry,' she spat, storming towards the door. 'I'll go where you can't find me, and I'll take Alice. You'll never see her again, if that's how you feel.'

'You are not taking Alice,' thundered Grandie.

'I will and I am. I'm her mother, you can't stop me,' she shouted through her frustrated tears.

Her words penetrated my heart. Feeling shocked, my eyes misted with tears.

'How can you do this to me? You know how much I love that girl. If you walk out that door with Alice we're finished ... forever.' He moved towards the table and thumped his hand down, sending a cup and saucer crashing to the ground.

Mum was about to fling open the door and I was suddenly terrified of being caught standing on the other side. She couldn't discover me listening to their conversation. For a split second, Mum hovered with her hand on the door handle and gave a dismissive shrug. 'If that's what you want ...'

Sensing my knees were about to crumble, I quickly crouched down at the side of the grandfather clock and held my breath. Her voice trailed off as she flounced past me and disappeared up the stairs. She didn't spot me, much to my relief.

Forcing myself to stand up, I stole a quick look into the living room before racing back through the kitchen and thrusting my feet back inside my boots. I ran and ran over the fields until I flung my hands around Billy's neck, who nuzzled my pockets looking for carrots.

I thought back to Grandie who had been slumped down in his chair. He'd raked his hand through his hair before doing something I'd never seen him do before: he cried.

I'd no idea what he and Mum were arguing about but just twenty-four hours later I was strapped into the back of a taxi, tightly hugging my teddy bear. Of course, I'd asked where we were going but Mum wasn't forthcoming with any answers.

5

'Stop asking questions Alice, you'll see when we get there,' was all she offered me.

Mum's best friend, Connie, had clutched on to her arms at the bottom of the steps to the farmhouse. 'I don't understand why you're leaving. Where are you going? What's happened?' The barrage of questions tripped off her tongue, but Mum never answered any of them. In a trance-like state Mum muttered something then swiftly pressed a kiss on to Connie's cheek before hugging her and clambering into the passenger seat of the taxi. She never even gave as much as a fleeting glance backwards.

I had no idea where we were going or why. All I knew was I had this wretched, nauseous pain in the pit of my stomach. Feeling scared, I snuggled my teddy bear and blinked back the tears. As the taxi pulled away from Honeysuckle Farm, I looked up and took a last glance towards the farmhouse. There was Grandie, standing in the bedroom window. He placed a hand on the pane of glass in front of him and I did the same. His tearful, saddened eyes never left mine but as the taxi reached the ornate black iron gates at the end of the drive he got smaller and smaller, before he finally disappeared out of sight, and the pain twisted in my heart.

Little did I know that this would be last time I saw Grandie for thirteen years.

Chapter 1

New York City, thirteen years later ...

Hearing a knock on the door, I knew immediately it would be Molly, you could set your watch by her. Molly Gray had been my best friend for the last three years. She was a proper city girl, born and bred in New York and living in a second-floor apartment near the corner of 57th Street and 9th Avenue on the west side of town. I, on the other hand, had arrived thirteen years ago as a terrified and bewildered child, and I had always felt I struggled to fit in. I was now living in a dingy flat in a less salubrious area of Manhattan, a place full of unfamiliar sounds and smells and where everything and everyone were constantly on the move. It was a million miles away from the country village upbringing I'd had, and often, I'd long to hear the familiar sounds of a cockerel or the bleat of a lamb. Occasionally I'd dream that I could freeze the constant motion and walk the streets silently, at my own pace.

Every Sunday morning, come rain or shine, Molly would power her legs around Central Park for a good hour or so before grabbing a coffee and a catch-up at mine when she'd finished.

'The door's open,' I shouted, 'I'm in the kitchen.'

Molly soon appeared in the doorway, her eyes sparkling and her cheeks aglow.

'Morning,' she panted, switching off the latest gadget that was measuring her performance and heart rate. 'Not a bad time,' she muttered to herself.

Her slender body was poured into the tightest, most flamboyant running gear you'd ever set eyes on and an abundance of rust-coloured hair was escaping her pony-tail as she hooked it behind her ears.

'This was sticking out of your mail box,' she said, placing the flyer down on the table in front of me before slumping on to the chair. 'That's right up your street,' she said, sneakily pinching a piece of buttered toast from my plate then grinning at me.

Auditions for Wicked
The Majestic Theatre
Broadway, New York City

'What, are you saying I'm a witch?' I smiled up at her, hugging my third mug of coffee of the morning.

'A good witch,' she chuckled, 'but this morning looking

more like one of those English eighties rock stars. What's with the make-up thing?' she waggled her finger towards my face before standing up and sliding her Nike-swathed feet over the brown tatty lino that had seen better days towards the coffee pot.

'It wasn't the best night I've ever had, let's put it that way,' I answered, placing my mug on the table and looking up at Molly.

'I'll pour us both a coffee and you can tell me all about it. It can't be that bad.' Her tone was sympathetic.

'Sorry, but there's no more coffee, I've run out ... again.'

Molly peered at the coffee pot then back to me, her expression a mix of surprise and sympathy, but she had no idea how difficult things really were. I immediately felt guilty for not sharing my woes with her, but the last thing I wanted was pity.

'You can have this one,' I offered, sliding the mug over the table towards her.

'It's okay, you look like you need it more than me. I'll grab a water from the faucet.'

'I don't get paid until tomorrow.' I sighed, 'But there's a couple of slices of bread left if you fancy some more toast.'

Molly gave me an inquisitive stare before pulling open the door to the refrigerator. Every shelf was bare except for a mouldy block of cheese wedged right at the back.

'What are you planning on eating today?'

I shrugged, feeling totally helpless. I hadn't even thought that far ahead yet. I didn't want to think that far ahead.

'Dunno, I'll probably end up with a couple of Twinkies,' I replied partly in jest, but deep down I knew if things carried on the way they were this could become reality.

'Have things really got that bad?' Molly's tone was now a little more serious.

'Oh Molly, I just can't make ends meet, no matter how hard I try,' I answered, not meeting her gaze. 'It's really difficult to find work, with a decent wage, working decent hours. Every job I go for has already been filled or the salary only just about covers my rent, leaving nothing for anything else. I don't want to be working dead-end jobs; I want a career, I want to work in the area I'm trained for, but I just don't get past the auditions. Something has got to give. I can't carry on like this.'

Molly shut the refrigerator door before squeezing my hand, but stopped short of telling me it was going to be all right. It wasn't. In fact, it hadn't been all right for the last few years, but lately things had been slipping further out of my control and I was unable to hide it any more. There was a pile of unpaid bills sitting on the table in front of me and to make matters worse, I was already a month behind with my rent.

'Let me help you.'

I didn't realise I was holding back the tears, but I clearly was, as her kind gesture soon had them flooding down my cheeks.

I shook my head, 'Thank you, that's a kind offer but no, you have your own bills to pay. This is my problem, not yours.'

'Don't be crazy Alice, you're my friend, my best friend. I

can stretch to some groceries for you and help you sort out this mess. Have you told your mom?' she probed lightly.

'No,' I confirmed, 'the diner she was working at has just closed down and I know she's in a similar situation. I didn't want to go worrying her.'

Molly gave me a concerned look and pulled out a chair and sat down at the table opposite me.

I thought back over my last three jobs and blew out a breath. I'd handed out leaflets in Times Square for a pittance, worked unsociable hours in a twenty-four-hour burger joint which was usually frequented by drunks and undesirables, and currently I was employed as a cleaner at a theatre on Broadway. The money barely covered my rent, never mind extras for food or nights out. I couldn't afford new clothes and every day was a struggle. This wasn't how it was supposed to be.

Last night had been a turning point for me, I'd decisively told myself that something had to change. I needed to take control.

'I had dreams once Molly, and look at me now. Can you remember when we first met?'

Molly smiled, 'Of course I remember.'

Molly and I had met three years ago while doing an impression of a tin of sardines on the subway. It had been rush hour and we'd been travelling in the same direction towards Times Square, holding on to the same metal handrail. We'd both noticed him at the same time.

'Look at those lashes, jealous!' Molly had whispered to me and I'd chuckled.

I couldn't help but stare at his bright-blue eyes, his rugged cheekbones and those eyelashes. Molly had been right, they were incredible. Any girl this side of the city, actually any side of the city would have died for those lashes. His attire, which consisted of a bright-purple velvet suit, a brown top hat and a gold bow tie, was causing a little commotion with another group of girls sitting nearby. And I was mesmerised too, he had a certain aura about him.

The train slowed down and he jumped off at 42nd Street. But just before he did, he'd turned to us with a twinkle in his eye and whipped out two golden tickets to Willy Wonka's Chocolate Factory.

As we hopped off the train close behind him, we watched as he disappeared through the hordes of people.

'It's not every day you get a ticket to chocolate heaven,' Molly sighed, and I laughed, stuffing the ticket inside my handbag. We walked and giggled all the way to Times Square.

In that short walk, something between us just clicked and we got on like a house on fire. I told her I'd just graduated from performing arts and about my dream to perform on Broadway.

Molly invited me for a coffee and we strolled up 6th Avenue in the New York sunlight towards the radio station, the place where Molly had worked since leaving school. She told me she'd started off as a general dog's body, answering the telephone, making endless cups of coffee and generally avoiding the wandering hands of the guy on the news desk. But now, with her quick wit, hard work and determination she'd secured a place behind the mic and worked the afternoon show between five and seven o'clock on weekdays.

I was in awe of her, and as we walked through the glass doors of the studio, it felt like stepping into a different world. In the foyer were signed photographs of numerous famous people that had been interviewed at the station and Molly told me that she'd met most of them. It was exciting to think she'd rubbed shoulders with the rich and famous and was becoming successful in her own right. I too wanted my name up in lights, I wanted to be interviewed by radio stations and see my name splashed across magazines.

Now that I'd graduated, there was a fire in my belly. I was searching for jobs on Broadway and was excited for what the future would hold.

After the coffee, Molly invited me to join her in the studio and sit in on her radio show. The excitement kicked in as she gestured for me to sit opposite her. I watched in amazement while she put on her headphones and pulled the mic towards her and got the show underway. After the first song had played, Molly snapped a photo in the studio with us holding up the golden tickets and tweeted #findwillywonka. Within the hour, Twitter had responded and the actor Joe Tucker had replied.

That same evening Joe had invited us to one of his shows. It had been sensational, the performance out of this world. He'd met us for a drink afterwards and in his kindness arranged numerous auditions for me, but time after time the competition had been fierce, and I just hadn't been good enough to secure a part, and the rejection letters littered the door mat. As each month passed, I felt stardom slipping further and further out of reach and I began to feel like a failure, struggling to fulfil my dream career. That's when I'd begun to take any job, work any hours to pay for my own place and how I'd found myself in the situation I was now in ...

Molly took a sip of her water. 'Come on then, what happened last night?' she asked, dragging me from my memories.

I shot a look around the dingy kitchen. Wallpaper was peeling from the damp spot in the corner of the room, the brown lino was curling at the edges and there was barely any light seeping through the kitchen window. Every surface seemed to be piled with flyers, newspapers and unpaid bills.

I exhaled, then took a breath.

'I needed time to think, so took a walk along 5th Avenue, until I found myself looking up at the Empire State Building. You know ...' I paused, 'I've never been up to the top of that building until last night. I was standing there, looking up towards the lights at the top, when I heard someone calling my name. I couldn't believe it when I saw Madison, a girl I went to college with. She was selling tickets outside and slipped me a free pass to the top. And as I was making my way towards the 86th floor I could feel myself becoming teary, something inside changed,' I began to explain.

'What do you mean?'

I blinked back the tears and swallowed down the lump in my throat. 'The view was spectacular, and in all the time I've lived here, in New York, I've never seen anything like it. I stared out across the city ... at the million lights sparkling in the night sky, and it was simply breath-taking. And it might be the most beautiful place in the world, Mol ... but,' I prepared myself as the words left my mouth, 'I'm not happy.'

Almost immediately, Molly reached over the table and grasped both my hands.

'Oh, Alice,' she said softly, 'what can I do to help?'

I could tell by the look on her face she'd no clue to how I was feeling. Of course, living in New York had its good moments, but there was something inside me telling me I just didn't belong here anymore, I didn't fit in – and I never really had. Even at school, I was the girl with the pale freckled face, the English girl with the funny accent who always stood out.

Mum would never talk about the reason we moved to New York, and as time went on it became even more difficult to broach the subject with her.

My voice quivered, 'I'm not sure there is anything you can do ... I must have been standing at the top of the Empire State Building for ages, lost in my own thoughts, staring out over the city. And then, all around me, applause erupted. I looked round to see a crowd of people had gathered around this couple. There was a man bending down on one knee looking up at a woman grasping a burgundy box. You could see how much he loved her and right there and then, he proposed! What a proposal, Molly! It was so romantic, all hearts and flowers, something out of a fairy-tale but ... it just made me think, what have I got here?'

'You're not too shabby,' she gave me a half-hearted smile, trying to lighten the mood. 'I know loads of men who'd give their right arm for a date with you ... except maybe I would lose the eighties rock make-up first.'

'I'm lonely Mol, sat here in this dingy flat with hardly any money, working any job I can to make ends meet. Surely there's got to be more to life than this?'

Over time I'd begun to resent this flat more and more. In the last week alone my sleep had been disturbed nearly every night. Music pounded through the wafer-thin walls from the flat above, the lampshade shaking from the vibrating drum and bass. Often, I'd spend my nights shouting expletives and banging on the ceiling with the handle of the broom, and when that didn't work I'd bury my head under the pillow in an attempt to block out the sound.

'I'd never realised things had got this bad,' said Molly, her attention unwavering. 'Let me see if there's anything at the radio station.'

'It's too late,' I said softly, 'it's too late.' Casually leaning both my hands on the table, I sighed.

Molly gave an infinitesimal nod, taking in what I was saying, and we sat there in silence for a moment.

'In time, you'll meet the right man,' she offered.

I managed a smile. 'It's not just that.' There had been something on my mind for a while, a niggle, an itch that needed scratching, but I just hadn't said the words out loud.

I took a deep breath. This was the time to clear my conscience and confess all while I had Molly's full attention. She was my best friend and I'd no idea how she was going to react to my next bit of news. But I managed to splutter the words out: 'I'm thinking of going back to England.'

I watched as the words registered on Molly's face. Her expression changed then she sprang upright in her seat like a jack-in-the-box being unleashed for the very first time.

'Alice, England's over 3,000 miles away,' she finally said, breaking the silence. It was difficult for her to keep her voice steady.

'I know, but it's been playing on my mind for a while,' I answered truthfully.

Molly's bottom lip wobbled. 'How long is a while? And why didn't I have any idea about any of this?' She fiddled with the strap of her Garmin with a grief-stricken look on her face.

'Maybe the last six months or so, but even more so since I received this,' I admitted, exhaling slowly and turning my laptop towards her so she could read the message I'd received at the beginning of the week via Facebook from Grace.

Grace Anderson and I had known each other from the year dot. Our mums had been the best of friends and as children, we'd gone everywhere together. Not only were we in the same class at school but we'd shared a passion for dance and drama, and every Saturday, dressed in all things pinkish, Grace's mum

Connie had dropped her off at Grandie's ballet school, where my mum had worked as a dance teacher. Everyone thought we were sisters as we twirled with our identical long plaited coffee-coloured hair, blue eyes and a string of freckles across our noses. Back then, we had been inseparable, the best of friends until the day I left.

When I'd left, I remembered Grace clinging to me on the step, making me promise to write to her as soon as I could. I never broke that promise and never lost touch. Over the years, staying in touch had become easier. We'd followed each other's lives on social media and I'd been thrilled to see that she was living her dream, starring in the theatre in Birmingham, even though I had to admit I was a tiny bit jealous that her career had worked out much better than mine.

I felt my pulse quicken as Molly began to read Grace's message:

Dear Alice
I hope you're behaving in that big old city and it's treating you well.

Please forgive me for the late-night message, I've toyed for the past twenty-four hours about whether to say anything at all but decided that if I were you, I'd want to know. I'm afraid your grandfather isn't well. His health has been deteriorating over the last couple of months and he's been admitted to the local hospital. Mum is still cleaning and acting as general housekeeper up at Honeysuckle Farm. He's mentioned to her he would like to see you one last

time, which I know may be difficult in the current circum-
stances, but I feel you needed to know.

If you decide you want to come back, there's always a
spare bed at mine. I would love to see you too!

Grace xx

'Does your mom know about this?' Molly's eyes were wide
as saucers as she tucked her feet back underneath her.

I swallowed hard and shook my head.

'You'll have to tell her you are going back to England. You
can't just up and leave without saying a word.' Molly managed
a glimmer of a smile, 'You need to go, Alice.' Her voice faltered
as she handed the laptop back to me and I slowly closed the
lid. 'You need to see your grandfather. They don't live forever,
and time is precious.'

I knew Molly was right, I didn't have any intention of just
upping and leaving but I didn't relish the idea of telling Mum
either. I'd no clue how she was going to react. Grandie's name
had not been mentioned for years, in fact it was never
mentioned again after the day we left. My stomach was
churning just thinking about it.

'Don't worry, you have me to help you through it,' Molly
said, giving me a reassuring smile.

'Thanks, Mol, it means a lot.'

'Are you definitely sure about this?'

I nodded, 'Definitely sure. I need to see him again. It might
be my last time.'

'I know,' Molly's voice was barely a whisper.

'Grace wouldn't message me if it wasn't serious and something inside me is telling me I need to try and put this situation right.'

'What do you mean?' she asked tentatively.

'I loved Grandie, I still love Grandie, but at the time we left, I didn't have any choice, I was ten-years-old. But I do have a choice now. I'm my own person and whatever went on between him and Mum is not my argument.'

Molly gave a brief nod of understanding. 'Do you have any idea what the argument between them was about?'

'No,' I shook my head and felt myself tremble, remembering back to that day. 'I've no idea, all I know is that Grandie was angry, shouting she'd betrayed him in some way.' The pain twisted in my stomach just thinking about those words.

'Do you remember much about England?'

I nodded and smiled, and a warmth filled my heart just thinking about it. 'Grandie lives at Honeysuckle Farm, and we lived in the annexe attached to the farmhouse.' I hadn't realised how much I missed him, until now.

'Sounds very grand.'

'It is,' I cast my mind back, remembering the three-storey building full of exposed brick, wooden beams and huge stone fireplaces which roared every winter. 'And there was a secret spiral staircase at the back of the house.'

'Very quaint, like something out of a romantic novel.'

I smiled. Honeysuckle Farm was idyllic, set in acres of land with stone walls, ponies and chickens. 'One day, you need to come and visit.'

'I'd love to.'

'Then there was the dance school where my love of ballet and drama began. Mum was a teacher there and helped to run the business. The idea was that she'd completely take it over from Grandie when he retired.'

Molly frowned at me with concern, 'Do you know what happened to it? Is it still up and running?'

'I'm not sure, I'm assuming eventually it closed down.' My tone was pained, thinking about it. I'd never even asked Grace whether it was still there. As time passed it had never really crossed my mind what had happened to it, but it was that little place that had moulded my dreams into becoming a performer. I'd loved dancing there.

'Such a shame.'

I nodded, 'You'd love Brook Bridge; it's a pretty village, a typical idyllic setting with lovely tea shops too, all things rustic.'

'Very England!'

I felt a sudden warmth surge through my body, a feeling of belonging at my memories.

'It was a wonderful place, but I've no idea what it's like now.' I began to wonder if it had changed and how different it might be.

Suddenly Molly's mood dampened. She bit down on her bottom lip and her eyes drooped. 'If nothing else, moving here meant we met.'

'Mol,' I exclaimed, 'I'm going back for a short while, a few weeks at most. I need to recharge my batteries. I think I need a change of scenery, and hopefully I'll come back with a new lease of life.'

'So, when are you going to tell Rose?' asked Molly as though she was reading my thoughts.

I exhaled and took a deep breath. 'I'm just trying to work that one out,' I said, turning it over in my mind.

'And when are you thinking of leaving?'

'I'm going to look at flights today. I applied for a credit card and it came through yesterday. The quicker I go, the quicker I'm back.'

'Alice Parker, I'll be counting the days until you return.' She threw open her arms and I fell into them, hugging my friend tight.

As much as I'd miss Molly, the thought of going back to England by myself caused a feeling like excited fireflies exploding in the pit of my stomach. Was this a chance to get my life back on track? I couldn't wait to see Grandie and Grace, and of course Honeysuckle Farm. The only pang in my heart was that Mum wouldn't be going with me.

Chapter 2

Twenty-four hours later the warmth of the early evening air had enticed out most of the city dwellers and Molly and I were sitting on the comfy seats of the rooftop jazz bar overlooking the neon signs and giant billboards that illuminated the city. The clear, azure sky was the perfect backdrop for the skyscrapers that glistened in the evening light. I loved this bar, it was all gypsy swing, stunningly crafted cocktails and just a stone's throw from the radio station where Molly worked. The ambience was perfect, with a low-lit interior, wall plants and fairy lights that draped the bar. The rooftop was small and intimate with a band playing on the little stage in the corner.

Molly had talked me into coming out. It was her treat, she said but as her boyfriend Jay was the bar manager of this drinking establishment, we rarely ever paid for our drinks. Jay had reserved our favourite table and the moment he spotted us he beamed, then saluted us.

Within seconds he appeared at our side with two prosecco cocktails balancing on a round silver tray.

'Now that's what you call service.' Molly gave Jay a warm smile and a kiss on the cheek. 'Can we open a tab?'

He winked, 'Not on my watch, you provide the smiles and I'll provide the drinks,' he replied with a sparkle in his eye before pressing a swift kiss to my cheek.

'Deal,' both Molly and I said in unison, then laughed.

Molly had met Jay at this very bar nearly five years ago and they'd been the perfect couple ever since. He too was a proper New Yorker, born and bred, and his smile would be one I would miss when I returned to England.

'Busy day?' he asked, placing the cocktails on the table in front of us.

'Yes, the radio show was fun tonight and missy here,' she smiled towards me, 'worked her last shift as a cleaner and has begun packing her case.'

'Huh?' asked Jay, puzzled.

'I knew you weren't listening to me when I was telling you!' Molly jabbed him in the ribs in jest.

'Telling me what?! I'm always listening,' he tipped her a wink, 'but maybe not at 3 a.m. when I've just finished my shift and all I want to do is sleep.'

'Mmm, you're forgiven,' she answered playfully.

Jay turned towards me, 'Where are you going?'

'I'm taking a trip ... back to England,' I answered.

'I wasn't expecting that,' he said, cocking an eyebrow and

sitting down on the arm of the chair. 'Any reason why?'

'My grandfather is ill, and it's been a very long time since I've seen him. It may be the last time I ever see him,' I said, giving Jay a watery smile.

'Will you come back?'

'Of course, I'm just unsure when at the minute, but I won't stay away too long,' I promised.

'I will miss you, my Mary Poppins.'

I smiled at Jay. The moment I'd first walked into the bar with Molly, Jay had guessed I was English. Over time I'd obviously picked up an American twang to my voice but there was still a hint of an English accent underneath. He'd called me Mary Poppins – a nickname that had stuck.

'You too, Jay.'

'When do you go?'

'Day after tomorrow.'

Jay fell silent and took a second to absorb this information. 'So soon.' He looked towards Molly whose eyes had misted over. 'Drinks definitely on me tonight.' He touched my arm tentatively before returning to the bar.

For a moment, Molly and I stared out into the impressive night sky in silence, sipping our cocktails and lost in our own thoughts until she broke the silence.

'Who am I going to drink with when you're gone?'

'You make it sound like you have no other friends! You have a whole gang at the station.' I smiled at her.

'It's not the same though, is it?' She poked out her bottom lip sulkily. 'You're my best friend.'

'I'll be on the other end of an iPad, we can FaceTime each other and I'll be back before you know it.' The words left my mouth, but they didn't sound convincing, not even to myself.

Molly pointed her index finger at me. 'You'd better be, or I'll come and find you.'

Even though we'd both laughed it felt like there was an air of uncertainty hanging over me. Did I really want to come back to this life? I couldn't see how my misery would change here, with the same old same old, day in and day out.

The band in the corner were now in full swing and a jovial group of thirsty drinkers had arrived, enjoying the beginnings of a night at the bar. Jay was busy entertaining them and preparing their drinks.

Molly eyed me carefully, the straw of her cocktail poised at her lips. 'Do you want to talk about this afternoon?' she asked. 'I was surprised when I received the text.'

I swung my gaze back towards Molly, swallowed hard and felt the colour drain from my cheeks. I knew it was the question she'd wanted to ask all evening.

'I would have gone with you, you know,' she continued smoothly, 'you didn't have to face it on your own.'

That afternoon, I'd never been so nervous in my whole life. Auditioning for a lead role in a production was one thing – the nerves always kicked in – but that didn't even come close to how I'd felt visiting Mum and telling her I was travelling back to England. My hands were sweating, I'd felt nauseous and I honestly thought I was going to pass out.

'I know, thanks. But once I'd got it into my head that I was going, there was no stopping me. I had to get it over and done with.'

'And dare I ask?' Molly sat back to look at me carefully.

Mum had opened the door with a beam on her face, then right on cue, made her usual comments, like how she wasn't expecting me and to excuse the state of the flat. Of course, the flat was immaculate with not a thing out of place. Then, just like every other time when I'd turned up out of the blue, we had the usual spiel – if she'd known I was coming she would have fetched some groceries, etc., etc. I knew she was struggling to stay afloat as much as I was, and I'd often thought about moving back in with her but when I started college I'd become independent. I wanted to do things my way, I'd needed to grow as a person and going back to live with her would have been tiresome for both of us in such a small space.

I drained my glass. 'The subject of Grandie was difficult to raise, believe me. I felt like I was walking on eggshells. In the end, I just showed her the message from Grace on my phone.'

'And?'

'And she stared at it for a minute but didn't say a word. She carried on folding the washing like she hadn't even read it.'

A curious look appeared on Molly's face. 'Then what?'

'I told her I was going back to England. All she said was, "You do what you need to do." I could see it troubled her, the colour drained from her face and there were tears in her eyes, but she just stared at her hands which were visibly shaking. It upset me to see her that way.'

'Does she know when you're leaving?'

I nodded, 'Yes, I told her. She stood up and disappeared into her bedroom for a while and I could hear banging about. Then she reappeared clutching a small blue book.'

'What was it?'

'A bank book ...' I took a breath. 'She told me that ever since I was a little girl, Grandie had been putting money into a savings account for me. She'd no idea if he still did it, as the book couldn't be updated, but once I'm back in England I can check at the bank and withdraw the money.'

'How much is in it?' Molly enquired with a questioning look.

'Five thousand pounds, but that was the amount thirteen years ago.'

I'd been astounded when I'd opened up the book. I'd no idea that Grandie had been saving for me. Mum claimed she hadn't mentioned it before because, after her falling-out with Grandie, she hadn't wanted to take anything from him. She was uncertain how to withdraw the money with only the old-fashioned bank book, but now I was returning it should be easy to sort out. The money was mine and all I would need was my birth certificate and driving licence to prove my identity.

Molly gave a low whistle, 'That's an unexpected surprise.'

I nodded. 'To be honest, it couldn't have come at a better time. And it means I don't have to put my flight on a credit card. You know how those things frighten me, and the interest soon mounts up.'

'Yes,' Molly agreed, 'but with this money you can pay it off as soon as possible and have enough left for your flight home.'

'Absolutely,' I smiled at her. 'I even asked Mum to come with me, but she just shook her head.'

'Did you attempt to change her mind?'

'Of course, I tried, but she just wouldn't discuss it. She told me to leave it, repeated that I had to do what I had to do, then stood up and started folding the washing again in a kind of trance. It was like I'd never said anything in the first place.'

After telling Mum it had felt like a weight had been lifted off my shoulders, but I was worried about her. She looked fraught, her shoulders were slumped and now it seemed like *she* had the weight of the world on her shoulders. I knew I couldn't push the conversation any more but one day I was determined to uncover the secret that had driven us from England.

'It must have been one hell of a disagreement,' Molly probed.

'It was, and there's only two people who know the truth, and that's Mum and Grandie. Mum isn't talking – she never has – but I can see she is hurting. She must miss him too.'

'It'll be pride.'

'Stubborn pride. How can you let things slide so badly?'

'I'm not sure, but there's one thing I've learnt in life, there's nothing as funny as folk or family disagreements.'

I knew the argument I'd witnessed had been heated and

had split the family up but the whole situation still puzzled me. We'd had a good life at the farm, everything had been peaceful and calm and we'd both had a relationship to treasure with Grandie, up until that day.

In New York, Mum had done a variety of jobs, just like me. Mostly jobs she detested, with unsociable hours, but she made enough money to put food on the table. On the surface, she put on a front for everyone, but underneath I knew she was sad and had lost the zest for life she once had in England.

There she'd been a respected dance teacher, working in the family business. Each year she'd choreographed the village show and the local children and elderly had flocked to her lessons, enjoying every second of them. She must miss her life back in England. If only I could turn back time to the day before the argument, both our lives might have panned out differently.

I managed a weak nod. 'What if he dies Mol, and she hasn't put things right?' A tear slipped down my cheek just thinking about it. 'Surely she wouldn't be able to live with herself?'

Molly jumped up from the chair and immediately wrapped her arms around me with a hug. 'You can't beat yourself up over that, that's her decision. You've asked her to go back with you and she's said no. What more can you do? It's her choice. You're doing the right thing, doing what you need to do. That's all that matters,' she reassured me, but it still didn't stop me from feeling anxious leaving Mum behind. I wanted her to come with me.

'I'm going to miss you, Molly.'

'Don't go all soppy on me, you'll have me crying,' she insisted, trying to keep her voice steady.

'Hey you two, no time for tears in my bar.'

Our eyes slid towards Jay who'd appeared at the side of our table. 'And your glasses appear to be empty,' he grinned, slipping another two flutes of fizzy prosecco cocktail down in front of us and picking up the empty ones before balancing them on his tray.

'You know what Jay, you are the best barman in the city,' Molly tipped him a wink.

'Thanks Jay, you're a superstar,' I added with a watery smile.

'Do get I a hug, Ms Poppins, before you go?'

'You certainly do,' I replied, standing up without any hesitation.

Jay hugged me tight. 'Hurry back soon, it's not only Molly who will miss you.'

'Make sure you look after her while I'm away.'

I tipped my head towards Molly who blinked away her tears.

'Without a doubt,' he answered, flinging his arms open wider. 'Come on, group hug. And when you get back, I'll take my two favourite ladies out for a night on the town.'

'That's worth coming back for,' I smiled at them both, trying to put on a brave face through my tears but knowing it was unlikely I'd be back any day soon.

Chapter 3

I lay on top of my bed with my laptop open and scrolled through my messages. There was nothing of much interest except a few audition emails, notifications of upcoming Broadway Shows which I'd subscribed to. I sighed then hit the unsubscribe button. What was the point in torturing myself, reading those emails? After all, they only ever resulted in yet another rejection letter.

Logging on to Facebook, I clicked on Grace's profile which was a portfolio of success compared to my own disappointing timeline. Currently, she was starring in the musical *Mamma Mia* in the city of Birmingham. I'd followed her career over the last few years and marvelled at how well she was doing. She was living the dream – our dream – the dream we'd had as small children, two best friends. Of course, I was happy for her, but a part of me felt envious of the roles she'd played and what she'd achieved.

I noticed Grace had uploaded an album of photographs, herself and the cast from her latest production enjoying a night out. She looked stunning, her long russet wavy hair bounced on top of her shoulders, and her eyes sparkled. The Cath Kidston floral dress she wore with her vintage-stitch scallop-edge cardigan looked like something straight out of a fashion magazine. She was standing alongside different groups of people in the various photos, drink in hand and always wearing a perfect smile. I casually flicked through the album, but I didn't know any of them. They all had that immaculate polished West End look about them, bright smiles and not a hair out of place.

As my eyes flicked over the next photo the hairs on the back of my neck prickled and a flurry of goosebumps ran down my spine. My eyes locked with a pair of mesmerising hazel eyes and an almost perfect symmetrical face. This man had stopped me dead in my tracks, which took me completely by surprise!

'He's undeniably a damn fine-looking man,' I mumbled to myself as my breath caught in my throat and I hovered over his name tagged in the picture ... Sam Reid.

'In fact, that's what you'd call orgasmic.' I knew I was talking to myself, but I couldn't take my eyes off the photo. I stared at him for a moment longer and felt my body flush with warmth. Something inside me had awakened. I was, purely and simply, attracted to him. There was a softness to his eyes and a gentleness in his smile which drew me in. He sailed the fine line between handsome and downright sexy. This was a photo of a person I'd never met but felt an immediate connection to, a feeling that had been missing from my life for a long time.

'Who are you talking to?' Molly asked, appearing in the doorway with a grin. 'Do I need to send for the men in white jackets?'

Even though I'd been expecting Molly, I jumped out of my skin. 'Ha, funny, just talking to myself, as you do,' I answered, smiling. 'In fact, I'm just looking through Grace's uploads from last night,' I said, scrolling back to the first photograph.

Molly pointed at the screen and sat down next to me. 'I love Grace's dress. Very quintessentially English.'

'She knows how to dress.'

'And who's that?' Molly's eyes were wide, her finger pointing at exactly the same photograph that had caught my eye.

'Sam Reid, according to Facebook.'

I looked closer at the photo again. He was standing next to Grace with his arm draped around her shoulder wearing a faded vintage T-shirt and Levi jeans.

'I wouldn't mind ruffling my face against that chest,' Molly rolled her eyes.

'Molly! You're taken,' I said, slightly miffed, even though I knew she was joking and Sam Reid lived on the opposite side of the world, and who knew whether he was in a relationship or not?

'That T-shirt is fitting snuggly around ... well, actually, every muscular part, and those eyes, oh and that shaggy, mousy hair ...' She tilted her head and dreamily put her hand on her heart.

'Just for you, Molly. Stalk all you like while I nip to the restroom.' I stood up and stepped over my packed case before glancing at my watch. 'Time's ticking, the taxi will be picking me up in fifteen minutes,' I said, with mixed feelings, sad I'd be leaving Molly behind, but with a realisation that life wasn't offering me any new challenges of late. In just a few hours I would be flying halfway across the world and who knew what my adventure might entail? I felt a twinge of excitement at the thought of it.

'I know, I don't want to think about it, but this Sam Reid is going to help us pass the time before you fly off back to the land of farmyards and people who speak like the Queen,' she attempted an English accent before tugging the laptop towards her and tipping her head towards the screen.

'They don't all have accents like the Queen, you know,' I insisted with a smile, disappearing inside the bathroom.

'Works on the same production as Grace,' she shouted after me, 'according to his Facebook profile, but I can't see whether he's single or not. There's no relationship status.'

'Not everyone lives their life through Facebook, you know.' I grinned at my own reflection in the mirror, waiting for Molly's outburst.

'Mmm, is that a dig at me?' she exclaimed huffily, knowing full well she checked in at every bar, and documented her life like it was a Reality TV show.

'If the cap fits.'

'You have some very funny sayings, however ... oh no!' she suddenly exclaimed the second I walked back in the room.

'What have you done?' I asked, noticing the mischievous glint in her eye.

She tried to arrange her face into an innocent expression. 'I hope you don't mind but I accidently pressed the friend request button when I was scrolling through his profile.'

'Oh God! You haven't?' My eyes fell towards the screen.

Molly scrunched up her face and bit down on her lip.

'He'll have no clue who I am!' I said in mock indignation but secretly curious to see if he noticed I was friends with Grace and accepted the request. I closed the lid on the laptop and stowed it away in my bag.

'Something tells me it's going to be an interesting trip back to little old England! I'll be watching your every move, Alice Parker, whilst I'm missing you like hell!'

I swiped her arm playfully. 'By the time I get to England you'll find yourself blocked from all my social media!'

'Such a spoilsport,' she laughed, rolling her eyes. 'Sometimes the English are so uptight!'

Chapter 4

Taking a deep breath, I paid the taxi driver and climbed out of the cab. I'd arrived at Newark airport wheeling my case behind me with my rucksack slung over my shoulder. The blast of air conditioning inside the terminal building was a welcome relief after the blistering heat outside, but a twinge of sadness hit me as I made my way through the revolving glass doors.

In the pit of my stomach there was an unsettling feeling regarding Mum. I'd looked over my shoulder as I'd climbed into the taxi, hoping to see her, but she wasn't anywhere to been seen. I'd texted her to let her know I'd left for the airport and slight relief flooded through me when she replied, telling me to have a safe journey and that she loved me.

Shoving my sunglasses high on my head, I glanced at my watch. I'd given myself loads of time and once I'd checked in I'd have enough time to relax and settle my nerves.

Thankfully, according to the departure times on the plasma screen, the flight to Manchester was on time. I'd only travelled once before on a plane and that was when we'd arrived in America, but I'd always kept my passport up to date. Deep down I knew I'd return one day.

Inside the terminal building the white floor tiles gleamed as people hurried over them, pulling suitcases, checking watches and tapping on mobile phones. Everywhere people seemed in a state of mad panic. There were two glass elevators leading to the upper levels and kiosks dotted about manned by harassed-looking cashiers. I chewed on my lip and looked around in bewilderment, everywhere was so busy. My stomach was churning with nerves, I'd no idea where to go or what to do.

'You okay?' I must have had a mortified look on my face when I heard a voice and looked up to see a friendly airport official smiling back at me.

'I'm not sure. I've no idea where I'm going.' My ticket and passport were tightly clutched in my hand like my life depended on them.

'It's not as difficult as it looks,' he said. 'Let me help you.' He nodded his head, 'You can check in at the machines over there.'

I looked over to where he was pointing. There was a red-faced businessman banging one of the machines and a mother at the next one cradling a crying baby whilst looking in confusion at the screen.

Oh God.

'Here, I'll help,' he said kindly, leading me towards the machines. 'They don't bite, and are quite straightforward.'

None of this seemed straightforward to me. Public transport didn't bother me, I used the subway on a daily basis, hailed taxis and pounded the sidewalks of New York, but this looked like another planet, everything seemed so alien.

'Thank you, Lewis, you're so kind,' I said, glancing at the shiny name badge attached to his jacket, relieved he'd offered to help.

We waited our turn and I watched him as he scanned my passport into the machine. And as if by magic it came up with my name and my flight number. He asked me a series of questions and then said, 'Here you go Miss Parker,' with a broad grin on his face, handing me a luggage tag.

'Is that it?' I asked, smiling my thanks but feeling a little daunted, noticing a queue had formed behind me.

'All done, as easy as that. Wrap the tag around the handle, place your bag on that conveyor belt over there and follow those stairs.' He pointed to a set of white steps. 'You'll go through passport control and then into the departure lounge. You have a safe journey back to England,' he said, smiling.

I couldn't thank him enough and twenty minutes later, I was standing in the departure lounge, which looked more like a mini shopping mall to me. There were several large open areas dotted with blue fabric-covered seats that were filled with people reading or scrolling on their phones and children colouring in books. I spotted an empty seat next to the huge windows that looked out over the runways. Inquisitive children stood and watched the planes taking off and landing, their hands pressed against the glass.

For the next couple of hours, I tried to relax but sitting at the airport seemed so surreal. I cast my mind back to thirteen years ago, when we'd left Staffordshire and travelled to Terminal 2 at Manchester Airport. I had just my backpack and my favourite teddy bear tucked safely under my arm. We'd boarded a flight to a brand-new life and I remembered feeling scared. My mum had grasped my hand tightly, as though she was scared to let go. At the time, she'd seemed edgy, always looking over her shoulder. Maybe she was looking for Grandie, but he never came. I'd no idea why she'd chosen New York, no idea at all, but that decision had changed my life.

I took a breath. I was actually going home and couldn't quite believe it. I'd no idea how Grandie would react to my return and there was no denying that, as much as I wanted to see him again, feelings of trepidation poured through my body.

Surprisingly, time passed quickly and before I knew it my flight was announced over the tannoy.

'Just boarding,' I sent a quick text to Molly, feeling a sudden surge of triumph. I was about to board a plane. I was really doing this.

My phone pinged almost immediately: 'Missing you already, safe flight and don't forget to message me as soon as you land.'

I then sent one last text to Mum: 'Just boarding, love you too.' Switching off the phone and stuffing it into the dark recesses of my rucksack, my stomach was churning. Bravely, I followed the masses down the air-bridge towards the aircraft.

Making my way to seat 39A, I couldn't believe my luck when I noticed a well-dressed man with excellent cheekbones and a beautiful mouth flicking through the pages of a newspaper in the seat next to mine. Maybe there was a God, and this man had been sent to keep me occupied on my long journey to England. I smiled broadly at him as he looked up and met my gaze. This was his cue to chivalrously offer to hurl my hand luggage into the overhead locker, but that wasn't to be as I felt a tap on my shoulder.

Spinning around, I met the gaze of an attractive woman. 'This one's my seat,' she smiled. 'I wouldn't wish my husband's grumpy mood on anyone today.' She acknowledged him with a fleeting nod.

'Sorry, my mistake,' I said, feeling disappointment and quickly fumbling for my ticket, a blush rushing to my cheeks. 'I'm 36A.'

Turning back, I located my seat and, miraculously, the seat next to mine was still empty. I heaved a sigh of relief when I finally settled down into the cramped window seat clutching my Kindle. My bag was stowed and the locker was closed. It wouldn't be long until we took off and in approximately seven hours I'd be arriving in England.

As a child, I could remember being truly happy running around the farm without a care in the world with Marley the puppy by my side. Happiness to me was the gorgeous smells seeping from the Aga, the smell of home-baked bread, the casseroles bubbling away on top of the stove. I'd loved splashing in the stream, blackberry picking, collecting the eggs from the hens and riding Billy through the long grass in the summer sunshine. And suddenly I missed it all. Maybe, I could have all that again? Maybe I could change Mum's mind and persuade her to come back with me? Then I felt a sudden burst of jitters. What if everything had changed? What if Brook Bridge village wasn't how I remembered it and Grandie didn't welcome me back with open arms? After all, that was a possibility. I'd no idea what I would do then. I shuffled in my seat anxiously, wondering suddenly if actually I was doing the right thing.

'I think I'm next to you.'

My reverie was broken.

A lady hovered in the aisle and gave me a warm smile, which put me at ease.

My guess was she was mid-sixties and her accent was Mancunian … an accent I hadn't heard for a long time.

'Be my guest,' I smiled back, switching on my Kindle, the arrival back in England still firmly on my mind.

'An American accent with an English intonation,' she said, collapsing in the seat next to me.

I nodded. 'I'm going back home, it's been a while.'

'I can relate to that,' she answered. 'Work?'

I shook my head, 'My grandfather is ill.'

Her face turned a little more serious. 'I'm sorry to hear that, dear,' she said sadly, pulling out a magazine from her bag and fastening her seatbelt. 'I hope he'll be all right,' she said with genuine concern. 'Grandparents are precious things. You make sure you spend as much time as possible with him. I'm Hetty, by the way, your new neighbour – well, for this journey anyway.'

'Alice,' I smiled, thinking how right she was and that I was doing the right thing travelling back to see Grandie even though a couple of moments earlier I had doubted myself.

Hetty waved the magazine in the air, 'I don't know why I read this trash, waste of money. I've no idea who half these people are, usually those reality stars, if you can call them stars. Why would anyone want to parade their private life on the screen for everyone to see?'

'Fame and money, I guess.'

'Whatever happened to having a proper talent?' She rolled her eyes, and ripped open a packet of boiled sweets.

'Take one ... for your ears when we take off,' she offered.

'Thank you. What's taking you back to England?' I asked my new-found friend.

'This little bundle of joy,' she said, bursting with pride and showing me a photo of a baby swaddled in a blue woven blanket on the screen of her phone. 'My very first grandchild, Elvis.'

'Destined for great things with a name like that,' I grinned. She glanced down at the phone, 'I'm not sure he suits the name but who am I to interfere? And I can't wait to have Granny cuddles.' She slid the phone away.

Over the course of the next ten minutes, the plane was pushed back and I heard the engines start before the noise increased to a roar. The plane began to roll, slowly at first, but within a few seconds I was being pushed back firmly into my seat and before too long we leapt off the tarmac and were soaring into the sky. My lip had wobbled a little when we'd taken off and my throat was dry. Thoughts of Mum flooded my mind and I felt guilty leaving her behind, but something inside me was telling me to go. I just wished she'd see sense and put the past issues behind her. Grandie was old, he'd dedicated most of his life to us, surely the right thing to do now at a time like this would be to swallow your pride and see him one last time.

I watched the houses and trees get smaller and smaller as the plane climbed into the clouds and within minutes all I could see was the intense blue sky.

'I hope you've brought a coat with you,' Hetty chuckled. 'That'll be the last sunshine you'll see for a while. It's always raining in Manchester.'

I smiled, leaning back against the headrest, remembering all the times I'd pulled on my Wellington boots and splashed through the puddles on a Saturday morning on the way to the dance school.

With one last glance towards Manhattan, I lowered my oversized shades on to the bridge of my nose and closed my eyes. My mind drifted towards the farm, my childhood home, a place of outstanding beauty. I could still remember my bedroom, a large room situated at the rear of the annexe. The window overlooked the amazing view across the valley. In spring, I'd been mesmerised by the white, cotton-wool clouds bobbing along and in winter by the angry, dark clouds that were pushed by the sharp gusts of wind.

Every morning, Grandie used to wander across the court-yard towards the annexe clutching a mug of steaming tea for Mum and without fail he would kiss me goodbye before school. I was his girl, and we'd been so close back then. I started to worry again, how it was going to be when I saw him. What would I say? What would I do? And the question burned inside me, how would he feel about me? It must have broken his heart when we'd left, and I felt sad and angry that I'd had to miss out on the last thirteen years. I'd missed the place and I was only just beginning to realise how much.

Before I knew it, I was being shaken gently. 'Wake up.'

I opened my eyes and soon realised, I'd slept for the whole of the flight.

'Welcome to Manchester, England where the local time is 6:45 a.m.,' the purser announced over the intercom.

'I told you,' Hetty grinned, tipping her head towards the window. 'See, it's raining in Manchester.'

Immediately, I sat upright. 'Gosh, how did I sleep for the whole of this time?' I couldn't quite believe it, stretching out my legs in the cramped leg space as best I could.

'You're very lucky. I've been plotting his murder for nearly seven hours.'

'Huh?' I answered, puzzled.

She raised her eyebrows towards the man sat on the opposite side of the aisle. 'He's snored for the whole time,' she rolled her eyes. 'It's driven me insane.'

'Oh no, I hope ...'

'I never heard a peep out of you,' she confirmed with a sparkle in her eye.

The pilot steered the plane towards the terminal and cut the engines. As soon as the aircraft came to a standstill the clicking of seatbelts echoed around the cabin, followed by the clunking of the overhead compartments being opened.

It didn't take long to get through passport control, collect my luggage from the carousel and make my way through customs. I pulled my case behind me and encountered a sea of faces staring back at me, people holding up signs eagerly waiting to meet their loved ones.

I'd arranged to meet Connie outside the terminal building and Grace's message had instructed me to stand still, and she would find me. I hadn't seen Connie for such a long time and wondered if she'd even recognise me.

Hetty had been right, the blue sky I'd left behind was nowhere to be seen and instead there was an army of black angry-looking clouds marching above, being hurried along by a sharp wind. The rain was belting down and the puddles splashed under my feet as I pulled up my hood and snuggled deep down inside my hoodie, waiting outside for Connie.

The nerves were kicking in as I waited, flicking a glance at all the cars pulling up and others whizzing by.

Then I heard a voice: 'Oh my goodness! Look at you, Alice Parker, you're all grown up!' I spun round to see a white-haired woman dashing towards me.

'Connie!' I exclaimed, feeling relieved that her arms were open wide and her smile was very welcoming.

'Welcome home!' she shouted, pulling me into a suffocating hug. 'It's good to have you back.'

The hug was heartfelt and tears welled up in my eyes. 'Thank you!' I gasped, taking in a lungful of air the second she let go of me. All my nerves disappeared in an instant.

She stood back and took a proper look at me. 'My word, you look just like your grandfather.'

I felt a sudden surge of happiness being compared to him, even though I had no idea what he looked like now.

'How is he?'

'Frail, but he has all his faculties and talks about you all the time.'

'Does he? Does he really? Does he know I'm coming?'

Connie shook her head. 'We didn't say anything, just in case your plans fell through. We didn't want to raise his hopes. No Rose?'

I shook my head, 'Afraid not.'

'Such a shame. Anyway, let's get you home. We can chat on the way. Grace can't wait to see you!'

We hurried towards the car, splashing in rainwater, and once my suitcase was loaded into the boot, we began the journey back to Brook Bridge Village.

'How are you feeling?' asked Connie, once she'd carefully manoeuvred the car from the busy slip road on to the inside lane of the motorway.

The second the plane had landed there was no denying I'd

felt apprehensive, even a little panicky, not knowing what was waiting for me. What if ... what if I'd made the wrong decision coming back? What if Grandie didn't want to see me? But once my feet were firmly back on English soil, all my apprehensions dissipated and I couldn't help but recognise that comforting feeling, the smells and the familiarity that swathed me as a child, feeling safe and happy.

'I'm glad to be home.' I replied, meaning every word.

Chapter 5

Connie slowed the car and changed gear before driving around the roundabout and up the cobbled High Street that I'd walked along so many times as a child. I was back in the village for the first time in thirteen years and I felt a tingling of excitement along my spine.

My eyes were wide, staring out of the passenger window, taking everything in. It felt like time had stood still and I'd never been away. Opposite the village pub stood a row of cottages, painted in different colours, facing on to the main street. I smiled to myself. Grandie and I used to take a stroll most evenings after school, which was basically code for going to the pub where Grandie sneaked a crafty pint and I was treated to a packet of salt and vinegar crisps. We'd sit on the benches outside and he would test me on the colour of the houses, for educational purposes, he said. Of course, I knew my colours at that age, but it was just our little bit of fun together. These were happy childhood memories. Apart from the new housing development that had sprung up on the outskirts of the village, everything appeared exactly the same.

'There's Mr Cross,' I exclaimed in amazement, as I saw him disappearing through his front door. He owned the small bookshop on the corner of Bridge Lane in the heart of the village. 'He doesn't look any different,' I remarked. He was just as I remembered him, dressed in a green checked wool jacket with brown leather patches on the elbows, over his smart sweater. 'And does Mrs Berry still own the sweet shop?' I asked, watching it whizz by.

'She sure does, the kids still swarm in there after school, like bees around a honey pot.' Connie smiled at me before turning into the next street.

'What about The Old Teashop? Please tell me that's still here?'

'You do have a good memory! Yes, Mrs Jones is still there and over the years she's won many awards for her delicious cakes.'

'I must make sure I see her while I'm here. I wonder if she'd recognise me.'

'I think she might. Looking at you is like looking at your grandfather. Your characteristics and mannerisms are exactly the same, but that accent of yours might cause a stir with the locals. It's not often you hear an American accent round here.'

Connie flicked on the indicator and turned left into Croft Lane, 'That's Grace's house, the one with the duck-egg-blue door.' She nodded to a row of three cottages all with pink coloured roses entwined around their stunningly crafted oak beam porches. Each cottage had its own individual swinging garden gate. Colourful blooms drooped from the hanging baskets and the grass was neatly edged and mowed.

'So pretty, a scene from a countryside magazine.'

'She's been there a little over two years now. You do know Grace and Finn have split up, don't you?' asked Connie, still staring at the road ahead.

'I do, but we have a lot of catching up to do,' I said, knowing how devastated Grace had been when she'd discovered Finn had been having an affair after they'd moved in together.

'She isn't going to arrive home for another hour. The show finished last night and she's out to lunch with some of the cast members who are moving back to London. Do you fancy coming back to the farm and having a look around at the old place before she's home?'

Gripped by intrigue and excitement, I responded, 'Do I ever,' feeling the corners of my mouth lift. Just thinking about the old place sent a tingle through my body. I wondered if it would still be the same as I remembered and how I would feel seeing it again after all this time. It was only a matter of seconds before I'd find out.

'But what about Grandie?' I asked, eager to see him.

Connie took a swift glance towards me. 'I know you are desperate to see him, but he's got visitors today. Why don't you freshen up, unpack and settle in. And, we'll go first thing tomorrow? There will be plenty of time to talk then too.'

I nodded. Even though I felt a pang of disappointment, I knew Connie was right. I didn't want to go steaming in there, in front of other people, giving him the shock of his life, and tomorrow we had all the time in the world.

Two seconds later, as we travelled up Horsey Lane, the familiarity swathed me, and a swarm of butterflies erupted inside my tummy. Connie slowed the car right down in front of the wrought-iron gates and I reminded myself to breathe calmly, my heart thumping with a mixture of trepidation and anticipation. I couldn't wait to see my childhood home once more. There was a time when I thought I'd never see it again and now here I was, waiting anxiously for the gates to open. It was so surreal!

Connie pressed a small black remote control on the dashboard of the car, and the gates creaked and slowly began to open.

I glanced up the driveway towards Honeysuckle Farm. Thankfully, the rain had finally ceased, and the sun was shining through, glinting off the red tiled roof of the farmhouse. A vivid rainbow arched over the enormous cherry trees that flanked the edges of the driveway, their branches swaying lightly in the breeze.

'Home,' I breathed to myself.

The view was spectacular and took my breath away. It was a world away from the cloud-reaching skyscrapers of New York. Here bursts of colour bloomed from every flower bed, the gardens maintained like the perfectly manicured grounds of a stately home.

The three-storey farmhouse was every bit as idyllic as I remembered, just perfect in fact.

Everything felt calm and peaceful.

'How are you feeling?'

'A little strange, if I'm being honest. It's weird. I used to live here. I used to run around splashing in that stream and, oh my ... there's Billy.' I stared with surprise towards the chestnut Welsh pony who was currently scratching his bum against the old apple tree. Happy tears were now pricking my eyes.

'Yes, he's still going strong,' smiled Connie, slowly driving the car up the long gravel driveway. 'And look at that rainbow, now that's a welcome home. Very impressive!'

Connie cut the engine and we climbed out of the car.

'Can you smell that?' I grabbed hold of Connie's arm while I sniffed the air.

'Smell what?' answered Connie with amusement.

'The country air, the smell of the farm, eau de cow muck. I've missed that.'

Connie chuckled, 'I can't make up my mind whether I'm laughing because you've missed the smell of dung or because you sound funny with that accent. Even though it's you, you don't sound like you ... if you know what I mean.'

'Home sweet home,' I said with a contented sigh.

For a moment, I was rooted to the spot and silent. Staring up at the farmhouse, I couldn't take my eyes off it and could visualise the last time I'd seen Grace and Connie standing there, waving goodbye to me the day I left. I shot a quick glance up to the bedroom window, hoping to see Grandie staring back at me, but of course he wasn't there.

My sudden silence must have worried Connie because she reached out and squeezed my hand.

'I didn't think you'd ever be back, you know.' She gazed in the same direction as me, and her voice wavered a little.

'It's like you've just read my mind,' I said softly. 'I've been thinking about it for a while but I think Grace's message gave me the push I needed.'

'It must be hard, with the way things are between your grandfather and your mum.'

'I don't understand it. Mum won't talk about it. I've no idea why we left, do you?'

Connie shook her head, 'The circumstances were all very peculiar, and Ted wouldn't talk about it either. Whatever went on between the pair of them left him heartbroken and I really have no clue. He never fully recovered from you both leaving so suddenly.'

A wave of guilt hit me. I knew I couldn't do anything about it at the time but maybe I should have taken the plunge and got back in touch sooner. He'd been on his own all these years.

'Families, eh?' I said slowly, once more turning the bizarre situation over in my mind.

'Come on, you're here now, that's all that matters.' She gave me a warm smile as I followed her up the stone steps and waited behind her while she turned the key in the lock. The second she pushed open the door I heard a woof, then the sound of paws clattering along the wooden floor of the hallway. My heart began to beat faster and furiously, surely not ... I held my breath and couldn't believe my eyes as a black-and-white spaniel woofed again.

'Marley! Oh my God, Marley!' I dropped to my knees, the tears falling from my eyes. Being happy to see him again was an understatement. Marley wagged his tail and circled round me, sniffing frantically. Wrapping my arms around him, I buried my head into his neck and breathed in his familiar smell, then ruffled the fur on the top of his head as he began licking my face.

'I can't believe ... I just can't believe it. I didn't think he'd still be here.'

Connie was smiling down at us. 'Now that is what you call a welcome home. He's a very old man now.'

'Do you think he remembers me?'

'I think it's safe to say over the years I've never witnessed a welcome like that before.'

When I stood up, Marley kept close to me. I paused beside the imposing grandfather clock and looked around wide-eyed. Mixed emotions poured through my body. A part of me felt sad, knowing Grandie had rattled around in this place on his own since we left, and another part of me felt proud that he'd kept the farm.

'How has he managed, living here all this time by himself?' I asked, peering around. Even now, this place still looked humungous to me.

'He hasn't. Once Grace left home I sold our house and moved into the annexe. Up until then, I was here every day from eight in the morning and most evenings past eight too, but once Ted began to struggle to move around the place, it seemed the simplest solution would be to move in. I could never abandon him, he's like family to me. He's looked after me for all these years and Grace and I have never wanted for anything.'

'He's so lucky to have you.'

'I'm the lucky one. I've loved my job here and I never want it to end.' Connie's voice faltered, and she blinked back the tears.

I knew what she was thinking and touched her arm gently. 'Let's not think about that,' I said softly, linking my arm through hers. 'Grandie will live forever, he's a tough old cookie.' Of course, I knew this wasn't true but like Connie, I couldn't bear to think about life without him being there. I was going to cherish every moment I had with him.

'Let's hope so,' she gave my hand a little squeeze. 'He moved his bedroom to the dining room once he began to find it difficult climbing the stairs. I prepare all his meals and usually he only uses the small sitting room off the kitchen. This place has been his home for over sixty years. Jim's still here too. Do you remember him?'

It only took me a second to place Jim. 'Yes ... yes of course I do, Jim the gardener with his flat cap and green overalls.'

'Probably still the same flat cap and the same pair of overalls,' joked Connie. 'He still maintains the garden and the general upkeep of the place.'

We walked up the hallway and I hovered near the antique

dresser full of framed photographs. 'Look at this one,' I said, clutching the silver frame. 'Mum looks so young and I'm riding Billy. I must have been about five years old.' I cast my mind back to that day. The sun was shining, and I rode Billy through the field of buttercups. Mum and I sang songs from every musical we could remember, and picnicked in the bottom field. I messed about in the stream while Mum lounged on the red tartan rug reading a book.

'Happy times.'

On our way towards the kitchen, Connie led me through the vast gallery. Heavy tapestry curtains adorned the huge windows at the far end of the room and the wallpaper of the hunt, with horses and foxes, still hung on the walls.

I glanced towards the stone fireplace and there she was, still watching me with a sparkle in her eye, like she'd done when I was a child. I paused and looked up at the magnificent painting.

'Grandma's still here then?'

'She is, the beautiful Florrie Parker, your grandfather's one and only true love. I don't think he ever had another relationship after she passed away.'

'That's so heart-breaking ... Mum never speaks about her, actually never talks about anything that's to do with England,' I said sadly, still staring up at the portrait.

I'd never met my grandmother, she'd passed away before I was born, but Grandie used to say I was just like her, beautiful inside and out and full of character. She reminded me of royalty, the queen of the manor. Her hair was just so, and her skin peachy white. When I'd walked through the room I'd always felt her eyes were twinkling at me.

Connie turned her head to look at me. 'Cup of tea?'

'Perfect.'

The kitchen looked just exactly how it did thirteen years ago. Floral curtains framed the windows that looked out over the fields. Pots and pans hung off the old wooden beams that ran across the ceiling. The racing-green Aga gleamed and there were even the same tea and coffee canisters that stood proudly next to the kettle. I paused at the window and peered out. I could see the top of the hill, where Brook Bridge woods met the top of the field. Grey stone walls criss-crossed the land and a tiny stretch of road snaked into the distance. The cattle in the nearby field were grazing, the calves swishing their tails beside their mothers. That view was achingly familiar, a view I'd loved as a child and one I'd missed. Feeling a little emotional, I gave myself a little shake. It was so different to New York City. This place felt like home.

Turning, I sat down at the oversized pine table while Connie made the drinks. Marley nestled close to me.

'How long will Grandie be in hospital for?'

Connie looked in my direction for a fraction of a second before rummaging in the top cupboard for a couple of mugs.

'I'm not entirely sure. Hopefully the doctor will be able to update us tomorrow,' she said, sitting down opposite me.

On the journey home, Connie had told me about Grandie's fall. She'd been watching him from the window of the annexe.

One minute he'd been there and the next he was gone, toppling down the steps that led to the patio. She'd found him within seconds, but he'd banged the side of his head on the corner of the stone wall and had felt dazed. The doctors had stitched him up and decided to keep him in for observation.

Finally, the kettle whistled and Connie stood up and made us both a cup of tea.

'Thank you, Connie,' I said. 'I really appreciate everything you do for him.' Being back here, I could see for myself that the upkeep of the farmhouse would be a struggle for anyone on their own, never mind an elderly person like Grandie.

'You don't need to thank me. Your grandfather gave me a job when I was at the lowest point of my life and I'll always be grateful.' She sat back down and slid the mug across the table towards me.

'I couldn't have carried on being married to Paul. It was a big decision to go it alone with a child but he'd stripped me of my self-confidence and self-worth and something had to change.'

'What happened between you two? Did he have an affair?'

'That's an understatement,' she rolled her eyes, 'but I'm over it now and I haven't set eyes on him since the day he left.'

'What about Grace?'

'She's not seen him either. He's never been in touch, disappeared off the face of the earth. I withdrew from relationships for a while and concentrated on making a happy life for me and Grace.'

I gave her a tentative smile. 'And now?' I said, raising an eyebrow.

'Life twists and turns in many ways,' she answered, cupping her mug of tea. 'Jim ...' she paused, 'me and Jim are together. We've been lucky to have been friends for years. When I first moved into the annexe, I'd discover fresh food parcels on the doorstep every morning.'

'How romantic,' I smiled, thinking how lovely it was that their friendship had blossomed over the years ...

Connie blushed and suddenly Marley woofed, sat up and began thumping his tail on the floor.

'Brought together by asparagus and strawberries,' another voice suddenly chipped into the conversation.

Immediately, we both spun round to see a teary-eyed Grace beaming back at us.

'Oh my life ... Alice Parker, you're home!' she shrieked.

Huge happy tears threatened to break loose at any second. Grace squealed, then I squealed, scraping my chair backwards as she rushed towards me with her arms flung wide, then clamped them around me.

We bounced up and down like kids on pogo sticks. 'I can't believe you're actually here ... Alice Parker, look at you, even more gorgeous in real life, you haven't changed a bit! ... Except for that dodgy-sounding accent!' she exclaimed breathlessly.

I loved the way she'd said my full name in an English accent.

'What's wrong with my accent?' I laughed, emphasising it

even more. 'And after that many hours on a plane I wouldn't class myself as gorgeous. My make-up slid off several hours ago!'

'Who needs make-up?' She took a step back and looked me over again. 'You're real, you're actually here. We've got so much catching up to do!'

Connie watched us with amusement. 'How did you know we were here?'

Grace turned towards her mum and kissed her on her cheek. 'You weren't at mine and you kind of live here, which is a bit of a giveaway. So, I thought I'd come over. I couldn't wait any longer to see Alice,' she said, swinging back towards me.

'Grab a seat, I'll make you a drink,' Connie said, standing up to boil the kettle once again.

'How're you feeling? Tired?' asked Grace, slipping into her mum's seat, grabbing my hands across the table and clasping them tight. 'The jetlag will kick in soon. I still can't believe you are here ... I'm babbling now, aren't I?' she trilled, and I bit back a giggle at her excitement.

'At the minute, I'm not too bad, I think my body is running on adrenalin! And luckily for me, I managed to sleep the whole of the flight.'

'I've been on edge all day!' she said, taking the drink from Connie. 'I actually woke up this morning and prepared myself for the worst. I was worried you would change your mind about coming.'

'I almost did. I can't believe that yesterday I was in New

York and now I'm back here, in Brook Bridge village.' I grinned at Grace, 'It's so surreal.'

'That's what aeroplanes are for! How're you feeling about seeing the village again, this place?'

'I didn't know how I'd feel, but now I'm here, I have to admit I've missed this place more than I realised. And Marley ...' I shot him a glance, 'I never thought I'd ever see him again.'

Connie and Grace both smiled at me.

'It's great to see you back here,' Connie chipped in.

'It feels so right to be back, it's been far too long. The only upsetting thing is, I wish Mum was with me.'

Grace gave me a sympathetic smile before sipping her tea.

For the next half hour, we reminisced about life before New York: our trips to the sweet shop to buy penny chews and the time we'd got stuck up the old apple tree in the orchard and the fire brigade was nearly called out to rescue us.

'Are you up for the pub later? No pressure if you'd rather chill and grab a bottle of wine and put your feet up?' asked Grace when we'd finished our drinks.

'I'm up for the pub,' I replied, remembering the Sunday afternoons I'd be sat by Grandie's side while he enjoyed a game of dominoes with his friends – such fond memories. 'But I'll apologise in advance if my head suddenly droops and you find me fast asleep at the table.'

'You just shout up when you've had enough.'

'What's the plan now?' Connie interrupted. 'Shall we head back to yours, Grace, or do you want me to rustle you up some food here?' she asked, taking the empty mugs and rinsing them out in the sink.

'What's Jim doing?' Grace turned towards her.

'He's sorting himself out tonight, so I thought I'd grab a bite with you girls.'

'Shall we eat back at mine, then, and get you settled in?' Grace turned back towards me.

'That sounds like a perfect plan,' I beamed, standing up. 'I still can't believe I'm back,' I said, repeating myself and taking in my surroundings once more.

'There's no place like home,' Connie smiled, grabbing the car keys from the table. 'Come on, you pair, I'm ravenous and you must be too, Alice?'

'I am, now you come to mention it. I managed to miss all the food on the plane.'

'You probably didn't miss much,' grinned Grace.

Marley was now fast asleep in his bed at the foot of the Aga. Kneeling down, I patted his stomach and he peeped out of one eye before shutting it firmly again. 'See you very soon.'

After locking up the farmhouse we clambered into the car, Grace sitting in the back with me. Connie started the engine and we began to drive towards the wrought-iron gates.

I glanced back over my shoulder and glimpsed the farmhouse once more before the car manoeuvred through the open gates on to the lane. I shuddered at the thought of leaving it behind again and that's when I knew. The tiny niggle deep in my brain had finally worked its way to the surface after all this time. The overwhelming feeling of security and contentment had enveloped me the second I stepped off the plane. Deep inside, I knew I didn't have any intention of returning to New York. I'd come home, and all I had to do now was convince Mum to do the same.

Chapter 6

'Here we are,' Grace jumped out of the car and smiled proudly. 'Welcome to my home, Wild Rose Cottage.'

She opened the gate and we headed up the path.

The front garden was utterly gorgeous, striking in fact. There were so many flowers blooming, the beds were bursting with colour. 'This is so beautiful and quaint,' I said, admiring the pink roses straggling through the hedgerows. 'Very English countryside.' It was a far cry from my own front garden in New York, mainly because I didn't have one. The door to my block of flats was grey with a chrome keypad to enter the darkened stairwell, and I didn't even have the luxury of a flowerbox hanging from my front window. Where I lived was completely dull and colourless.

'Look at those roses ... simply stunning.' I leant forward and inhaled the rich scent from the prized flowers that danced in the light breeze.

'I worked hard on this little piece of paradise when we bought this place and never in a million years thought I'd end up living on my own here after such a short time,' Grace said, fishing the keys out of her bag. 'It was difficult at first, but I've made it just the way I want it. It's my home and I love it.' She pushed open the door and we followed her into the small hallway.

'Meet Harry.' Grace knelt down and scooped up a long-haired black-and-white cat. 'He's the only reliable man in my life and that's the way it's staying – well, for now, anyway,' she grinned, handing me the cute bundle of fluff who immediately purred and butted his head gently against my face.

'He's adorable,' I exclaimed.

'Let me take your suitcase and show you up to your room. Follow me,' Grace insisted, hanging her coat on a peg and climbing the stairs while Connie disappeared down the hallway.

'There's a bathroom in there and that's my room,' she nodded towards the door at the far end of the landing. 'You're in here,' she said, pushing open the door with her foot while dragging the case behind her. I put Harry down on the floor and he immediately jumped up on to the bed and gently padded the duvet with his paws. I took in my surroundings.

'Look at this place, very shabby chic.' On the bedside table there was a lamp and a small vase of colourful flowers. The antique rose bouquet bedding looked so inviting on the single bed and lengths of triangular floral bunting featured strongly, as did the twinkling of fairy lights draped across the light-pink pastel walls, giving the room a very homely feel. There was a single wardrobe, a dressing table and a pink stripy rug that lay on the exposed wooden floor and an idyllic view out of the bedroom window. 'Now this is what you call a room with a view,' I said in utter amazement, staring out on to the fields beyond. Again, so different from the view I was used to back in New York.

'It's quite a sight, isn't it?' Grace stood by the side of me and looked out of the window. 'Eventually, this room was going to be a nursery, but how things change in such a short space of time!' She spoke with a twinge of sadness to her voice.

'I don't know what to say,' I admitted, thinking of how happy Grace had seemed when she'd announced the news that they'd finally got the keys to this place.

'What can you say? Finn wasn't the person I thought he was. Within hours of finding out he'd been having an affair, I stripped the house of all his belongings and changed the locks. You'd never have known he'd ever lived here. He moved straight in with her and signed the house over to me.'

'Guilt?'

Grace nodded, 'Probably. At times, the mortgage is a struggle with the type of work I'm in. Things can get a bit tight, but I've had a good run with *Mamma Mia* and managed to save enough for the next couple of months, in case I find it difficult to get work.'

'Have you got anything else lined up?' I asked, lifting my case on to the bed. I thought back to my own dreary flat in

New York, so unlike the soft comfort of Grace's home. I could cope with Grace's kind of tight, if this is what I had to come home to every day ... a beautiful cottage with spectacular views and no drum and bass pounding above my head into the early hours. This was heaven, pure heaven.

'There's a few auditions coming up which my agent has put me forward for, so fingers crossed, but you need to tell me what you've been up to. After graduating from performing arts ... well done you, by the way ... your lack of status updates must mean you're extremely busy.'

'Yes, very busy,' I answered. The words tumbled out of my mouth before I'd thought about what I was going to say. I didn't want to stand there and admit I was a failure or share with Grace that I was living in a run-down flat, struggling to pay my bills with barely any money to my name. What would she think?

'Yes, in fact ...' again I wasn't thinking, 'I'm just waiting to hear about an audition ... a huge show opening on Broadway.'

Inside I was screaming to myself, *Alice, what are you doing? Just tell the truth!* I couldn't believe I'd lied to Grace. I felt so underhanded, but she'd assumed I had it all, and I couldn't face admitting to her that the truth was so very different.

Grace was successful, living the dream, and I wasn't. I didn't want the focus of conversation to be on me – I'd only just arrived. The last thing I wanted to do was talk about how it had all gone wrong for the girl in New York City. The reason I didn't post regular updates on Facebook wasn't because I was too busy. It was more down to the fact that I didn't have anything to say. Surely, there was no harm in telling a tiny white lie.

'How exciting! I knew you'd make it big and in New York too. You had that raw talent ... anyone could see that, even at an early age. I tell all my friends about you ... my friend is a star in New York! Everyone is jealous ... I can only dream about being that successful.'

How dreadful did I suddenly feel, misleading Grace like that? I needed to put her right straight away ... but I didn't. I swallowed, opened my mouth, but no words came out. I hadn't meant to give her the impression I was something special, I was far from special, but for the first time in a long time, it was heart-warming to think someone actually thought I could be successful and capable of achieving my dreams too. That part gave me hope and boosted my confidence a little. So I wasn't quite ready to spout out how difficult things were back in NYC. Did anyone really need to know?

My heart squeezed with guilt for giving Grace the wrong impression, and giving myself a small shake, I managed a slight smile.

'At least you can recharge your batteries while you're here on holiday,' said Grace.

The word 'holiday' echoed in my head. Usually a holiday was a short period of time away from your work and then you returned home, but already, within a couple of hours, I felt more relaxed than I had in a long time, away from the bright lights of the city. Brook Bridge village was already drawing me in and I hadn't even seen Grandie yet.

'What are you pair doing up there?' Connie shouted up the stairs. 'The food's ready.'

Grateful for the change of focus and thankful this conversation was over for the time being, I gave a small sigh of relief.

'Coming,' Grace shouted. 'Are you okay with Harry sleeping on your bed?' He was now curled up in a tight ball and fast asleep at the foot of the bed.

I smiled at him, 'He's absolutely fine there, I don't mind at all.'

Animals had been a huge part of my life when I lived in England and I missed the unconditional love they provided. I can remember feeling disappointed when I signed the lease for my flat back in New York, and the very last clause stated no pets were allowed, not even a goldfish.

'Can I quickly use the bathroom to freshen up?' I asked, taking the washbag out of my case and pulling a brush through my hair.

'Of course, there's a bundle of fresh towels in there. Help yourself to anything, treat the place like it's your own.'

Five minutes later, feeling refreshed, I wandered towards the kitchen. Connie had rustled up a delicious-looking ham-and-egg salad with homemade onion chutney and fresh crusty bread. 'Eggs from the chickens at Honeysuckle Farm,' she smiled. 'Simply divine, and homemade pickles too.'

'This looks delightful,' I hungrily announced, sitting down at the table opposite Grace who was scrolling on her phone. 'Thank you.'

'I've received a message from Molly on Facebook,' Grace

flicked her phone towards me, 'asking if you've arrived safely.'

I gasped. 'I forgot to message her and Mum when I landed. I'll do it now. Talking of Facebook, I flicked through your latest photo album.' I wasn't sure why but the photograph of Sam Reid immediately popped into my mind. 'You looked amazing.'

Grace picked up her knife and fork. 'Thank you. The cast's last night together – it's always sad when a production comes to an end. I'm actually feeling pretty gloomy about it. It becomes your whole life and then suddenly there's nothing, but you'd know that feeling.' Grace flicked a glance in my direction.

I didn't say anything but felt yet another pang of guilt at not confiding in them both about my current situation.

'In fact, were your ears burning? You were the hot topic of conversation,' Grace now teased, giving me a wink.

'Ha! Me?' I asked in wonderment when I realised she wasn't joking. 'How come?'

Grace took a mouthful of water and put her glass back on the table. 'I mentioned you to one of the cast members, told them my best friend from across the pond was a superstar and you were jetting in from New York for a visit.'

'Far from a superstar,' I managed to say.

'Says the one who is far too busy to update her social media due to her hectic schedule!'

Grace gave me a knowing smile and I could feel my cheeks redden at the mere thought that my little white lie was already coming back to haunt me only seconds later. Why did I have to give the wrong impression? The embarrassment and guilt were gnawing away at me, I knew I was no superstar. 'Over-exaggeration,' my voice came out a little sharper than expected.

'Don't be modest, credit where credit's due, and it was only Sam I was chatting to.'

My ears pricked up, 'Sam?'

'Yes, Sam ... Sam Reid, the lead role in the production we've just finished.'

My heart was racing now.

'He was very impressed I had a friend who lived in New York City, in fact we need to have a drink with him while you're over here.'

Of course I was nervous about meeting the man in the photograph I'd admired from afar – but also a little excited. 'I think I saw him in one of your photos: tight T-shirt, Levi's jeans.'

'You did notice him and scrutinised his photograph, by the sound of it,' smiled Grace.

'Maybe a little,' I smiled, feeling the crimson flush to my cheeks.

'You'd get on well, both of you are top of your game ... are you blushing?'

'Leave the girl alone, give her time to settle in before you go teasing her,' Connie joined in, trying to rescue me from Grace's scrutiny.

The blushed cheeks had everything to do with Sam Reid but were also helped along by the high pedestal everyone seemed to be putting me on, which I'd encouraged by not offering the truth straight away about my life and career.

'What about the kids we went to school with? Sarah, Sian, Lizzie and Ben, are they still living around these parts?' I asked, safely steering the conversation away from my failing career.

'They all moved on after university. Sarah's a vet, Sian's a doctor and Lizzie works on one of the national newspapers in London. They all discovered life outside the village, but Ben is still here.'

'Works for his dad's building firm. The yard is still in the same place, just off Captain's Lane, and doing very well, by all accounts. The new development we drove past on the way in is all down to them,' Connie chipped in.

I gave a low whistle. 'Definitely doing all right for himself.' Inside my mood slumped a little further. It seemed there was only me out of the old gang that wasn't in the least bit successful. For the past twelve months, I knew I'd been stuck in a rut, unable to see my way out of it all. Every day it had been a struggle, the same old same old, and there had even been days when I didn't want to climb out of bed and sweep the stage of the theatre. I wanted more, and I knew I was capable of more. Things needed to change and hearing about how successful my old school pals were gave me a jolt. Inside a spark of determination ignited, just like the feeling I'd had when I was a little girl dreaming of a life on the stage.

'Is the dance school still open?' I looked towards Connie and took a sip of my drink.

She looked up, 'Afraid not. It closed down the day you left.'

I raised my eyebrows. 'The day we left? Really? That's so sad,' I answered, feeling a gush of emotion, but I suppose in all honesty that was what I'd expected to hear.

'It was very sad, it affected the whole community. All those children and adults suddenly without dance classes. Some had been coming to the school for years. It affected Ted's mental state in a big way. He felt like he'd let everyone down, so he hid away in the farmhouse for a while. He couldn't face anyone, the questions ...'

'Was there any chance of him handing it over to anyone else?' I asked, already knowing the answer and unable to keep the slight note of sadness from my voice.

Connie regretfully shook her head. 'No, that was Florrie's school, a family business. He would never have entrusted it to anyone else.'

I pressed my lips together, not knowing what to say.

'I suppose without the support of Rose he would have found it difficult to manage. He didn't want to interview new staff,' added Connie, her eyes blinking sadly at me. 'It was one of those things ... timing.'

'What happened to the school? Did Grandie sell it?' I asked, thinking it had probably been bulldozed for houses by now.

'No, he didn't sell it. Funnily enough, Jim and I were talking about it only this week. The dance school is still locked up and Jim checks on it on a weekly basis.'

'Really?' I asked, amazed. 'And it hasn't been used since?'

Connie said sadly, 'Ted couldn't bear to part with it ... Memories, I suppose.'

I wasn't sure why but all of a sudden I felt emotional, my eyes prickled with tears and my throat became tight. Even though it hadn't been my choice to leave back then, a wave of guilt washed over me. The day we left for New York, Grandie had lost everything: us, the dance school and his life within the community. It was so sad to hear.

I slapped the table as a thought occurred to me. 'I'd love to see it, while I'm here,' I blurted, hoping that was a possibility. 'Jim has the keys, you say?'

'Absolutely,' replied Connie. 'And of course you can. I'm sure your grandfather won't mind at all.'

Delighted by Connie's enthusiasm, I realised the dance school still held a special place in my heart. That had been my grandfather's empire, his passion and a huge part of my childhood. How would it feel to step back inside that building? A shiver of excitement ricocheted through my body at the very thought.

We spent the next twenty minutes enjoying our food and chatting about all the people I might remember in the village. The pair of them reeled off a long list of names, mainly from the dance school days, but I couldn't remember half the people they mentioned.

'Dessert?' asked Connie, standing up and collecting the empty plates from the table.

'Not for me, thank you.'

'Or me,' Grace smiled up at her mum. 'Sit down, I'll clear away in a moment.'

'If you're sure?'

'Of course.'

'I hope you don't mind, but I'm going to get going, leave you girls to it,' she said, slipping her arms into her coat and grabbing her bag from the worktop.

'Thank you for picking me up from the airport,' I said, smiling up at Connie.

'You are more than welcome. Shall I collect you around eleven-ish tomorrow and we can visit your grandfather? Would that time suit you?'

'Perfect,' I answered with a little apprehension. I was beginning to feel nervous about seeing him again.

Connie must have noticed the look on my face. 'There's no need to be nervous, I promise.'

Grace stood up and kissed her mum on the cheek before Connie disappeared out of the cottage.

'Here, have a look through that while I wash up.' Grace handed me a programme from the latest production she'd performed in.

'I'll help you clear up.'

'You will do no such thing,' Grace insisted. 'Sit and relax, it won't take long.'

'I could get used to this.'

Grace began to run the hot water while I browsed through the thick booklet she'd handed me. 'Wow! Good photo of you there,' I cooed, incredibly proud of her. 'Just think where it all started, in a little village dance school.'

'I know, two superstars from the same community.' She flashed me a grin, placing the dishes on the drainer.

This was my opportunity to come clean, to tell Grace I'd never made it on to the stage, I'd never passed an audition or even got a call back. My face would never be printed in a programme. But I didn't tell her. Instead I kept quiet, not wanting anyone's pity. I didn't want people to know how badly I'd failed, so I brushed over it once more, hiding the fact that I was a disappointment.

Turning the pages casually, I knew at any second Sam Reid would once again be staring back at me, and there he was on page twelve, making the hairs on the back on my neck stand to attention.

Grace must have noticed I'd gone quiet and glanced over my shoulder.

'Sam Reid, Birmingham Hippodrome's favourite heart throb.' Grace pressed her lips together then whistled softly.

'Which I'm assuming is undisputed.' I knew I was staring gormlessly at his picture. 'It's a hard job but someone has to do it,' I murmured, still not able to tear my eyes away from the page.

'Absolutely.'

'Will Sam Reid be joining us in the pub tonight?' I bit down on my lip to stop my smile from escaping.

'No, afraid not, but I'm sure it's more than likely you'll bump into him very soon.'

'It's a pity he's not out tonight.'

'You're staring!'

'His eyes are mesmerising. There's something about Sam Reid.'

'Which is?' Grace quizzed.

'Very photogenic.' I paused. 'What's the relationship status of this man?'

With a wide grin Grace smiled in my direction, 'That'll be single!'

Chapter 7

After a quick shower, I hung up my clothes in the wardrobe and chose an unassuming outfit of white skinny jeans, accompanied by a light-blue stripy blouse before sitting at the dressing table. I used a couple of wands of mascara and a dab of nude shiny lip gloss, brushed through my hair, squirted my perfume and declared myself ready.

The jetlag was beginning to kick in now, but if I could manage to keep going for a few more hours, I'd hopefully fall quite easily into the UK time zone.

Grace rapped on the door. 'You still awake?' she asked, leaning against the doorframe.

'Just about,' I said, standing up and slipping my comfy battered pumps on my feet. 'You have permission to flick my ears if I fall asleep on you.'

'Ha! You'll be fine. Once you're there you'll get a second wind ... just shout up as soon as you want to come back,'

Grace said with a smile. 'The pub is only five minutes' walk away, if that.'

'Which one are we going to?' I asked, grabbing my bag and a cardigan.

'The Malt Shovel, the one on the high street.'

As Grace and I set off up the lane with our arms linked and the warmth of the evening sun on our faces, a sense of contentment flooded my veins as the pub grew close. This was the pub Grandie and I used to sit outside regularly ... happy memories from a time before everything changed.

The outside benches were already jam-packed with drinkers chatting and laughing while enjoying the weather. Grace led the way through the heavy oak door then pushed through the thirsty customers and waved towards the barman. I was taken aback by the charm of the place; as a child, I'd never really noticed. It was so different from the rooftop bar overlooking Manhattan. The quintessential low ceiling held aloft by wooden beams, the stone floors and the fireplaces gave the whole place a cosy feel. The mahogany shelving in the corner was littered with bric-a-brac and books. From the flashing fruit machine in the corner came a clatter of falling money as a man stood and scooped up his winnings.

Grace stopped in a space and I lingered behind her. As soon as he finished serving the girl at the side of us, the barman turned towards Grace with a full-on beam.

'Good evening, do you remember Alice?' Grace gestured towards me.

I smiled. His face looked familiar, but I couldn't quite picture him. 'Hi,' I said, narrowing my eyes and scrutinising him.

'That's not a local accent ... American?' He scrunched up his face and bit down on his lip.

'No shit, Sherlock,' chuckled Grace. 'Definitely an American accent.'

He studied my face.

'Lived around these parts until she was ten. My mum works at the farm owned by her grandfather ...'

As the penny dropped his face changed from a look of confusion back to a grin. 'You're kidding me ... Alice ... Alice Parker.'

'The one and only,' Grace responded whilst glancing back in my direction.

I smiled at him even though I was none the wiser who he was.

'This is Henry Carter. You must remember Henry, Ben's younger brother.'

'Alice Parker ...' he took a breath, 'the one who broke my brother's heart when you moved to New York.' He thrust his hand over the bar and I heartily shook it.

'My God, Henry! You've grown!' I said, amazed. His curly blond hair fell across his golden skin and his blue eyes flashed instant warmth.

'That's what normally happens,' he goofily grinned.

'I didn't really break his heart, did I?' I quickly added.

'He never got over it.' Grace winked at Henry.

81

'Stop teasing, the pair of you!' I smiled. 'How is he?'

'He'll be in later, ask him yourself. He'll be made up to see you, no doubt. Now, what can I get you both to drink?'

'Gin and tonic please,' I piped up.

'I'll have the same,' answered Grace.

'These are on the house, welcome home Alice! Go and grab a table and I'll bring them over.'

'Thank you,' we both said in unison.

'What a lovely welcome. If I'd known it was this friendly I would have been back sooner!' I pulled out a chair and settled down at the table.

Grace laughed and slipped into the chair opposite me. 'You've always been welcome, you know that. So, thirteen years of catching up, where the heck do we start?'

'School, first dates, college, work, the list is endless.'

There wasn't much I didn't know about Grace's life. Her constant updates on Instagram and Facebook kept me informed. I knew about her break-up, every job she'd ever worked, every show she'd ever performed in, whereas my Facebook was sparse, past posts were carefully selected and never gave anything away about my real life and how bad it had become.

I lifted my hair off my neck, twisted it up into a bun and secured it with a bobble from around my wrist.

'Where to start?' I sat up straight, 'But what I do know is, being miles apart hasn't affected our friendship, it still feels like we are the best of friends.'

Grace agreed, 'I know ... that's what a true friendship is

all about. We might not live in each other's pockets, but I agree, what's 3,000 miles between best friends?'

'Here you go, ladies.'

We both looked up to see that a smiley Henry had appeared at the side of the table. He placed two gin and tonics down on the beer mats in front of us.

'I hope you don't mind, I texted Ben to let him know you were here.'

'How lovely,' I didn't mind at all, 'it would be nice to see him after all this time.'

'And how's your grandfather? He's been absent for a while, usually props up that bar on a Sunday afternoon with his pint of ale.'

'I bet ... That's why I'm back, he's not too well at the moment,' I answered, taking a sip of my drink.

'I'm sorry to hear that.' He gave me a sympathetic smile.

'Old age, they call it.'

'Give him my best.'

'Will do.'

'I never want to get old,' Grace chipped in the second Henry returned to the bar.

'You and me both,' I said, having sudden visions of reaching the age of eighty, still living in the same damp cold flat, wrapped in numerous blankets, still unable to afford the heating and listening to the dreadful music pounding through the ceiling until the early hours of the morning.

'Boyfriend?' she asked, narrowing her eyes at me.

I shook my head, 'Not at the moment.'

'In between jobs, though.'

I nodded, which wasn't strictly a lie but not entirely the truth.

'Anyway, what happened with Finn?' I'd noticed Grace's relationship status change to single a while back and we'd chatted briefly over messenger but the situation had been too raw for her to talk about. She'd been in the middle of a production and the only way to cope was to get herself through each day as it came.

Grace looked like she was on the verge of tears. 'I should have known after the shoddy proposal it wouldn't go the distance. He went down on one knee after a skinful of beer and a night of karaoke followed by a greasy kebab ... living the dream,' she said sarcastically.

'I wasn't expecting you two to split, though ... everything always seemed ...'

'Okay on Facebook?' she interjected, rolling her eyes.

'So, what happened?' I asked tentatively.

'Where do I start?' Grace's voice rose an octave. 'Never live your life through Facebook, because when it's over you look a right idiot.' She blew out a breath and stretched out her legs before blinking away the teary mist from her eyes.

'To be honest, it came as a bit of a shock to me too. One minute, he was there, next he was gone from my life forever. It felt like my heart had been ripped out, it hurt so much.' Her voice was shaky.

I reached over and squeezed her hand. 'Do you want to talk about it?'

She sighed, flipping a beer mat over in her hand, and nodded. She paused for a second and took a deep breath. 'He blamed me, said it was my fault that we'd drifted apart, which I think is a bit of a cheek as I wasn't aware we'd drifted at all.'

'How did he make that out?' I raised my eyebrows.

'He said he got lonely every night.'

'When you were out working?'

'Yes, but he knew that had always been my job. I perform on stage, the schedule is gruelling – you'll know that – but that's what makes me, me. That's the person he fell in love with. I haven't changed.' She took a breath. 'And when he accused me of having an affair with Sam, the leading man, I couldn't believe it. It was ridiculous.' She took a sip of her drink.

The hurt on Grace's face was clearly visible.

'At a guess, maybe it was his own insecurities.'

'More like the best form of defence is attack. I've never been interested in anyone else and even when I acted opposite Sam Reid every hour for months, I wasn't even tempted. I wouldn't have done that to him. Especially, knowing what Mum has been through with my dad, the affairs ... the lies. I wouldn't dream of putting anyone through that pain.'

'That's because you're a good person.'

'It wouldn't have been so bad, but trying to shift the blame on to me! If he'd told me he was unhappy, that's one thing, but to carry on behind my back for nearly six months ... I felt a fool. I'd no clue, working every night. He was always back before I got home, playing the dutiful boyfriend.'

'How did you find out he was seeing someone else?'

'It was my day off and I'd nipped into his office to take him out for a surprise lunch, but the surprise was all mine. The reception desk was empty, so I didn't think anything of walking straight through to his office to see if he was there. He was there all right, having it away with her in the office. So clichéd, grim doesn't even cover it.'

I stared open-mouthed at Grace. 'What did you do?'

'Kept my dignity, turned around and came home. I dumped all of his belongings in bin-bags and left them out on the front garden, then began to worry about how I was going to pay the mortgage by myself. He moved in with her, but rumour has it, it fell apart soon after. But I'm not totally sure, as I cut all ties. Everyone was shocked, even his parents were devastated. I'm just glad I didn't give him any more years of my life or had children with him. Can you imagine?'

Listening to Grace, I could hear the wretchedness in her voice. It was clear she was still devastated by the whole sorry situation. Her heart had been well and truly broken.

'Honestly, he's mad to give you up.'

'It doesn't take away the pain though, does it?'

I shook my head. 'How did you cope at work?'

'Sam was a legend. Can you imagine going on stage night after night, forcing a smile on your face, when all you wanted to do was hide under your duvet? He held me up, made sure

I was fed, watered and kept me distracted at work. He was good to me.'

'Just a friend?' I narrowed my eyes at her, hoping the answer was yes.

'Don't you start. I've had enough of those accusations from Finn.'

'Sorry, I didn't mean to upset you.'

'You haven't. Finn only accused me as he was trying to cover up his own guilty feelings.'

'And how are you coping now?' I asked, drinking the last dregs from my glass.

'Good,' she said, 'in fact, damn good. Working hard in the job I love so much, and your timing couldn't have been better. With the show finishing I've got time on my hands and I'm looking forward to spending it with my oldest friend.' Her eyes sparkled as she smiled kindly towards me.

'I can't believe I'm actually here, Grace.'

If someone had told me two weeks ago I would be sitting in a pub in my home village of Brook Bridge I would have thought they were completely mad. How things can change in such a short space of time. I know Grandie being ill was the push I'd needed to make my excuses to come home to England, and maybe my return wouldn't have happened if it wasn't for Grace's message, but I was here now with a sense of belonging, already feeling like I'd never been away.

'Now, less of the doom and gloom, tell me all about New York. All that razzmatazz, I bet it's a-m-a-z-i-n-g living and working there?' She strung out the word amazing while shimmying her jazz hands in the air. 'Is it really the city that never sleeps? I bet you live in a fancy flat with all the mod cons, probably even have famous neighbours! And tell me all about the productions you've finished? You should post more photos, you know.' Grace finally came up for air.

I didn't know how to reply. Right here, another perfect opportunity presented itself to come clean, to confide in Grace that my life wasn't all that great ... *Tell her the truth.* The words whirled in my head. Taking a breath, it was now or never, but where did I start?

I gulped and opened my mouth to start talking.

'Alice Parker is back in town!' a voice boomed.

On this occasion I'd been saved by Ben Carter, who I recognised immediately. He hadn't changed one little bit.

I beamed at his enthusiasm, his arms were flung wide. 'Alice Parker, a vision of utter loveliness, I knew you'd come back for me one day!'

'Always the joker,' I burst into laughter, springing to my feet and tightly hugging him.

'And always the flirt,' laughed Grace.

He kissed me lightly on the cheek, taking me by surprise, then stood back and held my hands. 'I honestly never thought you'd cross my path again. Married ... single?' he added, and raised his eyebrows at me hopefully. 'And what's with that accent?'

'That might be down to living in New York for thirteen years! How are you?' I grinned in an attempt to steer the conversation away from my non-existent love life. 'Grab a chair, come and join us.'

Ben swivelled a chair round and sat at the table. 'Drinks ... your drinks are empty, my round.' He waved his hand above his head. 'Henry,' he bellowed, 'we need drinks! What are you both having?'

'Gin and tonic, very kind.'

Ben looked over his shoulder, but Henry was busy serving other customers at the bar.

'Two seconds, don't go anywhere.' He leapt up and I noticed Henry tip him a wink to help himself.

'Hurry back, Alice was just about to tell me all about her life in New York.'

There was an excitement in her voice which made my mood slump a little again.

She flapped her hand at me. 'Come on then, let's hear all about it. And Molly, she's a star too ... a radio presenter ... Friends in high places?'

Ground, swallow me up ...

I was beginning to perspire at the very thought of this conversation and smiled wistfully towards Grace. 'We can save all about me for another day,' I offered, hopefully managing to steer the conversation away from me yet again. 'I want to hear all about Ben and this building business he's in.'

Grace eyed me carefully, her expression knotted with concentration. 'I get it ... you don't want to sound big-headed in front of Ben ... city girl ... life in New York ... hitting the big time ... but I'll be grilling you later.' She was, of course, totally oblivious to my discomfort as I cringed inside. I may be a city girl but hit the big time I had not.

'Exactly, can you imagine? He'll think I'm a big-headed American,' I said, feeling shifty, but relieved I'd bought myself a little time before I had to face the embarrassing conversation that was whirling around in my head.

'It's all about Ben, then, as soon as he comes back ... he'll like that,' she chuckled. 'Honestly, he's the biggest flirt in the village, very full on all the time.'

'I'm assuming single, then?'

'Very much so,' laughed Grace.

True to her word, when Ben returned Grace began talking to him about his business and how his dad was going to make him a partner in the company.

Her kindness since I'd arrived made my little white lie even more unbearable. I knew I needed to put this situation right ASAP, but the more she thought I was something I wasn't, the harder it was becoming to tell her the truth.

Chapter 8

The following morning, as soon as the breakfast dishes had been cleared away, the anxious feeling in my stomach began to surface again.

Grace must have noticed my shift in mood. 'You okay?' Her eyes roamed my face, full of concern as she passed me a cup of tea.

I managed a brief smile and sat down at the kitchen table. 'Just feeling a little ...'

'There's nothing to worry about, nothing has changed. He still loves you,' Grace interrupted, trying to reassure me. It was like she'd just read my mind.

I slid my eyes doubtfully towards her and smiled briefly. I wanted to believe her, of course I did, but such a long time had passed. I'd no idea how Grace could be so certain how Grandie would feel. A lot had happened in the last thirteen years and that familiar feeling of dread, the fear of rejection, was swirling in the pit of my stomach once more. What if ... what if he didn't want to see me?

We both turned our heads towards the kitchen clock. 'It's nearly time,' Grace said softly as I exhaled and followed her into the living room. Standing side by side, we stared out of the living-room window, waiting for Connie to arrive. As soon as we spotted the car turn into the top of the road we looked at each other nervously.

My heart raced. 'How do I look?' I asked anxiously, smoothing down my top.

'You look great, now stop worrying,' she insisted. 'Ted is a gorgeous man, you have nothing to worry about,' she assured me. 'Now go and make an old man happy.'

For a split second, I stared out of the window, expression-less, then waved at Connie before plastering a smile on my face. Grace handed me my bag and pressed a kiss hastily to my cheek and ushered me towards the door.

My stomach flipped, and my legs were trembling as I walked towards the car. I looked back over my shoulder, trying to smile bravely. We exchanged looks then Grace gave me a thumbs-up.

Nervously, I climbed into the passenger seat of Connie's car and took a breath.

'Ready?' asked Connie. The car engine was running and her hand rested on the gear stick.

'Ready,' I swallowed, painting a smile on my face and really not knowing what to expect.

This was it, I was on my way to see my grandfather for

the first time in thirteen years. After Grace's reassurance, my spirits lifted a little, but I knew in my heart I had to do this, despite his fall-out with Mum. And I desperately wanted to see him again.

We spent most of the car journey in a companionable silence, Connie leaving me to my own thoughts. She concentrated on the road ahead while I gazed out of the window, watching the pretty houses whizz by with their colourful hanging baskets and freshly cut, striped lawns. On the edge of the village ran Brook Bridge stream, a popular spot with dog walkers.

Once we drove past the church, we were out of the village and my mind kept flipping back to the argument I'd witnessed as a small child between Grandie and Mum. My heart still banged against my ribcage at the thought of the drama I'd witnessed. What on earth had happened that day?

Both of their tempers had flared like I'd never seen before, their unkind words firmly planted in my mind. Seeing the two people that I loved most in the world arguing so vigorously had been painful enough, but the most awful thing was that argument had changed my life forever. If the truth be told, the more I thought about it, the more I resented it. I'd lost my home, my friends, my Grandie and my life at Brook Bridge. Why hadn't the row just blown over? Why had Mum allowed it to change my life so fundamentally and catapult us to the other side of the world? I wondered if Grandie would be willing to talk about it now. Would I finally discover what it was they were rowing about that day?

I tried to dismiss all thoughts of the past and blinked away the memory. Today was about building a new relationship with my grandfather, one that I'd missed dreadfully. Hopefully we could start to look towards the future, not the past.

I felt the corners of my mouth lift just thinking about Honeysuckle Farm, a magical place that gave me comfort and joy – a stable family home that even now made me feel truly blessed to have such wonderful childhood memories. I'd no idea why Mum would ever want to leave this idyllic countryside and live on the other side of the world, surrounded by the bright but anonymous lights of the city, its vista dominated by skyscrapers, when we'd lived in the most beautiful place.

It didn't take long to drive to the small cottage hospital and once Connie had parked the car we walked towards the entrance, past the ambulances that were lined up outside.

Once inside, I could feel myself beginning to tremble.

Bright smile, Alice.

'I'll take you up to Ted's room and then I'll sit in there,' Connie nodded, towards the small café area situated on the ground floor. 'I'll grab myself a coffee and I've brought a book to read, so you take all the time you need, there's no rush.'

'Thank you,' was all I could muster, holding on to my tears.

We followed the gleaming white floor and the polystyrene-tiled ceiling towards the second floor.

'Okay, there's his room.' Connie stood still and tipped her head towards the door in front of us before swiftly kissing my cheek. 'Good luck,' she whispered and without saying another word she turned to go.

'Connie,' I swallowed down a lump in my throat and immediately she spun back round towards me. 'What if he doesn't want to see me? What if he rejects me?'

Connie quickly stepped forward, giving me a warm smile, then held both my hands. 'Don't be so tough on yourself, your grandfather loves you, that'll never change. Now go and make his day.'

Her kind words caused a gush of tears to spring to my eyes, as I tried to compose myself standing there, watching her disappear along the corridor then out of sight.

For a split second, I hovered outside the door of Grandie's private room. Nervous didn't even come close, as a huge dollop of fear descended over me. I was relieved he wasn't on a ward surrounded by other people because I had no idea how this reunion was going to be. Would he reject me in anger, or welcome me back with open arms? Either way, it was going to be emotional. I was filled with excitement and fear, and there was only one way to ease that grinding knot in my stomach. I exhaled, and with my heart in my mouth I slowly pushed open the door, my hands unhelpfully shaking.

The sun shone through the cracks in the blinds, painting narrow, vertical bands of light on the magnolia walls. With a hundred fireflies fluttering around my stomach, my eyes darted towards the bed.

There he was.

Grandie was lying underneath a white cotton sheet with a blue blanket over the top, pulled up under his chin. His eyes were closed, and I tiptoed towards the blue plastic seat – the kind you find in every school, village hall and hospital – on the other side of the room. His hair was wispy grey, his cheeks hollow and pale. He looked so frail, thinner than I remembered, and wires protruded from a gap in his pyjamas and hooked up to the monitor at the side of the bed which bleeped every few seconds.

Gripped by emotion, I tried to keep hold of my tears, but it was in vain and they rolled down my cheeks as I quickly brushed them away. I'd missed him so much and my heart filled with love for him and regret for all the years that had been lost and couldn't be replaced. I'd never felt as helpless as I did in this moment.

I quietly pulled up the chair and sat by the side of his bed, not wanting to wake him, he looked so peaceful lying there. I tightened the band of my ponytail then folded my arms and held my breath. Would he even recognise me when he woke up?

In the peace and quiet of the warm hospital room, I suddenly felt tired. I'd managed to sleep a little last night but not until I'd tossed and turned until 3 a.m., desperate to drift off. No doubt the jetlag had prevented me from falling asleep until close to my usual New York bedtime. I stretched out my legs in front of me and could feel my head beginning to droop as my eyelids closed together.

The next thing I knew, I heard a cough and began to stir.

I must have nodded off altogether. Opening my eyes, it took me a second to realise where I was. A quick glance at my watch told me I'd been dozing for twenty minutes or so. Then, looking over towards Grandie, I met his inquisitive stare. A weird tension simmered under the surface while he battled to focus. I shifted self-consciously in my seat and for a second no one spoke.

He sat up straighter and reached towards the bedside cabinet, grasping at a pair of glasses which he slowly balanced on the bridge of his nose without taking his eyes off me. He didn't say anything, just blinked and stared.

'Hi, Grandie,' I said softly.

'Alice ... Alice, is that you?' Grandie murmured with an element of surprise in his voice, raising his bushy eyebrows. His voice sounded just as I remembered it.

I let out a long breath, 'Yes Grandie, it's me.' I leant forward and held both his hands gently.

He gasped and his mouth fell open, then the corners of his mouth began to lift.

A wave of emotion caused me to blink back the tears.

'Look at you, look at you, and that accent!' He cupped his hands around mine and took a breath. 'You gave me a shock, you did, a good shock.' He quickly added, 'All grown up and beautiful ... beautiful. I never thought ...' His voice trailed off and he removed his glasses and dabbed his watery eyes on the sleeve of his PJs.

'How are you, Grandie, how are you feeling?'

'Grandie ... Grandie,' he repeated, 'I never thought I'd hear you say that word ever again. I can't believe you are here. You've made an old man very happy.'

He gave me such a big smile that I couldn't stop smiling too. 'You don't know how pleased I am to hear that.' The relief that he hadn't rejected me swept through my body.

'I feel like a silly old fool and useless lying here. Fancy falling over,' he smiled. 'It's just bruises and a bump, nothing to worry about.' He touched the bandage on his head. 'It looks worse than it is.'

'What's the machine for?'

'Monitoring my heart rate, I think. Thankfully it's still beeping which means I'm alive,' he gave a small chuckle.

I patted his arm soothingly, 'That's good to hear!'

'How long have you been here?' he asked, pushing himself up in bed and reaching for the glass on the bedside cabinet.

'Here, let me pour you some fresh water,' I offered.

'I'd prefer something a little stronger.'

'I'll remember for next time,' I grinned, taking the glass from him and rinsing it out at the small basin in the corner of the room before filling it back up from the jug of water that was by the side of his bed. 'I arrived back in England yesterday.'

'I'd no idea you were even coming, not that I'm complaining. Where are you staying? How long for?'

I handed him the glass, 'With Grace. And Connie picked me up from the airport. It was good to see them both again. They've made me feel very welcome, like I've never been away. It's been too long.'

He nodded. 'They are worth their weight in gold. I can't believe they'd keep this a secret from me.'

'They are,' I admitted, thankful they'd looked out for him all these years.

'Tell me ... about you ... What do you do?' his eyebrows waggled with intrigue. 'I want to hear all about my Alice.'

The past thirteen years whirled in my mind, and in particular the last few of those years. I was battling my own conscience, it was so hard to know what to say next. If I told Grandie the truth about my life right now, he'd only worry, and I didn't want him fretting about me while he wasn't in the best state of health. But I didn't want to lie either. I felt guilty enough misleading Grace. I knew I had to put that right, and I would, this evening.

'Please tell me you're still dancing?' Grandie looked hopeful.

I swerved the question: 'I studied performing arts in New York and I graduated with flying colours,' which wasn't a lie.

'I'm so proud of you Alice, more than you'll ever know,' he thumped his chest and his heart monitor beeped loudly.

My hand flew to my own chest and my eyes swung towards the monitor, struggling to catch my breath. 'Gr-Grandie,' I stammered, my eyes as wide as saucers, panicking that something was wrong.

'It's okay, it's okay,' he glanced briefly back towards the machine as the bleeping began to behave itself once more. 'It's only me setting it off.'

'Grandie, don't do that!' I'd jumped out of my skin as the beeping increased tenfold.

'Sorry! I didn't mean to do that ...' he smiled. 'I'm still here.'

He began to chuckle and I couldn't help feeling grateful for his sense of humour.

'I knew the minute you were born, you were a performer, it was in here' – this time he placed his hand lightly on his chest. 'I'm a dancer, you're a dancer, it's in our genes and there's no changing that. I'm glad you carried on down that path. New York, you say ... a world away from Brook Bridge village, but ample opportunity, I suppose, to make a decent life for yourself.'

He wasn't wrong, the two places couldn't be any more different.

'Didn't you know that's where we were going?'

He shook his head, and the pain in his eyes was clearly noticeable. 'At first, I'd no idea,' he said, letting out a long breath.

Just hearing the sadness in Grandie's voice smashed my heart into a million pieces.

'It was only when Grace received your first letter that Connie told me where you were. We couldn't believe it ... New York!' He struggled to catch his breath. 'Before then I'd no way of finding you or contacting you. Believe me, I wrote to you many times. I asked Connie for the address – you see, it was on Grace's letter – but I never posted them ... I didn't know if they'd be passed on.'

'It's okay, let's not dwell on that. I'm here now,' I reassured him, patting his hand.

'Very true,' he smiled.

'And I'm going nowhere.'

'I just wish ... those lost years.'

'I know Grandie, don't get upset,' I soothed.

He nodded. 'I'm glad you kept up with the singing and dancing.'

This was my cue to tell him that my career wasn't all that great, but looking at him lying there, it could wait – for now.

'Me too, I used to have the best teacher,' I beamed, remembering back to all the times he'd be at the side of the stage encouraging me during classes, and every evening he made me grab hold of the bannister in the hallway of the farmhouse and took me through all my ballet positions.

We stared at each other for a split second with such warmth.

'I'm so sorry,' I said, desperately struggling to keep my voice under control.

'What have you got to be sorry for?'

I touched his hand and gave it a quick squeeze. 'For leaving. I didn't want to leave you. I've missed you so much.' It was too late, my voice cracked. I was feeling so overwhelmed.

'I've missed you too,' he said, handing me a tissue from his pyjama pocket. 'It's clean,' he added quickly with a smile.

'Thank you,' I said, dabbing my eyes.

'You do know this wasn't your fault?' His gaze met mine.

'I have no idea what happened or why we ended up in New York,' I said, desperately trying to make sense of it all.

'Look,' he swallowed, 'what happened, happened and we can't change that. I'm just grateful you are here now, that's all that matters to me. You came back to me.'

'I sure did.'

We stared at each for a moment, taking in the sight of each other, then suddenly a question began to burn inside me. Before I could stop myself, the words slipped past my lips: 'Aren't you going to ask how Mum is?' I asked cautiously.

Momentarily, his gaze flickered towards the window. 'Alice,' his voice was pained and I could see he'd no intention of entering into this conversation now or any time soon.

'She's okay,' I added.

He nodded his acknowledgement. An awkward silence hung in the air.

'Are you going to tell me what happened all those years back? Mum's never spoken about it, you know.'

His wounded eyes locked with mine. 'Not now, Alice.'

I nodded my understanding. His mood had slumped and I was keen to see the smile return to his face, even though I was desperate to push further. I didn't want to cause him any more pain.

Luckily for the pair of us, the slight tension was lifted by the timely arrival of the nurse to check his machine readings. Once she was satisfied with the various numbers, she noted them down on the chart attached to the bottom of his bed and smiled at us both before leaving the room. 'I didn't mean to upset you,' I said.

'You didn't, but I've got something to run by you.' His voice was low.

'That sounds worrying.' I perched on the edge of my seat in anticipation.

'Not worrying,' he reassured me, 'but ...' He took a breath. 'There's something I've been waiting to ask you for a very long time.'

'Okay,' I answered, wondering what it could be.

'Are you happy in New York, Alice?'

This question took me completely by surprise and I hesitated. Was this the time to come clean and admit how bad my life in New York really was? To tell him my living conditions were appalling and finally admit to someone that the only job I was fit for was working as a cleaner in the theatre, not as the star of the show.

I blew out a breath, my shoulders sagged and my head was swimming. What could I say?

'Call it intuition, even after all this time, but you're not sitting here telling me how fantastic it all is. I see your smile, but your eyes look sad.' His own smile had now been hijacked and his expression was one of concern. 'Talk to me.'

He still had the measure of me after all this time.

'You're right, it's not going great, but it's a long story,' I said, relieved I wasn't going to cover up my life and pretend it was all hunky-dory, like I'd done so far with Grace.

'I'm not going anywhere.' His voice was soft and his eyes urged me to start talking to him.

Feeling my lip wobble, I took a very deep breath. 'Grandie, it's not all that great.' For the next ten minutes I bared all and left no stone unturned. It wasn't easy telling him how unhappy I was, living in New York. A part of me felt disloyal towards Mum. But he listened intently as I wearily told him how I'd never fitted in, and struggled to land a decent job to pay the rent on my dingy flat and stay afloat. When it came down to it, living in the city didn't make me happy, everything was too fast-paced, and for the short time I'd been back in the country-side I'd felt more at home than I'd felt in the last thirteen years.

By the end of the conversation we were both brushing away a flurry of tears.

'I'm so sorry Alice, you deserve the best.'

'It's not your fault,' my voice was barely a whisper. 'It's just been difficult the last few years.'

'There's nothing to feel ashamed about. It doesn't change who you are as a person, and what I see in front of me is a kind, beautiful young lady who hasn't quite found what she is destined for, but you will ... I promise you that.'

Telling him how I was feeling had lifted the weight off my shoulders. It had been difficult to talk to Mum about it because sometimes I felt if I told her about my unhappiness, it would be a kick in the teeth for her. She would blame herself and there was no disputing she'd always done her best for me and loved me with all her heart.

'Every day I've willed you to come back. I thought about you every single moment and today you've made my dreams come true. I can't believe you are finally here.'

'I am.'

He held my gaze. 'Here's the thing Alice, I'm not getting any younger and it would be great to live forever but ...' he paused, 'open that drawer for me.' He nodded towards the bedside cabinet. 'Go on, open it.'

I stood up and pulled open the top drawer of the cabinet. 'Do you want the Bible?' I asked, perplexed.

'No,' he smiled, rolling his eyes, 'I don't.'

'There's nothing else in there except a bunch of keys.'

'That's what I'm after,' he replied, holding out his hand.

Handing the bunch of keys over to him, I sat back down.

'These keys have been my life,' he explained, grasping them with such passion. 'The keys to every possibility. This ...' he said, 'was bought on a trip to Blackpool with your grandmother.' I glanced down at the keyring and smiled at the photo of them both sat on a donkey wearing 'Kiss me quick' hats.

'You remind me a lot of her. She was a wonderful woman – kind, loving, lived life to the max, the life and soul of any party,' he said, teary eyed. 'And taken much too soon.'

'I wish I'd known her.'

He acknowledged what I said with a warm smile.

'These keys could be yours.' He stared straight at me.

I gave him a quizzical look. 'What do you mean?'

'Honeysuckle Farm, the annexe ...'

My eyes widened.

'It could all be yours. I've waited all these years to say these words and really I had no idea whether this moment would ever arrive.' Taking a sip of water, he smoothed down his pyjama top and composed himself, then carried on.

'Alice, I would dearly love Honeysuckle Farm to become your family home.' His eyes were bright, and I could hear the excitement in his voice.

I was shocked, lost for words. Not in a million years had I been expecting this. Things like this never happened to me.

'That place has been in our family for generations and I couldn't bear it to be sold to just anyone. I want you to have it, but on two conditions ...'

'Which are?' I asked, knowing that this inheritance should rightly be Mum's. She was, of course, his next of kin.

'That I can carry on living there until the day I take a trip through those pearly gates ...'

'Grandie,' I interrupted, not wanting to even think about him no longer being around.

'And ...' he held my gaze, 'that you take this key and re-open the dance school ... put some oomph back into this community and get them dancing again. At least think about it.' He looked at me earnestly.

My brain took a second to register what he was actually saying. What an offer! I didn't know what to say. 'Are you serious?'

'I am.'

Elated, I gasped. Without a doubt, this generous offer would solve all my problems, giving me something to focus on and work towards. My pulse raced and my heart thumped nineteen to the dozen. 'But I live in New York,' I blurted out.

'And you've told me how unhappy you are there.'

Immediately, my thoughts were falling over each other to make sense of this proposal. I was fighting a mixture of compelling emotions, each one of them vying for dominance. On the one hand, his offer was like winning the lottery, but with uncertainty rushing to the fore, I thought of Mum. She lived in New York and I couldn't abandon her there.

'It could all be yours Alice, all you have to do is say yes.' There was no denying, by the tone of his voice and the look on his face, that he meant it.

I only managed a nod. Conscious of the lump in my throat, I didn't dare to speak. Was it practical to even consider coming back to England?

'I put my heart and soul into that business, and do you know why?'

My eyes darted back towards him.

'My dad, your great-grandfather.'

I stared at him, listening.

'Alfie Parker was, in my opinion, one of the greatest theatrical stars to grace the West End. I may be biased,' he gave a little chuckle, 'but in his day, people like him were frowned upon,' he said solemnly.

'What do you mean ... people like him?' I asked, puzzled.

'Men that wanted to dance. Those were the times when society dictated that you should be employed in a suitable job. Which meant finding work in the factories, the Royal Mail, or on the railways. But Dad never gave up on his dream. He believed in himself, fought endless stigma, jeers in the pub, and he taught me to dance too. His passion was to convince all walks of life that it was okay to dance. When I met Florrie, she spurred me on to carry on with my dad's passion and open up the dance school, and so we did it together. That dance school became the hub of this community.'

'He sounds like a true inspiration.'

'He was,' Grandie said proudly. 'You'd have loved him.'

I was in no doubt.

'But I've no business experience,' I said, thinking out loud.

'We can overcome every obstacle, Alice. This could be the making of you, your own dance school. Ballet for the children, foxtrot for the pensioners. It made me a decent living – what do you say? Are you willing to give it a try?'

I didn't know what to say, I really was stuck for words.

'You can surround yourself with a good team – I'm sure Connie and Grace would help you. But it will mean telling Grace the truth about New York. Although, I'm sure she'll understand. And I'm here too.'

This was certainly an opportunity, and I nodded, taking in every word.

'Dare I ask, what are you thinking?'

I stared up at him in quiet contemplation, blown away by the whole proposal, and I blew out a breath. In my head, I was fighting my own conscience – loyalty to Mum, loyalty to him – I was certainly stuck in the middle. If I accepted his offer, the direction of my life would completely change. Sometime in the future I'd own my own farmhouse, a home of outstanding beauty and my own business. Granted, I would have to build it up again from scratch, but I wasn't adverse to hard work. I even had visions of the annexe being turned into a holiday cottage in years to come. Excitement was bubbling in the pit of my stomach, a feeling that had been missing for a very long time.

Then the self-doubt began to kick in. I wasn't able to land a part in a production, so how would I even be good enough to open up a dance school and teach the community? I'd been a failure in New York, why would it be any different here?

And then, of course, there was Mum. I could hazard a guess how she would feel about it all. Could I really be that selfish and put my own career and desperate longing to return to Honeysuckle Farm before her? She was waiting for me back in New York. And if I did take up this incredibly generous offer, Mum would be left all alone, miles away from me.

It was all so complicated.

For a second, I could feel Grandie studying my face before I slid my eyes to his briefly. My thoughts were all over the place, a mix of both fear and delight. Standing up, I stared out of the window, my head full of possibilities, and I could barely breathe. This was an opportunity to make something of myself, something for me ... but what if I failed? What if I didn't do Grandie proud and it was a disaster? Then what? I would have let him down and the whole community, and again, how did Mum fit into all this? Would she ever be willing to come home?

Grandie broke the silence: 'It's a good future, Alice. You wouldn't want for anything.'

I swung my gaze back towards him. 'But this means staying in England, leaving Mum on her own in New York. I can't do that.'

At first, he didn't answer me. 'That's something you need to work out for yourself,' he replied, with just a hint of bitterness.

I was hoping for more, I was hoping the invitation would be extended to her too.

Was it silly to even consider returning to England on a more permanent basis?

'What do you think, Alice?'

'I just don't know.' My heart was fighting my head. 'I'm only meant to be gone for a few weeks, not a lifetime.'

'I understand that.'

But did he really, did he really know what he was asking me to do?

'Here, take these.' He placed the keys in my hand and cupped his tightly on top of mine. 'Go and look for yourself, the dance school is still there. Get a feel for the place,' he urged. 'See it in all its glory, and at least tell me you'll think about it.'

'Okay ...' I paused, 'I'll think about it.'

'I can see it in your eyes, this place is your home. Take those keys – you belong here, Alice.'

All I could manage was a nod. My head was whirling with exciting possibilities and my heart was thumping fast.

'Come back Alice, come home.' His words echoed around the room. Despite my reservations about Mum, the offer was more than tempting. Since leaving England all those years ago I'd felt isolated, like a part of me was missing, then all of a sudden I'd been offered a lifeline. Feeling a spark of excitement and hope ignite inside me, I smiled up at Grandie. I couldn't deny this was the perfect opportunity to get my life back on track.

Chapter 9

The next morning my eyes gradually focused on my surroundings and a quick peep at the clock told me I'd finally slept a full eight hours without waking up. Feeling rather refreshed and pleased with myself that I'd finally beaten the jetlag, I threw back the duvet and pulled open the curtains. My mood dampened a little when I noticed there wasn't a chink of sunlight in sight, only dark clouds looming in the sky. All the cows in the far field were lying down under the enormous oak tree, obviously shielding themselves from the rainfall that was about to teem down at any moment.

Slipping my feet into my slippers, I padded downstairs towards the kitchen. This morning I was home alone. Grace had left early for an audition across town and hopefully she'd be back around lunchtime so we could grab some food at the café. Last night, I hadn't shared Grandie's amazing offer with either Grace or Connie, I'd wanted to mull it over a little longer by myself before I told them the real truth about my life in New York.

After switching on the kettle, I noticed a note left in the middle of the table:

Sorry, Alice! I've used the last of the milk. Take some money out of the pot and grab a couple of pints from the corner shop. Grace x

Grace kept an old coffee canister by the side of the breadbin full to the brim with loose change. The kettle clicked off and I tipped a handful of coins into the palm of my hand before staring out of the window. The shop was only at the bottom of the road, I could be there and back in a few minutes, before the rain started.

Despite my desire to quickly get changed, I slipped my feet into my pumps, grabbed the keys from the kitchen table, then hurried towards the shop.

I'd convinced myself my PJs could actually pass as everyday lounge wear, until I witnessed the odd looks and mutterings from an elderly couple who were standing in the queue behind me in the shop. Swiftly paying for the milk, I stepped outside just as the heavens opened.

Damn.

Admittedly, this was not the best idea I'd ever had.

This wasn't just rain but huge, fat dollops of water. The sort of rain that drenched your body in seconds. Clutching the milk, I ran as fast as I could, dodging the puddles until the garden gate was in sight. Suddenly, I heard the roar of an exhaust and glanced over my shoulder to see a car within inches of me.

Jumping away from the curb, it was too late. Like a rabbit caught in headlights, I froze then squealed as a tidal wave of cold, muddy water was thrown over my entire body.

'Idiot!' I raged, staring in dismay at the car with my arms held open wide as the water dripped from my face. 'Don't mind me,' I shouted after the car, which suddenly pulled in and parked a little further up the road. The engine cut out and the car door swung open.

'Urghh,' I grumbled, swiping the water from my bare arms.

'I'm sorry, I'm sorry, I didn't see the puddle,' he said, all apologetic.

I was momentarily thrown by the pair of deep-hazel eyes staring back at me. The same pair of eyes that had locked with mine from the computer and the theatre programme, the same pair of eyes that belonged to Sam Reid.

'You ...' the words died in my throat. 'Look at the state of me,' I croaked, shivering in the cold. My hair was completely flattened, the rain dripping off the end of my nose, and I was soaked through to the skin.

He took a cautious step back and his eyes swept over my entire body. I could feel the burn in my cheeks intensify.

'I'm looking ...' he said, running his hands through his wet, unruly hair. I glared up at him, his shirt now drenched from the rain, clinging to every muscle in his chest. Then I followed his gaze and was mortified to see my sodden, wet top clinging to my breasts.

Oh God.

I quickly folded my arms, trying to draw his gaze away from my chest to my face.

'Obviously, my clothes are ruined,' I said with a twinge of irritation.

'They kind of look like pyjamas to me,' he grinned, dazzling me with his perfect white smile.

'I would like to stand here arguing but it's raining, I'm cold, and I want coffee.' I was justifiably outraged. 'I could have drowned.'

I knew as soon as the words left my mouth that they were a little over-dramatic.

'That's a little unfair,' he protested, with a look of amusement written all over his face. 'I didn't wake up and say to myself, I'm going to drive through a rather large puddle and attempt to drown a beautiful girl in the street.'

'Oh really, are you sure?' I huffed, trying not to focus on the word beautiful but feeling my heart start to thump a little faster and my annoyance soften a little.

'I'm quite sure,' he grinned, thrusting his hand forward. 'Can we start again? I'm Sam.'

I hesitated before shaking his hand.

He raised his eyebrows.

'Alice,' I finally said.

'That's an accent not from around these parts.'

'America,' I grumbled.

'And where are you going this morning, dressed to impress, Alice?' he grinned, his eyebrows shooting up. 'Can I give you a lift somewhere? It's the least I can do.'

'Actually, I'm already home.'

'Home?' he queried, giving Wild Rose Cottage a sideward glance.

'I live here.' Which I knew wasn't strictly true.

'Call it male intuition, but I kind of think we may be bumping into each other a lot,' he smiled.

'Don't count on it,' I said, making sure I didn't show I was suitably flattered by his flirtatious smile. 'I need to go inside before I die of hypothermia.'

I turned and walked towards the gate and he followed me.

'What are you doing?'

'I'm going home.' He jangled his keys in the air and I watched in astonishment as he strolled, larger than life, up the path of the cottage next door. It was safe to say my jaw had fallen somewhere near my knees – Sam Reid lived next door?

'You live there?'

'I do indeed!'

Oh God.

'I'm sure I'll be seeing you very soon, Alice ...'

'Parker,' I finished off his sentence.

He held my gaze for a second longer than necessary before I turned quickly away, feeling my face heat up a notch. There was something about Sam that had me blushing uncontrollably.

There was no denying I was secretly delighted that Sam

lived next door. I knew after only being in his company for five minutes that I wanted to spend more time getting to know him. Fumbling with the keys to Grace's cottage, I summoned up enough courage to glance back over my shoulder one last time, only to find his eyes locked with mine, and we grinned foolishly at each other.

I pressed my lips tightly together to hide my smile before squelching into the hallway, relieved to be back in the warmth. When I closed the door, I did everything in my power not to whoop out loud.

Sam Reid lived next door! Even though I was cold and wet, this little bit of information warmed my heart.

'Urgh, urgh,' I shivered, peeling the wet shoes from my feet and looking down at my dishevelled, dirty, sodden clothes. After putting the milk in the fridge, I jumped into the shower and let the hot water cascade over my body, relieved to finally feel warm and human again.

About thirty minutes later I finally sat on the sofa, hugging my hot morning cup of coffee. I powered up my laptop while flicking through the programme of *Mamma Mia* that had been left on the coffee table.

Thoughts flooded my head. All these years it had been my dream to appear on stage and see my face in one of these magazines, but was I really destined for that? It hadn't worked out so far. My head was still swimming with Grandie's proposal and I sighed. It was a perfect opportunity, a fresh start, if only I could persuade Mum to come back too.

I turned to the page that featured Sam, and the pair of eyes that belonged to the boy next door once more stared back at me.

Reaching for my phone, I punched a text to Grace.

'Why the heck didn't you tell me that SAM REID lives next door? Sorry for the shouty capitals but don't you think this was important information?'

Almost immediately my phone pinged, 'I thought you'd find out soon enough!'

I rolled my eyes, 'You could have told me!'

Grinning at Grace's message, I logged on to Facebook. I'd had boyfriends over the years, but nothing that had ever set my world alight in quite the same way as Sam Reid looking at me. His air of confidence and that twinkle in his eye ensured that I was instantly attracted to him.

Noticing I had a new notification, I clicked on the icon. 'Sam Reid has accepted your friend request.'

I swallowed, feeling a little flutter of pleasure knowing I now had full access to his profile.

For the next ten minutes, I clicked on everything – his photos, his status updates and people's comments. He had over six hundred friends and now one more was added to his list ... me.

Once more I received a notification and clicked on it. 'You are now connected to Sam Reid,' the message read, 'say hi with a wave.' The green circle next to his name showed me he was online. For a second I hovered over the button wondering whether to press it, but I couldn't believe my eyes when he beat me to it.

'Thanks for the friend request x'
The smile hitched wide on my face.
'You're very welcome! x'

Chapter 10

Later that day, the rain had dried up and the sun was shining down on my face as I sauntered up the long drive towards the farmhouse, clutching Grandie's keys.

Grace was back from her audition but with a few errands to run, Connie had given her a lift into town. With both of them busy for a few hours, I'd taken the opportunity to wander up to the farm and have a good look around. I knew at some point today I needed to phone home and talk to Mum, but I was putting off the conversation for as long as I possibly could.

Grandie's proposal was playing on my mind, and I wanted to spend a couple of hours with only myself for company. After letting Marley out of the kitchen and giving him a fuss, we both headed into the courtyard. Billy was in his stable, his head hanging over the door, and as I rubbed his nose he nudged me back. I used to spend hours stroking his wiry mane and there was something very relaxing about grooming a pony. I stood still and furtively took a glance around; of course there was no one there. 'Right Billy, you up for a ride?' Billy threw his head back and gave a soft neigh. 'That's a yes then,' I smiled, thinking it had been a long time since I'd sat on a horse. There was a time I'd loved ambling around the field on his back with the wind blowing in my hair and my wellies dangling from my little legs that had been too small to reach the stirrups. Glancing around the stable, the tack was still hanging up in the very same place. The saddle looked tiny, but I pressed my lips into a small smile and slipped the reins over his neck.

'Just like old times, Billy,' I said, patting his neck before unbolting the stable door. Standing on an old crate, I swung my leg over him and settled on his back.

'Whoa!' I said out loud, trying to steady myself. It seemed higher up than I ever remembered, but then I had to stop myself from squealing in delight as instinct kicked in and I gripped the reins.

'Are you ready, Marley?'

He padded excitedly from one paw to another, wagging his tail.

With Marley by my side, I kicked my legs softly and Billy began to plod slowly forwards. There was a bridle path that ran all around the edge of the farm and we clomped towards it through the barns and buildings. The hens scattered and clucked at the sound of the hooves on the rough concrete surface and quickly disappeared to the other side of the yard.

There was squawking coming from the far barn, the noise of a hen laying her eggs. It was a sound I'd never heard in New York and one I'd missed.

I remembered the day of my eighth birthday when Grandie had given me my very own chicken, and I'd named her Enid. Everyone at school had thought it was super cool to own your own hen and it was that very day I became a business-woman when Grandie had put me in charge of the eggs. Every day, I had to collect them, which wasn't as easy as it sounds, as they were never laid in the same place. I'd discover bundles of colourful eggs in the hedgerows, in hay bales and even in Grandie's old straw hat which he'd left in the barn.

Each morning, I would place the egg boxes along with an honesty box outside the gates of Honeysuckle Farm and each night after school I'd run home and count the coins.

That summer, I'd helped Grandie lug huge wicker baskets to the apple orchard to collect the windfalls and distribute them to the neighbours – apple pie a-plenty. I smiled now at my memories as we plodded along in the sunshine. 'This is the life,' I said out loud, soaking in the peace and quiet, a far cry from the busy pace of New York City life.

Once on the bridle path, the view was spectacular. A cow mooed, making me jump, her head poking through a hole in the hedgerow, and the sheep were dotted about in the fields at the bottom of the valley. I ducked my head under a low-hanging branch, then stopped to admire a deer that loped through the woodland. It was such a beautiful sight it made my heart swell.

Stopping Billy with a pull on his reins, I took a moment, glancing back over my shoulder. There was Honeysuckle Farm in all its glory. Like Grandie had reminded me, the farmhouse and the land had been in his family for generations. Mentally, I'd already moved back here, I didn't want this place being sold to just anyone. This place was brimming with our memories, our family history. My chest heaved and I reached out a hand and patted Billy's neck. This was home, but if only it was that simple. Deep down I hoped Mum would see sense because I could never envisage anyone else living here, it wouldn't seem right.

Kicking Billy on, we arrived back at the stable thirty minutes later. After thoroughly enjoying myself and feeling relaxed, I jumped off and tied him to the wooden post before giving him a handful of carrots. Marley headed towards the water trough and gulped the water before lying down on the ground. Noticing the pitchfork resting against the barn, I began to shovel the manure out of the stable into a wheel barrow. It had been a long time since I'd shovelled manure, and the fork seemed a lot smaller than when I was a child, and easier to manage. I noticed I was slipping back into country life quite easily.

Out of the corner of my eye, I spotted Jim in the greenhouse harvesting tomatoes. He was just how I remembered him, wearing the same green overalls and the same green wellies. I made a mental note to say hello before I headed back to Grace's cottage.

The ride on Billy had put me in an excellent mood and

feeling relaxed and content, I groomed him before letting him loose in the bottom field. He headed straight towards the stream for a drink.

Feeling at home, I decided to have a mooch about and noticed the ramshackle barn just to the left of the annexe. Sliding the rusty bolt on the door, I pushed it open and glanced around. This was a place I used to often hang out, making my own amusement, jumping off the hay bales and climbing up into the rafters, which had been boarded out. There were stacks of flowerpots, garden tools hanging off the walls and my old yellow bike with two flat tyres. I couldn't believe it was still there after all this time and it looked so tiny leaning against the wall. There was an old-fashioned lawnmower covered in cobwebs and bags of chicken feed stacked up in a corner. I scooped up a handful of corn from the open sack and threw it outside for the chickens to peck on.

'Hey, what sort of welcome is that? You don't need to pelt corn at me!'

Startled by the voice, I spun round – my heart beating wildly – and met the smile of Ben.

'Sorry! I didn't mean to scare you. What are you doing here?' I asked, walking back out into the sunshine and sliding the bolt back across the door.

'Clearing out the gutters and doing a spot of painting for your grandfather. He often uses our company.'

'Aww, I see.'

'What are *you* doing here?' he asked, taking off his jacket and hanging it on the hook outside the barn door.

'I thought I'd enjoy some time with this fella,' I ruffled Marley's head, 'and for old times' sake I've just taken Billy out for a ride along the bridle path.'

'Judging by the colour in your cheeks, you enjoyed it.'

'I did.'

We began to walk, and Marley followed close at my heels.

'It's good to see you back here, where you belong. Your grandfather has missed you, you know. He's always talked about you.'

I nodded, 'I've missed him and this place.'

I saw the corners of his mouth lift slightly. 'You are funny with the slight American twang to your voice.'

I grinned, 'Give me a week or two and no doubt I'll slip right back into a Midland accent.'

'Remember how rich I thought you were when I found out you had a pony and lived here?'

'Lady Alice, you called me, then bowed. Bigger than Buckingham Palace, you said.'

Ben gave a chuckle, 'It is such a beautiful, calming place.'

'It is.' I stood still and scanned my eyes over the estate.

'I love the days I work here, that view, the peace and tranquillity is better than working on any noisy building site.'

We paused on the little wooden bridge across the stream. Marley was already knee deep, paddling in the water. Ben bent down and handed me a stick which I promptly threw into the water before leaning on the rail and staring out over the fields.

'Time for a walk?' he asked, and I nodded.

He followed me across the bridge and we headed towards the farmer's gate on the other side of the field.

'Have you ever thought about being anything other than a builder?' I probed, still thinking about Grandie's proposal. My dreams of stardom had never quite worked out and for the first time I was considering other possibilities. Maybe, re-opening the dance school was just the push I needed to get my life back on track.

'Nah, my passion for building started off when I was knee high to a grasshopper. Every school holiday I'd tag along with Dad, hang out around the building site, ride in the wheelbarrow and mill about in the empty shells of houses, mesmerised by how it all became a real house,' he laughed. 'I love my bright-yellow hat, and look at these muscles ...' he flexed his abs. 'Who needs a gym?'

I chuckled and rolled my eyes in jest.

'Don't get me wrong, there are good days and bad. Winter days are the worst, lack of progress due to the frost and days when you are so cold you can't feel your hands, but I wouldn't change it for the world. Especially when there's a patch of empty land and over time you transform it into a family home, right in front of your eyes.'

'What's it like being part of a family business?'

'Great, it gives me a sense of belonging, knowing I'm working damn hard and one day my own flesh and blood might take over my little empire and share the same dream.'

The glint in Ben's eyes and the passion in his voice were obvious to anyone.

He turned towards me, 'And look at you, always doing what you wanted to do, born to be a dancer, a performer. The whole village thinks of you as their own little superstar. We've all been half-expecting to see you on that dance show one day.'

I raised my eyebrows, unsure what he meant.

'*Strictly Come Dancing* or whatever it's called. I'm not really up on TV shows,' he said blithely with a twinkle in his eye, 'but I bet you'd get a Ten from Len.' He gave me a wink.

I swiped his arm playfully, 'Do people really expect me to be on a TV show?'

'Maybe a slight exaggeration, but things seem to be going great for you over in the States.'

I sighed before I could stop myself.

'What's with the sigh?'

'It's nothing,' I said unconvincingly.

'Come on Parker, are you missing New York?' He stared at me before perching on top of the farm gate. 'Suddenly, you look like you've got the weight of the world on your shoulders.'

He didn't know the half of it. My mind switched to my own dilemma: Mum or Grandie, England or New York?

Sitting side by side, I closed my eyes and tilted my face towards the sunshine. 'More than you'd ever know.' The words slipped out and I pressed my lips together.

'Hey, I've got a spare shoulder, you know, if you want to talk.' He playfully bumped his shoulder against mine and I wobbled on the top of the old rickety gate.

'Don't do that, I'll fall,' I smiled warmly towards him, then fixed my gaze on Marley who lolloped after a hare which promptly disappeared amongst the hedgerows, leaving him sniffing frantically.

'I wouldn't know where to start ... Did you ever feel it was an easy option, working for your dad when you left school?' I asked, steering the conversation back towards him.

Ben blew out a breath. 'You're joking, aren't you? It was far from easy, with his outstanding reputation around these parts. He's never had to advertise for work, it's always been word of mouth. There were times when he was harder on me than the other builders and for the first few years I was allocated all the menial, dirty jobs that no one wanted to do. And of course, I was chief tea-maker, which drove me insane! However, with all that practice, there's no disputing I make a decent cup of tea now.'

'Every cloud,' I smiled, jumping off the gate.

We strolled back up the lane. Marley ran in front, nose to the ground, and led the way to the stile behind the annexe.

'I certainly had, and still do have a lot to live up to. Yes, when we left school the lads were envious. I didn't have to go for interviews, or go to college, and I've learnt on the job, but there was always that niggle in the back of mind – would I be good enough, could I actually run the business by myself one day and step into Dad's shoes? But there was fire in my belly to prove my worth and if you don't give it a go, how will you ever know? Without blowing my own trumpet – which obviously I am – I think I'm doing all right so far.' His face was unmistakably brimming with pride.

I listened to his words ... if I didn't give it a go, how would I ever know ...? But what if I accepted Grandie's offer and made a complete hash of it?

'Come on, let's get back and you need to do some work or I'll be reporting you to the boss,' I joked.

'So, what's with all the questions?' he raised an interested eyebrow.

I didn't want to give anything away, not until I'd spoken to Grace. And, of course, there was a conversation that I needed to have with Mum.

My gaze dropped to the floor and I took a deep breath. 'I've not told anyone yet,' I paused, 'but I've got a decision to make.'

'What decision?'

'Do I stay or do I go?'

'Huh? I don't understand. Stay or go where?' he asked, squinting at me in the sunlight while steadying my climb over the stile.

'I've said too much already. As soon as I know you'll know. But you, Ben Carter ...' I wagged my finger at him, 'have been a big help today. Now go and get to work.' I pushed him lightly towards the farmhouse.

He laughed with bewilderment. 'Glad to have helped, even though I've no clue how.'

He waved his hand over his head and whistled his way to a set of ladders that were propped up against the side of the house.

His words turned over and over in my mind. After locking

Marley back in the kitchen, I punched in Grace's number on my phone. She answered almost immediately.

'Are you back at the cottage?'

'Just walked through the door ... why? Is something going on? You sound kind of ...'

'Yes,' I interrupted, 'there is more than something going on. Can you meet me at The Old Teashop in fifteen minutes?'

'I'm intrigued ... Of course, see you there,' said Grace, hanging up the phone.

I was still very much in a quandary when I walked back towards the village along the country lane. I was hesitant about telling Grace the truth about my life, but it didn't sit right with me that I'd lied to her. Although I was feeling anxious about telling her, I knew I couldn't put it off any longer. The conversation with Ben had hit home. If I didn't give Brook Bridge a go and re-open the dance school, how would I ever know if it was meant to be? But on the other hand, what if I wasn't up to the job? I wasn't Grandie, or Mum. What if I didn't live up to their reputation or no one wanted me to teach them to dance? It was a scary prospect.

Brook Bridge village could hold the key to my future happiness, but first I needed to tell Grace the truth. And secondly, I was hoping she was going to help me come up with a plan to convince Mum to come back to England.

Chapter 11

Standing in the quaint courtyard, I took in the view, which was still exactly as I remembered it as a little girl. There was a multitude of artists selling their paintings and photographers snapping pictures outside the small cluttered shops filled with leather goods smelling of incense. Giggling children ran over the stone bridge clutching their melting ice-creams while dog walkers happily strolled through the courtyard towards the fields and stream.

The afternoon sun was high in the sky, and the tables outside The Old Teashop were busy. Customers were sat under the yellow-and-white awning, enjoying cake and coffee while chatting to their friends. I knew Grace would be here any second and already I was beginning to feel worried. I'd no idea how she was going to react when I told her I was destitute, and my career wasn't actually a career. But with Grandie's offer on the table, I needed to own up.

I pushed open the door and the bell tinkled above my head. The Old Teashop was just the same – all things vintage with its china tea-cups and colourful, triangular bunting draped across every wall. The front counter revealed an array of beautiful cakes in numerous glass-domed stands and immediately my mouth watered when I spotted the lemon drizzle tray bake which had my name written all over it. Mrs Jones was stacking a batch of Eccles cakes next to the chocolate-coated gingerbread men, which were topped with chocolate chips and Smarties and screaming out to the younger customers. She looked exactly the same, her face still as kind as I remembered. Her plump figure gave her a matriarchal aura, complemented by her rosy cheeks and grey hair which was pinned up in a bun.

'What can I get you, dear?' Mrs Jones looked up and met my gaze. Her eyes flickered and I knew she'd recognised me but couldn't quite place where from. I gave her a warm smile. 'Hello, Mrs Jones, long time no see.'

She screwed up her face and the penny dropped.

'Christ on a bike! ... oh my,' cried Mrs Jones with her infectious smile that oozed such warmth. Quickly, she hurried to the front of the counter, wiping her hands on her pinny. 'Oh my,' she repeated once more, her eyes wide as she grabbed both my hands. 'It is you, isn't it?'

'It was last time I looked.' I couldn't help the huge beam on my face. What a welcome!

'Our dear Alice, finally home, and that accent, very ...'

'American,' I finished off her sentence. 'It's good to see you, Mrs Jones.'

'Dorothy, don't be calling me Mrs Jones, I feel old enough as it is,' she chuckled, before enveloping me in a tight hug.

'Let me look at you,' she said, finally releasing me from her grip and taking a step backwards. 'All grown up, a beautiful young lady ... Bert! ... Bert! ... Bert!' she bellowed towards the kitchen door. 'Look who's here,' she said without taking a breath.

Dorothy's husband Bert poked his head around the door. 'Where's the fire?'

'Look who it is, it's young Alice, back from America.' She finally caught her breath.

'Well I never, so it is!' exclaimed Bert, tipping his cap and heartily shaking my hand.

'How are you, Mr Jones?'

'Bert, call me Bert ... Mustn't grumble. Still taking orders from Dorothy, nearly fifty years married to this wonderful woman and ready for retirement a long time ago,' his eyes twinkled towards Dorothy.

'He does tease, he wouldn't have it any other way.'

'Golden wedding anniversary?'

'It's in a couple of weeks but I keep telling him there's still time to trade him in.' She gave a small chuckle.

Just at that moment, Grace walked through the door. 'Afternoon, Dorothy. I see you've discovered who's back in town,' she grinned, joining in the jovial atmosphere.

'We can't believe it. She's certainly her grandfather's granddaughter.'

'Aye ... look like Ted, you do,' agreed Bert.

'And how's your mum? Is she here with you?'

'She's fine, Dorothy, but not here with me on this occasion.'

'That's a shame, we would have loved to see Rose, wouldn't we Bert?'

He nodded.

'You girls take a seat.' Dorothy ushered us to a table in the front window which overlooked the courtyard outside. 'Best table in the house. Now let me get you each a slice of cake and a cup of tea.'

'Thank you, lemon drizzle for me,' I smiled, not having to think twice about it.

'Me too, great choice,' said Grace, sliding into the seat opposite me.

Dorothy gently shooed Bert back into the kitchen before disappearing back behind the counter.

'Now that's what you call a welcome!'

'Lovely couple, this place won't be the same when they retire,' said Grace fondly.

'How did you do at your audition? Any news yet?'

Grace shook her head. 'No, they email you, but there's another one in a couple of weeks, *Romeo and Juliet*, you should give it a stab too?'

'A show like that would go on for months,' I answered, knowing I'd swerved the question. I'd battled with crushing disappointment for years so I wasn't about to put myself up for an audition against the likes of Grace who obviously brimmed with talent. The feeling of failure would be too much to bear.

Grace gave me a wicked smile. 'That's the plan. See, there's a method to my madness!' she laughed, wagging her finger at me in jest before I glanced down at my phone.

I had one new notification on Facebook, and quickly swiping my phone, I noticed I had a new message waiting for me. Nervous butterflies began to flutter around my stomach when I saw it was a message from Sam:

'How's little Miss America today? If you're free for coffee anytime do let me know. Sam x'

'You're smiling,' noticed Grace as I looked up from the screen.

'I'm not,' I grinned even though I knew there was a huge beam spread right across my face.

'Anything interesting?' asked Grace, narrowing her eyes at me while I punched back a quick reply:

'I'd love that, Alice x'

'Maybe,' I teased as Dorothy appeared at the side of the table with a pot of tea and two slices of the most delicious-looking cake I'd ever set eyes on.

'These are on the house but promise me you won't disappear before saying goodbye.'

'Too kind, and of course I won't.'

Mrs Jones turned and bustled back towards the counter. 'Our Alice back in town, I can't quite believe it, brightened up my day,' she was excitedly still mumbling under her breath.

Grace poured us both a cup of tea. 'Right, Parker, get talking, what's going on with you?'

In the pit of my stomach I wasn't looking forward to this conversation, but I knew I needed to confide in Grace. I agonised for a split second and took a deep breath. How did I start this conversation?

'Hey, come on, it can't be that bad. Ted is okay, isn't he?' she asked tentatively, sensing my hesitation.

'Yes, it's not Grandie.'

'Then what is it? You can tell me.'

A little smile appeared on Grace's face, followed by a look of anguish.

Feeling nervous, I took another deep breath and exhaled sharply. 'I've not been totally honest with you.'

Grace met my gaze and held it.

'What do you mean?' she questioned.

'I couldn't audition for *Romeo and Juliet* in a million years ...'

'Why?'

'I'm struggling, Grace, and I mean struggling,' my voice was low and my lip began to tremble.

It was Grace's turn to listen and I began to talk.

I told her everything, absolutely everything, from feeling like I'd never belonged in New York to failing every audition and living in the most run-down flat. I told her about my life being a mess, and how it had been easier to paint a smile on my face and hide how difficult things had become.

The whole truth was laid out in front of us.

I gulped in some air while Grace hugged her cup of tea. I

watched as her eyes widened. There was no mistaking the look of shock on her face.

'Are you mad at me?' I asked, but not sure if I actually wanted to hear the answer.

A lump formed in my throat while Grace's eyes searched mine. 'Of course I'm not mad, I'm just lost for words, which is actually a first for me.' She gave a slight smile then exhaled. 'It's a lot to take in, this is all so awful for you. Why didn't you tell me things had got this bad?'

'I'm sorry I wasn't straight with you when I arrived. I feel dreadful misleading you, really I do, but I felt ashamed, a failure.'

'Please, don't ever feel like that or beat yourself up about that. Things happen. I'm so sorry it hasn't worked out as you'd hoped, I really am.' Her tone was warm and kind.

'Me and you both,' I admitted, feeling glad I'd finally confided in Grace.

'I wish there was something I could do. But you, Alice Parker, aren't a failure, and you can stop with that talk right now.'

'I feel so useless, though, Grace. I had dreams like you. But all I can manage is a job sweeping the theatre stage.'

After we both tucked into our cake, Grace posed the question to me that was already on my mind: 'What I don't understand is why you are both still there? What's keeping your mum in New York?' she asked, trying to grasp the whole situation.

I knew exactly what was keeping her in New York ... good old-fashioned stubbornness.

'The argument with Grandie, it's never been put to bed, but that's not all ...'

'There's more?' she asked, taking a sip of tea.

'I've not told anyone else but this morning, after you left, I disappeared up to Honeysuckle Farm.'

I reached down and fished out the keys from my bag and put them on the table in front of her.

A look of confusion passed over Grace's face. She still had no clue what was going on.

'Okay, they are a bunch of keys but what are they for?' Grace arched an eyebrow.

I took a deep breath. 'This one ... Honeysuckle Farm ... this one ... I'm assuming is the spare key for the annexe, this one ... I'm not so sure about, but this one ... the dancing school,' I said, my eyes wide.

'And what are you doing with them?' Grace moved her tea-cup to one side, folded her arms and waited for me to answer.

'These ... are ... the ... keys ... to ... my ... future,' I said slowly, stringing it out for dramatic effect. 'If I choose to accept, it could all be mine – Honeysuckle Farm, the annexe and the dance school,' I explained, watching Grace's face change as my words registered. 'Grandie has offered it all to me.'

'Woah! Information overload, this is amazing! How the heck have you kept that to yourself? Would this mean you staying in England? How do you feel about that?'

'Excited ... scared ... I feel at home here, this is my home ...

but I can't stay, can I? I'm torn between doing something that I want to do and my relationship with Mum.' My voice faltered just thinking about Mum.

'So, if there wasn't this issue between them both, would you stay?'

'I don't think we would be in New York in the first place, if I'm truly honest,' I said sadly. 'I know it sounds silly when I've only just arrived but in here ...' I thumped my chest, 'it feels right. England is where I belong.'

'It doesn't sound silly at all.' Grace sat back in her chair, her hands cupped around her tea-cup, her mind clearly in overdrive while she sipped slowly.

'But this will solve all your problems,' she squeezed my arm over the table. 'You'll have a home, a business. That dance school would be back up and running in no time. It's meant to be. This is your time.' The excitement danced in Grace's eyes.

'It does solve all my problems, and it doesn't,' I answered solemnly, trying to keep a level head, even though inside my stomach flipped at the thought of staying in England. 'How can I leave Mum in New York? She'd never speak to me again! It's just not that simple.'

'Tricky one.'

We sat in silence for a second. 'But surely you aren't going to say no? You'd be mad to say no. You need to talk to her. Tell her how unhappy you are.'

'Firstly, the inheritance should technically belong to Mum, as she's Grandie's next of kin. How is she going to feel, knowing he wants to give her legacy to me? It would be like a kick in the teeth for her.'

'Okay, I kind of see your point, but it's your grandfather's choice and they haven't spoken for thirteen years – that's a long time. What the heck did they fall out about anyway? Did he give you any more clues?'

I shook my head. 'No, and I wish I knew,' I told her, sighing.

'Must be one hell of a falling out. I spoke to Mum about it, but it's a mystery to her as much as it is to you.'

'Do you think they still keep in touch?' I probed lightly, knowing Mum had never spoken about Connie in recent years.

Grace shook her head. 'I asked Mum that very same question last week when I knew there was a possibility you were coming back.'

'And?'

'She said the last time she spoke to your mum was the day we waved you off, the day you left for New York. She was teary when we talked, and felt hurt that she didn't have a clue about it all, especially with the two of them being best friends for all those years. What happened that your mum couldn't trust mine or confide in her?'

I blew out a breath, 'I've no idea. The plot thickens and then there is the dance school.'

'A fantastic opportunity.'

'But how can I re-open the dance school and run it as a business? Firstly, there's Grandie, his reputation,' I continued. 'He and Grandma were local celebrities, they performed on the stage. Would I ever be good enough to teach people to their standard when I can't even land a part in a show? It's a lot to live up to! What if I fail at that too? I don't want to let anyone down,' I spluttered, sitting back in my chair and waiting for Grace's reaction.

'If you don't give it a go there will always be that niggle in the back of your mind. You'll regret it.'

Grace was saying exactly the same thing as Ben.

I tried to put on a brave face, but a tear slid solemnly down my cheek, which I quickly brushed away with the back of my hand.

Grace's eyes swept towards me. 'There's only one thing for it.' She gave me a knowing look then picked up her mobile phone.

My heart was racing now and my mouth was dry.

'Which is?' I asked, watching Grace slide the screen on her phone.

'Let's ask Siri! Should Alice Parker live in New York or England?'

We both smiled, the mood lightened a little. 'Grace Anderson, you are nuts.'

'Ha! That's not in dispute!'

In an ideal world, I knew what I wanted to happen, but it was unlikely I could ever persuade Mum to swallow her pride and travel to England to see Grandie.

'These things have a knack of working themselves out, try not to worry,' Grace added softly with a reassuring smile.

'I know,' I said, relieved to have Grace on my side.

'But first things first, you need to call your mum, and talk to her.'

I knew I couldn't put it off any longer. Of course, I'd sent the odd text telling her I'd arrived safely and explaining how welcome Connie and Grace had made me feel, but there was this huge elephant in the room and we weren't even in the same country. The one person each of us avoided talking about ... Grandie. Letting out a huge sigh, I told myself I'd ring her that afternoon. Perhaps, if I just came out and said it, it might jolt her into realising there was a possibility that I might well stay in England.

'I'd be surprised if either of them can remember what they even fell out over. I'm going to phone her as soon as we get back to the cottage.'

'I think it's for the best, get it out of the way. At least this way you are being honest with her.'

Grace was right.

'How's the cake?' Dorothy appeared at the side of the table with her hands cupped together.

'Perfection,' I smiled, 'the best lemon drizzle I have ever tasted.'

'And I second that,' chipped in Grace.

'That's what I like to hear, satisfied customers.'

'I've got to nip out, but please tell me, dear Alice, you are staying around for a little while.'

'A few weeks at least.'

She placed her hand on my shoulder, 'Good, good, that's what we like to hear.'

'Dorothy,' called Bert, 'you've forgotten your bag and the file.'

She chuckled, 'That's old age for you.'

'Going anywhere nice?' asked Grace.

'You know ... WI business,' answered Dorothy, clutching her bag and file.

'WI?' I mimed at Grace, thinking it was some sort of code.

'Women's Institute,' she mouthed back.

'It's Village Day, you see. The committee needs the final schedule. It's getting close now. You will still be here for that, Alice? Oh, we hope so.'

'You still have Village Day?' I was amazed.

Village Day was just that, a day where all the local businesses, scout groups, schools and community groups gathered on participating floats and paraded through the village. Everyone would bring their picnic blankets and camp on the grass, enjoying a day of stalls packed with cakes, home-made produce and knick-knacks. There was fun for all the children, games to play and a show put on by the local schools and groups each year on the make-shift stage in the middle of the green.

'We do, but each year we do miss the dance school's performance. There has been a massive void since it closed down.'

'I'd forgotten all about Village Day.'

'Here, take a leaflet, there's still time to schedule a performance. Maybe you girls could dance for us this year?' Dorothy looked hopeful.

But before I could answer, I noticed the smile fall from her face. Her expression hardened and was it my imagination, or did Dorothy bristle?

Following her gaze, I watched Sam sauntering past The Old Teashop. His earphones were firmly planted in his ears and he was looking in the direction he was walking. My heart flipped at the mere sight of him. Dorothy muttered under her breath, 'You keep walking. You're not welcome in here.'

Catching Grace's eye, I was shocked. 'What's that all about?' I mouthed, but she didn't answer.

Dorothy's eyes burned angrily and she didn't take her eyes off Sam until he'd disappeared out of sight. There was no mistaking the fact that the jovial atmosphere in the café had somewhat plummeted.

A flustered Dorothy was still mumbling something under her breath when she turned round towards me. 'Alice, my dear Alice, I'm so sorry you have to put up with the likes of him walking the streets.'

Words failed me.

'This village will never forget. Taken too soon,' she said, her eyes glistening with tears. 'We will never forget.' She patted my arm before leaving the shop and pulling the door shut behind her.

'Oh my God, what the heck was that all about?' I asked Grace in bewilderment, feeling the strange tension in the air.

Grace shot me a warning glance before looking towards the kitchen door. 'Not here,' she said, her voice barely a whisper.

To me, Sam seemed a normal bloke walking through the

streets minding his own business. What had he done to warrant comments like that from Dorothy? And what did it have to do with me? I had no clue what had just happened but I had every intention of digging further.

Chapter 12

Seconds later we both said farewell to Bert and Dorothy and strolled back through the courtyard.

'What was that all about?' I asked again, completely and utterly mortified at what had just happened inside The Old Teashop.

Grace quirked an eyebrow.

'And why did she apologise to me?' I added, feeling baffled.

'A long story, and that's village life for you. People never forget.'

'What do you mean? Hang on ... you'll have to hold that story right there, that's my phone ringing,' I said, quickly rummaging through my bag. I glanced at the screen, 'It's Ben.'

'Back in the country for two minutes and he has your mobile number,' she gave me a teasing look.

'Sshh! Hi, Ben!' I answered, as we turned on to High Street. Grace was trying to earwig in on the conversation but stopped as soon as she saw the puzzled look fleet across my face. 'Yes, I can come now.'

'What was all that about?' asked Grace, the second I hung up. 'Is everything all right?'

'I'm not entirely sure but he's asked if I can nip over to the farm now.'

'Do you want me to come with you?' asked Grace.

I shook my head, 'No, I won't be long. I'll see you back at the cottage.'

'Okay, if you're sure.'

'What were you just about to tell me about Sam?'

'Don't worry, that'll keep for later.'

I nodded and began walking towards Honeysuckle Farm. As I sauntered up the drive towards the farmhouse, the familiar smells were wonderful. The underlying aroma of the cows, the straw from the stable and the burning of rubbish in the bottom field. I felt a bubble of happiness rise in my chest every time I was here, but thoughts of Mum were never far from my mind. How could she give all this up?

I felt at home here, and right now, this second, my heart was telling me that Brook Bridge was where I needed to be, but I knew that choice was going to have devastating consequences for my mum.

In the shrubs, the chickens were pecking around and the cockerel puffed out his plumage before letting out a throaty crow. The barn doors were thrown wide open and Billy was in his stable gnawing at the hay bag. After giving him a quick pat, I glanced around and spotted Ben whistling to himself up the top of a ladder while painting the guttering.

'Hi,' I called, and Ben spun round. He was dressed in overalls which were tied around his waist by the sleeves, and his T-shirt was splattered with speckles of paint. A smile crept across his face and he began to climb down.

'Perfect timing, I was due a break.' He slipped a hand on the small of my back. 'You look nice.'

Today, I'd chosen an ordinary outfit: denim jeans, a pale-blue T-shirt and my tatty old grey pumps. 'Thanks.'

'So, what's all this about?' I asked with intrigue.

Ben took off his gloves and placed them over a rung of the ladder.

'Over there,' he nodded towards the brick wall that ran around Grandie's sun garden. 'There's another building behind that wall.'

My eyes darted over to where Ben was pointing.

'No, there can't be.'

'Honestly, I was up the ladder and spotted it.'

'That wall separates the farmhouse from the annexe. There can't possibly be another building anywhere there,' I said, puzzled. 'You've probably mistaken the roof of the annexe or something.'

'Seriously, there's something there. Here,' he held the ladder steady, 'climb up and see for yourself.'

I smiled at Ben wanly and shuffled restlessly before I stepped on to the bottom rung.

'Keep calm, Alice,' I said to myself, knowing I wasn't at all keen on heights.

'Don't let go of that ladder,' I instructed in a firm tone as I looked up towards the sky.

'Don't worry, I've got you.'

Putting one foot above the other, my heart was in my mouth as I began to climb.

'Stop around there,' I heard Ben call up.

Holding on for dear life, my knuckles were white as I carefully swung my head round. 'Whoa! That view, it's amazing.'

'I never tire of that view,' Ben laughed. I wasn't sure whether he meant the view over the valley or the fact that he was looking straight at my backside.

'Now look towards the wall.'

Shaking my head in disbelief, I saw that Ben was right. There was some sort of roof draped in overgrown ivy and what looked like a small courtyard.

'I don't believe it. There's definitely something there,' I said, staring for a moment before lowering myself down slowly and gratefully, planting my feet firmly back on the ground.

'Connie and Jim must know something about it,' I said. 'Is Jim around?'

Ben shook his head, 'Market day, won't be back until 6 p.m.'

'Whatever it is, it's certainly well hidden.'

Ben raised an interested eyebrow, 'A secret room, very mysterious and exciting. What's the plan of action?'

'Find the way in,' I said without hesitation.

'I'll start this end, you start over there,' suggested Ben and immediately the pair of us set to work, trailing the length of the wall, thrusting our hands behind the entwined ivy, searching for a way in.

'It's just stone here,' I said, disappointed, tapping at the wall.

'Keep moving along, there has to be a way in somewhere,' reassured Ben with an encouraging smile.

For the next five minutes, we carried on prodding behind the shrubbery until I heard Ben shout from a little further up, 'Here, over here, this part isn't brick, it's wood.'

I looked over with a sharp intake of breath and the skin on the back of my neck prickled.

'There's definitely something here ... come and feel.' Ben's voice had risen by a thrilled octave.

My heart was thumping as I arrived at his side. He tugged at the ivy, ripping it straight off the wall to create a small opening.

'Yes, you're right,' I breathed excitedly, feeling the wood, 'and that's definitely a handle of some sort.'

'Go to the far barn, there's a pair of shears hanging on the wall. Let's get this cut back, see what's behind,' he ordered, still ripping away at the overgrown plant with his hands.

My heart raced as my legs powered towards the barn and I yanked the shears from the wall.

'Here,' I said, panting, a little out of breath, thrusting the shears into Ben's hands. He began to snip back the trailing plant. I watched in amazement, cupping my hands around my face as the wooden door became visible.

'What is this place?'

'I'm not sure, but we are about to find out.'

Ben cleared away all of the ivy and we stood and stared at the peeling duck-egg-blue painted wooden door with a huge, tarnished brass knob.

'After you.'

My heart was hammering against my chest as I took a huge deep breath and grasped the knob with my unsteady hand.

Nothing.

It was locked.

Damn.

We stared at the lock beneath the knob.

'Well, that's that then, it's locked. Looks like the mystery is going to stay just that, a mystery, unless you've learnt how to pick locks while living in New York?'

I shook my head, 'Unfortunately that was never on my list of things to do.'

I sighed, my mind whirling. I didn't want to be beaten now.

'I'd say that was quite a big key too, not your run-of-the-mill mortice lock,' said Ben.

Once more I grasped the knob and bumped my shoulder against the door. 'Not quite as easy as it looks in the movies,' I sighed. The door didn't budge an inch.

'You'll hurt your shoulder if you carry on like that,' said Ben. 'Why don't you just ask your grandfather about it? Ask him for the key.'

'Key ... that's it, you are a genius,' I beamed. He looked at me with bewilderment as I began to frantically rummage around in my bag which I'd thrown to the ground earlier.

My hands were visibly shaking as I held up a bunch of keys. 'It's got to be this one. I'd no idea where it was for.'

We both stared at it, then the lock.

'It definitely looks like it would fit. Come on, what are you waiting for?' asked Ben impatiently.

Feeling apprehensive, my heart was thumping and my breath caught in my throat as I placed the key in the lock and turned it.

Click.

Both Ben and I locked eyes before I turned the knob and pushed.

'OMG,' I muttered under my breath as we walked in. I shot Ben a quizzical look. 'What is this place?'

The air was dusty and it smelled damp.

He simply shrugged.

As I edged forward slowly, my eyes widened. It looked like some sort of office-come-dance-studio, which was enclosed inside a small walled garden. The huge, smeared, dirty windows at the far end let in a little light and there was another wooden door leading into a very small courtyard.

In the corner was a small desk with numerous papers stacked in a pile, adorned with dust. A pair of abandoned spectacles lay on top. A ballet barre ran along the far side of the office with mirrors from floor to ceiling, and hanging on the wall were numerous framed photos of ballerinas alongside some very famous ballet production posters.

'There's everything here from *The Nutcracker* to *A Midsummer Night's Dream*,' I said in awe, staring at the posters.

On the small wooden table in the corner of the room sat an old-fashioned tape recorder. I blew away the dust from the top of the black machine then opened the cassette compartment.

'Gosh, they used these things back in the days of the dinosaurs,' I said with amazement, taking out the cassette tape and flipping it over.

'Plug it in, see if it still works.' Ben placed the tape recorder on top of the desk, and switched on the socket.

'There's a red light on it,' I exclaimed, hurriedly stuffing the tape back inside the player. 'It's working.'

As I pressed play we waited in anticipation. There was a click followed by a whir and I gasped as the truly timeless classic, *The Nutcracker* composed by Tchaikovsky, began to fill the room.

The music brought back memories and immediately, happy tears filled my eyes. It was such an emotional piece of music and I remembered one Christmas, curling up under a blanket on the settee with Grandie in front of the roaring log fire. We watched the ballet on an old video cassette. I'd been mesmerised, it was pure magic.

Lost in my memories, I sat down on the old dusty chair, closed my eyes and let the music envelop me.

'It's so beautiful,' I said, my body lifting as though it were being controlled by some invisible force. All of a sudden, I found myself standing in the small cramped space in the middle of the room.

I balanced on one leg and stretched the other leg out behind.

Holding my back upright, I gracefully reached both arms out in front. For a split second, I let the music take over, a feeling of floating on air captivated my whole body. Turning myself elegantly in tune with the music, my arms and legs began to glide and spin. Everything was in sync, even my breathing, but as I spun I locked eyes with Ben and halted.

'Don't stop ... don't stop!' urged Ben. 'That was amazing! Absolutely amazing.' Ben's praise was coming thick and fast.

I could feel myself breathing in and out, my chest rising and falling.

'More ... more,' he said in a playful chant. 'That was breath-taking. You, Alice Parker, were born to dance.'

'I can't,' I said, suddenly feeling inadequate. I thought back to all those rejection letters and emails. My shoulders drooped and I slumped into the chair.

'I don't understand, what do you mean, you can't?'

He balanced on the edge of the desk and waited for me to speak.

'Are you okay?' A worried look was now written all over Ben's face.

I wanted to open up to Ben, he was one of my oldest friends in the village.

'It's just ... for a split second, I felt like the old me again.' I sighed.

'What do you mean, the old you?'

'I'm not quite what I seem,' I admitted, pressing the stop button on the tape machine and switching the socket off at the wall. 'I feel like a phoney.'

Ben looked puzzled.

A little sheepishly I revealed the truth to him about my life in New York and the fact that I'd never made it as a dancer or even performed on Broadway.

He blew out a breath, ran his hands through his hair and gave a low whistle. 'I wasn't expecting that.'

'People always seem to assume I'm something I'm not, and I wish I was that person, I really do, but ... I've never made it past the audition stage. I've never been good enough to land a role that was of any significance. Everyone else is of a higher standard, or their face fits. I stopped attending auditions because I couldn't face another rejection letter landing on the doormat.'

'You've got a skill, a gift you should be proud of. Have you ever asked for feedback? Asked for help?'

I shook my head. 'Grace is trying to talk me into going for an audition with her next week but, how can I? I've messed up every audition so far. Why would this one be any different?' I sighed.

'That would mean you'd be here for a while. I thought you were only here for a holiday?'

'I was ... I am ... but those questions I was asking you, about business, working for the family ... I was asking because Grandie has offered me the dance school.'

Ben's face flashed with excitement. 'What an amazing offer!'

'Mmm, it is and it isn't. I live on the other side of the world and so does Mum,' I answered, wanting to join in with his enthusiasm.

'But if you don't give it a go?'

'But what if I fail? What if I can't teach dance?' I said, hearing the frustration in my own voice.

A slight smile spread across his face. 'I'm not good at this type of stuff, me being a builder, but as my gran used to say, always believe in yourself. Things happen for a reason. It will work itself out. It always does.'

Silently, we walked over towards the windows at the back of the room.

'Have you seen out here?' he asked, changing the subject.

There was a small tranquil courtyard with two wrought-iron chairs and a table. A purple-and-blue flowering climber clambered over the wall while the ivy toppled over from the other side. Even now, there was a burst of colour in this little hidden space.

I caught Ben's eye. 'Do you think this was Grandie's office?'

'It appears that way, maybe he ran the dance school from here and used this space to choreograph routines or some-thing.'

As Ben was talking, I turned around and my eyes flickered towards a rusty old filing cabinet in the corner of the room. Surely it wouldn't hurt to take a sneaky peek inside there. Pulling open the drawer, I shuffled through some of the papers.

'This paperwork goes back years. There's still invoices in here from way back for every student that danced at the school ... and accounts too. Why would all this stuff still be here after all this time and why let this place get so overgrown that it becomes hidden?'

'Who knows?' Ben spun another glance around the place.

'It's an absolute mystery,' I said, perching on the dusty chair and rifling through an old newspaper that was stuffed in the back of the drawer. 'It just seems such a shame. Maybe when the dance school closed down that was it, he just turned his back and shut the door.'

I sat down at the desk and began to thumb through the ancient newspaper. My eyes locked on the headline on page five which was boldly staring back at me. My heartbeat quickened, promptly followed by a queasy feeling which swirled in the pit of my stomach.

I bit down on my lip and could feel myself beginning to tremble, my eyes filling with tears.

'Alice, are you okay? What's wrong?'

Ben looked towards me and waited for me to answer.

I turned the paper towards him.

'Dancer killed on opening night,' Ben read out loud.

'My grandma, according to this,' my voice faltered.

A tear slid down my cheek as I read the story in the paper:

Oscar Bennett has been convicted for his part in a conspiracy to commit burglaries and robberies across the West Midlands and cause death by dangerous driving.

At Stafford Crown Court on Wednesday (June 3rd) it was revealed that the men were involved in stealing prestige vehicles and using them to commit a string of violent crimes.

On the night of May 6th the court heard that Oscar

Bennett had stolen a car and lost control of the vehicle, mounting the pavement and instantly killing Ballerina Florrie Rose Grant on the opening night of The Nutcracker *at the Birmingham Hippodrome, Birmingham. Florrie Grant was married to dancer Ted Grant, leaving behind one daughter, Rose. The married duo, who both danced* The Nutcracker *in the very same theatre over twenty-five years ago, were attending as guests of honour.*

Oscar Bennett was found guilty and sentenced to ten years in prison.

'It was a dreadful tragedy,' Ben offered in a sympathetic tone. 'My own grandma told me the story, I can't remember why it came up in conversation but she said it affected so many people in this village.'

Through my blurred eyes I looked up at him. 'What, you knew?' The knots in my stomach took my breath away.

He solemnly nodded. 'Everyone in Brook Bridge knows. Your grandma is truly missed in this village. Ted and Florrie were the heart of this community. I take it you didn't know?'

But Ben replied to himself before I could draw breath, 'By the look on your face you didn't have a clue.'

'No, I didn't know.' My voice was shaky.

I was distraught, the tears flowing freely. This was tragic. Why did no one think to tell me? Distressed didn't come close to the way I was feeling. Crushed to the core, I re-read the article. Poor Grandie, poor Mum. Florrie ripped from their lives by a senseless crime.

Swallowing down the lump in my throat, I said, 'I didn't know a thing, all I knew was that she died before I was born, and I suppose when I was old enough to ask questions, I couldn't because we'd left, and Mum never spoke about either Grandie or Grandma again.'

'Here, take this,' he said, passing me a tissue from his pocket, 'It must have come as shock to find out this way.'

I managed a nod and let out a long breath, my blurry eyes still staring at the newspaper article. That day must have shattered Mum and Grandie's entire world.

'What am I going to do now?'

'How do you mean?' Ben's sympathetic eyes fixed firmly on me.

'Things are strained with Mum as it is. Can I really go telling her what I've discovered and ask questions?' The photograph of my grandma on the newspaper page was staring back at me, the resemblance between the pair of us was striking. I'd never really noticed from the painting that hung in the gallery at the farmhouse, but this was uncanny.

'Surely it's no big secret? It's in the paper.'

I shrugged. 'A paper from years ago, one that I shouldn't have seen. If we hadn't broken in here, then I would never have found out.'

'But everyone in the village knows about your grandma's tragic death, it's not a secret. Talk to Grace and Connie about it, they might presume you already knew.'

It had never even crossed my mind that Connie would know, but of course she would. Not only was she Mum's best friend at the time, she also worked for my grandfather.

'I just find it strange that it would never be talked about.' I'd no idea why, but the gut feeling in the pit of my stomach was telling me there was more to this story. I looked up at Ben through my teary eyes. 'Do you think that's why he stopped dancing, stopped performing and just ran the dance school?'

'Maybe,' he shrugged his shoulders.

I read through the article one more time and swallowed. Grandma's life had been taken away from her by a common criminal. Her life over in a split second.

This surely must have brought Grandie and Mum closer together. I knew it did. We'd lived here for ten years until that night, when that dreadful argument spiralled out of control and Mum packed our things and left.

Sitting there in the office, I felt saddened by the tragedy of my grandmother's death. Why had no one ever told me what had happened? I'd never really given it much thought before, I'd just thought ... in fact, I had no idea what I thought.

'Come on, we need to get out of here before Jim catches us or Connie arrives home,' I spluttered, suddenly feeling uneasy that I'd gone rifling through Grandie's personal hideaway without permission.

'And you'd best get back to work. Ben ... please can you keep all this to yourself until I've had a chance to chat with Connie and Grandie?'

'Of course,' he answered.

Within seconds the room was locked, and Ben had returned

to work. I tripped numbly along the lane back towards Wild Rose Cottage with thoughts of the past playing over and over in my mind. Reaching the end of the road and with my mind somewhere else, I stumbled on the edge of the kerb, lost my balance and fell to the ground with a bump.

'Are you okay?' The voice behind me sounded concerned and I looked up to find the gorgeous eyes of Sam staring back at me. He extended a hand to me, pulling me to my feet, my face dangerously close to his.

'I think so,' I said, my eyes not leaving his. My heart was beating so loud I thought he might hear. 'I must have tripped, I wasn't looking where I was going,' I said, brushing myself down. I'd no idea where he'd sprung from. 'What are you doing here?'

Sam smiled down at his attire.

'Jogging,' I answered my own question, my eyes skimming over his body which was dressed in trendy sports gear. He had that toned, lean thing going on which gave me tingles in my tummy.

'Where are you going?' he asked.

My eyes lifted back towards his and I held my breath, praying he couldn't read my mind. I thought he was perfect. 'Home,' I managed to say, then sucked in a sharp breath.

Feeling a pain in my knee, I looked down to see the trickle of blood seeping through the ripped knee of my jeans.

'You're bleeding. Here, sit yourself down on this bench, catch your breath,' Sam insisted. He extended his arm and draped it around my shoulder while supporting my elbow with his hand. His hazel eyes bore into mine and I could feel my entire body trembling.

'Honestly, I'm okay,' I answered, even though my knee was smarting. 'I should have been looking where I was going.'

'Things on your mind?'

'You could say that.'

Sam bent down in front of me, the pain now coming through in short, sharp bursts. He slowly rolled up my trouser leg then reached over and squeezed my hand, giving me a reassuring smile. 'I think you'll live but you'll need to bathe that, get the grit out. Are you able to walk or is it piggy-back time?' he said, giving me an amused look, the trace of a smile playing on his lips.

He was definitely flirting a little.

'Piggy-back every time,' I mused, biting down on my lip as I imagined myself being hauled on to Sam's back with my arms tightly wrapped around his broad shoulders.

He flashed me the most gorgeous of smiles that made my heart skip a beat, then held out his hand. I pressed mine into his, he steadied me and we began to slowly walk up the lane.

'Thanks Sam, I feel a bit of an idiot.'

'No need, just one of those things,' he said, still smiling, as he raked his other hand through his hair.

'And I've delayed your run.'

'Any excuse to help a pretty damsel in distress.' His eyes caught mine and I glowed inside. Surely, he could feel the attraction between us too.

'How long are you staying in England?' he probed.

I was just about to answer when we heard the sound of a van slowing down beside us. Turning round, we saw Bert leaning over and winding down the passenger window.

'What's going on here?' he puffed, eyeing me astutely, his manner rather abrupt, taking me by surprise.

'I've tumbled over the kerb, and Sam is helping me home.'

'I'll take it from here.' Bert's tone was very direct and what-was-that-look he gave Sam?

For a moment, a heavy silence settled over us, the tension uneasy.

It was obvious to anyone that there was some sort of friction between the pair of them and with me rushing off to the farm earlier, Grace hadn't had time to tell me about the situation that I'd witnessed in The Old Teashop this morning.

'Honestly Bert, I'm fine, Sam's going to walk me back to the cottage,' I said, not wanting to be dictated to. 'We can manage.'

Bert shot a glance towards my leg. He wasn't taking no for an answer. 'I'll take you up to the farm, that's closer. Connie's just arrived home with your grandfather ... jump in.' Bert locked eyes with Sam who shifted uncomfortably and slowly dropped my hand.

I was feeling a little annoyed at Bert's insistence but the moment I'd discovered Grandie was out of hospital, I knew I needed to see him.

'You go,' Sam insisted, not making eye contact with me.

'Are you sure?' I asked.

His face had paled and the closeness that had been there between us earlier had suddenly vanished.

'Yes, you go, it's for the best,' he said and, taking me completely by surprise, he turned and powered his legs and began jogging up the lane, leaving me standing there.

What did he mean, it was for the best? One minute he was walking hand in hand with me, mildly flirting, and next he can't get away from me fast enough.

Feeling frustrated, I climbed into Bert's van. What the hell just happened here?

Bert was silent as he put the car in gear and began to drive. 'Bert, I have to say I'm rather taken by surprise. That all seemed less than friendly to me.'

'You need to stay away from his sort.' Bert didn't look in my direction as he swung the van into the driveway of Honeysuckle Farm.

'His sort?'

'Yes, his sort. Speak to my Dorothy. She'll tell you all about it.'

Before I could ask any more questions, Bert had parked the van and the door swung open. I looked up to see Ben standing there. 'Great timing, looks like your grandfather is home!' he beamed and tipped his cap at Bert.

'Great news!' I sounded more cheery than I felt.

As I began to climb out of the car I felt Bert's hand on top of mine. 'Talk to Dorothy.'

Utterly confused, I let myself into the farmhouse where I was greeted by Marley.

'Connie, Grandie, are you here?' I shouted up the hallway. Within seconds Connie appeared in the doorway of the kitchen wiping her hands on a tea-towel. Immediately she noticed my ripped, blood-stained jeans which I'd almost forgotten about in the last five minutes.

'Oh gosh, what have you done?' she fussed, ushering me to a chair in the kitchen before running some warm water in a bowl.

'I slipped off the kerb, it looks worse than it is ... ouch,' I blurted as Connie began dabbing away the small stones that were wedged in the cut with a cotton-wool pad from the drawer.

'Where's Grandie? Is he home?'

'He is.' She stopped dabbing and looked me right in the eye. 'Alice, can I ask you? Did you go into your Grandie's old office today?'

My stomach gave a lurch. 'Yes,' I answered sheepishly. 'Ben noticed it from the top of the ladder and curiosity got the better of me. Is there a problem? Is Grandie upset with me?'

Connie placed a plaster on my knee. 'That should be okay now,' she said, rinsing the bowl out in the sink. 'I would say he's a little shocked to see his office uncovered after all this time. He's gone for a lie down.'

'I didn't mean to hurt anyone,' I added tentatively.

'Where did you get the key from?'

'Grandie. He gave me a bunch of keys and once we'd uncovered the door I realised one of those keys fitted the lock. Why was it all shut away?' I asked, as Connie slid a mug of tea in my direction.

'Painful memories for Ted. That was the hub of their life. The dance school was one thing, for the community, but that was where they danced together of a night-time. Where each of them would choreograph their routines, support each other and practise, but once Florrie ...' Her voice wavered and she blinked away a tear.

'Connie, I've only just discovered what happened to Grandma.'

Connie looked at me with sorry eyes and reached over and rubbed my hand. 'You poor love,' her tone soft when she realised it was all so new for me.

'No one ever told me, Mum never spoke about her – well, not to me anyway. Did you know what happened?'

Connie nodded, 'Yes of course, the whole village was in mourning,' she shivered, 'it was devastating for everyone.' I could see the goosebumps prickle on Connie's arms and she quivered.

Taking a deep breath, she said, 'I was there that night.'

My jaw dropped open. 'At the theatre?' Her face turned a ghastly shade of white. 'And?' I narrowed my eyes at Connie. 'Please tell me.'

Connie took a breath. 'It was a big night for Ted and Florrie, they were special guests of the theatre and the press were waiting to take their photographs. It was the first time the show had opened again, since your grandparents had performed *The Nutcracker* all those years ago. They were local celebrities, guests of honour. Ted had secured a couple of extra seats which he'd given to me and your mum.

'I'd arranged to meet your mum outside the theatre just before 7 p.m., but by ten past she still hadn't arrived. Florrie had travelled alone from an afternoon event and was due to meet Ted there too. As far as we knew, she'd been stuck in traffic and was also running late. We were waiting outside when Ted suggested we move into the foyer before taking our seats.' Connie blinked away her tears. 'So, we did ... and that's when we heard it,' she exhaled.

'Heard what?' I questioned.

'The thud, the screams and the screech of a car. We ran outside, there was a huddle of people gathered around a body on the floor ... Florrie. The ambulance arrived, but they couldn't save her. She didn't make it to hospital.'

The emotion poured through my body, the tears began to fall. 'I don't know what to say.' My voice trembled.

For a brief moment, Connie closed her eyes. 'It was just at that moment that your mum appeared from nowhere ... Ted was sitting on the pavement, with your grandma locked in his arms. It was a devastating scene. The police arrived and told us the car was stolen and the driver had mounted the pavement. The bastard was arrested on the spot and thankfully charged and eventually sent down, but it was never going to bring Florrie back.'

Listening to Connie, I felt like I'd been kicked in the stomach. The pain was so raw, just thinking about what everyone had gone through that night. I sat still, numb. I had no idea what to do or say. What could I say? Grandma had been wiped from their lives through the actions of a selfish human being.

Visions of my mum filtered through my mind, how her life had changed in a split second. Thinking about her grief, what she'd been through saddened me. Bringing me up without a mother figure in her own life must have been difficult at times.

Discovering the truth about all of this threw me into further turmoil about the dilemma I'd been faced with. I questioned my own decision to stay in England. After all this time, what would it do to Mum if I abandoned her, especially after what I'd just discovered? I was torn between my love for her and wanting to make a successful life for myself – a home, a business. For all these years she'd been loyal to me, cared for me, had always been there for me, and suddenly my head had been turned by the prospect of this brand-new life back in England.

A pang of guilt hit me. How could I be so selfish? I loved Mum so much and a future without her in it was unthinkable.

Connie touched my hand and gave it a quick squeeze. 'It may be over twenty years ago, but the events of that night never left any of us. Your mum's life was catapulted into one of grief and disarray. She was in the early stages of pregnancy, carrying you, and she lost so much weight with stress, we thought she might lose you.'

I gasped, 'It's all so awful.'

'To be honest, when you came along – three weeks early, I may add – you were certainly a blessing in disguise. It gave us all something to focus on. You brought joy back into everyone's life and your grandfather doted on you.'

My eyes met hers. She was visibly upset and swallowed hard.

'The night Rose went into labour, we were all here, sat in the living room. That day had already been a difficult one.'

'Why?'

Connie's shoulders sagged. For a second she squeezed her grief-stricken eyes tightly shut. 'Because it was Florrie's birthday. It was the first birthday we'd spent without her. We'd spent the day at the cemetery.'

I dropped my head in my hands and sobbed. 'Are you saying my birthday is the same as Grandma's?'

Connie nodded. 'Yes,' she said softly.

I took a moment to compose myself but at last someone was talking, I was getting more information about the past. 'Every year, I must remind them of Grandma.'

'Don't fret about that, that's not a bad thing. She was a remarkable, caring person, beautiful on the outside and in, a rare quality in people of this day and age. Go and talk to your grandfather, he's not angry with you, he just still misses Florrie so much.'

I nodded, stood up and walked into the hallway. Taking a deep breath, I began to climb the stairs.

Chapter 13

I gently pushed open the bedroom door, barely able to breathe. Once standing inside the room, I realised I'd forgotten how magnificently spacious it was, with beautifully restored period interiors. In the middle of the room was a lavish four-poster bed with a gold-embroidered bedspread and through another open door there was the marvellous marble bathroom.

Everything was just so; there was a dressing table with a silver brush and an old-fashioned perfume vaporiser. A pair of ballet shoes hung over the mirror and two chairs positioned in front of the window overlooked splendid views.

Grandie was sitting on the edge of the bed staring out on to the farm gardens and the fields beyond which stretched for miles and miles. His eyes teemed with tears, his wedding photo grasped in his hand.

I felt my heart sink to a new depth.

'Hi Grandie,' I said, in a wavery voice.

He looked up and slowly placed the photo down at the side of him. He extended a shaky hand towards me. I quickly grabbed it and sat down next to him.

For a moment, he didn't say a word. He just clutched my hand then cupped his other hand over the top before turning towards me.

It was me who broke the silence. 'I didn't mean to upset you,' my voice caught in my throat. 'Curiosity got the better of me, which I know is no excuse.'

His face paled. 'I know, I know,' he stuttered, 'to see the door open ...' He patted my hand. 'It doesn't matter,' he said, sadly.

'It does matter, I should have asked you first before I went poking my nose in.'

'How did you discover it?'

'It was Ben, he noticed it when he was at the top of the ladder. When I had a look, I couldn't believe it. Why is it all overgrown,' I asked cautiously, 'hidden away?'

Grandie dabbed his eyes with a handkerchief from his pocket. 'Because it was all too painful. Florrie and I had this place and the dance school to rattle around in, but that little room was where we escaped, let the magic happen. Our own private space where we could be ourselves and dance together. Happy memories – and sad ones too – but once Florrie was gone, I couldn't step foot inside there again. The grief was too much for me to handle.'

Grandie looked around the room. 'The same as this place. This was our bedroom, everything is just how it was when she was alive. Some people may find that a little morbid, but I find it strangely comforting. Soon after we lost her, I moved over to the other side of the house, but Connie still comes in here to dust and vacuum each week.'

'It's a magnificent room, and look at those views, they're incredible.'

The corners of his mouth turned slightly upwards. 'Florrie used to sit in that chair and read and read. When she wasn't dancing she was reading. I'd sit opposite with my newspaper, the pair of us could sit in a comfortable silence for many hours.'

'You still miss her.'

'Without a doubt, every day. No one could ever replace or even come close to the love we shared, she was one in a million.'

'I know how she died. I read the newspaper article.'

I could see him take a deep breath. 'Is that the first you knew of it?'

I nodded. 'Why did no one tell me?'

'I suppose we muddled through. The events of that night still haunt me, and you were only a little girl, but I'm sorry you found out this way.'

I nodded. 'Maybe that was the same for Mum too. She's never spoken to me about it at all.' I took a breath. 'Connie has just told me that I share the same birthday with Grandma too. I never knew that either.'

'You do ... that date became doubly painful once you'd left.'

I couldn't imagine what he'd gone through each year, the grief of losing Grandma then the pain of losing me.

I shook my head. 'But this is what I don't understand. Shouldn't this have brought you and Mum closer together?' I swallowed. I knew I was pressing him but now he'd begun to open up about Mum a little, I needed to ask.

He dabbed his eyes once more and looked like he'd swallowed a large lump in his throat.

His voice was shaky, 'There was a time when Connie and I were so worried that Rose would suffer a miscarriage – her weight plummeted with grief. Rose and Florrie were close you see, they had a special mother-and-daughter bond. But luckily for us you got here safe and sound,' he placed his hand on my knee. 'You brought hope back to us, new love. It was you who gave me the strength to start living again.'

'And Mum?' I pressed the conversation again.

'We were very close when you were born,' was all Grandie offered.

'It sounds like you both helped each other get through this,' I added softly.

He nodded. 'The whole community was affected. Over the years, Florrie and your mum taught so many children and adults to dance in the village. Flowers stretched for miles and miles outside the entrance of Honeysuckle Farm. The children from the dance school all hung their ballet shoes on the gates, it was heart-breaking for everyone. You'd have thought she was royalty,' he added, giving a small chuckle. 'She touched the hearts of many families around here.'

'I only wish I had the chance to spend time with her.'

He nodded his understanding. 'You are very much like her, the same striking blue eyes, beautiful and kind.' He paused and took a deep breath, and his voice wavered. 'Your grandma would have been so proud of you, just like I am. Re-open the dance school, Alice. It's been closed far too long and I'm not getting any younger.'

The tears were now rolling down my cheeks. 'But ... but what if I can't do it? What if I let you down?'

He raised his eyebrows.

'I may not be good enough to step into your shoes, Grandma's shoes, or Mum's, for that matter.' Self-doubt oozed out of my every pore.

'You are a gem Alice, and you just need the chance to be polished so you can shine brighter and brighter. This could be your calling. Open up the school, the whole community will be behind you.'

'I'm so tempted, but you know the dilemma I'm in.'

He remained silent, but his eyes were earnest.

It was time to bite the bullet while I had his full attention.

'What if I could persuade Mum to come back to Brook Bridge, put the last thirteen years behind you both? We could open the dance school together, as a team ... a family.' As far as I could see, there was nothing keeping her in New York. 'What do you think?'

He shook his head. 'Your mum would never come back.'

I bit down on my lip. 'Why did it go wrong? Why did we leave for New York? What happened between you?'

The question hung in the air.

'That is something you'll have to ask her.'

'But I'm asking you. How can I make a decision on my future without knowing all the facts?'

'All I can tell you is that this place is your home, you belong here, and you have all this waiting for you.'

Technically, I knew this wasn't all mine. This should be Mum's inheritance. Grandie was asking a hell of a lot, basically telling me to cut ties with her. Their argument wasn't my argument. Surely they could both understand that, but how could I be disloyal to Mum?

'You, Alice, are such a beautiful girl. Your mum did well bringing you up to be such a loving, considerate woman, but sometimes you have to make choices in life – follow a path that you want to follow. It doesn't mean everyone will like it at first, but in time ...' he broke off.

My mind whirled. Was he saying that if I took this opportunity he thought Mum would actually follow me back to England? But how would I know that for sure? There weren't any guarantees.

'Do you want her to come back?' I asked, feeling utterly confused and frustrated by the whole situation.

Grandie swerved the question completely: 'Let's go and get a cup of tea.'

'Please, Grandie, I'm not a child any more. Everything is not fixed by a cup of tea. Don't you think I deserve the truth?' I pleaded as he placed his cane on the floor and pushed himself up.

'Connie will be wondering what's keeping us.'

Needless to say, my efforts to get to the bottom of it failed.

I was close to breaking point, the sheer frustration of the situation was taking its toll. Why would no one tell me what was really going on? What happened all those years ago to tear them apart, when it was clear to me by the tears and the tormented look on his face that he still loved Mum?

But with Mum in New York, I knew I was going to have to dig deeper to uncover the truth. I decided to ring her and tell her I'd made the decision to stay in England and re-open the dance school and I wanted her to do it with me. At least then, the offer was on the table. If she decided to turn it down there was nothing more I could do.

Chapter 14

My head was in a whirl on the walk back from the farm. The pain in my knee had subsided but the much-needed phone conversation with my mum was playing over and over in my mind. What was I going to say? And how was she going to react? I had no idea.

The second I stepped into the hallway of Wild Rose Cottage, Grace beckoned me into the kitchen.

'You look like you've got the worries of the world on your shoulders,' she noted, placing two glasses of water on to the table alongside the mouth-watering prawn salad she'd prepared for dinner.

'You don't say. That was an afternoon I wasn't expecting,' I said, deflated, kicking off my pumps and plonking myself down heavily on the kitchen chair.

I blew out a breath and folded my arms on the kitchen table. Immediately the smile slid from Grace's face. 'It's serious, isn't it? What's happened?'

For the next ten minutes I told Grace everything, from the discovery of the secret room to the newspaper article and the unexpected arrival of Grandie, home from the hospital, and our emotionally draining chat.

'That's an awful lot to take in.'

I nodded. 'Am I okay to ring Mum before we eat?' I was frightened that if I didn't call her that very second, I wouldn't do it at all.

'Of course you can, the food will keep.'

'Thanks, Grace.'

'You must be genuinely considering Ted's proposal, other-wise there would be no need to mention it at all to your mum,' she raised her eyebrows at me.

'You know what, Grace Anderson? Sometimes you are just too clever for your own good. All I can do is give her the choice to do it with me.'

'Not just a pretty face,' she grinned. 'Good luck.'

Feeling nervous, I disappeared upstairs clutching my phone and settled cross-legged on my bed. With my heart thumping, I braced myself. This was the hardest conversation I was ever likely to have with Mum, but she must have known there was a possibility that once I was here, I might not want to go back.

Was it such a crazy plan to up sticks to England and move into Honeysuckle Farm, leaving my life in New York behind?

'You can do this, Alice.' The words rattled inside my head over and over again. 'The sooner you talk to her about this, the better it'll be.'

Deep breaths, deep breaths.

Feeling apprehensive, I began to dial the number.

Needless to say, the second the phone connected I was shaking like a leaf. My head was throbbing and my hands were sweaty but there was no going back. I couldn't play piggy in the middle forever.

After three rings, Mum picked up the phone.

'Hi Mum, how are you?'

'Alice, it's lovely to hear from you. It's stifling hot and the air conditioning is playing up, but I mustn't grumble. What's the weather like there?'

'Sunny at the moment but we've had a lot of rain too. I've been to The Old Teashop café for cake. Dorothy and Bert pass on their best and said it would be lovely to see you again.'

'How lovely of them both, pass on my best too.'

'Grace and Connie say hi,' I chirped, thinking I would lead her into the next conversation gently.

'Are you getting on okay?' she asked.

'Yes, it's like we've never been apart.'

Then there was a slight awkward silence, but it was now or never.

'Mum,' my voice faltered, 'there's something I need to talk to you about.'

Again silence.

'Are you still there?' I checked, feeling uneasy while fiddling with the top of my sock.

'I'm here,' she said finally, her voice quivering. Deep down I think she knew the conversation with Grandie would happen sooner rather than later. I tried to keep my voice upbeat: 'I've been back to Honeysuckle Farm and guess what, Marley is still there and Billy. I couldn't believe it.' I knew I was beginning to babble.

I could hear Mum breathing on the other end of the phone and could visualise her sitting at the kitchen table, staring out of the window.

'How lovely.'

There was another long pause.

'And I've visited Grandie in hospital, but he's back home now.' There, the word Grandie was out in the open, hanging in the air, so there was no going back. I decided to bite the bullet and just keep talking. Even if she wasn't going to enter into a conversation about him, at least I knew I had her attention and she was listening.

'He's had a fall.'

Still Mum didn't say anything.

'He's okay, but he's very frail, Mum.'

I thought I heard a sniffle at the other end of the line – or was it just a crackle? – I couldn't quite decide.

'There's something else too.'

'What is it, love?'

I was taken aback by the sound of her voice. She definitely sounded shaky. I knew I had to tread very carefully.

'He's not getting any younger and I think the time has come when he wants to put all his affairs in order, for his own peace of mind. He wants to give me the farm, Mum, and the annexe, but there's one condition.'

'Which is?' She spoke slowly but I could hear the intrigue in her voice.

'He also wants to give me the dancing school. He wants me to move back to England and re-open it as a business.'

I heard a sharp intake of breath from the other end of the line.

'We could do this together, Mum, we could move back to England and re-open the dance school together in partnership.'

For a moment, there was silence.

'I'm sure that wasn't your grandfather's suggestion.'

'It's my suggestion. We could work together, doing what we both love doing best ... singing and dancing, nurturing talent, preparing them for auditions. Our very own business ... me and you in partnership.' Even I could hear the sudden excitement and enthusiasm in my own voice.

'I'm sure that isn't what your grandfather wants.'

'But it's what I want. He'll come round, especially if it means me moving back to England.'

'Is that what you want? You want to move back to England? Where has this idea suddenly come from? You are only meant to be away for a few weeks.'

'What's keeping us in New York, Mum? What life do we have there?'

'It's where I live, it's where we live now.'

'I know all this must seem a little too much, out of the blue,' I said softly, 'but it's not like either of us have jobs that are tying us there and we both rent apartments. You are wasted cleaning diners when you could be back here, teaching dance and living at Honeysuckle Farm. It feels like home here, Mum. It's our home.'

'And you think your grandfather is just going to let me waltz back into my old life, teaching dance and living at the farm? That's never going to happen, Alice.' She sounded a little hysterical now.

'To be honest, Mum, one of you needs to make the first move. If the truth be told, we don't know how long he has left, and could you actually live with yourself, knowing you had the chance to put it all right, but didn't take it?'

'That is a low blow, Alice, and you know it.'

Now it was my turn to remain silent. I recognised that tone of her voice, the tone when I knew I'd over-stepped the mark.

'He made it crystal clear to me that I was never to come back – never to darken his door again – and since he has never told me otherwise ...'

'All that was said in the heat of the moment, all those years ago! Isn't it time everyone let bygones be bygones?' I tried to be the voice of reason, keeping my voice calm.

'You've no idea what went on, Alice,' she carried on without taking a breath.

'Well, why don't you tell me then?' The frustration was now clear in my tone.

'This conversation ends here, Alice,' she said, firmly taking control.

Silence again.

I could feel tears pricking the back of my eyes.

'Mum, this is ridiculous. He's an old man and surely some

sort of fallout from years ago can be put behind you?' I said, wistfully.

'I'll ring you again next week to see how you are.'

'Mum, please.'

Without saying anything more, she hung up.

Even though it was a relief to get the conversation over, I never even had a chance to tell her I'd discovered what had happened to Grandma. And as soon as I put the phone down there was a soft rap on the bedroom door.

Grace stepped into the room and gave me a hug. I'd been holding onto my tears but the second Grace's arms wrapped around me they were unleashed.

'Sorry, I was kind of eavesdropping outside ... difficult conversation?'

I managed a nod as we both sat down on the bed, crossed-legged, facing each other.

'What was the outcome?' she asked tentatively.

'Not the one I was hoping for.'

'Did you discover what the falling out was over?'

I shook my head. 'I'm still clueless.'

'Do you think it's anything to do with money? People always fall out over money.'

'I've honestly no idea.'

'How did she take Ted's offer?'

'I kind of put a new spin on it, told her he'd offered me the farm, the annexe and he wanted me to re-open the dancing school, but that I wanted her to move back to England with me so that we could open it together as a business, a partnership.'

'Good plan, and her response?'

'She hung up on me! This whole thing is just causing everyone more upset.'

'Stalemate. Someone has to make the first move.'

'That's my point. I need some fresh air. Have you got time for a quick walk to the dance school? I've not even seen it yet.'

'Absolutely. I've not been inside that building since the day you left.'

'Come on,' I said, grabbing my phone, 'there's no time like the present.'

'You know what I think, Alice Parker? I think your mum will mull over that conversation and come to her senses.'

'I hope you're right, because I've made a decision,' I announced, feeling my spirits perk up.

'Go on ...'

'I can't face going back to my dreary life and Grandie's offer is too good to pass up. I'd be mad not to give it a go.'

'You are definitely staying?' Grace's eyes widened.

'I am. There ... I've said it out loud.'

Grace threw her arms around me. 'For what it's worth, I think it's a great decision.'

'Me too. I feel like it's my time now, I want to do something for me. Does that make me sound selfish?'

'Of course it doesn't.'

My decision was made.

Even though Mum was still firmly on my mind, I just had to accept Grandie's offer. He had welcomed me back with open arms, and it wasn't my job to sort out their relationship. That was down to them, especially if both of them were being stubborn and keeping me in the dark. What more could I do? I felt a great weight lifting off my shoulders.

'Right,' I said bracingly, 'come on, let's go and have a look around the dance school.' I could hear the excitement in my own voice as I let out a breath.

Brook Bridge village was home again and as we grabbed our bags I felt a real sense of belonging once more.

Chapter 15

We'd only managed to get as far as the doorstep of the cottage when Grace stopped in her tracks.

'Phone, I've forgotten my phone.' Grace rummaged through her bag before racing back inside the cottage, leaving me standing in the fresh air. I looked up when I heard a car door slam and noticed Sam. He'd changed from his sports gear and was now dressed in casual jeans and a navy-blue polo shirt. He was collecting his shopping from the boot of his car, and when he looked up our eyes met. His face lit up briefly, but he shifted his gaze to the ground and quickly turned away. Surely he wasn't going to ignore me?

Taking a deep breath, even though I was feeling anxious about Sam's odd behaviour, and with my heart beating in double time, I decided to go over.

'Hey?' I said softly.

He looked up once more. The waft of his aftershave caught on the light breeze and flipped my tummy straight away.

'Hey, how's the knee?'

'All sorted now.'

The conversation seemed to end there. He looked like he was about to say something else but changed his mind. There was a sudden awkwardness between us and I felt an instant pang.

Hearing the door of the cottage close, I realised Grace was on her way out. 'I'd best go,' I managed to say, thankful my voice wasn't shaky.

He nodded, but there was a sadness in his eyes as he held my gaze. I was confused. There was a connection between us and I knew he must feel it as much as me. I watched as he carried his shopping up his path, exchanging a few words with Grace before disappearing inside his cottage. Every time I looked at him my heart melted, but was the blossoming friendship between us over now? Before it had really begun? His behaviour had changed towards me in a matter of seconds once Bert had pulled over in that van. Why was he giving me the cold shoulder all of a sudden?

Putting on a brave face, I walked towards Grace, not quite knowing what to do about the situation. How things can change in such a short space of time!

'You okay?' Grace noticed. 'You seem distracted.'

I gazed up wearily.

'You're teary? What's going on?'

I couldn't help it. All day my emotions had been all over

the place and I couldn't understand why Sam would suddenly treat me this way. Maybe I was being over-sensitive, but something just didn't feel right.

'I wish I knew,' I sighed. 'There's something strange going on. One minute Sam and I are getting on like a house on fire, and then Bert pulls over in the van and everything seems to change in a split second. Sam's now acting cool towards me.' My voice cracked, 'I've no idea what is going on.'

'Van? What happened with Bert?'

I shared with Grace what happened that afternoon. 'Why did Dorothy treat Sam like that in the teashop and why is Bert warning me to stay away from Sam?' I didn't understand any of it.

Grace linked her arm through mine and with a fleeting glance over my shoulder I saw Sam was standing in the window watching us. We began walking. Grace was quiet and I eyed her carefully. 'Why do I get the impression there is something you aren't telling me?'

'You like him, don't you?'

'I do, yes ... so tell what's going on. Why are Dorothy and Bert acting that way towards him?'

Grace held my gaze, I waited for her to say something.

'Please don't think I don't support you and your family, of course I do, but I like Sam, he's always been good to me. I really don't want to take sides.'

'Sides? Sides about what?' I was beginning to feel anxious.

Grace looked panicked.

'Surely it can't be that bad.'

'Unfortunately, in such a close-knit community people never forget and Florrie was a huge part of this village, everyone loved her.'

I was on the verge of tears again. 'What's Grandma got to do with this?' I enquired, forcing myself to sound far brighter than I felt.

'Oscar Bennett ...'

That was the second time I'd heard that name today.

'The man who killed your grandma.'

'What about him?' I asked. My heart was now beating ten to the dozen.

'Oscar Bennett was Sam's uncle.'

I gasped, 'You're joking?' My head was spinning with this snippet of information.

She shook her head, 'Unfortunately not.'

I took a second to digest the information, which had completely taken me by surprise.

'You said, *was* his uncle?'

'Oscar Bennett was killed in a road-traffic accident after he served his time in prison,' continued Grace.

I sucked in a breath, 'If truth be told, I'm not too sorry about hearing that piece of news, but what has any of this got to do with Sam?'

'People who were close to Florrie never moved on. Oscar Bennett had brothers, they are still notorious petty criminals around these parts.'

'And Sam's tarred with the same brush as his family?'

'Exactly.'

'That's a huge grudge to be holding for all these years.'

'Even now, most of the petty crime in the area has something to do with them.'

'But Sam isn't a part of it?' I asked, thinking how unfair it was to be accountable for someone else's actions after all this time.

'No, from what I understand he doesn't even speak to them. He goes about his own business and against the stigma, and by sheer hard work and determination Sam has become successful, the top of his game. No matter how some people act towards him, he holds his head up high.'

'If things are that bad for him, why does he stick around?'

'Because one day he hopes people around here will see past the fact that he's related to Oscar and will accept him for who he is, and not for the reputation of his uncle.'

We walked in silence as I thought about what Grace had just told me. Just seeing the animosity towards him made me realise how over time certain situations can get way out of hand. I knew all about people holding grudges for far too long, hiding secrets and letting things fester without talking them through. I only had to look at the situation between Grandie and Mum. Even though I was emotionally involved in the situation, it was obvious to me that Sam was being treated unfairly and my heart truly went out to him.

One thing was for sure, he definitely had staying power to put up with being treated like a pariah. Why wasn't it obvious to the rest of the village that there was no connection between

Oscar and Sam except a bloodline? They weren't the same people, both had their own minds.

'What are you thinking?' Grace broke the silence. 'You're not mad at me, are you?' Her expression was earnest.

'For being friends with Sam? Of course not, what sort of person would that make me?' I said softly, feeling a little overwhelmed by it all.

There was no denying today had been an emotional day for me, discovering the truth about my grandma's tragic death. But that wasn't Sam's fault. He hadn't been driving that car.

Then an uneasy thought crept into my mind. Why had Sam's behaviour suddenly changed towards me when Bert had pulled up in his truck and told me Grandie was out of hospital? He must have realised at that moment who I was – Florrie Parker's granddaughter. That would explain his change in behaviour. I knew I needed to talk to him, but what if he didn't want to talk to me and kept his distance? I felt a pang at that very thought.

'I need to talk to him, Grace.'

'You will, but look, we're here now.'

We paused on the pavement, shielding the early evening sun from our eyes while looking up at the large sign on the front of the building.

'Florrie Rose School of Dance,' Grace read out loud.

'My grandma,' I said simply, as goosebumps tingled my skin.

Chapter 16

The last time I'd stood here was as a ten-year-old child, happy and carefree, before life got complicated. I couldn't quite believe I was back here again, it seemed so surreal. A fizz of excitement popped inside me and there was no mistaking the huge beam etched on my face as I clutched the keys tightly in my hand. This place could actually be mine, the key I held could be the key to my future.

Grace was watching me with curiosity. 'Are you ready for this? I'm excited, so goodness knows how you are feeling!' She draped her arm around my shoulder and gave me a quick hug.

'Ready as I'll ever be,' I said, placing the key in the lock and turning it slowly, savouring the moment. 'I can't believe I'm here, it's so bizarre.'

'Me neither,' Grace answered, hovering behind me on the pavement. I pushed open the door then waited.

'What are you doing?' she asked, puzzled, looking over my shoulder.

'Listening for the beeps, but it doesn't appear to be alarmed. Are we ready for this?'

'Eek!' squealed Grace in my ear.

'I take it that's a yes,' I chuckled.

'I'm feeling a tiny spark of jealousy,' Grace admitted, following me inside the foyer. 'This could all be yours.'

'Look at this place!' I said, rolling my eyes around the room.

It was as though time had stood still. Even though Jim had been keeping an eye on this place, dropping in every now and again, everything looked like it had remained untouched. There was still an old jacket hanging on the coat stand behind the reception desk, and a shrivelled-up plant on the window-sill.

Pulling on the cord of the blind, I spluttered as a cloud of dust mushroomed into the air. The sunlight flooded the room and Grace gasped.

'OMG, the noticeboard is still up,' she exclaimed, pointing to the large cork board hanging on the wall.

'Extra show rehearsals for ballet,' I read out.

'And look, there's our names.' She ran her fingers over the cast list.

The A4 paper pinned to the board contained information for all the dance classes: ballet, jazz, tap and modern. Under each class was a list of the names of the children who attended, and on a separate sheet were the adults.

'Big band night was popular,' I mused, looking at the list of names. 'Dorothy and Bert were regulars.'

I was in awe of the place – all those names, all those classes filled to the brim, bringing hours of joy to the students – and now Grandie was giving me the chance to bring this place back to life. All this was going to be mine.

'Why didn't Ted keep it going? There were other teachers here apart from your mum.' Grace turned towards me.

'I think he was heartbroken, and it was a family business,' I answered, still taking in my surroundings.

It was a little sad knowing the school had closed down after Grandie and Mum argued, but knowing what I knew now, Grandie would have found it difficult to carry on without Mum. And he wouldn't have wanted just anyone taking over, he'd have wanted to keep it in the family, just like Honeysuckle Farm.

'Come on, let's have a look through here.' Grace followed me towards the double doors at the far end of the foyer, which I pushed open.

'I used to think this room was massive when I was a kid,' smiled Grace, immediately grasping hold of the ballet barre. 'First position, second position ... I feel like I'm ten years old again.' She laughed.

The room was exactly how I remembered it, mirrors all down one side, a small stage area at the far end framed by red velvet curtains that were still hanging, giving it all a very regal effect. Folded chairs were stacked to the side of the stage alongside the old, battered, out-of-tune brown piano that Mr Cork the caretaker used to play in times of need.

'Everything's still here, by the looks of things, even the lost property,' remarked Grace, as she opened the cupboard door and was faced with a heap of old clothing. 'Aww, look how tiny these are,' she said, holding up the cutest, tiniest ballet shoe. 'Very adorable.'

'This place, it wouldn't be that hard to re-open,' I said admittedly.

'A fresh lick of paint, the windows cleaned, a brush and a mop, you could have it up and running in no time,' Grace agreed.

'I think you're forgetting a tiny detail,' I smiled, pinching my thumb and forefinger together. 'The students.'

'Advertising ... distribute leaflets to all the local schools. The local WI and community groups would jump on board. Dorothy would pin up a poster in The Old Teashop, word of mouth ... this is just what Brook Bridge needs.' Grace had it all fathomed out as she followed me into the kitchen.

'This place reminds me of a school canteen,' I pointed to the large stainless-steel water urn hanging on the wall and the small tables and chairs dotted around. 'We used to sit and have our snacks there, do you remember?'

'And you've got to love the hatch,' Grace giggled, poking her head through it.

'Everything is still in here – cups, mugs, and cutlery,' I said, sliding open the kitchen drawers and peering inside. 'It even comes equipped with stale biscuits!' I held up an out-of-date packet of Rich Tea.

'Eww!' Grace scrunched up her face. She sat down on one of the tiny tables and I heaved myself up on to the hatch.

'Come on then, I'm dying to know.' Grace locked eyes with me. 'What do you reckon to all this?'

'I reckon ...' I thought for a second, 'I reckon after seeing this place again, I've got to do this!' My face broke into a huge grin.

'Are you serious?'

'I think I am!'

Grace let out a whoop. 'With you at the helm, what can go wrong? It's going to be the making of you, and not to mention a little goldmine.'

The excitement in the pit of my stomach was telling me exactly the same thing too.

'I'll help you devise a leaflet, decide what classes to do, what age groups to teach and what interest we can drum up.'

'We ...?'

'Yes, we! You didn't think I'd let you do all this by yourself, did you? And I bet if we sweet-talk Mum, she'll help you with the book-keeping until you get up and running. She takes care of the accounts up at the farm.'

Listening to Grace's excited chatter, I could see this place transforming right before my very eyes.

'I'm really going to do this!' I squealed, feeling that this was my future, a project I could really get my teeth into. The excitement rushed through my body just thinking about it. I really hoped Mum would get behind the idea when she realised I was serious about staying here.

'If anyone can do it, you can,' said Grace, smiling winningly.

'So, how long do you think it would take to get this place up and running?' I gazed around the room, thinking. In the cold light of day it did all look very tired, the décor needed a little updating and the studio needed a deep clean, but this place could be brought back to life in no time at all.

'Six months, maybe less. The building is sound, it's just cosmetic. A fresh lick of paint will transform this place in no time at all and I'm sure we can talk Jim into helping too. This school,' she paused and looked around, 'is crying out to become the heart of the community once more.'

'I hope you're right.'

'I'm always right,' she grinned.

'Knock, knock, anyone there?' we heard a voice shout and Grace jumped off the table.

Bert's worried-looking wizened face appeared around the door.

'Girls, you nearly gave me a heart attack ... and I don't want to be having one of those at my age.' Bert gave a small chuckle but his hand was clutching firmly against his chest.

'Or any age,' smiled Grace.

'The front door was ajar. Is everything okay?'

'Yes, we were just reminiscing,' I said brightly.

Bert walked into the room and sighed contently. 'Look at this place. Dorothy and I loved our Thursday nights here. Twinkle-Toes, she used to call me, even though I stepped on her toes more often than not. I won't repeat what expletives she called me then.'

Both Grace and I laughed.

Bert told us about the fun this little place had brought to the community of Brook Bridge. It wasn't just the hours of dance he'd enjoyed but the friends he'd made too – good solid friendships. My heart swelled when he told us of the summer day-trips to the seaside that Grandie and Mum had organised for everyone and the winter quiz nights at the pub.

'When you get to our age we need places like this to bring us all together. There were plenty of laughs to be had and always something to look forward to, and now ... and now ... look at me, getting all maudlin. This place will always be special to me and Dorothy ... happy times when I was a little more nimble on my feet. These days all I have to look forward to is the *Daily Mail* crossword and keeping a watchful eye over the ovens at The Old Teashop so the cakes don't burn.'

A wave of pure sadness washed over me and that's when it hit me. This place wasn't just a dance school, it was much more than that to everyone who lived in Brook Bridge. It had been a hive of activity that brought everyone together to enjoy dance and each other's company.

'We hoped this place would re-open again but as time passed, everyone realised it was more and more unlikely.'

'Some things are worth resurrecting,' chipped in Grace, cocking an eyebrow in my direction with a huge beam.

Bert's eyes crinkled with hope. 'Are you thinking of re-opening, Alice?'

A smile hovered on my lips as I looked between Grace and Bert. 'Absolutely, Bert!'

'I knew it!' exclaimed Bert, 'I knew this place would get under your skin, I said those very words to Dorothy. Wait until I tell her! Young Alice following in Ted's footsteps. Florrie would be so proud of you. We all still miss her very much, especially my Dorothy.'

'Bert, about this afternoon ...' He looked towards me as I spoke. 'Grace has filled me in ...' I took a breath, I didn't want to sound disrespectful. 'Grandma's death was a long time ago and I know Dorothy and yourself were the best of friends with her, but if I'm moving back here I need calm, I can't take on anyone else's battles. Do you know what I'm trying to say? I want to look towards the future. This dance school will be open to everyone.'

He nodded his understanding. 'Say no more, lass.'

'And I hope you and Dorothy will be back through those doors.'

'You try and stop us! This is great news for the village.'

'I'm glad you think so.'

Bert tipped his cap, his eyes a little teary. 'This place saved Dorothy and I after Janice passed away. It was a place where we'd lose ourselves in the music and dance away the grief.'

Janice had been Dorothy and Bert's only daughter. She'd passed away twenty years ago after a short battle with breast cancer.

'One of the cancer charities we donate to on Village Day is in memory of Janice,' chipped in Grace. 'Great cause.'

Bert mopped his eye with his hanky and composed himself. 'It is, everyone is very generous. Ted and your mum were always a great part of the day, and if Ted wasn't under the weather I'd be asking him for help right now, instead of trying to grapple with the technology of today.'

'Help with what?' I asked, intrigued.

'Our golden wedding anniversary ... that daft wife of mine still believes she's Ginger Rogers and I'm Fred Astaire.'

Grace raised her eyebrows. 'Meaning?'

'Meaning, I've been watching those tube videos.'

Grace gave a small laugh, 'YouTube.'

'Dorothy has always loved to dance, and I wanted to surprise her. I'd visions of twirling her around the stage on Village Day, foxtrotting around in front of the whole of Brook Bridge. It would make her anniversary special, you see. And I like my Dorothy to be happy ... makes my life easier if she's happy.' He tipped us a wink.

'Aww!' exclaimed Grace, 'how romantic. If you weren't taken, Bert, I'd snap you up for myself. You are a definite keeper,' she marvelled.

Bert chuckled, 'This is true, I've been telling her that for years,' he said, taking the weight off his legs and leaning against the edge of the table.

'But I'm no Anton du Beke,' he quirked a bushy eyebrow. 'The old pins don't move like they used to and for the record, I'll wear a tuxedo but there's no way I'm pouring this body into any type of colourful Lycra for the whole of the WI to witness – or Brook Bridge village, for that matter. I have my limits.'

'We hear you, Bert,' I grinned.

'But ...' his shoulders sagged, 'I'm struggling.' He attempted a half-hearted smile. 'These feet haven't danced for over a decade and can I remember the steps?' He rolled his eyes. 'No ... that's why I was going to ask Ted to give me a few pointers. I don't want to let my good lady down.' He blew out a breath.

Anyone could see the love in Bert's eyes for his beautiful Dorothy. He really wanted to give her a golden wedding anniversary to remember.

Grace caught my eye and grinned. 'I'm sure Alice can help you. You can be her first student!'

Witnessing the glint of hope in Bert's eye, I asked, 'The foxtrot you say, Bert?'

'Dorothy's favourite dance.'

'One of my favourites too. I'd love to help.'

Bert's gaze locked with mine. 'Really? You'd do that for me ... for us?'

'Yes, really! I can't have you letting down Dorothy after all this time. I wouldn't be able to sleep at night! Let's give her an anniversary to remember.'

His eyes lit up as he sprang upright, closely followed by Grace. Unable to take the huge grin off his face, he said, 'But promise me I don't have to wear Lycra.'

'No Lycra,' I agreed, with a grin.

Bert darted towards me, his hand stretched out. 'Thank you, young Alice, but let's keep this to ourselves, we mustn't tell Dorothy.'

'Your secret is safe with us!'

'When do we get to work?'

'How about tomorrow morning?' I suggested, feeling my heart give a little leap at his excitement and the challenge ahead.

Bert saluted. 'Bright and early, which means I'd best keep off the cider tonight. Will we be seeing you later?'

'Later?' I asked.

'The barn dance at The Malt Shovel,' he answered.

'I forgot all about it. It's usually a good night.' Grace looked at me.

I shrugged, 'We can nip along.'

'Good, good, now I'd best be off, and thank you, young Alice, you've made an old man very happy.' He shook my hand heartily before turning and whistling his way through the door. Both Grace and I stood and watched him leave with huge grins on our faces.

'See, your first customer,' Grace whispered in my ear. 'New beginnings.'

I blew out a long, calming breath.

'Team Bert and Dorothy, let's give Dorothy a golden wedding anniversary to remember. I just hope I'm up to the ...'

'Stop right there, Alice! You'll be fantastic,' she reassured me, with a twinkle in her eye.

'I hope so,' I replied, not wanting to let anyone down.

Chapter 17

'When I agreed to go to the barn dance at the pub there was no mention of dressing up in ridiculous clothing,' I argued, adjusting the spotty red bandana around my neck while gazing down at the borrowed, ripped-denim dungarees that Grace was forcing me to wear.

'It'll be great fun, you'll enjoy it,' said Grace, tugging a brush through my hair.

'Ouch,' I exclaimed, 'you are the world's worst hairdresser.'

'Sticks and stones and all that, just hold still, will you, I'm nearly done,' she ordered in a firm tone. I didn't dare move.

A couple of seconds later, she handed me a mirror. I stared at my two long plaits and the huge ribbons tied around the bobble. 'I look like I belong on a farm.'

'Job done then, I've got the look perfect.' She swiped her hands together in a pleasing manner. 'You do belong on a farm – or you will soon.' She gave my shoulders a quick squeeze. 'There's just one more thing you need.'

'Which is?'

Grace disappeared towards the cupboard at the bottom of the hallway. 'I know they're in here somewhere,' she called, rummaging around. 'Here they are ... found them.'

She poked her head back around the kitchen door holding up the most battered pair of cowboy boots I'd ever seen.

'They are certainly well used,' I mused, taking them from her.

'Correction, well loved!' she smiled. 'They were given to me by the prop department when I was starring in *Calamity Jane*, but they were so comfy, I kind of forgot to give them back.'

'Perks of the job!'

'They'll finish off your outfit perfectly.'

'Thank you ... I think,' I laughed, pulling them on to my feet.

'I'm glad Bert reminded us about tonight, it's an event not to be missed. Apple cider made from the local orchards, live music, hog roast and all the village folk,' she said with a grin.

'All the village folk?' I asked, casting a thought towards Sam. After we'd arrived back from the dance school Sam was still on my mind. I'd messaged him on Facebook, general chitchat, just keeping it light until I could talk to him face to face, but as yet there had been no reply.

'There's usually a good turn-out every year. Are we ready to go?'

'Ye-haw-cowgirl, let's get to this hoe down,' I slapped my leg, getting into the spirit of things.

We set off and walked over the bridge, past the little parade of shops, and emerged through the cut-through at the end of the High Street. We followed the sound of music and the gang of people in front of us dressed in denim cut-offs, gypsy tops and cowboy hats.

As soon as the pub was in sight it looked spectacular. Every tree, every bush and every stall was draped with sparkling fairy lights and bunting. Before I could say anything else, a tall balding man, dressed up as a cowboy with dark-rimmed glasses, jangled a bucket of loose change in front of us as we neared the entrance.

Throwing a handful of coins into the bucket, we stepped into the grounds of the pub. There was an oversized marquee up ahead, and we were welcomed by an impressive number of bales of hay, giving it an authentic feel. Some were neatly stacked against the sides of the tents while others were set out in squares, covered with people sat eating, drinking and chatting.

Everyone we passed gave us a welcoming smile as we were swept along in the joyful atmosphere.

Inside the marquee, there'd been a burst of shabby chic, floral bunting criss-crossed the ceiling and tables were draped with beautiful polka-dot tablecloths. At the far end a folk band were playing and already a handful of people were dancing on the makeshift dance floor.

Opposite the entrance to the marquee the smell of a hog

roast turning on the spit was mouth-watering. It was accompanied by huge aluminium pots of homemade beef stew on the table inside an open-fronted food tent. A group of men were huddled around the makeshift bar, clinking their glasses and laughing heartily. I'd been a little apprehensive when Grace first mentioned it but being here amongst the friendly faces and jovial chatter, I soon felt at ease.

'Drink?' asked Grace.

'Oh, go on, if I must!'

'Inside to the main bar or outside?'

Before I could answer a voice hollered, 'Grace! Alice!'

We spun round to see a beaming Connie and Jim manning the cider tent. Grandie was sitting next to them in a wheelchair with a blanket thrown over his lap.

'I didn't know you were coming,' I beamed at him.

'Going stir crazy after hospital. Thought the fresh air would do me good and this apple cider is going down a treat.'

'What's with the chair?'

'Between you and me,' Grandie leant forward in his chair, 'Connie thinks it's a safety precaution, there's a method to her madness ...'

I smirked.

'She thinks if I have too many of these,' he held up the near-empty bottle of cider, 'and I'm sitting in this contraption, then I'll be safe from falling over and hitting my head again.' He rolled his eyes in jest.

'I am here, you know,' she swiped his arm, 'and can hear every word.'

'I'm in no doubt,' Grandie replied with a playful tone.

'The hospital wouldn't have provided it if they didn't think it was necessary, and we won't be staying long. Just enough to show our faces and say a quick hello to everyone.'

By the looks on Jim and Grandie's faces, they had different ideas and in one smooth move Jim flicked the lid off another bottle of cider and swapped it for Grandie's now-empty bottle.

'I saw that!' Connie didn't miss a trick. 'Drink, girls?'

'If these pair haven't already drunk the bar dry,' grinned Grace, ferreting around inside her pocket for some loose change.

Jim handed over a couple of bottles. 'Strong stuff, don't have too many without lining your stomach first,' he warned, with a warm smile on his face, 'and put that away, these ones are on me,' he insisted, throwing some money into the bucket which was acting as the till.

'Thanks Jim, much appreciated,' said Grace before turning and pressing a swift kiss to Connie's cheek. 'We're off for a quick wander. Catch you all later.'

We began to walk through the stereotypical country revellers. In front of us there were straw-hatted, booted cowboys leaping around to music from a shrieking fiddle while supping from their bottles of cider.

'Fancy a quick jig?'

I must have looked stricken.

'Only joking, I think I need a few more of these first,' Grace chuckled, linking her arm through mine.

'There are people everywhere,' I said, glancing over to a

group of men who were competing in a tug-of-war event.

'Apart from Village Day, there isn't much to do around here and this type of event brings everyone together, a real community gathering. It gives the local people the opportunity to sample each other's produce too,' she nodded towards a rosy-faced Dorothy serving up slices of cake from a trestle table up ahead.

Bert cast his eyes over the crowd and spotted us. He tapped his nose and winked in our direction, reminding us to keep his secret.

There was commotion everywhere I looked, even excited toddlers were joining in on the act, stomping their wellies to the beat of the music while clutching hot dogs oozing with ketchup.

The aroma of the scrumptious food guided us back towards the huge pig turning on the spit. We queued behind the lingering crowd. 'Jim was right, this is strong stuff,' I said, 'very ... cidery!' taking another gulp.

Grace giggled, 'You daft bugger, that's made with some of the apples from Honeysuckle Farm.'

'Really?'

'Yes, really.'

'Who'd have thought, homemade cider on my very doorstep? Refreshing and going down a treat.'

Finally, we reached the front of the queue. The guy standing behind the trestle table, dressed in a blue checked shirt, tipped his cowboy hat.

'What can I get for you ladies?' he asked, in an exaggerated countryside accent, chewing on a piece of straw and shooting us both a cheeky grin.

'Two of those please,' Grace nodded towards the pile of hot sliced pork buns. Grabbing a serviette, we thanked the cowboy and parked ourselves on a hay bale overlooking the dance floor.

We placed our drinks on the ground and tucked into our food. I lost count of the number of nods of the head and waves of the hand Grace received – everyone seemed to know everyone here. Living in New York, you barely knew your neighbours, they were just people you occasionally nodded to on the stairwell, or politely said hello to when taking in a parcel.

After we'd devoured our oversized buns overloaded with hog and I'd wiped the apple sauce from my chin, I headed inside to use the bathroom while Grace walked back over to the cider stall to chat with Connie and the others.

The pub was heaving, the thirsty revellers five deep at the bar. Instead of fighting my way back through the crowd, it was easier to slip out the side door back on to the High Street, where I noticed Sam's car parked opposite the post office – and there he was, standing in the queue for the cash machine, dressed in his usual pair of Levis, complemented with a tight white T-shirt that clung to his perfectly toned torso. With my heart thumping wildly against my ribcage, I hovered by his car, hoping for a chance to speak to him alone. He crossed the road towards me, stuffing notes into his wallet.

'Sam.'

He looked up and met my gaze. Immediately, I could feel the crackling in the air, the instant spark between us.

'Hey,' I said softly.

'Hey back,' he said, his eyes skimming over my outfit. 'You pull the country look off very well.' His hazel eyes sparkled playfully.

'Mmm, I'm not convinced, especially when Grace dug out these old things,' I waggled the cowboy boots. 'She pinched them from her *Calamity Jane* performance.'

'They finish off the outfit perfectly.'

I was relieved there seemed to be no tension between us, and Sam was chatting to me without any awkwardness on his part.

'Are you coming in for a drink? My treat,' I asked hopefully.

As soon as I asked the question, Sam shifted uneasily from foot to foot while looking over his shoulder. His mood seemed to change within a matter of seconds. 'Not tonight, it looks busy in there.'

'Heaving,' I said, unable to hide the disappointment from my voice.

'I'll catch you soon. Have a great time.' And with that he turned away and unlocked his car.

'How soon?' I pushed, wanting him to commit to a time. He stopped and turned back round. Now something uneasy descended over us and I didn't like it.

'Sam, is everything okay?' My voice was earnest. 'You seem ... a little different towards me.' There, the words were out in the open. 'Can we talk, I need to tell you something.'

I wasn't giving up and gestured towards the bench at the front of the pub.

He nodded, locked his car and followed me over to the bench. He gave a fleeting glance towards the group of people huddled at the entrance of the pub before he sat beside me. His hand brushed against mine, sending a hundred fireflies hurtling around my stomach.

'If I can feel that, surely you can too?' I said softly, barely able to breathe.

He exhaled gently, 'I can.' And for a split second, his fingers entwined around mine, the feel of his touch sending shivers down my spine and making my skin prickle with goosebumps.

'I think I know what you want to tell me,' he said.

'You know, don't you?' My voice was calm even though my heart was hammering in anticipation of the answer.

Sam looked towards me. He bit down on his bottom lip, and with his unblinking eyes stared at me, then nodded.

'I realised the second Bert pulled up in his van and told you your grandfather was home. Alice, talking to me will give you no end of trouble. You don't need to be dragged into my family problems.'

My heart felt like it had snapped in two.

'Isn't that my choice?'

'Most people around here have a low opinion of me and ...' he held my gaze with his own, his round hazel eyes irresistible, 'and ...'

'I don't care what anyone else's opinion of you is,' I interrupted.

He looked towards the pub and shrugged. 'You will, Alice.' He let out a long breath and stood up slowly.

I swallowed, 'I won't. I don't care what anyone says or thinks. The past is the past and that's where it should stay.'

He took a breath in before speaking, as though weighing up what to say next. 'You get back to your friends and family, they will be wondering where you are.'

I felt a tear slip down my cheek and he extended his arm and gently brushed it away. 'Don't cry.'

I stared up at him through my watery eyes. 'Come here,' he said softly, pulling me in for a hug. I nestled against his chest and inhaled the gorgeous aroma of his aftershave. I could feel the heat radiating and hear the gentle thud of his heartbeat. Then he slowly released me before tilting my face to his. We stared at each other for a long moment, our faces centimetres apart.

'I need to go,' he whispered before he kissed me lightly on the cheek and turned to walk away.

'Don't go,' I pleaded, my heart breaking in two.

Suddenly, a voice boomed from nowhere, interrupting our moment together. 'Alice, is he bothering you?'

Startled, I spun round to see a thunderous-looking Ben standing at the entrance of the pub with Henry by his side.

'No, not at all,' I answered, meeting Ben's gaze head on.

'It doesn't look that way from here,' he continued.

'Ben, I'm absolutely fine,' I said, this time a little more firmly.

Bystanders now seemed to be staring in our direction.

Sam had stopped walking and turned back towards me. 'And this is exactly the reason why I need to go,' he whispered softly.

I watched as Sam started up the engine of his car and drove away up the road. Once he was out of sight I swung round angrily towards Ben. 'What was that all about?' I demanded, perturbed that my time with Sam had been cut short.

'Whatever are you doing with the likes of Sam Reid?'

'Who I spend my time with is my business.' My tone was cool and direct, and I'd clearly taken Ben by surprise.

I heard Ben mumbling under his breath, but I'd already walked off up the road. How must Sam be constantly dealing with such behaviour? I knew exactly how it felt, feeling like an outsider, and over time it chipped away at your confidence.

Ten minutes later I was back at Wild Rose Cottage wiping away my tears of frustration. I'd knocked on Sam's front door but there was no answer. I texted Grace to apologise and explain where I'd disappeared to, and she replied saying she was on her way back home. I was angry and disappointed that my night had been cut short and I hadn't even said good night to Grandie.

For the first time since arriving back in Brook Bridge I began to question whether it was all that it was cracked up to be. If this was the way villagers treated people, holding a grudge for over two decades, then did I really want to be a part of it? Maybe Mum was right leaving. After this evening, I wasn't sure if this village was the answer to my problems.

Chapter 18

The next morning, I woke up with the sunshine bursting through the curtains and the birds chirping outside my window. Within a split second, fleeting images from the pub flooded my mind once more as I remembered the way Sam had been treated.

When Grace had arrived home the night before, we'd shared a bottle of wine and I'd recounted the events, describing how for the first time I felt a little unsettled being back in the village. I thought my life was about to change for the better but after witnessing the hostility towards Sam that still lingered, I wasn't impressed with some of the Brook Bridge residents.

Grace had divulged that there had been rivalry between Ben's family and the Reids for decades. Ben's grandmother had been Florrie's best friend, and even after her death the family grudge between them had never disappeared. But after all this time, was there any need to continue to carry such animosity? Hadn't time moved on? Given what I'd witnessed outside the pub, Sam had kept his cool, walked away. There hadn't been any retaliation, so it appeared to me that he didn't want any part of it. And I couldn't blame him. I could sympathise. I too was fed up with people falling out over ancient feuds.

I sat in bed for a little while before I threw back the duvet and walked gingerly into the bathroom. Once inside the shower, I let the water cascade over my body while I thought about the day ahead. This morning I'd arranged to meet Bert at the dance school and once his lesson was over, I was going to take a walk up to Honeysuckle Farm to see Grandie before, hopefully, tracking down Sam.

Fifteen minutes later, with my hair washed and my make-up on, I wandered downstairs to the smell of bacon cutting through the air.

Grace smiled at me.

'Breakfast,' she said, placing a bacon sandwich and a mug of tea on the table in front of me. 'Sleep well?'

On the whole I had, which was no doubt helped by the boost in alcohol consumption after Grace's arrival home.

'Yes, not bad.'

'And the plan for today?' she asked, sitting down opposite me.

'Firstly, I'm foxtrotting with Bert.'

'No Lycra,' Grace reminded me, and I smiled. 'See, there is a smile in there somewhere,' she teased.

'Just a little one,' I said, squeezing my thumb and forefinger together, 'but there's stuff playing on my mind. I don't know what to do.'

'What sort of stuff?'

'I was beginning to get excited about the dance school. I had it all mapped out in my mind – new dreams, something for me to focus on. I thought I'd waltz in and get the place fit for purpose again. I had visions of running dance classes at the weekend for the children, then during week nights I was thinking I could jive with the WI on a Monday, tango with couples on a Tuesday, paso doble with pensioners on a Wednesday and charleston with everyone else on a Thursday, leaving me Friday nights free to recharge my batteries. I wanted everyone flocking back to the dance school – a feel-good community atmosphere bringing all the generations back together with one common goal – to have fun and learn to dance, but now ...'

'But now ...?' urged Grace.

'After last night, it doesn't feel like a feel-good community.' I looked at her incredulously and exhaled.

'Don't let what happened last night spoil your vision.'

I didn't answer. Reality had hit – maybe village life wasn't a bed of roses. Why couldn't people just be kind?

'Ben will be jealous.'

'Jealous?'

'Yes, look at you ... gorgeous ... and seeing you with Sam will have taken him by surprise.'

'It was obvious to anyone walking past that Sam wasn't

bothering me. Ben caused a scene for no reason. What are Grandie's thoughts on Sam and his family?' I asked, suddenly realising I had no idea.

'You'll have to ask him that one,' answered Grace. 'He's never spoken about it – well, not to me, anyway.'

Taking a bite of my bacon sandwich, my eyes threatened tears as I pondered the complexities of the past. Why did it all have to be so complicated?

'But ...' Grace carried on as I cast my eyes towards her, 'don't let that situation cloud your judgement. That's their problem, not yours. Just like whatever went on between your mum and grandfather, it's not your argument.'

'Look at me, stumbling at the first hurdle.'

'Don't panic, no one is stumbling. More like thinking about it all too much.'

I nodded, taking a swig of my tea.

'Don't think about it, just get on and do it.' I knew Grace was talking sense. I couldn't dwell on who was talking to who or what grudges they held. I needed to focus on my own life, my own business, and that started right now, this morning ... I couldn't wait to begin teaching Bert.

Chapter 19

The sun was shining and there wasn't a cloud in the sky as I ambled up the path of Wild Rose Cottage. I really wanted to catch Sam before I made my way over to the dance school but when I glanced over towards his cottage, the curtains were still drawn and there was no sign of life. It would have to wait until later.

Within minutes the school was in sight and my heart began to pound a little faster when I noticed a figure skulking at the side of the building. Squinting ahead, I was relieved to discover it was only Bert, who was acting very strangely.

'Morning, Bert,' I chirped. 'Why are you being very cloak and dagger?'

'Huh?'

'Hiding at the side of the building,' I said, fishing the keys out of my bag.

'I can't be seen. Dorothy is already on the warpath, wondering where I'm sneaking off to.' His voice was low.

Glancing up the street, there wasn't a soul around. 'I think it's safe to come out, Bert, there's no one in sight.'

'Good ... good,' he said, repositioning his cap on his head and taking a look up the street for himself. 'But you never know, she has the habit of popping up when you least expect it. She gave me that look ... you know, when I left the house.'

'Dorothy?'

'Yes, Dorothy. The look where she narrows her eyes and I feel guilty for even breathing,' he chuckled. 'Do you know how difficult it is to sneak out, even at my age? That woman must have some sort of psychic powers, knowing when I'm up to something.'

'I think that's just called being a woman,' I grinned at a flustered Bert, who sidestepped into the foyer like a dancing ninja once the door was open.

After flicking on the lights, Bert followed me through the entrance hall into the main rehearsal room. He slung his coat on the back of a chair and placed his flat cap on a table before ruffling his hand through his hair. I walked to the far end of the room and opened the blinds, allowing the sunlight to flood the room.

As I turned back around, I caught Bert eyeing himself up in the mirror.

'These mirrors don't do much for my self-confidence,' he admitted, breathing in and holding in his stomach. Turning a little red in the face, he exhaled and a coughing fit quickly followed.

'The things I do for that lady,' he murmured once he'd recovered, wiping his mouth with a hanky and twisting his body from side to side, scrutinising it from all different angles in the mirror.

'Everyone should have a Bert in their life,' I smiled with amusement, setting up my iPad on a nearby table. 'So, the foxtrot, you say.'

'Dorothy's favourite dance,' he answered, finally taking his eyes off the mirror and turning his attention back to me.

'Let's start with a few warm-up exercises. I don't want you pulling a muscle before we've begun.'

'Could you imagine how I'd explain that one away?'

'And then we'll shake ourselves out.'

'Sounds painful,' said Bert in a playful tone.

For the next five minutes, I took Bert through a series of exercises to warm up his muscles. He already looked frazzled as he wiped away a bead of sweat from his brow, and we hadn't even begun dancing yet.

'Let's start with basics.' I pulled my jumper over my head and slipped my feet into a pair of heels which I'd brought with me. 'Are you ready?'

'I think so,' he smiled, his watchful eyes observing my every move.

'The foxtrot is a smooth dance and we travel round the floor in a clockwise direction,' I began.

'Noted,' replied Bert, hanging on to my every word.

'The way we count the foxtrot is slow, slow, quick, quick, where the slow takes up two beats and the quick takes up one. The man, that's you ...'

'It was, last time I looked,' interrupted Bert.

'The men start with the left and take two walks forward, side step and then close ... like this.' I demonstrated the moves, my heels echoing on the wooden floor as I moved. 'Then the ladies start with their right foot and they take two walks back, a side step then close. Got that?'

'I think so,' replied Bert, his gaze firmly focused on my feet.

'Up you get, put your arms out, imagine you're holding Dorothy while you practise your steps.'

'Like this?' asked Bert, standing in the middle of the floor. I nodded, 'Now forward with the left.'

Bert put his wobbly foot forward.

'Then side with the left, like this.'

Bert copied me.

'Close right foot to left and then we do it all again.'

After a few more attempts it was coming back to Bert and he was smoothly co-ordinating the steps with a daft grin on his face.

'I feel wonderful, this is wonderful,' he said, stretching his arms wider. 'I feel like I'm a young man again.'

Just seeing the twinkle in Bert's eyes and the enjoyment written all over his face made my heart swell.

'Keep it going, and remember, clockwise around the room.'

Once Bert had mastered his steps, he watched me while I performed the ladies' part.

'Pretend I'm Dorothy,' I smiled as I took my position in the middle of the room. 'Dorothy will put her weight on her left foot, right foot free, then back with the right foot, back with the left foot, then side with the right and close left to right and again. Shall we try together?'

'Yes,' agreed Bert, taking his place opposite me.

'Basically, now you lead and I follow.'

'Dorothy won't like that, you know,' he teased, 'she wears the trousers in our house and I've always had to follow her lead.' He gave a light-hearted chuckle at his own joke.

'Well, enjoy your moment, Bert, because for three whole minutes you'll get your chance to shine, and for once Dorothy will have to take your lead.'

'I've waited fifty years for that moment.'

I couldn't help but feel warmth towards Bert. Even though he played the hen-pecked husband, it was obvious to anyone that his love for Dorothy was very much alive and kicking.

'Okay, lead and follow. Apply pressure from your frame. Lead Dorothy into those walks.' I was really enjoying myself and my mood had certainly been lifted since last night. My mind began to tick while I put Bert through his paces, and Grace's words whirled in my mind: 'Do what you want to do. You only have one life, so live it. Be happy.'

Bert was concentrating hard, mumbling the steps under his breath.

'When you move to the side, take me with you,' I shouted out clearly as we began to dance around the room. 'You need to connect with Dorothy and apply a little more pressure from your whole body, then step and do the walks. Take her to the side from the right and gently bring her along with you from your frame ... That's it, Bert, nice and smooth ... perfect!'

'I've got it, I've got it ... it's all coming back to me,' the joy in Bert's voice made my heart melt. His wrinkled face was alight with excitement and his cheeks were aglow. He glided smoothly over the floor, taking me with him.

'Shall we try this to some music?' I suggested now that Bert had the hang of things.

As the music filtered from my iPad we took our positions and as soon as I counted Bert in, he began to lead. At first, he stumbled a little, found it difficult to step in time with the music, but gently I talked him through it.

'We don't want any stops in the body as we move through the feet. Keep your knees flexed and extend the leg and roll on to it, side and close. Try not to step and stop,' I instructed softly. Bert listened to every word and the determination showed on his face. After a couple more attempts he understood and we were soon gliding around the dance floor until the music stopped.

'I didn't want that to end,' breathed Bert, catching his breath, 'that felt magical.' His eyes were watery with emotion.

'I can't wait to see Dorothy's face when you take her by her hand and lead her up on that stage.'

'Dorothy ...' he exclaimed, checking his watch. 'We've been over an hour. I'd best hurry, otherwise she'll be giving my lunch to the dog.'

'I didn't know you had a dog.'

'We haven't,' he laughed, placing his cap swiftly back on his head and slipping his arms through the sleeves of his jacket. 'Alice ... I can't thank you enough for your patience. You're
such a kind-hearted girl, giving up your time to help me.'

'You don't need to thank me, it's been a pleasure.'

'You are such a fantastic teacher. Can we go over it a couple more times before the big day?'

'Of course,' I answered, having enjoyed every second of the lesson. Teaching Bert had left me feeling uplifted, giving me the confidence boost I needed. Maybe this was the way forward, doing something I was good at.

He took my hands and squeezed them tight. 'My Dorothy's face is going to be a picture. She needs some cheering up at the minute.'

'Why?' I asked, releasing myself from his grip and stuffing my jumper inside my bag.

He sighed. 'She takes on too much, that one. It's this Village Day, you see. I don't know why she takes it upon herself to organise it every year, it will be the death of her.' He raised his bushy eyebrows, 'This year there's no one to bring the day to an end – there won't be a grand finale.'

'What do you mean?' I asked.

He paused for a moment. 'Stella's son was booked, she's Dorothy's friend from the WI. He's been on TV, one of those talent programmes – a magician, she said. But he's cancelled at the last minute and now she's searching high and low for a replacement, but at short notice everyone is busy.

'When is it, again?'

'A couple of weeks' time. Not much time to book another act. The WI are up in arms – you'd think it was her fault this magician guy had cancelled.'

'Let's focus on the positives. At least they will have you twirling Dorothy around that stage.'

'There is that,' he forced a smile, but I could see he was upset about the strain it was putting on Dorothy.

'Anyway, I'd best be off, and remember, this is our little secret.' Bert tapped his nose and disappeared through the door.

The second Bert left the building my mind began to whirl. Was this meant to be? As I packed up my iPad a smile hitched itself on my face.

After locking up the dance school I whistled my way back to Wild Rose Cottage. My mind flitted back to Dorothy's dilemma and I'd begun to have a crazy thought. What if ... what if ...?

'What are you smiling at?' Grace's head was poking out of the bedroom window of the cottage as I pushed open the garden gate.

Looking up, I said, 'Put the kettle on and I'll tell you all about it.'

'Oooh, intrigued, I'm on it!'

Grace was sitting opposite me with a goofy grin while hugging her tea. 'Alice, you are a genius, that's a brilliant idea. Have you run it past Dorothy?' The praise was coming thick and fast.

I shook my head. 'But is it biting off more than I can chew? There's only two weeks to organise this.'

Grace thought over my madcap idea for all of a second. 'I'll help, and we can rope Mum in too, she loves things like this. All hands to the deck.' Grace was clapping her hands together like a demented sea lion. 'Gushing friend moment coming up,' Grace warned me as she stood up and flung her arms around me.

'*Brook Bridge Goes Strictly*!' she announced. 'I can see it now, all the WI in their sequinned sparkly dresses ... pirouetting their way around the stage in front of the judges ... Can I be a judge? Please let me be a judge!' She gave me a lopsided grin and placed her hands in a prayer -like stance. Grace was running away with herself now.

'But what about the men, where are we going to find the men from?' I interrupted, racking my brains. 'I'm up for the challenge but it's going to be difficult enough teaching the women to dance from scratch in a couple of weeks, never mind finding a group of men and persuading them to take part too. Then there's the costumes et cetera, et cetera.'

'I can see your point.' Grace sat back down, her thinking face was apparent.

She exhaled sharply. 'OMG, I've got it.' Her eyes were wide and danced with excitement. 'What about if we rope in Sam?'

'Sam? Why Sam?'

'Think about it, most of Sam's friends are my friends and what do they do for a living? Dance! Each lady can be whisked off her feet by a handsome, good-looking man, and all in the name of charity.'

'I'm not sure, Grace,' I said, feeling a little dubious and knowing that Sam wasn't Dorothy's favourite man about town.

'You would have time to teach the ladies and the men will take care of themselves. No one would know Sam was even involved, if that's what you are worried about.'

'It's not me that's worried, I'd love to have Sam on board. It would certainly help me out,' I answered, turning it over in my mind.

'Shall I ask him?'

I took a moment. 'No, let me.'

'Okay, your call, but do it today, let's get this show on the road,' she said with such passion, humming the *Strictly Come Dancing* theme tune while dancing her way around the kitchen. I couldn't help but smile at her enthusiasm, while thinking about this morning. I'd really enjoyed teaching Bert today. Maybe this was my calling and co-ordinating *Brook Bridge Goes Strictly* would help me decide whether I was up to the job of teaching a group of people. Turning my thoughts to Sam, I knew asking him to help out would certainly solve a problem, but would he really be willing to help the community out, especially when he'd been receiving the cold shoulder from most of them?

'Grace ... this could be just the thing for Sam.'

'Huh?' she answered, perplexed.

'If Sam was on board, wouldn't this be the perfect way to reunite the community, look to the future and hopefully for him to be accepted – especially by Dorothy and Bert, and maybe even Ben?'

'Alice Parker ... you may have a point.'

'Okay, I'll talk to Sam and then share my idea with Dorothy.'

'She'll be made up; Village Day is saved!'

For the first time in a long while, I felt I had a purpose, a direction. All I had to do now was convince Sam about my idea.

Chapter 20

A couple of hours later I walked anxiously up the path towards Sam's front door. I'd made the nerve-wracking decision to invite him out for dinner to talk things through. What's the worst that could happen? Obviously, he could turn down my dinner invitation, but if that was the case I'd decided to play the plucky American stereotype for once in my life and take dinner to him. So, all in all, he'd no choice in the matter.

After smoothing down my top and taking a deep breath, I rapped on the door then dug my hands into my pockets, while nervously shuffling my feet from side to side.

I knocked again, but still no answer.

Damn.

I'd rehearsed the whole conversation over in my head and never once considered he wouldn't be home. Staring up at the cottage, I considered taking a glimpse through the downstairs window, but what if Sam was there and was ignoring the knock on the door?

Plucking up my courage, I cupped my hands around my eyes and quickly took a peep, but the room was empty. However, it was at that moment I heard a noise coming from the back garden and decided to follow the path around the side of the property, my feet crunching on the shingle as I walked.

Hearing a noise, Sam spun round and met my gaze. He looked startled to see me.

'Sorry, I did knock on the front door but there was no answer.' I made my apologies quickly.

My whole body tingled in his presence. He was ridiculously, ludicrously good-looking and looked like he'd just showered. His messy hair was wet, slicked back and his lounge pants looked super sexy clinging to his toned waistline.

'That's because I'm here, minding my own business, in my own garden.' His manner was abrupt, and it was obvious to anyone he didn't want me there, but hitching my mouth into a huge smile, I wasn't going to let that deter me.

'About last night, we need to talk,' I offered softly.

'I don't think so.' Sam dismissed the conversation almost immediately, leaving me standing there feeling squashed and confused. It wasn't the reaction I'd expected or wanted.

'Alice, I meant what I said last night. Associating with me will bring you nothing but trouble.'

He casually stepped backwards towards the open back door. 'No, please wait,' I pleaded.

He locked eyes with me again.

'Okay, here's the thing. Last night Ben was out of order, anyone could see you weren't bothering me.' I was now thankful for his attention, but he still didn't answer. His face was solemn, and he carefully eyed me.

'I can imagine it's very trying, putting up with hostile behaviour ...' I took a breath.

For a second, I thought he was going to turn and walk away and the rehearsed words disappeared from my mind.

'And ...' I said, stalling for a little more time.

'Look,' interrupted Sam, 'I appreciate you coming round, but you are only here for a few weeks, so maybe it's best you don't go getting involved in things you know nothing about, or putting yourself in the firing line with the locals because of me.'

'I'm not. I don't care what any of them think ... I only care about what I think ... and I do care ...' I now had Sam's full attention, he hadn't disappeared inside just yet. 'Give us a chance?'

'Alice ... my family.'

'I don't care who your family are.'

'You will, when people won't let go of the past and becoming my friend proves difficult for you.'

'At least give me the chance to try,' I pleaded, feeling myself trembling a little.

'Like I've already said, I don't want to make things difficult for you while you're here.' He tried for a smile but faltered.

I was relieved that his tone had softened a little.

'You won't, you aren't. Funnily enough, for what it's worth, this American can make her own mind up.' I cocked my head to one side and gave him a bashful grin. 'I take people as I find them, so I was thinking ...'

'Americans can think as well, can they?' he interrupted with a wicked glint in his eye.

Thankfully, the frosty atmosphere was melting a little, so I decided to bite the bullet.

'And they can invite people out for dinner too.'

'Dinner? Are you asking me out for dinner?'

I nodded, feeling my pulse quicken, waiting for him to answer.

He narrowed his eyes and was mulling over the invitation.

'Tonight?' I said with authority, like the pushy American I was trying to be.

'I've plans this evening ...'

'Oh,' I wasn't expecting that he'd have plans, but why wouldn't he? The world didn't just revolve around me.

'Okay,' I continued, the disappointment in my voice sounding loud and clear.

'But ...' He was thinking something over.

'But ...?' I added.

'I'm going to the theatre ... Come with me?'

He didn't have to ask me twice. 'It's a date,' I beamed, my heart leaping at the invite.

Sam was now looking at me with an amused expression written all over his face. 'A date?' he questioned playfully.

'I'll be ready,' I answered, with a huge grin etched on my face.

'Good, glad to hear it.'

'Great, see you later.' I quickly turned with a spring in my step and disappeared down the path before I embarrassed myself any further or Sam had time to change his mind.

As soon as I walked through the gates of Honeysuckle Farm, Marley was sniffing amongst the hedgerows and the second he heard the clang of the gates his head turned, and he launched his little legs down the long driveway towards me.

'Hello, boy,' I said, bending down and ruffling the short fur behind his ears before he turned and scampered back towards the farmhouse and waited for me at the bottom of the stone steps.

As I approached I heard the sound of muffled chatter from around the side of the house and walked round the corner to unexpectedly find Ben standing outside the barn with his phone firmly clamped against his ear. Our eyes met but I immediately broke from his gaze and turned, quickly strolling back towards the front of the farmhouse. At some point I knew I was going to have to speak to him, but I hadn't anticipated that he would be working at the farm today. The second he saw me I heard him make his apologies on the phone and hang up the call.

'Alice,' I heard him shout, 'wait.'

Spinning round, I saw that Ben was striding up the steps

behind me. My heart was thumping, I really didn't want this conversation now.

Ben flashed me a beaming white smile. 'I'm glad I caught you. Can we talk?' he asked, his manner now sheepish.

There was an awkward tension hanging in the air between us. 'I'm here to see Grandie.' I knew I wasn't doing a good job of keeping my feelings under control, but I was still mad with him. There was a certain uncharacteristic sharpness to my tone and even though Sam had advised me not to get involved, I couldn't help my reaction.

'Dinner, let me take you out for dinner … tonight?'

'I'm sorry, I can't. I'm out tonight.'

'Tomorrow?' he urged.

I was about to answer when Ben continued, 'The Reids – they aren't a good sort, you know.'

I raised an eyebrow and shook my head in disbelief. 'I don't want to hear this, Ben. I need to go.' I didn't want to get into a discussion about it, and I wasn't going to let him or anyone else spoil my good mood. And with that I turned and walked through the door of the farmhouse without a second glance backwards.

Pushing open the kitchen door with Marley close to my heels, I saw Grandie sitting in the old, red, checked, battered armchair in the corner of the room, chatting with Dorothy.

They both looked up. 'Another visitor!' Grandie exclaimed joyfully, placing his walking stick on the floor and attempting to push himself up out of the chair.

'Don't get up,' I insisted, scooting over to him and pressing a kiss to his cheek. 'You stay there.'

'We were just talking about you,' smiled Dorothy.

'All good, I hope!' I replied, placing the kettle on to the hot plate of the Aga. 'Does anyone else want a coffee?'

'Thank you, but we've just had one,' answered Grandie, 'but see that cupboard up there,' he waved his stick towards the cupboard at the side of the plate rack, 'there's some shortbread in there, even though it won't be a scratch on Dorothy's ... bring it out.'

After dishing up the shortbread on to a plate and placing it in the middle of the table, I sat down. 'So, anything happening I should know about?' I asked, flicking a glance between them both.

'Dorothy's here with a dilemma and is picking my brain, but I'm not being much help at all, I'm afraid,' he sighed, suddenly looking somewhat defeated.

'It's not your fault at all, just bad timing.' Dorothy's shoulders sagged. 'Maybe I'm just being picky, but I can't see how Mr Cross playing his ukulele will be the grand finale that we've come to love every year, but maybe beggars can't be choosers at such a late stage. We might have to go with it if we can't come up with a Plan B.' Dorothy actually looked horrified at the very thought of Mr Cross playing his ukulele.

I put on my best encouraging smile. 'What's all this about?' I knew full well the pair of them were discussing Village Day but of course I couldn't divulge that Bert had shared that little snippet of information whilst escaping from Dorothy's scrutiny for an hour.

'Village Day – the magician has gone up in a puff of smoke

and now, we've no closing finale ...' Dorothy now looked visibly upset.

I sipped on my coffee. 'What about Connie, has she got any bright ideas?'

Dorothy regretfully shook her head. 'I think between us all we've exhausted every avenue.'

I knew I was probably jumping the gun a little – after all, I hadn't even spoken to Sam about it yet – but seeing their disappointment, I wanted to put a smile back on their faces. So, the words shot out of my mouth: 'Maybe I could help.'

All eyes were fixed on me, even Marley seemed to stand to attention and patted my knee with his paw.

'How's that, dear?' asked Dorothy.

'How about ...' I began nervously, 'how about ...' I swallowed and looked at their expectant faces.

'Spit it out,' encouraged Grandie, 'we aren't getting any younger.' He gave a small chuckle.

'How about *Brook Bridge Goes Strictly?*' My idea was now unleashed to the world – well, to the three of us sitting in Grandie's kitchen, anyway.

Grandie and Dorothy both looked confused.

'But it would depend on the co-operation of the WI.'

Dorothy sat upright and folded her arms on the table. 'Do you mean like the show on the telly?' Her eyes were wide.

'I mean exactly that,' I said with enthusiasm, shimmying my jazz hands into the air. 'I could teach the WI, we could dance the cha cha, quick step, waltz, samba, paso doble – anything, really. And on the side of the stage we could have a panel of judges – me, Grace, Grandie and Connie – and score you all, like they do on the telly.' I waited with bated breath to gauge their reaction. 'One of the WI could be crowned the winner of Brook Bridge.'

Dorothy and Grandie locked eyes. Then I watched as a huge beam spread across their faces.

'Marvellous, marvellous idea!' he exclaimed. 'You, Alice … are a genius!'

The mood in the room had suddenly lifted, the doom and gloom replaced by excitement.

'You'd do that for me, for us, for the village?' Dorothy was overwhelmed, waiting for me to confirm that she wasn't hearing things.

'Yes, of course! But the WI will have to put in the hours over the next couple of weeks. It will be hard going, learning the dances from scratch,' I added, with my professional teaching voice.

Suddenly Dorothy was back on track, brimming with purpose. She turned and grabbed hold of my hands, 'You, my girl, are a life-saver … a life-saver,' she echoed, her eyes glistening with happy tears. 'We need outfits, dresses, sparkle, glitz and glamour. I'm sure Connie will take over the costume department. We can raid the local charity shops and sew a few sequins on some old dresses.' She clapped her hands with glee, but then I noticed the same solemn expression fleet across her face, like I'd seen earlier.

'But what about the men? Who are we going to dance with?'

Grandie looked towards me. 'My knees aren't up for whirling around the stage at my age – or those lifts, my back wouldn't stand for it.'

'Don't be daft, Grandie, I don't expect you to be doing lifts,' I smiled, and relief fleeted across his face.

But since I hadn't had the chance to discuss it with Sam yet, and knowing that Dorothy wouldn't be too keen on the idea at first, I brushed over the question for now.

'Don't you worry about that, leave it in my capable hands.' I knew I sounded much more confident than I felt.

'Good, good,' said Dorothy, 'this has brightened my day up no end. I must ring the girls.'

'How many of you are there?'

'Six, including myself.'

That was a perfect number to teach, I thought. We may just be able to pull this off.

'You rally the troops and we'll arrange a time to bring them over to the dance school. Do you think the ladies will be on board?' I'd never thought to ask.

'Without a doubt!'

'Brilliant, they will need to learn the routines first and once we've got the basic steps, we'll take it from there,' I said, hoping Sam would agree to help me out.

'You really have thought this all through,' Grandie congratulated me.

'It'll be fun.' After teaching Bert, I really was looking forward to putting the ladies through their paces.

'I'm proud of you, Alice, stepping up to the mark,' Grandie

glowed with pride. 'Now pass me one of those shortbread biscuits, I've suddenly got my appetite back.'

'And you, my dear girl, have saved Village Day!' added Dorothy with a full-on beam.

'Well, maybe from Mr Cross's ukulele,' I giggled, helping myself to a piece of shortbread.

It was a fantastic feeling, knowing how excited they both were about my idea. I just hoped I'd enough time to teach them all to dance, but there was still a slight niggle in the back of mind regarding Sam. How easy was it going to be to persuade him that this was a good idea? And if he agreed, I then had to convince the villagers to give him a chance too.

Chapter 21

'On a scale of one to ten ... how excited are you about this date with Sam?' teased Grace, straightening my hair then backcombing the fringe and pinning it back to give it some height.

It was six thirty in the evening, George Ezra was singing his heart out from the iPod and I was sitting at Grace's dressing table on her insistence that she gave me a helping hand to look drop-dead gorgeous for my theatre date with Sam.

'It's not a date as such.'

'You said it was a date,' she insisted.

'It's a figure of speech,' I argued, even though I was hoping it was exactly that – a date.

'Despite what some villagers think of the Reids, Sam's a decent guy,' said Grace, staring at me through the mirror while wafting the can of hairspray all over my hair.

'Go easy,' I spluttered.

Grace gave me the once over and swung the chair back towards the mirror. 'Ta-dah! What do you think? Glam or what?'

'It looks stunning,' I answered, pleasantly surprised, staring at my reflection.

'Now, you need to decide what you are going to wear.'

'Maybe a summer dress? Flats and a cardigan?' I suggested.

'Sounds just the ticket,' said Grace, swiping a handful of clothes from her wardrobe and laying them out on the bed for me to choose. 'What about this one?'

She handed me a duck-egg-blue floral dress which I held up against my body while staring into the mirror. 'I'll try it on,' I said, slipping into the bathroom.

Two minutes later, I stood in the doorway of Grace's bedroom. 'Well? What do you think?' I asked, giving her a twirl.

'Perfect, now pumps or flats?' She held up both.

'Flats,' I answered, slipping my feet inside a pair of ballet shoes.

'Looking gorgeous, and I now declare you ready,' Grace smiled, handing me a handbag. 'Now it's time,' she tapped her watch, 'to go and have fun.'

Grace followed me down the stairs and after I grabbed my cardigan she playfully pushed me out of the front door.

There was a taxi outside with its engine running and as I began to walk down the path Sam caught my attention. The second he opened his front door and stepped out on to his path, my heart soared and my eyes travelled up the length of his body. I had to do everything in my power not to gasp out loud. Goose pimples flashed across my skin and my stomach flipped. He wouldn't have looked out of place on the front of a men's fashion magazine wearing a crisp white shirt, tucked into a pair of Levi's accompanied by brown loafers.

I began to feel extremely nervous and gave Grace a fleeting glance over my shoulder. Her eyes sparkled and she gave me the thumbs up before slowly shutting the front door.

Sam's eyes lit up the second he saw me and his handsome face broke into a huge beam. We met at the garden gate, and he took my hands and kissed me softly on the cheek. I blushed and lowered my eyes. 'Not a bad-looking date,' he teased. I was hit with the woody scent of Sam's aftershave which immediately made me go weak at the knees and sent a shiver down my spine. He smelt divine.

'Thank you, you're not so bad yourself,' I said coyly, suddenly feeling shy.

He gestured towards the taxi and in a gentlemanly manner opened the door as I climbed inside.

My heart thumped wildly as he fastened his seatbelt and his hand lightly brushed against mine. After telling the driver where we were going, he settled back into his seat.

We watched the village pass us by and soon the cab was speeding up the A38. There was a comfortable silence and every now and then I sneaked a look at him, only to find him smiling back at me.

When we arrived at the theatre, Sam casually took hold of

my hand as we strolled through the doors. My heart gave a little leap at his unexpected touch.

Inside the theatre, there was a buzz of excitement everywhere. It was mainly couples sitting and chatting at the bar in the foyer, sharing a bottle of wine. I stared up at the magnificent posters and the screens advertising the upcoming performances.

'What are we watching?'

'*A Midsummer Night's Dream*,' answered Sam.

'One of my favourites.'

The rest of the lobby was swarming with people queuing for programmes and refreshments. With only fifteen minutes until the performance began, the double doors into the auditorium were swung open and people began to filter through to take their seats.

'Floor or circle?' I asked Sam, wondering which queue to join.

'Neither,' he grinned. 'Come on,' he took my hand and led me through a door at the side of the bar. I trailed behind up a flight of stairs leading to a rabbit warren of tunnels. There was no one else in sight.

'Are you sure we should be up here?'

Before he could answer, a member of staff appeared from nowhere and greeted us both.

'Good evening Mr Reid. Good evening, Madam.'

'Good evening,' I replied politely, taking it all in and wondering what was going on.

'Let me show you to your box.'

'Box?' I uttered under my breath. My eyes caught Sam's and I smiled shyly. He looked even more gorgeous under the dimmed light.

'Let me show you to your seats.'

As the lady drew back the curtain a tingle of excitement ran through my veins. 'Look at this,' I said out loud in amazement, feeling like an excited child on Christmas Eve.

The box was extravagant with two red velvet chairs facing out over the balcony and a small table, on which sat a bottle of champagne chilling alongside two glass flutes.

'Can I get you anything?' the waitress asked politely.

Sam gestured towards me.

'I'm okay, thank you.'

'I think we are just fine for now,' he smiled.

'I'll be back during the interval.' And with that she turned and drew the curtain behind her.

I couldn't hide my excitement. 'Sam, I don't know what to say. This is just perfect.'

He grinned, placing his hand on my knee. 'Let me pour you a drink.' He reached for the bottle and promptly popped the cork and handed me a glass.

'Cheers,' he held up his glass.

'How have you managed to book a box? Aren't they like gold dust?'

Sam chinked his glass against mine and smiled, 'After performing here on many occasions I've become friendly with the manager.'

I couldn't quite believe it. I was in awe, my jaw was somewhere below my knees at the extravagance of it all.

Leaning forward, I peered over the balcony admiring the view below.

The audience were settling in their seats and talking amongst themselves. I felt like royalty when someone below nudged the person next to her and they glanced upwards, deciding whether they recognised us or not.

'That couple are watching us, I think they think we are someone famous,' I whispered, not really knowing why I was whispering, as they couldn't hear me.

Sam grinned and held my gaze.

For a moment, I actually thought he was going to lean over and kiss me. I was hoping.

'You have an eyelash on your cheek,' he said, being very attentive and gently brushing it away before giving the couple who were still staring a quick wave of the hand.

I giggled, 'They certainly will think you're famous now.'

Sitting here with Sam, I felt at ease. There were no awkward silences and conversation flowed easily. I knew at some point this evening I needed to bring up the conversation about Village Day, but things were going so well that I didn't want to spoil things or create any tension.

'This is one of my favourite performances,' smiled Sam as the auditorium fell silent.

The lights dimmed and the curtains drew back, revealing the stage right below us.

I gasped, 'What an amazing view.'

I knew I was gawping with a huge smile on my face, but I couldn't help it. Sam was watching me with amusement.

We pulled up our chairs to the edge of the balcony and as the orchestra struck we entered the enchanted world of Shakespeare. I couldn't tear my eyes away, watching the lush forest besieged by a love triangle. I completely lost myself in the dance and music of it all.

'Hey, you're tearful,' Sam noticed twenty minutes later.

Choked up, I fanned my hand gently in front of my eyes. 'It's the music, the romance of it all, it gets me emotional every time,' I admitted, dabbing my eyes with a tissue.

'It's those feuding fairies that get me every time,' he smiled warmly, slowly slipping his arm around my shoulder and pulling me in close and holding me there, and it felt like the most natural thing in the world.

As soon as the first act ended, I felt saddened, not because I was disappointed in the performance but because I didn't want it to end, even though there was still the second half to look forward to.

As soon as the lights flooded the auditorium, people began to move from their seats and disperse towards the exits.

'At least we don't have to go and queue at the bar,' said Sam, topping up our drinks.

I thanked him before making my excuses and taking a quick trip to the bathroom, primarily to check the state of my make-up. After blubbing into a tissue, no doubt my mascara was streaked down my cheeks.

Pleasantly surprised when I looked in the mirror, I powdered my face, swiped blusher across my cheeks and, after a quick dab of lip gloss, I rang Grace who immediately picked up.

'I feel like a princess!' I exclaimed, overwhelmed. 'We have champagne, and the best seats in the house.'

'So, it's going well?' laughed Grace.

'Very well, the view is amazing and the company ... even better.'

'Sounds like you are quite smitten, my girl,' stated Grace.

'Maybe,' I answered, my mouth hitching into a smile every time I thought of him.

'You enjoy every minute.' And with that Grace hung up.

Returning to the box, I slipped back into the seat next to him.

Sam's pose was relaxed, one arm draped across the back of my chair, his legs crossed and stretched out before him. He was sipping his champagne. My heart beat faster at the sight of him. I wanted this night to go on forever.

'You okay?' He gave me a warm smile.

'Couldn't be better,' and I truly meant it.

He passed me my glass then rested his hand gently on my knee. 'How good was the first half? I feel emotional myself,' he said, gazing into my eyes. 'There's something so magical about the theatre.'

A man in touch with his emotions! I was impressed. My thoughts quickly flashed back to Bert and Dorothy. They'd got Sam all wrong, and by persuading Sam to help me with Village Day, I was determined to prove to them how genuine he was.

'I know this isn't the right moment,' I said softly, not making eye contact and staring over the balcony into the crowd, 'but I am sorry about yesterday ... Bert ... then Ben.'

'You don't need to be sorry,' he sighed, 'the contention stems from years ago. My uncles and the Carters were rivals from way back, even before Uncle Oscar went to prison ... They used to gather down in the local town to fight. Enemy alpha males always wanting their gang to be on top – it's carried on for generations.' Sam took a sip of his drink and turned towards me. 'My mum doesn't even have anything to do with her own brothers and I haven't spoken to anyone from that side of my family for years. We have no common ground. I don't aspire to their petty criminal behaviour. And I'm not interested in keeping any type of pointless feud going with the likes of Ben Carter because of generations before. I have dreams and I work hard in a career I love, but I am sorry my uncle stole the car that killed your grandma.'

I could hear a twinge of sadness in Sam's voice. 'You don't have to be sorry for something that had absolutely nothing to do with you.'

'Hearing you say that, means a lot.'

'Call it common sense.' I smiled warmly, resting my head against his shoulder and looking up at him. His eyes held mine, then he kissed me lightly on the top of my head before resting his arm around my shoulder and pulling me in close.

Just at that second, the lights dimmed and the theatre fell silent. We both fixed our eyes towards the stage.

The orchestra sounded and the curtains opened. Act Two was underway.

* * *

An hour later the equally stunning second half came to a close. The evening had been perfect. My eyes were still glistening with tears, lost in the true romance of the performance. 'I've had the most fantastic evening, Sam. Shakespeare gets me every time.'

'You are a big softie,' he grinned, holding my hand whilst hailing a taxi with his other hand.

'Where to?' asked the driver through his open window.

Sam looked my way. 'Are you hungry?' he asked, holding the cab door open as I climbed inside.

I shook my head, I wasn't.

'Shall we go for a drink?'

Again, I shook my head and made eye contact with the driver in the mirror. 'Can you take us back to Brook Bridge village, please?'

Sliding into the seat next to me, Sam gave me a quizzical look. 'You okay?' he asked tentatively.

'Don't worry, the night's not over yet, I've got something to show you.'

Sam cocked an eyebrow.

'Not like that,' I laughed, swiping his leg in jest, even though the fluttering in my stomach was now an anxious one as the driver pulled away from the theatre, because we were heading towards the Florrie Rose School of Dance.

Chapter 22

Twenty minutes later the cab stopped on the corner of the High Street back in Brook Bridge and we climbed out.

'Where are we going?' asked Sam.

'My dreams, the ones I've had since I was a little girl, are beginning to change and that's where I'm taking you now.'

A look of puzzlement flashed across Sam's face.

'Your dreams ... Tell me all about your dreams ... Who is Alice Parker?'

'You'll see. Come on, let's walk and I'll talk, and all will become clear.'

'I'm intrigued,' he said, taking my hand. 'How did you end up in America?'

We walked in silence for a moment while I gathered my thoughts. 'How did I end up in America? Now there's a question.'

Sam looked at me in puzzlement and I continued:

'America ...' I took a deep breath, 'I wish I could tell you that my dad was some influential businessman whose multi-million-pound empire catapulted us over to the other side of the world.'

'But it sounds like you're not going to tell me that,' Sam replied, with slight hesitation.

I felt myself sigh and my shoulders sag.

'Oh Sam, it's actually all a bit of a mess. The truth is, firstly, I don't know who my father is and secondly ... I don't actually know why we left for America.'

'What do you mean?' he asked with genuine concern.

'One minute I'm an average ten-year-old, enjoying life at the farm, messing about with my pony, dance lessons at the weekend ... then I'm hoisted on a plane to the other side of the world, surrounded by skyscrapers and bright neon lights.'

'Are you serious?'

'I may have made it sound a little more melodramatic than it was,' I paused, 'but actually, probably not.'

'So why the big upheaval?'

'Your guess is as good as mine,' I replied, wondering whether I wanted to spill everything to Sam. I took myself by surprise: 'There was a disagreement between my mum and my grand-father,' I continued, now unable to stop myself. Sam listened intently.

I felt my chest tighten and my breath quicken. 'I overheard Grandie telling Mum how disappointed he was with her, for some reason. Things got out of hand and, cutting a long story short, they haven't spoken since – thirteen years, in fact.'

'It must have been some argument.' He raised an eyebrow.

I shrugged, 'No point asking me, I've never got to the bottom of it. My grandfather's health is deteriorating, he's the reason I'm here. I knew I had to come home to see him ... before it was too late.' My voice wavered.

He touched my arm tentatively.

'Mum's still in New York and I've no idea what to do about it all. In fact, it's just all a mess.'

'Is she still refusing to see him?'

I nodded, feeling the tears well up in my eyes. 'See him, talk to him.'

Sam slipped his arm around my shoulder.

'I just wish they would heal the rift. He's not getting any younger and what if ... what if ...?' My voice cracked. My heart was aching. I knew that however much I tried to hide how I was feeling about it all, things were beginning to get on top of me and the emotion came flooding out.

'Hey, come here,' he said, gently gazing at my face before taking me in his arms. 'It will work its way out, it always does,' said Sam in a soft reassuring tone.

I snuggled close into his chest, burying my face into the soft fabric of his shirt. I felt safe with his arms wrapped around me, a feeling I could get used to. The comfort of another human being.

'Here, sit down,' he suggested, releasing me slowly from his grip.

We perched on a stone wall and he took my hand, resting it on his lap.

'Have you spoken to your mum and grandfather about any of this?' he probed lightly.

'Of course, but it's not quite as simple as that.'

'Why?'

Taking a deep breath, I said, 'Because my life has been hard going since I left this place.' With slight hesitation I continued, 'Don't get me wrong, New York is an amazing place.'

'I bet, I've dreamt about visiting there one day.'

'But it's not home, it's not who I am. I arrived as an English child with a funny accent, trying to fit into a school where the children had known each other from kindergarten. It was difficult. I was out of my comfort zone. I went from rambling around the fields of the farm and knowing everyone, to only being allowed on the streets of the city with my mum. I missed my grandfather, my friends, my animals and the life I had. I made a few friends, but I always felt like an outsider. When I graduated from college I thought things would get easier, but they didn't. I had a dream to perform on the stage and attended auditions, but time after time, all I ever received was rejection letters ... soul destroying.'

Sam leant forward and wiped a tear away that was sliding down my cheek.

'I thought about telling Mum how unhappy I was, but I never found the strength. She's always done her best for me and the worry etched on her face when I told her I was coming back to England pulled at my heart strings. I knew she was scared too, no doubt scared I wouldn't come back or would discover the truth of what went on. I hoped she would come with me. If my grandfather dies, how will she feel, knowing it was never put to rest?' I stared out into space.

'As hard as it may seem, they are adults, that's their choice.'

I nodded. Of course I knew that, and I had to respect their decision, but it didn't mean I had to like it.

Sam placed his arm around my shoulder and I rested my head against his chest.

'Families aren't easy, I think we both know that.'

We sat for a moment in quiet contemplation, before I looked up at Sam.

'But things are changing now. Let's walk,' I suggested, standing up and linking my arm through his, 'towards my future,' I added with a smile.

Sam gave me an inquisitive stare. 'Lead the way.'

Two minutes later I stopped on the pavement outside the dance school and took a deep breath.

'My grandfather has offered me a lifeline. This place,' I gently gestured towards the sign on the front of the building. 'The Florrie Rose School of Dance, named after my grand-mother,' I said proudly. 'Grandie is giving me this place.'

It took a second for the words to register, then Sam reacted the way I was hoping he would.

'Alice, that's fantastic!' He stood next to me staring up at the sign too.

'Not only does he want me to re-open this place, but he's offered me the farm too. I'll have a home and a business. This could all be mine on the condition that I move back to England.'

'And ...' his eyes were wide.

'And I've made a decision: that's exactly what I'm going to do. I'm coming home.'

Sam's beam mirrored the huge smile etched on my face.

'This is fantastic news, Alice!'

'I'm glad you think so. Fancy a look inside?'

'Do I ever!'

Flicking the switch, Sam followed me into the foyer. The light flooded the room and we wandered into the main dance room.

'Alice, this is a fantastic opportunity, you'll have this place up and running in no time.'

'I will, won't I?' I trilled, feeling enthusiastic about the prospect. 'A lick of paint, a deep clean, and then all I'll need is pupils.'

'They'll come flocking in, you don't need to worry about that.'

'Maybe this is what I'm destined for, Sam – re-opening this place, teaching people to dance, to excel and for the community to enjoy this place again.' I couldn't hide the excitement in my voice. 'When I came back to England, seeing Grandie again opened up a new future of possibilities. And I'm going to give this my all.'

'I have to admit,' he grinned, 'I'm a teeny bit jealous.'

'Don't get me wrong, I've had my reservations. What if I can't live up to the reputation of this place, what if I can't teach? But I've taken on a small project, let's call it a taster.'

Sam cocked an eyebrow.

'There's something I want to run past you, and before you make a decision, hear me out.'

'Okay,' he answered.

Taking a deep breath, I continued. This was my moment to convince him about Village Day: 'Putting the situation with Grandie, Mum and the dance school to one side for the moment, I've come up with a plan to save Village Day.'

'Save Village Day? What does it need saving from?'

'Mr Cross and his ukulele.'

Sam laughed.

'Dorothy organises the event, along with the WI, and the final act has pulled out at the last minute, leaving them in the lurch, the only other option being Mr Cross …'

'And his ukulele,' Sam finished off. 'But what's this got to do with me?'

'I've made a suggestion to help them out.'

'You're not going to do a duet with Mr Cross, are you?' he quizzed, concern written all over his face.

'No! Do I look like the type of person who plays a ukulele? In fact, don't answer that! No … I've suggested *Brook Bridge Goes Strictly*!' I shimmied my jazz hands and waited for his reaction.

'Which entails?'

'Me teaching the WI to dance on stage. We have a panel of judges and we'll crown one of them the winner! Also …' I continued, not taking a breath, 'it's Dorothy and Bert's golden wedding anniversary, and I'm teaching him to dance so he can twirl her around the stage, but that's a secret.'

'But I still don't understand why you need my help,' he said, puzzled.

'Because ... I've only got two weeks to teach the women how to dance, so I was thinking ...'

'You were thinking ...?'

'That's where you'd come in. You know people in the theatre who can dance. All we would need is maybe yourself and a couple of your friends to lead them around the stage.'

'Dorothy's not too fond of me, in case you are forgetting that tiny bit of information,' he said, looking slightly horrified at the suggestion.

'I'll speak to Dorothy ... we need to make this work. Considering the time constraints, it will be much easier if the men know how to dance.' I took a breath and gave him a pleading look. 'Will you think about it?'

Sam looked pensive. 'What if Dorothy doesn't like it, how are you going to tackle that? I really don't want to cause you any trouble. And then there's your grandfather. He's only just come out of hospital and doesn't need the past being raked up.'

'Firstly, I'll tell Dorothy that my involvement in Village Day is off if she refuses to have you involved. Okay, I'm letting them all down but I'm making a stand. If I'm doing this for the community, then all the community will be involved – otherwise, what's the point? And as far as Grandie goes, the past has never gone away and it's time to look to the future.'

'You are a feisty one, aren't you? And I admire your determination.'

'I like to think I stand up for what's right. Dorothy and the rest of the WI will soon see they have you all wrong.'

Sam was staring straight at me.

'So, what do you think?'

'Alice, one of my family killed one of yours.'

'It wasn't anything to do with you. And he went to prison, he served his time.'

'People don't forget.'

'Maybe not, but that doesn't stop us from being friends.' I held his gaze and refused to look away, taking his hand. We stared at each other for a second; my hand was trembling.

'Let's do this, all or nothing. How could the situation get any worse?'

Sam's face was serious, his eyes gazed into mine. Then I noticed the corners of his mouth begin to lift.

'Okay, just for you, I'll do it!'

I let out a squeal and threw my arms around him.

Sheer pleasure mixed with apprehension ran through my entire body when Sam agreed, especially knowing how certain members of the village behaved towards him. He didn't have to help me out and I was extremely grateful. I prayed it wouldn't make things more difficult for him in the village.

'And just one more thing ...' I said softly.

'Which is?'

I gently leant forward, and placed a soft kiss on Sam's lips.

'What's that for?' he asked, his lips still close to mine.

'Just for being you.' My voice wavered, exhilarated by the electricity between us.

He held my head gently in his hands and tilted my lips back towards his and then kissed me. Slow and soft, with his thumb caressing my cheek, and all my troubles instantly fell away.

Chapter 23

It was pitch black and the drone of a distant alarm disturbed me out of the finest dream I'd had in a very long time. There I was, curled up in the arms of Sam on the sands of a secluded beach, in our own little private cove with the sound of the waves lapping all around us ...

Damn that alarm.

Sitting up in bed, it took me a second to realise what the sound of the gong was, and over on the dressing table was my iPad flashing. According to the clock it was 3 a.m. What the heck was someone doing, FaceTiming me at this ungodly hour?

It was Molly. I swiped the screen.

'Huh,' I managed to say, trying to focus at the bright light.

'There she is, my gorgeous friend! How's England treating you?' She sounded far too cheery for my liking. She paused. 'Actually, not looking that gorgeous. You look half asleep.'

'Are you for real? I was fast asleep, never mind half asleep, and I've finally got over my jetlag, and you're waking me up at stupid o'clock.'

'Time difference,' she gasped, cupping a hand to her face. 'I've forgotten the time difference. Sorry, sorry, sorry,' she giggled.

'Are you drunk?' I scrutinised her cheesy grin. 'Yep, definitely drunk,' I said, pulling the duvet up to my chest and smiling at her. I did miss Molly. It might be three in the morning, but it was so good to see her. I actually felt a tiny pang.

'A little drunk,' she giggled again, pinching her thumb and forefinger together.

'Any reason in particular why you are ringing me?'

'Just because ... just because I miss you,' her words slurred a little. 'How's it going there? Have you booked your flight home yet?'

The question hung in the air and Molly seemed to instantly sober up. 'You are coming home, aren't you?'

'Here's the thing, Mol, I've every intention of coming home at some point, but a little dilemma has been thrown in my way. It's a long and complicated story.'

'Spill,' she stared intently at the screen, waiting for me to answer. 'I'm going nowhere.'

And so I told her all about Grandie's offer and, of course, the quandary with Mum and living in New York.

Molly's words were kind when she advised me exactly the same thing as Grace: 'You only get one life, so live it. Do what makes you happy.'

Of course I agreed with her, but it wasn't that simple. Could I put my own happiness before Mum's, and would I actually be happy if I stayed in England without her?

'Anyway,' I said quickly, trying to steer the conversation into another direction, 'tell me what you've been up to and how work is.'

Suddenly, a wide smile spread across Molly's face. 'Nothing much happening at the radio station. I got to interview Ben Affleck yesterday,' she said in a matter-of-fact tone.

'Whoa! Stop right there. THE BEN AFFLECK?' I knew I was nearly shouting now and for a second I forgot it was the middle of the night in England.

Molly brought her finger up to her lips and shushed me.

'And tell me how lovely Mr Affleck is.'

Molly swooned and brought her hand up to her chest. 'Absolutely lovely, and I told him about my mad best friend off on her adventures to England.'

'You didn't?'

'Of course I didn't, I had a fangirl moment and spent the whole time dithering over the airwaves while the rest of New York City were probably thinking, WTF?'

I chuckled at the look on Molly's face. 'So where have you been tonight to get you a little tipsy without me?'

'Jay's friend got engaged, so there was a small party after hours at the wine bar, and we both know what Jay's like with his free drinks.'

'Well, he is the best bartender in the city.'

'And what about that handsome Englishman?'

Remembering last night's kiss, a huge smile erupted on my face.

'You've met him, haven't you?'

'I have.'

'And?'

'Sam's lovely.'

'I bet.'

'Right Mols, I need to get some sleep.'

'Talk to me soon. Miss you.'

'I will, but at a decent hour,' I said, blowing her a kiss before flicking off the screen and sliding back under the warmth of the duvet. I briefly considered getting up and making myself a cup of tea, but before I had a chance to climb out of bed I heard the floorboards creak on the landing. Grace was up. I must have woken her while chatting to Molly.

Hearing a light rap on the door, I sat up in bed. 'Is that you, Grace?' I whispered, wondering why I'd said that because who else would it be, it's not as though burglars would be knocking on the bedroom door in the middle of the night.

'Yes, it's me,' said Grace softly, pushing open the door. She was clutching her phone.

'I'm sorry, did I wake you?'

'Wake me ... no. But why are you awake?'

'Molly just FaceTimed me, she'd forgotten about the time difference. What's up, can't you sleep?'

Grace perched on the end of the bed. 'I've just had a phone call from Mum.'

'Is everything okay?' I asked, sitting up, not having a good feeling about this.

Grace shook her head. 'Afraid not.'

My mouth suddenly became dry and my eyes welled up with tears. 'Please tell me it's not Grandie.'

Grace put the phone down on the bed and took hold of my hand. 'It is. I'm sorry, Alice – he's been taken to hospital. He's collapsed.'

Feeling the sudden wrench in my stomach, I felt like I'd been kicked a hundred times, and the tears began to roll down my cheeks.

'The ambulance has already left for the hospital, but Mum is driving over to collect you now.'

'Please tell me he's going to be okay?'

'He's in the best place. Get yourself ready, I'll give you a shout when she's here.'

Grace stood up and left the room. I heard her footsteps echo down the stairs and the light switched on in the kitchen.

Wearily I stood up, dragged on my jeans, T-shirt and my favourite big baggy olive jumper. I grabbed my phone that was on charge and my bag from the corner of the room, and wiped away a tear before scrolling down to Mum's number.

I took the plunge and began to type.

'I need you, Mum. Grandie has been taken to hospital, he's collapsed. Please come home and see him before it's too late.'

My hands were visibly shaking as I pressed send. All I could do now was wait for her response.

Chapter 24

Grandie looked so pale and weak lying in the hospital bed. He was hooked up to a machine and I could see his chest rising and falling rapidly.

Both Connie and I sat by his side, praying he was going to pull through.

'He's been so good to me,' Connie finally said, breaking the silence. 'I don't know what I'd do without him.'

I swallowed down a lump in my throat and blinked away the tears. I glanced at my phone one last time before switching it off to save the battery. There was still no reply from Mum. Granted, it was now midnight in New York, but surely she'd have picked up her message when I first texted over two hours ago.

As soon as Grandie arrived at the hospital, they took him off for a scan and we were still waiting patiently for the doctor to come and talk to us.

'Do you think he misses her?' I asked softly, not taking my eyes off him.

'I'm assuming you mean your mum?'

I nodded.

'I know he does,' answered Connie.

'How do you know? Has he said something to you?'

She paused. 'Not as such, but I know him. I spend a lot of time with him, and since you've come back he's been more pensive.'

'In what way?'

'The dresser in the gallery is jam-packed with old photographs, and the night before last he was sitting in the drawing room and was mooching through them all. I made him a mug of cocoa and that's when I noticed him clutching a photograph of your mum. He quickly hid it back in the pile and wiped away his tears when he noticed me, but whatever they fell out about is deep-rooted.'

'Do you think their argument is anything to do with me?' I'd been wracking my brains since I got here, trying to work out what it was all about.

Connie shook her head. 'I don't think so, Alice. Remember, your mum was my best friend, and I'm just as stumped as you are.'

'The day we left, did you ask her?'

She nodded.

'And?'

'Your mum couldn't look me in the eye. All she said was, no doubt it will come out one day and everyone would hate her. I thought she trusted me, but obviously not with this ... That hurt.'

'This bizarre situation has begun to make me think about something else too, Connie.'

'Go on,' she answered softly.

'Do you think this has anything to do with my father? Do you have any idea who he might be, Connie?' I asked impulsively.

I'd no idea where the question had suddenly come from or why tears had sprung to my eyes or why I was asking about it now. Over the years I'd never been curious about my father at all. Mum had always been enough for me, but who was my father? And, where was he? Like everything else in this family, he was another subject that no one ever spoke about.

I could see Connie battling with her own conscience. It was written all over her face that she knew something.

'Do you know who he was?' I probed further, feeling a teensy bit guilty for pushing her, but I couldn't help thinking that maybe this was something to do with the situation between Grandie and Mum. Maybe Grandie hadn't approved of him? I might be clutching at straws but maybe that was the missing piece of this jigsaw.

Connie didn't have time to answer as Grandie spluttered and opened his eyes.

'You're awake.' Feeling relieved, I smiled warmly at him.

He extended a hand, which I took.

'You don't get rid of me that easily,' he spoke slowly, his eyes drooped and exhausted.

'I'll get the nurse, she needs to know you're awake.' Connie stood up and kissed him on top of his head before disappearing out of the room.

'My mouth is dry,' he nodded towards the glass of water which I held to his lips before mopping his brow with a damp flannel.

'Is that better?' I asked.

'Yes, thank you.'

He clutched my hand and I noticed that he gulped. 'There's no big mystery, you know.'

'Big mystery about what?' I asked, confused.

'Your father.'

I swallowed – he'd heard me ask Connie.

'Really? How come I don't know anything about him or even who he is? It's never even been spoken about for all these years.'

'You've never brought this up with your mum before now?'

I shook my head. 'Never really thought about it much. There was the odd time when I'd wonder, but I've never had the urge to delve further. I was quite happy with it being just me and Mum. So, what do you know about him?' I asked, my hands fiddling with the hem of my jumper.

He smiled before speaking. 'Your dad was a local lad, William Hall, a decent kind. His family emigrated to Australia. Your mum dated him a few times, knowing that he would be starting a new life in Oz soon. She was keen on him, but they weren't in a serious relationship as such. I'm sure it would have developed further if he hadn't been leaving. The sad thing was, your mum only discovered she was pregnant after he'd left, and she'd no clue which part of Australia he'd moved to, or how to contact him – no social media back then.'

William Hall. That had been the first time I'd ever heard his name. I'd watched television programmes about relatives tracking down family members because they never felt complete until they discovered who their family were, but I'd never felt that urge – Mum was always enough. However, of course, hearing the name William Hall sparked a little curiosity. I liked the name – very English – and a part of me felt relieved that he hadn't abandoned me as such. I wondered if things would have panned out differently if he'd known that Mum was pregnant with his baby. Would he have stayed in England? They may have made a go of it, but I supposed I'd never know.

'So, he wasn't a crook?' I asked, thinking the worst.

Grandie seemed to stiffen a little and chewed on his lip. 'No, William Hall wasn't a crook, he was of good stock, unlike ...'

'Unlike who?' I arched an eyebrow, not knowing exactly who he was talking about.

Grandie began to cough and I quickly reached for the glass again and held it up to his lips. As he sipped on the water I was vaguely aware that Connie was back in the room and hovering behind me, but my eyes were firmly fixed on him.

'The nurse is just coming, you gave us all a scare there, Ted,' she said softly, sitting back down on the chair.

'Sorry,' he managed a smile.

The nurse walked in pushing a trolley, followed by the

doctor. She filled up his jug of water before examining the numbers on the machine that was bleeping away, and wrote something down on the chart that was hanging from the bottom of the bed.

'How are you feeling?' the doctor asked.

'Tired, in fact exhausted, my legs seem to feel particularly heavy.'

The doctor nodded while the nurse took his temperature, followed by his blood pressure.

'As soon as you came in we took you in for a scan and the results show you've had a small bleed to the brain.'

I couldn't help myself – as soon as the words left the doctor's mouth my eyes welled up with tears and they began to roll down my cheeks. Grandie squeezed my hand while Connie passed me a tissue to dab my eyes.

The doctor explained that he'd had a TIA, a transient ischaemic attack, a mini-stroke, caused by a blockage cutting off the blood supply to part of his brain, which was most probably a result of his fall and the bang to his head.

'We need you to stay in hospital, so we can monitor you over the next few days.'

'He's going to be okay though, isn't he?' my voice faltered.

'The symptoms usually last around twenty-four hours, and what Ted needs right now is rest.'

Connie and I agreed.

'Go home and get some sleep, come back later when every-thing will be brighter.' With that the doctor and nurse left the room.

'By the time you get back tomorrow, actually today, I'll be up on my feet dancing once more.' Grandie tried to make light of the situation but I could see the exhaustion and worry written all over his face.

'Don't go anywhere,' I said, by the warmth of my tone trying to cover up exactly how I was feeling. I knew this was a warning sign, his health was deteriorating. I gave him a hug but was careful not to squeeze him too hard. 'We'll be back later but try and get some sleep.'

He nodded his appreciation as his eyes began to droop. He looked pale and tired.

Connie and I walked through the silent, clean, white hospital corridors towards the car park.

'I messaged her before, you know,' I said, taking the phone from my bag and switching it on.

'Who?' asked Connie.

'Mum,' I answered, feeling anxious as I waited for the phone to find a signal.

'Any reply?'

I stared intently at the screen. As soon as the 3G kicked in my phone beeped.

Connie raised her eyebrows, 'Is that Rose?'

'Yes,' I said, quickly swiping the screen with my shaky hand.

'What does it say?' she asked, looking over my shoulder.

'How are you both? I love you.'

We stared at each other for a moment.

'What do you think?' I asked.

'I think that's progress. She's asked how you both are, which in my book, means she still cares very much.' Connie squeezed me tight, pressing her soft cheek to mine.

My heart leapt a little as I realised Connie was right.

This was the first sign of mellowing Mum had shown, which meant there was hope, however small. I was going to take this and run with it. All I had to do now was convince Mum to buy a ticket and jump on a flight to England, but one step at a time.

'My mission is to have her on that plane by the end of the week and there is only one way I'm going to achieve that.'

'What are you thinking?' Connie asked, narrowing her eyes at me.

I thought it over for a second. I knew I'd made up my mind to stay in Brook Bridge. My future was here – the school and the farm. Not only did I want her here with me, I needed the family feud to end. We all needed a fresh start ... There was only one way I could see to entice Mum on to that plane ...

'I don't like to admit it but,' I paused, 'emotional blackmail.'

Chapter 25

When Connie dropped me back outside the cottage it was just before eight o'clock. There was a couple chatting at the bus stop and early morning dog walkers were pounding the pavements. Even at such an early hour, the sun had already burst into the clear blue sky, promising a glorious day ahead.

I waved to Connie as the car pulled away from the kerb and I turned towards the cottage. All I wanted to do was climb into my bed. I was exhausted. The curtains to the cottage were still drawn; no doubt Grace was still fast asleep. I exhaled and pushed open the garden gate. Feeling a hand in the small of my back, I jumped out of my skin and spun round.

'Sorry, I didn't mean to frighten you.'

Sam was standing behind me, clutching a pint of milk. 'I didn't go shopping in my pyjamas,' he said, trying to make a light-hearted joke.

'That's good to hear,' I answered wearily.

'Are you okay? You look terrible ... Sorry, I didn't mean ...'

'It's been a hell of night,' I replied, completely exhausted and on the verge of tears, knowing how bedraggled I must look, staring down at my baggy olive jumper that didn't look flattering in the least.

'I thought we'd had a great night?' His concerned eyes stared deeply into mine.

'We did ... of course we did. It's not that. I've just got back from the hospital.' I tried for a smile, but my insides knotted with emotion and I did my best to hold on to my tears.

'Hey,' he touched my arm tentatively, 'what's up?' His tone was soft and sympathetic as he studied me closely. 'You okay?'

I shook my head, 'Not really, my grandfather's had a mini-stroke.'

'Do you want to come inside? I'll make coffee?' he held up the pint of milk.

'That would be great,' I said, giving him a warm, tired smile even though I was completely shattered and was looking forward to snuggling back under the duvet that I'd left hours ago. Another hour wouldn't matter if it meant spending time with Sam.

He held open the garden gate and we walked down the path together.

I'd never been inside Sam's cottage before, and when we stepped inside I noticed that it had the same layout as Grace's. Stripped wooden beams ran the length of the hallway and it felt extremely quaint and cosy. There were coat-hooks on the wall to the right of the wooden staircase and there was a small oak table to the left with a lamp.

'Come on, let's get the kettle on.'

I followed Sam into the kitchen. There was no clutter, no dirty dishes, even the tea towel was neatly folded over the oven door.

'Tea or coffee?' he asked, reaching towards the top cupboard for the mugs.

'Tea, please and one sugar,' I quickly added.

'Make yourself comfy in the living room,' he gestured towards the door. 'Put your feet up.'

The characteristics of the living room were completely cottagey. Again, the wooden beams ran across the length of the ceiling, a chair was positioned beside the log burner and a chesterfield and a coffee table were directly in front of the fire. There was a bookcase at the far end of the room stuffed to the rafters, books on every topic you could ever imagine. And there was an antique dresser that was packed full of framed photos and a docking station. I settled on the settee and heard the kettle click before Sam appeared, placing a tray of tea and biscuits down on the coffee table.

'Chocolate digestives, I'm impressed.'

'Emergency supply, and I kind of thought they may cheer you up,' he smiled, holding the plate towards me while passing me a mug of tea before settling in the space next to me.

'Is your grandfather going to make a full recovery?' he asked tentatively.

'Let's hope so.'

He nodded but I could tell something was on his mind. 'What is it?'

He blew out a breath, 'Don't think I've changed my mind, but maybe my involvement in Village Day isn't good timing, especially with your grandfather's health ... I'm only thinking of you.' He lightly bumped his shoulder against me and placed his hand over mine. 'I don't want to make anything more complicated for you, especially now.'

'You aren't making anything complicated for me, far from it.'

'Your grandfather is ill, your mum is 3,000 miles away and you've got a lot on your mind.'

Of course, I could see Sam's point, but I realised I needed his support now more than ever. 'Don't you go adding to my problems,' I half-heartedly joked, hoping Sam wouldn't back out on me.

He gave a soft laugh. 'Okay ... but if you change your mind ...'

'I won't.'

He gave me a lopsided grin that sent my heart into a spin. 'You are a force to be reckoned with, Alice Parker, and you intrigue me with that funny little accent of yours,' his eyes danced playfully. 'And I can't pretend you aren't on my mind. In fact, you were the first thing I thought about this morning when I woke up.' He entwined his fingers around mine.

'That's good to hear. You're on my mind too,' I murmured bashfully.

Sat there with Sam, it felt natural. I knew I had a lot going on in my life, but I felt relaxed in his company.

'Now you'd best get back and get some sleep.'

'Are you trying to get rid of me?'

'Far from it.' He gave me a sheepish grin, his eyes firmly locked with mine. He watched my lips, I couldn't breathe.

He moved closer towards me, our lips millimetres apart. Looking up from under my fringe, I felt dizzy with anticipation. Just like last night, I willed him to kiss me. He lowered his lips towards mine, neither of us faltered. Sending a shower of sparks through my body, I didn't want the kiss to end.

A few seconds later, Sam pulled me in close, resting my head against his chest. I stifled a yawn, feeling content, happy and tired all of a sudden.

'Your eyes are drooping,' he murmured. 'Feel free to fall asleep on me.' His tone was soft and inviting.

Feeling a bubble of happiness rise as I snuggled into him, I heard the thump of his heart. And there it was again, that tingle, and a flurry of goosebumps every time I was in Sam's company.

And I couldn't think of any place I'd rather be at that very moment in time.

Chapter 26

The cottage door swung open and Grace's eyebrows shot up. Her face was flushed. 'Thank God, where have you been? I've been worried sick!'

'Huh? What's up?' I answered, walking past Grace and lingering next to her in the hallway.

'What's up? Mum claimed she dropped you outside hours ago and there's been no sign of you since.' I could see the worry etched all over Grace's face. 'I was beginning to think you'd been kidnapped.'

'At my age,' I laughed. After bumping into Sam outside and being caught up in the moment, I'd never given it a second thought that Grace would be wondering where I was.

'I kind of fell asleep.'

'What, in the garden?' she asked, following me into the kitchen.

'As if! I've been at Sam's,' I said casually, trying to suppress my smile while I poured myself a glass of water.

She raised her eyebrows.

'I bumped into him outside after Connie dropped me home.'

'If you say so,' she teased, 'but never mind that now. Mum phoned to say she's picking you back up in an hour to visit Grandie again. We were both worried when you weren't home.'

'I'm sorry, I never thought ... An hour?' I began to panic. 'I need a quick shower and some food, I'm starving!'

'Worked up an appetite this morning, did you?'

'No comment,' I laughed.

Grace playfully pushed me towards the stairs. 'Go and get your shower and I'll quickly rustle you up something to eat.'

'Thanks, Grace.' I turned and bounded up the stairs with a spring in my step.

A few hours later Connie and I were back from the hospital. Grandie had appeared bright and cheerful, all things considered. The two of us had battled through the crossword in the paper to keep him occupied, with the help of Siri, which Grandie found extremely fascinating. 'The youth of today! If you wanted answers to questions in my day, you had to get on your bike, ride to the library and look up things in an encyclopaedia.'

'What's one of those?' I kept my lips flat-lined for a second before the laughter escaped.

Now feeling tired, I was looking forward to a girly night in with Grace.

Tomorrow was a jam-packed day. The ladies of the WI had

jumped at the chance of a night of glitz and glamour and were keen to begin their training routine for *Brook Bridge Goes Strictly*. There was so much to do. The dance school needed a good airing and a quick sweep of the floor; there was the music to organise and Jim had kindly offered to paint a backdrop for the staging. Connie had agreed to take care of the outfits and Sam had texted me to say his dance friends had agreed to take part, which was a huge relief. It was all coming together.

Grace placed two calorific hot chocolates down on the coffee table and slumped on to the settee, waggling her pink fluffy striped socks in the air.

'This is just what I needed.' I plunged the long-handled spoon into the top of the cream and scooped up the minimarshmallows while Grace stuffed a piece of margherita pizza into her mouth.

'How was Ted?' she asked, wiping her mouth with the back of her hand.

'He's looking a lot brighter but I think it's been a gentle reminder for him that he needs to take things easy.'

'It must be so frustrating when you've always been active, then to suddenly be told you need to slow down. Did you update your mum?' asked Grace, grabbing the remote control and flicking through numerous film options.

I shook my head, 'I'm still pondering ... kind of.' My mood flipped as thoughts of Mum flooded through my mind.

'About?' she asked.

'In fact, I'm not pondering at all, I've made a decision.

Please don't judge me, but desperate times call for desperate measures now.'

'Go on, I'm listening.' Grace looked worried as she waited for me to speak.

I took a deep breath, 'I'm going to twist the truth a little,' I admitted, feeling very underhanded. 'The minute I stepped off that plane, I felt like I'd come home. Before Grandie even offered me the farm, the dance school, I knew this was where I wanted to be.'

'But the only dilemma is Rose.'

I nodded. 'So, I've been thinking, and I know I am about to play with fire.'

'What are you going to do?' Grace sat up straight and looked at me wide-eyed.

'Stretch the truth?' My hands were trembling as I picked up my phone. 'I can't physically drag her here, but this situation can't go on. They need to see each other and speak, and how can they do that if they are miles apart?'

I began to type a text to Mum and just before I pressed send, I closed my eyes and exhaled.

'Done.'

'What did you say?'

'That Grandie is asking to see her.'

Grace gasped. 'Yikes, that is stretching the truth.'

'Believe me, I'm not proud of myself, but how else am I going to get her here? If this doesn't work, nothing will. I'll just have to deal with the consequences when and if I have to.'

I felt awful sending that text, it was dishonest, I was the first one to admit that. Everything could go wrong, even Grandie might never speak to me again when he found out what I'd done. I could lose it all. But hopefully Mum would take the bait, book her plane ticket and once they were both finally in the same room they would get over this silly feud and let bygones be bygones.

Grace gave me a warm, encouraging smile, but inside I was far from smiling. I was on tenterhooks, waiting for a reply, nausea surging through my body.

Within a few seconds my phone beeped and startled us both.

I couldn't even bring myself to read the message. 'Grace, can you read it?' I asked nervously, sliding the phone over towards her, my chest pounding.

Grace nodded, faltering for a moment before she picked the phone up.

'And breathe, it's from Ben.' She gave a forced laugh, the relief written all over her face.

I rolled my eyes, remembering the last encounter I'd had with him. 'What does he want?'

'He's asking if you can talk,' she said, handing back the phone.

I sighed, 'I've got nothing to say to him.'

Just as I balanced the phone on the arm of the chair, it beeped again. Grace noticed my hands trembling. 'I take it that's not Ben again?'

Shaking my head, I passed her the phone.

'It's Mum.'

Grace read out the text: 'That's all I needed to hear. I'll book a flight and be with you by the end of the week. Please sort me out a place to stay.' Grace stared at me, her jaw dropped somewhere near the floor.

'I've done it now, haven't I?'

'How do you feel?' Grace asked tentatively.

My head was spinning. 'I really have no idea,' I admitted, feeling my pulse throb in the side of my head, an outbreak of nerves making me shudder. 'What do I do now?!'

'We do nothing, we say nothing, we act surprised,' she said with a half-smile.

'What, like, "Ta-dah! Mum's turned up out of the blue!"' I waved jazz hands in the air.

'Okay, maybe not with jazz hands, but we say nothing until we know what flight she's on, and then we need to tell my mum.'

'What do you think Connie will say?'

Grace shrugged, 'We'll explain that you were desperate, you panicked when they took Ted into hospital.'

'So, we just sit tight, until we know more?'

'That's exactly what we do; no point rocking the boat until Rose is actually here.'

I nodded, struggling to take it all in.

'Thanks, Grace, I don't know what I'd do without you.'

'You've certainly injected drama into my life,' she grinned, 'but who wants a boring life anyway?'

Right at this second I'd give anything for a boring life. I'd never actually considered what I'd do if Mum agreed to come to England. It was safe to say she'd actually taken me by surprise. I'd no idea how any of this would play out, I'd just have to wait and see. But at least I was on the way to getting some answers.

Chapter 27

The following morning, after visiting the hospital, Grace and I let ourselves into the dance school armed with more cleaning products than they had on the shelves at the local supermarket.

Tucking my hands into the front pockets of the apron I had borrowed from Grace, I looked around the room before scooping up my hair and securing it in a messy bun on the top of my head. 'It won't take long to spruce this place up,' I said, my tone hopeful, pulling on a pair of pink Marigolds.

'We need a plan. Firstly, let's clean up the main dance room, the kitchen area, then the toilets,' I suggested, taking control and flinging open the windows at the far end of the room. 'That's better, a bit of fresh air.

'I've got some fantastic memories of this place,' I reminisced, thinking of my Saturday mornings dancing my little heart out on this very floor.

'And hopefully there will be many more to come,' added Grace encouragingly. 'In a couple of hours, we won't recognise this place.'

We jigged our way around the room, dusters and mops in hand, giggling away like a couple of teenagers. With buckets filled to the brim with warm water, we wiped the mirrors, brushed the stage, scrubbed the blinds and mopped the floor. And after two hours of gruelling cleaning, I pulled off my gloves and wiped my brow. The pair of us perched on the edge of the stage and admired our hard work. What a transformation! The whole place gleamed and a fresh floral aroma flooded the room.

I'd had a fantastic couple of hours singing, dancing and cleaning alongside Grace, and for the first time I wasn't dwelling on Mum at the back of my mind. I'd had some fun.

'Wow, just wow!' exclaimed Grace, meeting my gaze with a wide smile. 'It looks as elegant as the ballroom at Blackpool Tower,' she chirped.

I couldn't help but smile at her comparison. 'I wouldn't go that far,' I grinned, looking up at the newly polished glitterball that now sparkled with a new lease of life and shimmied coloured speckles of light around the room.

Feeling proud, my eyes filled with tears. This little place had come alive and there was fire in my belly. I didn't want to turn my back on the dance school. I wanted this to be the start of my new future. Somewhere I could call my own and be valued.

'Drumroll,' announced Grace. 'I now declare Florrie's School of Dance open and fit for purpose,' she chuckled.

I laughed at her outburst.

There was still a long way to go. The carpet in the entrance hall needed a deep clean. The bathroom needed a little modernising and the walls could do with a fresh lick of paint, but at least now, it was clean, aired and dust free.

'We've done well,' admitted Grace, smiling towards me and patting my knee. 'Even Darcie Bussell wouldn't have any qualms about pirouetting on such a clean polished floor.'

I'd lost count of the number of buckets of dirty water we'd emptied. I'd even apologised to the spiders as we sucked away the cobwebs from the corners of the rooms, but it had been worth it.

'We need a toast, a small tipple to mark the occasion,' suggested Grace.

'Tipsy while in charge of the ladies of the WI?' I chuckled, thinking the task ahead of me this evening was maybe already challenging enough.

'What time are they arriving?'

'Just after 7 p.m., and I have to admit I'm a little nervous.'

'Are you going to tell them about Sam's involvement?'

'I am, I'm going to be up front from the start. I've got nothing to hide and if they don't like it ... well, this place is important to me, the past is the past and that's where it needs to stay. This business needs to get off on the right foot ... no pun intended,' I said with determination.

'I think it's the way forward.'

I swallowed back an emotional lump in my throat. I was going to put my all into resurrecting this dance school and staying in England. Living in New York was becoming more of a distant memory every day.

Chapter 28

Just after tea-time the sky began to darken and in no time at all the heavens opened. I ran towards the dance school, clutching my bag while holding on to the hood of my coat and striding over the puddles, trying to keep the drenching to a minimum.

As I thrust the key into the lock there was a flash of lightning across the dense black clouds, followed by a boom of thunder. Once inside the safe haven of the foyer, I peeled off the sodden coat from my back and draped it over the coat-stand behind the reception desk and switched on the lights. I wasn't sure whether the WI ladies would venture out in such torrential rain, but at that very second, the door swung open and a gang of excitable wet pensioners tripped inside.

'What an evening!' exclaimed Dorothy, untying a plastic head scarf that was attempting to keep her hair dry. 'I've only had my hair done this afternoon and now look at it!'

'It looks perfect, not a hair out of place,' I said, holding the shoulders of her coat while she slipped her arms out.

Just at that second, we were silenced by a strip of lightning that tore across the sky, making the lights flicker.

'Ladies, ladies ...' Dorothy attempted to bring some order to their gasps, 'we weren't going to let the weather dampen our spirits.'

Everyone hushed.

Dorothy carried on, 'Let me introduce you to Alice, Alice Parker ... Ted and Florrie's granddaughter, who has thankfully saved the day for us with her bright idea.'

Everyone began to smile and say thank you, then they broke into a delighted applause, taking me completely by surprise but boosting my confidence.

'No need for that,' I smiled. 'Honestly, anyone would do the same and it's lovely to meet you all. There is tea and coffee in the kitchen, if you want to go through and grab a cup before we start?'

With affirmative nods, they made their way towards the kitchen. 'Dorothy, can I have a word?' I asked, feeling nervous, knowing what I was about to say next.

Dorothy hung back. 'Is everything okay, dear?' she asked.

'I hope so Dorothy, I really do.'

'Is it your grandfather?' Her voice quivered.

'Grandie is back in hospital but stable.'

Dorothy gasped, 'Oh you poor thing, all this worry.'

'It is a worry, but that's not what I need to speak to you about.'

She took hold of my hands. 'What is it? I'm here to help with anything.'

Knowing the friendship bond that had tied Dorothy to Grandma and feeling anxious, I took a deep breath: 'I'm coming home, I'm re-opening this place.'

The smile spread across Dorothy's face. 'Bert did mention it, but hearing those words from you ... Your grandma would be so proud of you. And what about Rose, is she coming home too?'

'I don't know but I've got to do what's right for me, that's why I need to speak to you.'

'I'm listening.' Dorothy's eyes were wide and I had her full attention.

'I'm not sure of the reason why we ever left for New York but all I know is, if I'm coming home I need to look to the future.'

'Of course you do, onwards and upwards ...'

'But,' I interrupted Dorothy while I was in full flow, 'But that means leaving all the feuds behind, all the bad feeling, moving on.'

'I don't understand.'

'It's Village Day, Dorothy.'

'You aren't backing out on us, are you? We're all so excited and ...' Her voice was shaky.

'No, I'm not backing out Dorothy,' I interrupted, 'but I need to be honest with you. I've asked Sam to help me.'

'Sam?' Dorothy hesitated.

'Sam Reid,' I said slowly.

Dorothy exhaled and paled instantly.

'What happened to Grandma had nothing to do with Sam and, as much as I respect both you and Bert, I don't hold a grudge, and isn't it about time everyone let go of the past?'

Dorothy remained silent.

'This place ...' I looked around, 'meant the world to Grandie and I'm going to put my all into it, but everyone will be welcome. Village Day is about bringing the community together, and that's why I think you should give Sam a chance. He's his own person ... and he knows some fantastic handsome male dancers that will swoop these ladies off their feet. There's a bigger picture here, can we just let bygones be bygones?'

I could see Dorothy was turning it over in her mind, then taking me surprise, the tears rolled down her cheeks. Quickly I passed her a tissue. 'I know you're right, Alice, love. We just miss Florrie.'

'I know you do, but you're directing your anger towards the wrong person.'

She nodded, and dabbed her eyes.

Feeling relieved the conversation was over, I said, 'Are you ready to join the others? They'll be wondering where we've got to.'

She touched my arm affectionately. 'You are a good girl, Alice. Come on, let's get this show on the road.'

All the ladies had now moved into the main dance hall, and were settled in the chairs that were laid out at the far end of the room. 'We can't thank you enough for helping us,' said Elsie, giving me a quick introduction to everyone.

'Look at this place,' revelled Stella, the chair of the WI. 'It's been years since we've been in here. It's not changed a bit.'

'You are all more than welcome, but there's a lot of hard work to be done and over the next couple of weeks you all need to practise, practise, practise.' I'd raised my tone a little to gain all of their attention.

Six eager heads nodded back at me.

'Shall I talk you through the plan?'

'Yes please,' came all their enthusiastic voices in unison.

I perched on the edge of the stage. 'Stella ...' She was a tall, slim, elegant woman with a blonde bob that bounced on top of her shoulders. She wouldn't have looked out of place at a make-up counter in the local department store. Even her painted nails matched the colour of her lips, not to mention her shoes. 'You are going to be dancing the waltz.'

She clapped her hands excitedly while the rest of the ladies gave each other an approving nod.

'Next, we'll have Elsie, dancing the quick step, followed by Freda with the tango, Ida with the Charleston, Mabel with the Paso Doble and Dorothy ...' I glanced towards her, knowing already she would be opening the show with Bert, 'you will be dancing the foxtrot.'

She gasped, 'My favourite dance of all time, thank you.'

'We can decide what order we'll be dancing in nearer the time, once we've mastered the steps. Is everyone happy so far?'

There was a consensus gabble of approval.

'On the day, there will be a panel of judges, but don't worry

– we will all be giving very kind comments and scores,' I gave them a reassuring smile.

'But who will we dance with?' asked Ida, turning and facing the rest of the women, followed by an undercurrent of mutterings. 'I'm not sure my Alfred will be up to it.'

My heart raced as all eyes were on me. 'My friend Sam Reid, who has just starred in *Mamma Mia*, will be helping us out on that front.'

All the women looked between themselves then turned towards Dorothy, who nodded approvingly.

'You won't be disappointed. Young handsome men twirling you around the stage, what more can you ask for?' I kept my voice full of enthusiasm and continued:

'I've downloaded each dance on to my iPad, which we can watch together now, then let's decide on a colour scheme for each of your dresses, and I think it's best if I arrange one-on-one time with each of you to put you through your paces over the next couple of days. Are we happy with that?'

Everyone was in agreement and for the next twenty minutes we all huddled around the screen watching the dancing.

'Beautiful,' murmured Stella, mesmerised by the waltz. 'Just beautiful.'

'He's very bendy,' chuckled Freda, twisting her head upside down and taking a better look. 'I'm not sure I can bend like that anymore but I remember a time with Fred the milkman, we got carried away on his early-morning ...'

'Whoa! Stop there,' interrupted Mabel. 'Let's not corrupt this young innocent girl in front of us.'

Everyone chuckled.

'Look at those lifts. We need those strapping young men to lift us like that.' Elsie's gaze flicked towards me.

'I think we'll be keeping lifts to a minimum, I don't want anyone ending up in A&E.'

After we'd finished swooning over the stunning footage of the elegant dancing we turned our attentions to the colour scheme. Making a note in my notebook of who was wearing what colour and various measurements, I'd pass on all the details in the morning to Connie who was going to trawl the local charity shops for anything suitable with glitz and glamour. Individual times were arranged for each of them to have one-to-one tuition with me over the next couple of days, and when everyone else had gone home Dorothy stayed behind to go over her steps with me.

'I'm sorry,' were the first words out of Dorothy's mouth once everyone had left the building.

'For what?' I asked, stacking the chairs away.

'If I made you feel uncomfortable,' Dorothy sounded sincere.

'You haven't … really. But I've learnt that harbouring feuds is draining and time-consuming – life's too short.'

'And I'm not sure how much life I have left,' Dorothy gave a small chuckle. 'You'll make a success of this place, I know you will.'

'I hope so,' I replied, knowing I'd enjoyed every second of this evening with the ladies. I knew I was going to pour my heart and soul into it.

'Right, let's go over your steps. We'll begin right at the very beginning.' I tapped my heels on the wooden floor and Dorothy mirrored my steps.

'I feel like a fish out of water,' she exclaimed, concentrating hard on my footwork. 'It's been years since I've danced.'

'It won't take long to learn these steps, it's like riding a bike.'

'I've not done that for years either,' she chuckled.

'It will all come back to you,' I reassured her, slowly talking her through the steps once more.

'With it being our golden wedding anniversary, I've asked Bert to dance with me, but it's his hips, it would be too much for him,' she said sagely. 'But hopefully it will be a treat for him to watch me dance on the stage wearing something all glitzy and glamourous.'

I bit my lip and said nothing. I couldn't wait to see Dorothy's reaction when Bert whisked her off her feet, around that stage. It would be the grandest opening to the show.

Dorothy puffed out her cheeks. 'I'm not as fit as I used to be,' she said, starting again from the beginning with her right foot. 'In my head, I'm still only twenty.'

I smiled, 'You are doing fantastic.'

'I knew the second I hit middle age, everything changed. There were no more drinking sessions at the pub or days at the races, it all became blended healthy juice meals that tasted bland, and yoga.' She rolled her eyes, 'And now what have I got going for me?'

'Fifty years of marriage, and you own the best teashop in the land.'

'And I wouldn't change that for the world,' she patted my hand affectionately.

After those words of encouragement, Dorothy danced her socks off for the next twenty minutes before thanking me for my time and heading home with a smile on her face to her beloved Bert. She'd grasped the basic steps and I'd given her pointers to focus on over the next few days until we met again. The evening had been a success and Village Day was well and truly back on track. The ladies were full of vim, vigour and determination. It gave me a warm, fuzzy feeling to see their energy and enthusiasm, knowing I'd played a part in it all.

Thinking I was all alone, I was startled by a voice that echoed through the foyer: 'Knock, knock, anyone there?'

'Sam?' I called out, my heart giving a little leap when I recognised his voice. 'I'm in here.' I'd had every intention of texting him once I'd arrived back home.

He appeared in the doorway, drenched to the skin. 'It appears to be raining,' he said, giving me a cock-eyed grin. 'Look at the state of me, and I've only come from the car. It's torrential out there.' He raked a hand through his unruly hair.

Believe me, I was looking. My eyes flitted over his sopping T-shirt that clung to his chest. I was doing my very best not to stare at his toned abs or breathe too deeply. My heart constricting at just how gorgeous he was, I said, 'What are you doing here?'

'Grace said you were here and should be finishing round about now, so I thought I'd pick you up. You'd get soaked walking back in this.'

I flashed him a grateful smile. 'My knight in shining armour! Thank you, that's very kind.'

'But I was also worried about you. How did it go?' his brow furrowed.

'With Dorothy?'

He nodded.

I tried to put on a serious face, but the smile hitched before I could stop it. 'I think I've given her food for thought.'

'You have?'

I nodded as Sam pulled me closer and wrapped his arms around my waist.

'It comes down to common sense, if you ask me. Whoever your family were, or are now, that's nothing to do with you … you are your own person. We are a community and you are part of that too.'

Sam was grinning down at me.

'What?!'

'You … when you're passionate about something you talk so fast, I can't keep up!'

We smiled at each other and his eyes sparkled. I lifted my hand up to Sam's face and stroked his stubble lightly. My eyes stayed locked on his. He pulled me in, pressed his body closer and lowered his lips to mine.

'Dance with me,' he murmured.

'Here?'

'Yes, here,' he said softly, holding my hands in his. The acceleration of my heart rate was instant and I honestly thought I was going to melt or combust. There was something about his gentlemanly confidence that made me go weak at the knees.

We moved slowly together, our bodies a revolving whirl of precision and grace in perfect sync. Every inch of me tingled with desire for this man as I floated and twisted weightlessly across the room in his arms. The intensity between us was as hot as fire as we lost ourselves in the music. And when eventually the tempo slowed, and the music that filtered from the iPad curled like a thread around us, he brought me closer than I ever imagined possible.

Closing my eyes and breathless, I rested my head on his chest and could hear the thumping of his heart. I felt a yearning for this man like I'd never felt before and when the music came to an end I had to remind myself to breathe.

For a moment, we stayed locked in each other's arms, then gazed at each other in a contemplative silence. Sam leant forward and gently tucked an escaped strand of hair behind my ear. 'You okay?' he finally asked, his lips close to mine.

I nodded, the emotion welling up inside me. 'That was perfect ... just perfect.'

He lowered his lips to mine, his kisses were long and deep, I savoured every moment, lost in the intoxicating trance of passion.

I'd never felt desire like it.

Chapter 29

As we locked up the dance school and made a hasty dash towards Sam's car, the rain was still pelting down. Once we were safely inside, he attempted to start the engine, but nothing happened. The car wouldn't turn over. A flash of frustration fleeted across Sam's face. One last time he tried again, before turning towards me: 'This knight in shining armour has failed.'

'It's not your fault, the thought was very much appreciated.'

'But now, we are going to have to make a run for it ... in this.'

We both took a glance out of the window. The rain seemed to have worsened, drumming against the windscreen and bouncing off the pavements. A couple raced along the street, clutching tightly to an umbrella that was blowing inside out.

We sat there for a second, hedging our bets, waiting to see

if the rain would give up even for a second, but judging by the blackened sky, it wasn't going to stop any time soon.

'Are you ready?' Sam asked.

'Ready as I'll ever be,' I answered, zipping up my coat and pulling my hood over my head.

Sam stepped out of the car and opened my door. He extended his arm and draped it around my shoulder.

'Run!' he ordered.

'Yikes! I'm drenched already,' I laughed, trying my best to miss the puddles.

We exchanged mischievous grins as we took off up the street, and my shoes were sodden in seconds.

Sam took my hand and pulled me along and we reached the gate of his cottage in no time at all.

Falling into the hallway, we were both soaked to the bone.

'Look at the state of us!' I couldn't stop laughing.

'Here, let me take this from you,' he said, peeling the coat from my back and hanging it up on the coat peg in the hallway. He flashed me the most gorgeous smile, which made my heart skip a beat.

'And take this,' he handed me a grey hoodie, 'put it on.'

'Thank you,' I said, slipping it over my head. The words caught in my throat as I snuggled inside his hoodie and breathed in the spicy aroma of his aftershave. It smelt divine and my heart thumped a little faster.

'It suits you,' his eyes glinted as he gave me the once over. My cheeks stretched into a gigantic smile.

There was no denying the spark, the chemistry, the raw

attraction between us, and this kind of intensity was new to me. Of course, I'd had dates in the past, boyfriends too, but those feelings weren't anything like what I was experiencing now.

Not only was the man standing in front of me incredibly gorgeous, but every time I was in his company my insides became a gibbering wreck.

'Go and make yourself comfy, I'll make us a warm drink.' He raked his hand through his hair and swept his wet fringe from his eyes before gesturing towards the living room and disappearing down the hallway.

As soon as he was out of sight I risked a hesitant look in the hallway mirror. My hair was limp and the tip of my nose resembled Rudolf's. This really wasn't an attractive look. Rummaging quickly in my bag, I pulled a hairbrush through my hair, touched up my make-up and prayed I looked at least half decent.

Sam appeared a couple of minutes later and handed me a mug of steaming tea which I immediately clamped my hands around.

'The weather in England, very unpredictable,' he mused, sitting down next to me.

'It's not that different to New York. One minute it can be sunny and the next, knee deep in snow,' I shared, remembering last February when one day I was walking around Central Park in a T-shirt, and the next week I was bundled up inside a parka. We sipped our drinks and finally I felt myself beginning to dry out.

'Any plans for tonight?' he asked.

Taking a quick glance towards my watch, I saw it was already fast approaching eight thirty. 'Bath and bed, I'm exhausted.'

'I'm not surprised. Your trip to England has been full on since you arrived.'

'What are your plans?'

'No plans ... no plans whatsoever.'

'Tonight was a good night. I really enjoyed myself, Sam.'

'That's good to hear.'

'Spending time with the WI and organising their dances and being a part of something made me feel kind of useful again, gave me back some confidence.'

'If you teach as well as you dance, this business will be a success from the off. So, the dance school, is it all systems go?' he enquired, sipping his drink.

'It is, and I can't wait to get started once Village Day is over.'

'And there's the added bonus for me.'

'For you?'

'I quite like the thought of Miss America sticking around,' he said, placing his mug on the table.

'You do now, do you?'

Sam reached out and took my hands. His quiet confident declaration was the sign I needed that he felt that spark too, and I shuffled a little closer to him. There was something about Sam Reid that made me want to spend more time with him.

'Honestly, I noticed you that first morning. There was something about that slight American twang, those two cute dimples and the way you were standing there, drenched on the pavement in your PJs. I mean, you have to be mad to wander up to the local shop in your PJs,' he grinned. 'In fact, bonkers.'

'Lounge wear, that's my story and I'm sticking to it!'

'PJs,' he insisted, his tone mischievous.

But before I could argue he kissed me.

Beep.

'What's that?' he whispered.

'My phone, damn that timing,' I smiled, slowly sitting up.

'Leave it.' Sam's face was flushed, his hair tousled and his eyes wanting more. I kissed him lightly on the lips before reaching inside my bag.

'I can't, it may be important, especially with my grandfather being in hospital and everything.'

'Sorry, that was selfish of me,' he said, sitting up slowly.

'Not to worry, it's only Grace.' I swiped the screen, 'She probably wonders where I've disappeared to again.'

My eyes widened as I read the text.

'What is it? Is it Ted?' asked Sam with concern, noticing my sudden change in mood.

'No, it's my mum. Apparently, she's been in touch with Connie to tell her she's arriving from New York at the end of the week.' I stared at Sam.

Suddenly I was feeling very nervous, and apprehension ran through my entire body. This was really happening. On

Friday, my mum would arrive from New York and in the not-so-distant future she would come face to face with her father once more, and the pair of them would discover I'd lied to entice her here. I knew this was what I wanted but now that it was really happening, I had no idea how to handle it.

I gulped.

'Surely that's a good thing?' asked Sam with curiosity.

'It is, and it isn't. I've kind of been a little deceitful in getting her here,' I admitted, biting down on my lip.

Sam raised his eyebrows.

'But one thing I'm absolutely sure of, time is going to tell very, very soon.'

Even though I knew my lie gave Mum the excuse she needed to travel over 3,000 miles, I was a strong believer in fate. All this – the first message from Grace, the trip to England, the dance school ... Sam – it had all happened for a reason and I was determined to do my damn hardest to uncover what the hell had happened thirteen years ago.

Chapter 30

The next morning, Grace was standing in the kitchen flipping pancakes while whistling along to a tune on the radio.

'Good morning,' she chirped the second she noticed me. 'Sleep well?'

I'd barely slept a wink and couldn't even blame it on the rain hammering against the window all night. It was more down to my own conscience stopping me from sleeping, and the words of Mum's text, 'That's all I needed to hear,' had been playing on my mind.

'You seem a little quiet, subdued,' noticed Grace, before I had a chance to answer. She slid a plate overloaded with pancakes into the middle of the table, 'Help yourself.'

'Thanks,' I said, blowing out a breath and pulling out a chair.

'At least it's brightening up now,' she observed, taking a

fleeting glance out of the kitchen window before sitting down opposite me. 'Come on then, what's eating you? Everything okay with Sam?'

Everything was more than okay between me and Sam, but I was beginning to wonder if that might change on Mum's arrival when she discovered who Sam was and that we were getting close. Would she hold a grudge, like others did in the village?

'Yes, all's good with Sam. It's just the arrival of Mum on my mind,' I sighed, taking a pancake from the top of the pile. 'I'm just feeling a little unsure about how it's all going to pan out.'

'Well, we'll know soon enough,' said Grace, drizzling lemon juice over her pancakes before shaking a teaspoon of sugar over the top.

'As much as I'm looking forward to seeing her, I'm not actually looking forward to seeing her, if that makes any sense.'

'I can imagine.' She leant forward and touched my hand.

'What did your mum say about my mum getting in touch again?'

'She was surprised, but she's kindly offered to pick her up from the airport and said she can stay in the annexe with her. But she did question whether your grandfather knew anything about it.'

'And?'

'And I told her you hadn't had time to tell him yet ... but you will.'

I didn't say a word.

'Alice, you're going to have to tell him. It will be a huge shock for him to see Rose after all this time with no prior warning, he's not a well man.'

'I know, I will,' I said, knowing that I wasn't at all looking forward to that moment. 'I don't think he'll be out of hospital before she arrives, which gives us all a little time to see how the land lies, what Mum's mood is like and how I'm going to handle it all.'

'Nervous?' asked Grace.

'Beyond belief. Did you let on to Connie how I got Mum here?'

'No, you'll need to tell her that too.'

'Maybe it won't come up in conversation?' I replied, suddenly feeling very guilty.

I saw Grace raise her eyebrows at me, knowing the tangled web I was weaving.

'Picture this ... Ted and Rose come face to face for the first time in how many years?'

'Thirteen.'

'What's the first thing they are going to say to each other?' asked Grace, scrutinising me closely.

I shifted uncomfortably in my seat and shrugged.

'Ted will say, "What are you doing here?" And Rose will answer, "You asked to see me."'

Grace was right. I looked up alarmed, placing my head in my hands, knowing I hadn't thought it through. 'I know I'm being dishonest but I'm hoping, praying in fact, that the second they set on eyes on each other it will all be forgotten.'

'A rift that has festered for thirteen years isn't going to be forgotten, but we can hope,' said Grace, sounding unconvinced.

We polished off the rest of the pancakes and I switched the kettle on before helping Grace to wash up the dishes.

'How did the rehearsals go last night?' she asked, hanging the wet tea-towel over the oven door.

'Yes, good! Everyone was enthusiastic,' I answered, thankful for the change of subject.

'And how did Dorothy take Sam being on board?'

'Surprisingly well,' I said, 'after I explained that Village Day was for the whole community, which Sam is also a part of.'

'It probably just needed saying out loud, but good for you! It must have been nerve-wracking for you. So, what are the plans for today?'

I slid a detailed schedule over the table towards her. 'You are taking it seriously!' exclaimed Grace, casting her eyes over the timetable and following me into the living room.

Slouching on the settee, I tucked my feet underneath me. 'To be honest, I'm thankful for the distraction. If I was sitting here with nothing to do, I'd just drive myself crazy over Mum's arrival.'

'And my mum said something about her being in charge of the costume department?'

'Yes,' I answered, sifting through a pile of papers I'd left on the coffee table. 'Here it is, everyone's measurements and colours. I'll nip it over to her later.'

'Mum did mention something else and I've been meaning to ask you, but … I wasn't sure whether it was a good idea bringing it up, with everything else you've got going on.' Grace eyed me carefully.

'Go on …' my voice lifted.

'Mum said you were asking about your father.'

I nodded. 'I was wondering whether he had anything to do with the fall-out.'

Grace sat upright on the settee.

'Have you ever asked your mum about him?'

I shook my head, 'No, never.'

I'd reached the age of twenty-three and had never given it a huge deal of thought. It wasn't something that had ever kept me awake at night, there was never a massive void in my life. My mum had been great and I'd never needed any more.

'And in all these years your mum has never mentioned it?'

I shook my head. 'I was taken a little by surprise when Grandie told me about him. I don't know what I was expecting – maybe a one-night stand or a low-life, which doesn't make it sound like I think very highly of Mum … but there wasn't a huge mystery, just a set of unfortunate circumstances. She'd met a guy, a decent lad, Grandie said. They'd had a couple of dates, but he emigrated to Australia with his parents and she only discovered she was pregnant after he'd left. Unfortunate timing.'

'So, he never knew?'

'It appears that way.'

'How are you feeling about it all?'

'In a way, kind of relieved he's just a normal guy.'

'Did your grandfather tell you his name?'

'William Hall,' the name left my lips.

The name turned over in my mind, William Hall.

'The question is then, I suppose, are you going to do anything about it?' probed Grace.

This was the very question that had been on my mind since Grace had brought up the subject. What could I actually do about it? Australia was a huge place and there must be hundreds of William Halls in the world, and who knows, he might not even be in Australia any more.

'Not sure what I can do, even though I'm kind of curious what he looks like. Do I even look like him?'

'Talk to your mum, surely it can't hurt? Maybe she would have an old photograph of him?'

'You never know. It's worth an ask.' I nodded, 'And I'm definitely now intrigued to discover more about him – what's his background, what does he do for a living? And not forgetting the possibility that he has his own family, which is more than likely.'

'You could have brothers and sisters,' Grace's eyes widened.

'I could,' I paused, the same thought crossing my mind.

Reaching for my iPad, there was a message visible on the screen. 'It's an update from Mum, details of her flight and that she's looking forward to seeing me.' I raised my eyebrows. 'Hopefully when she finds out I've told a weeny white lie, that won't change.'

'My guess is, you'll be in for a rough few days but I'm sure once they come face to face, it would be silly not to forgive and forget,' said Grace, clearly keen to smooth the way.

I put on a brave smile. 'I hope you're right,' I said, forcing a brightness into my voice I didn't feel.

After typing a reply back, I began to scroll through my homepage on Facebook, and Grace carried on talking but for a second I didn't hear a word.

'Earth to Alice ... earth to Alice. What's so interesting on there?' Her voice was gently enquiring.

Aware of the tiny knots forming in my stomach, I didn't know how to respond. My eyes pinged open and when I looked back at her, my heart was thundering in my chest, and I could barely breathe.

'What is it?' she asked slowly, placing the rehearsal schedule on the table. 'You've got a funny look about you.'

My stomach clenched, 'It's Facebook, the "People you know" suggestion.'

'And?'

I cast my eyes back towards the screen, then turned it towards her.

Grace shuffled up next to me, taking the iPad from my hand. 'William Hall,' she read out loud. 'You daft thing,' she said, laughing, 'that will be a freak coincidence, just one of those things,' trying to make light of the situation.

'That's what I thought, but look, we have one mutual friend,' I emphasised, pointing at the screen. 'Rose Parker,' I said simply, 'my mother.'

'Go on then, tap on the profile,' said Grace with urgency.

For a second, I hovered over his name before tapping on his profile picture. 'William Hall lives in Perth, Australia.'

Grace and I stared at the face looking back at us.

'Wow! This is amazing,' Grace gave a whistle, and flicked a glance between me and the screen. 'What do you think?'

'I think that's him. Right age, lives in Oz and appears to be friends with my mum, and there's no mistaking ...'

'The eyes and the nose,' Grace interrupted, 'it's uncanny, that's you.'

I was speechless. Adrenalin shot down my spine and my stomach was now performing double somersaults. 'I don't know what to think.' I thought today was just another day, but it turned out it was the day I found out what my father looked like for the very first time.

'Do you think she has been in touch with him all this time?' I asked Grace, feeling a bit dazed. 'Do you think he knows anything about me?'

'I've no idea, Alice,' Grace replied softly.

My pulse was racing as I stared at his profile, then I took a deep breath and began clicking on his photo albums.

My eyes welled up. 'Look,' I said, turning the screen back towards Grace. 'There's his family, a wife and two beautiful girls.'

I could feel the emotion rising inside, a mixture of fear, happiness and, of course, the unknown.

I rubbed my eyes.

'You're tearful ... here,' said Grace, passing me a tissue.

'What do I do now?'

I had a thousand questions swimming around in my mind and it was difficult to make sense of it all. I'd no idea how I was going to get through the day, knowing I'd potentially stumbled across my father, but there was nothing I could do until Mum arrived.

'Alice, you have sisters,' Grace said softly.

This caused my heart to squeeze a little and I managed a glimmer of a smile. Keep calm, I told myself, crying softly into Grace's arms.

Chapter 31

'Wake up, wake up.' I felt myself being shaken lightly. I tried to create a gap between my upper and lower eyelids in a vain attempt to loosen the grip of the mascara holding them together. My head throbbed, and then I remembered. Last night, I'd drunk myself silly with Grace after discovering my mum was in touch with William Hall, a man whom we suspected was my father, a man who probably didn't even know I existed.

Finally, I prised my eyes open. 'What time is it?' I groaned, 'and where's the fire? It feels like I've only just gone to bed.'

'It's eight-thirty,' Grace stated, throwing me a pitying look. 'Hangover, by any chance?' She smiled kindly, placing a mug of tea by the side of my bed. 'Here, drink this, two sugars in there.'

'Eight-thirty, why the heck are you waking me up at this time?' I grumbled, pulling the duvet back over my head.

'You told me to,' she laughed. 'You have thirty minutes to get up, shower, dress and attempt breakfast.'

'No breakfast,' the very thought turned my stomach.

Grace chuckled as she left the room. 'Get up, Elsie and the quick step will be waiting for you.'

Elsie was unswervingly sweet, and at the age of sixty-five a bundle of fun. She was a small voluptuous woman with rosy cheeks who worked part time for Dorothy at The Old Teashop. Yesterday, her enthusiasm to learn her steps had been faultless, but a dancer she was not. By the end of the session her Latin ballroom satin sandals with a chunky heel had trodden on my own feet more times than I cared to remember. However, she looked the part in her racy red-sequinned dress. Elsie had proudly announced it had been purchased from last year's village-hall jumble sale and had been a bargain at three quid, which I couldn't argue with. But with its plunging neckline, it was a revealing little number and what you might class as risqué. I didn't think it was designed with a sixty-five-year-old woman in mind but Elsie was delighted with it and that's all that mattered.

This morning we were trying again to learn the quick step, an early-morning start before she began her shift at the teashop. I'd advised her to wear trainers; hopefully she'd taken my advice, as I wasn't sure my poor feet could withstand another bashing.

Slowly climbing out of bed, I risked a cautious look in the mirror and really wished I hadn't.

I felt dreadful, I looked dreadful. I'd fallen asleep in my

clothes, my hair was messy, my eyes were swollen and I wasn't going to win any beauty contests any time soon. As the shower water cascaded over my face my thoughts switched back to last night. Grace and I must have drunk at least two bottles of wine, and thankfully Grace had taken the iPad off me before I had a chance to drunkenly message Mum or William Hall.

Ten minutes later, I'd climbed inside some clean clothes, tied my hair back and ambled downstairs into the kitchen where Grace was tucking into buttery scrambled eggs on toast.

'There's plenty left, if you've got time.'

I shook my head, not able to face any food. 'Why did I drink so much?' I groaned.

'It always seems like a good idea at the time,' she mused.

After a quick drink of juice, I grabbed my heels and welcomed the outside breeze, heading towards the dance school.

'Good morning,' chirped Elsie, sounding a lot brighter than I felt. She was knocking back a large espresso. 'I've been practising all night.' She gave me a twirl on the step as I unlocked the door and pushed it open.

'Dedication, Elsie, that's what you've got,' I smiled at her and was thankful that after the brisk walk I was beginning to feel human again.

Elsie followed me into the foyer, hung up her coat and whipped out a mobile phone from her bag. 'It's my grandson's,' she said proudly, 'and I've borrowed it. He's shown me how to load apps and I've been stalking that Bruno Tonioli on Bluebird.'

'Twitter,' I chuckled.

'I told my Cecil, he needs to start this dancing lark. It would tone up that belly and bottom of his no end,' she sniggered dryly, rolling her eyes at me.

'He doesn't know what he's missing. C'mon, let's see how you've got on.' Before I had time to press play on the iPad, Elsie was already in position in the middle of the dance floor.

'Left-foot start,' I instructed, and Elsie mirrored my move.

'Back ... side close ... side ... forward ... side close and side.'

Elsie had been practising hard, her face radiated happiness as she danced the quick step in time, around the room.

'Oh my,' she breathed, when the music stopped, 'that felt amazing, I feel like a million dollars. You, young lady, should be proud of yourself.'

'Me? What have I done?'

'Brought a smile to all our faces.'

'You are more than welcome, Elsie. I'm just glad I could be of some help. Shall we do it again, but this time I'll lead as the male,' I suggested.

For the next few minutes we glided around the room. Elsie had come on in leaps and bounds, she was a different woman compared to yesterday.

'Nearly there,' I announced, side-stepping on my heels as the music began fading out, and that's when I became aware of two people standing in the doorway.

With one arm linked through Connie's and the other

leaning on his walking stick, Grandie bellowed, 'Bravo, Bravo,' smiling at us both, his eyes proud and tearful.

'What are you doing here?' I asked, switching off the music and hurrying over to greet them.

'Ted Parker, how are you?' Elsie was already smothering his cheeks in kisses. 'Your granddaughter is simply wonderful, spending so much time with us all to whip us into shape. A credit to you.'

'You looked wonderful, Elsie, simply dazzling.' Grandie's kind words caused Elsie to blush.

'And we hear you are going to be a judge at Village Day ... I hope you're going to be the kind one.'

'Always, Elsie! I'm looking forward to it.'

After a quick conversation, Elsie gathered up her belongings and left for her shift at the teashop, leaving me in a complete spin that Grandie was out of hospital.

'What are you doing here?' I asked again, flicking a glance between him and Connie.

'Fit for purpose again,' he laughed, unlinking his arm from Connie's. 'They let me out early for good behaviour and Grace told us you'd be here. So, we thought we'd look in on you on our way home.'

'But the doctor says he needs to take it easy,' Connie reminded him in a firm tone. 'Tell him, Alice, he needs to take it easy.'

Grandie didn't let me answer. 'Look at this place,' he waved his stick in the air, causing him to slightly wobble. 'You've done wonders, I've not set foot inside this place since ... since ...'

'Now don't go upsetting yourself, Ted,' Connie soothed, patting his arm.

'This school meant the world to my Florrie. Just then, when you were dancing, I could picture her, leading the class at the front of the room, just like you, Alice.'

I was overwhelmed by his compliment. His admiration was strong and being compared to Grandma made me feel worthy and joyful.

'You are a natural, so patient, bringing out the best in people. Look at me, silly old fool,' he said, dabbing his eyes with a hanky. 'I'm getting all emotional,' he continued.

'It's understandable,' I cut in. Seeing Grandie upset caused me to swallow down a lump in my throat. A couple of seconds ago I was lapping up his praise but in a split second my mouth was bone dry and I was beginning to feel fretful, as I thought about the lie I'd told. Grandie had been so kind to me, and had offered me a chance to turn my life around. And how had I repaid him? Instantly, my mood was dampened. This was not what I'd planned. I'd had it all mapped out in my head: time to prepare both him and my mum, to ease the reunion slowly.

But now he was out of hospital, the timing couldn't be any worse.

What the hell was I going to do now when Mum arrived?'

One thing I knew for sure was that the next twenty-four hours were crucial in saving my own relationship with Grandie, before my mum had even arrived.

Chapter 32

Ten minutes later Connie had driven Grandie back to Honeysuckle Farm and I began taking down all the old leaflets and exam timetables from the old cork pin-board in the entrance hall of the dance school. My stomach growled, hungry now after skipping breakfast.

Sam caught my eye through the front window of the dance school. He was standing on the other side of the road next to a recovery vehicle, chatting to a man with messy brown hair wearing a red checked shirt who was wiping his hands on an oily rag. Two brightly coloured leads trailed from Sam's car to the van, and the car's engine was revving. Sam must have sensed someone was watching him and he looked over. His smile lifted and widened, then he waved at me.

Once the man had disconnected the leads and packed up his van, he slapped Sam on his back, climbed into his vehicle and drove off. Sam hovered on the pavement for a split second before locking up his car and crossing over the road, heading straight for the dance school.

'All fixed?' I asked as the door swung open.

He exhaled with relief, 'Just a flat battery, and now it's fully recharged, thankfully.'

'We all need our batteries recharging at some time.' I sighed. 'You okay?'

'Hangover, tired and worried sick, in a nutshell. I bet you're glad you asked now.' I attempted a smile.

Sam pulled a baffled face. 'Sounds to me like you need cheering up.'

'I need food. I skipped breakfast and now the munchies have kicked in.'

'Then let me treat you to brunch, I know just the place,' he grinned.

After I'd locked up the dance school Sam drove the car towards the edge of town and parked it down a side street. The red neon sign above the door read 'Harry's Café' and visible in the window were a couple of plastic tables covered in wipeable gingham table cloths, accompanied by the usual brown and red sauce bottles.

'A greasy spoon – you can't beat a full English fry-up with a hangover,' he assured me with a twinkle in his eye. I followed Sam into the café and he pulled out a chair. 'The best seat in the house, the window seat.' He handed me a paper napkin which I placed on my lap.

'Such a gentleman.'

Sam ordered at the spotless aluminium counter that ran the full length of one wall, and exchanged jovial banter with the waitress behind the counter before returning to the table with a pot of tea to share.

'Do you come here often?' I asked playfully.

'Funnily enough, I do, usually on the way to the train station. It sets me up for the day. Now, what's up with you?'

'Nothing ... everything.'

'Typical woman, can't make her mind up.'

I laughed.

'That's better, she smiles – and a wonderful smile you have, too.'

My heart stuttered as I stared at him. He had the ability to make me feel good even when I didn't want to.

'I've got a few things on my mind,' I admitted, knowing that my life was going to come crashing down around my ears very soon. Try as I might, I couldn't push that worried, anxious feeling from my mind. 'Grandie is out of hospital and Mum is due to arrive.' But I didn't mention accidently coming across my father on Facebook.

'And have you taken on more than you can manage with *Brook Bridge Goes Strictly*?' He raised a worried eyebrow, pouring the tea.

I was thankful for the distraction. Choreographing the dance routines and bringing a smile to the WI ladies' faces had given me something good for the community to focus on. I hadn't known how enjoyable teaching could be until I'd been given this chance to do it.

'There's a lot to do with the staging and the costumes but it all seems to be coming together.'

'Good, the lads are coming over one night next week.'

'Excellent!'

Sam nipped to the bathroom, just before the waitress placed two full English breakfasts and a plate of granary toast on the table in front of me, which my stomach was extremely grateful for.

Out of the corner of my eye, I noticed a shadow lurking outside the café window, then met the stare of Ben, his cool eyes studying me intently. He pushed open the shop door and was now hovering at the side of the table, his face like thunder.

I smiled.

'For a minute there, I thought you were having breakfast with Sam Reid.'

There went my smile. That wasn't the greeting I was quite expecting. 'I am,' I replied coolly, wondering where this conversation was going.

'What are you doing with the likes of him?'

My mouth dropped open, 'Like we've just established, having breakfast.'

'You never returned my call.'

So that's what this is about, I thought. He felt dejected that I hadn't texted or rung him back.

'I've been busy,' I said, which wasn't strictly a lie. 'I'm working with Dorothy and the girls on the grand finale of Village Day. *Brook Bridge Goes Strictly*.'

He nodded his acknowledgement, which suggested he thought my answer was feasible.

'How about dinner tonight or a drink?' he pressed, his mouth doing a funny twitching thing while he waited for me to answer.

'I really haven't got the time, with the rehearsals and everything ... but thank you,' I added politely.

'But you've time for breakfast?'

I was beginning to feel a little uncomfortable in Ben's presence now. Why was he continuing to be like this? And where was Sam? I was willing him to hurry back.

'I have. I've just finished a dance session with Elsie and I'm taking a quick break.' Why did I feel the need to explain myself? The anger was beginning to furiously bubble inside me.

'His sort aren't good.'

'Ben, I don't want to hear it. Whatever your opinion is of Sam, it's not mine.'

The fury in his eyes flashed before me. To me it looked like Ben was jealous of Sam, resenting the fact that I was sharing breakfast with him. Once upon a time, Ben had been my friend, but how things had changed in thirteen years. He'd changed. I didn't recognise the kind, caring lad I once knew.

Judging by the tone of his voice and after spotting me having breakfast with Sam, it was safe to say he wasn't happy. I had a horrible feeling about the thunderous look in his eyes.

'You and Sam? Are you ... are you?'

'It's none of your business,' I replied curtly, daring a quick glance towards the door and hoping Sam would return.

'Does your grandfather know about this?'

'What, that I'm having breakfast in a café on the edge of town?' I knew I was being facetious but he was being pathetic.

'Maybe I should mention it. That's where I'm off to now, the farm.'

I heard the tenor of his breathing change. Inside I was beginning to shake with rage. Was he actually threatening me? Before I had time to answer, he huffily walked out of the café.

I blew out a breath.

The absolute horror of his suggestion caused my heart to race. What if he did mention it to Grandie? I had no idea how Grandie was going to react, but thinking about all the possibilities, my appetite diminished fast and I began to feel sick to my stomach. Ben's manner was quite disturbing, but surely he wouldn't stoop that low.

'Sorry I've been so long. My phone rang.' Sam settled back at the table, picking up the sauce bottle, oblivious to Ben's fleeting visit.

I was staring out of the window. Sam followed my gaze and then he saw him too – Ben striding away, with his hands pushed deep into his pockets.

'Sam, I'm sorry, but I have to go,' I said with urgency, knowing I needed to hotfoot it to Honeysuckle Farm.

'What have I missed?' asked Sam, giving me an incredulous stare.

Chapter 33

To say I was a nervous wreck was an understatement, as I loitered on the steps of the annexe. Knocking on the door, I waited anxiously for Connie to appear. Half of me was praying she was out, but her car was parked at the side of the barn and when I heard her whistling her way to the door my heart pounded faster. She greeted me with a full-on beam. 'Good afternoon. I'm glad you're here.'

'Are you?' I asked, wondering why.

'Don't look so worried,' she smiled, opening the door wide so I could step inside. 'I've managed to pick up numerous dresses for Village Day from the charity shop. With a few alterations and added sequins they will ooze glitz and glamour.' Connie was thrilled with her findings.

'Now, that is good news.'

'I'll bring them over to the dance school and get to work on them straight away once they've been tried on.'

'Connie, you're a star.'

I was touched and flattered that everyone was pulling together to support me. The community spirit was heartfelt – well, all except Ben, who seemed hell bent on causing me trouble.

We looked at each other. 'I do need to speak to you about Rose's arrival, though,' said Connie. She eyed me, 'In fact, you do look kind of pale. Everything's all right, isn't it? C'mon dear, it can't be that bad, a problem shared and all that.' Her kindness was overwhelming. 'Tea, we need tea.'

'Thanks, I'd love a tea. It's just been a bit of a dramatic morning.'

'Sit yourself down and you can tell me all about it.'

'I'm not sure you'd want to hear it,' I replied fearfully, offering a slight smile even though inside I was far from smiling.

Connie sat down opposite me. 'In fact, you go first,' I offered, quietly inhaling.

'Well, the thing is, I'm quite surprised, Alice,' she continued.

I knew what was coming. I sat quietly on the edge of my seat and sipped at my drink.

'Ted hasn't mentioned Rose's arrival at all. Half of me was thinking he'd have broached the subject by now, but I suppose he may feel uncomfortable talking about it, and I didn't want to press him. I'm sure he's worried and anxious about tomorrow. Maybe I'll talk to him about it tonight, once he's had his tipple of whisky and is settled back in at home.'

'No don't, you can't say a word to him,' the words tripped

out of my mouth before I could stop them. 'Promise me.' The turmoil flushed through my body.

Connie's eyes widened as she fixed her gaze on me.

By the look on her face, I could see that warning alarms were probably ringing loud and clear in her mind. 'I'm not liking the sound of this. Why wouldn't I mention it to Ted?'

'Because he doesn't know she's coming.'

She breathed out slowly, staring straight at me, then rubbed her hand up and down her upper arm, clearly not comfortable with the situation.

'He doesn't know she's coming?' repeated Connie, most probably hoping she'd misheard me the first time.

Shaking my head in shame, I said, 'I kind of lied.'

'There seems to be no "kind of" about it.' She was still staring at me.

Utterly ashamed, tears sprang to my eyes. 'I've told Mum that Grandie is asking to see her, that's why she's agreed to fly home.'

Connie's eyes never left mine. Her trembling hand rose to her forehead and she wiped her brow with the back of her hand. The look on her face was pure shock and disbelief. 'Let me get this straight, you've cajoled your mum here under false pretences.' Connie was beginning to sound impatient.

'I have to admit, it's not feeling like one of my better plans.'

'So, Rose has booked a plane ticket, not knowing the true facts. She's under the impression Ted is going to fling his arms open wide and welcome her home after all this time.'

'I don't think she's expecting everything to be hunky-dory

but ... pretty much so,' I admitted, feeling stupid and helpless. 'You never know, when they clap eyes on each other, all might be forgiven for whatever went on,' I said with a little bit of hope in my voice.

Connie cocked an eyebrow at me. 'So, what's the plan of action when Rose arrives tomorrow? How do you think she's going to react when she discovers Ted hasn't asked to see her and she's travelled all this way? It's not as if New York is just around the corner! And then what do you think Ted is going to do when he discovers Rose is here, and you've lied to them both? Alice, this situation goes back years and neither one of us knows the root cause of it. Some things are best left alone.'

'But how can any of this ever be sorted if they are in different countries?'

'What do you think this is going to do to your grandfather, and to Rose? He's only been out of hospital for a matter of hours.'

'I've not really thought that far ahead,' I admitted, feeling a pang of guilt.

'Obviously,' Connie sighed, 'it's not for us to meddle in anyone's business, and believe me, I know it's frustrating. I lost my best friend all those years ago but we need to respect their decisions – they might not want to sort it out. It's their choice, not ours. Yes, of course it would be fantastic if everyone got on, played happy families, but I think we need to face facts. The probability of that actually happening is low, especially after all this time.'

'But I don't want to give up on either of them and I want

to stay in England. And I can't do that if my mum is living in New York! I know I've lied, but can't you see how desperate I am?'

Connie seemed to take pity on me and squeezed my hand. 'I know your heart is in the right place. But you could jeopardise your own relationship with both of them, and what is Ted going to think of me? He's been good to me, always looked out for me and Grace. I'll tell you what I think – he'll think I've been a willing party in all this deception, especially when he discovers I've picked Rose up from the airport. He's going to know I knew about this little charade. How's it all going to look?' Her voice was now unsteady and full of anguish.

I nodded my head shamefully. 'I'll tell Grandie, I'll tell him it had nothing to do with you whatsoever,' I offered, swallowing down the lump in my throat and feeling absolutely dreadful about it all.

Connie sighed, 'We can't change it now and all we can do is try to handle this situation as best we can.'

I nodded in agreement, not trusting myself to speak.

'What I'm suggesting,' Connie carried on, 'is that we don't tell Ted tonight. Let him settle back in without any extra worry. He needs a good night's sleep in his own bed. Then once Rose has landed, she needs to know the truth and you need to own up to your grandfather.'

'Okay,' I said. 'I'm not sure how Mum is going to react either.'

'I can hazard a guess,' Connie answered in a slightly unsympathetic tone. 'But you need to be straight with her too. Tell her how much you want to stay here and how worried you are about her staying in New York. Whoever was right or wrong all those years ago, let's just hope that after the initial shock of them finding out they are both in the same village ...' Connie took a breath, 'you never know, a miracle may just happen.'

'Do you think?' I said, hopeful.

'I've no idea,' Connie said simply.

'I am sorry,' I said, feeling absolutely wretched about the whole situation. I'd played with fire and I knew I was about to get burnt. 'But there's another dilemma.'

'Go on ...'

'Sam.'

'Sam Reid?'

I nodded, feeling myself beginning to tremble. 'He's helping me out with Village Day. I managed to talk Dorothy round but I've not had a chance to talk to Grandie about it ... I've no idea how he feels about Sam and I was waiting until he was out of hospital and things had settled,' I took a breath, 'and we've been getting close,' I blurted. 'Ben doesn't like it, he's implied he's going to tell Grandie and I've no idea how he's going to react.'

Connie listened intently. 'Ben can be hot-headed at times,' she declared. 'But don't you worry about him, we'll figure it out.'

'Thank you,' I said gratefully. 'I'm sorry to have let you down.'

'You've done it for the right reasons. Let's sit tight and see what happens, wait until the morning.'

There was nothing else I could do now except exactly that, but I was grateful for Connie's reassurance and relieved to get it all out in the open. It was comforting to know that even though I may have got things wrong, I had both Connie and Grace for support.

Chapter 34

It was just past eight o'clock in the morning and I'd slipped out of Wild Rose Cottage before Grace was awake. I'd had a restless night, knowing that Mum was arriving today and I hadn't told Grandie yet. I'd promised Connie I would do it first thing this morning and time was ticking. It had been a hell of a couple of days and in need of some fresh air, I grabbed my coat and headed towards the fields at the back of Honeysuckle Farm for a brisk walk. An aeroplane soared through the clouds above and I knew Mum would be on her flight and Connie would be on her way to the airport. It was only a matter of time before I knew how all this was going to pan out, and at Honeysuckle Farm it felt as though everything was closing in and was about to buckle underneath me at any given time. I didn't like the uneasy feeling in the pit of my stomach that I'd no control over.

With the early morning sun shining on my face, I followed

the stream and glanced towards the church, its steeple towering above the top of the hill. The view was breath-taking and stretched out for miles. As a child, I remembered Grandie and Mum had taken me to the church a couple of times. After the service, I'd sat on the bench with Mum while Grandie had tended to a grave. The memory was hazy, as I'd only been small. Then a thought struck me: it must have been Grandma's grave. Having the sudden urge to find it, I powered my legs through the long grass and soon arrived at the entrance of the church. The graveyard was well maintained with bursts of colour sprouting from every aluminium pot standing in front of the headstones. The grass was neatly mowed and there were benches sporadically dotted around the paths. I remembered I'd been sat on a bench near the back of the churchyard by an old oak tree. Feeling the tears well up, I sauntered towards it. My plan was to search for Grandma's headstone from the far end, then walk horizontally across each row until I stumbled across it. If Grandma was here, then surely I would find her.

There were two figures in the distance, a man stooped over a gravestone clutching a small bouquet of flowers. He arranged them in the vase at the foot of the headstone.

There was an aching familiarity about him and my heart began thudding inside my chest and goosebumps prickled my skin when I recognised Grandie. Connie was standing by his side. I didn't understand why Connie was here. Shouldn't she be on her way to the airport to pick up Mum? Their heads were bent low and Connie's hand was resting on the small of Grandie's back. I was puzzled, had Mum changed her mind? Was she not arriving today? I went hot and cold in rapid succession and, not knowing what to do, I slid on to a nearby bench and watched them both, until they turned and slowly walked towards me.

'Hi,' I said, as they approached. My voice must have startled them.

Connie looked at me, followed by Grandie. His eyes were watery, he was visibly upset.

'I'm surprised to see you here,' I said, my eyes searching Connie's for answers.

'Jim's running an errand for me this morning.' She gave me a look and I read between the lines. He must have gone to the airport to pick up Mum. 'So I could accompany Ted here today.'

'Are you okay?' I asked, not really understanding what was going on. Grandie looked like he had the weight of the world on his shoulders.

With a slight hesitation, he spoke. 'Alice, why are you here?'

For a split second I debated what to say. 'I've never visited Grandma's grave, and something was telling me to come. I'm sorry, maybe I should have spoken to you about it first.'

He gave me a loving smile before Connie patted his arm. 'You two need to talk. I'll be over there,' she said. 'Give me a shout when you're ready to go.' We watched Connie trail off towards the entrance of the church. 'Shall we sit?' I offered.

Grandie nodded and I helped to steady him on to the bench.

'Is it Grandma you're visiting?' I asked tentatively.

'Yes,' he replied, 'today ...' he took my hand and held it tight, 'is our anniversary. We got married in this church.' He took a fleeting glance towards the steeple. 'People always say it's the best day of your life and I can't argue with that.' His voice quivered. 'I really wish things could have been different.'

'Me too, I would have loved to meet her.'

'Come on,' he said, pushing himself up by his walking stick, 'I'll show you where she is.'

We walked slowly in silence towards the spot where Grandie had been standing minutes earlier. He stopped and gestured to the well-kept grave, 'Here she is.' He smiled fondly towards the headstone.

Sadness crept through the whole of my body and my eyes shimmered with tears.

In Loving Memory of Florrie Rose Parker
Beloved wife of Ted Parker
Treasured mother of Rose Parker

He eased his hand into mine, 'I do miss her, you know. I miss them both.' His eyes slid briefly from mine and he gently let go of my hand.

I swallowed down a lump, 'Both? Do you mean Mum as well?'

He didn't answer.

'Talk to me, Grandie.' The frustration in my voice was loud and clear.

'I'm feeling tired,' he replied, 'let's head back to the farm.'

I exhaled. As much as I loved the stubborn old man, I was beginning to tire of being kept in the dark.

He turned and slowly walked towards Connie, who was waiting at the gate of the churchyard in the car.

I felt so exasperated about the whole situation. Mum and Grandie were both as obstinate as each other, holding on to their grudge because of their pride.

Connie drove us back to Honeysuckle Farm and the second the front door opened we were greeted by Marley, excitedly wagging his tail and padding around us in circles. Connie made haste into the kitchen to make tea but not before insisting I now tell Grandie of Mum's imminent arrival.

Scared, I caught sight of my deflated face reflecting back from the hallway mirror, then followed Grandie into the living room. We sat facing each other, Grandie in his favourite chair and I settled on the sofa, crossed-legged like I always used to sit when I was a little girl. I was fearful, an uneasy feeling swathed me. The mood was sombre and I knew that before I came clean I was going to press him once more for answers. His breathing was shallow and neither of us spoke for a moment. Then, taking a deep breath, I broke the silence.

'Just then, in the churchyard ... did you mean Mum?' I probed softly. 'You must miss her, tell me you miss her.'

He pressed a hand to his chest and his gaze fell to the floor.

'Of course I miss her. I've always missed her.'

This was the first time he'd admitted it to me, and I felt a sense of relief wash over me. Maybe there was a chance this could all be fixed?

Taking the plunge, I continued, 'There's something I need to say, Grandie.'

He looked up, 'What is it, Alice?'

'There's something inside me telling me it's the right thing for me to stay, here, in England. You have given me the most fantastic opportunity, and this place ... this place is my home.'

His eyes lit up.

'But ... like I've said before, I want Mum to come into the business with me, to move back to England and run the school like she used to.'

Grandie's face drooped and he remained silent.

'She's my mum,' I said nervously. 'How can I possibly choose between the two of you? I love you both, surely you understand that.'

I noticed a tear roll down his face.

'I'm sorry, I don't want you to be upset,' I said softly and I really didn't, 'but I know you can see the predicament I'm in. I need to offer this chance to Mum with your blessing, and then it's up to her if she accepts.'

Deep down, I think he knew that this would be the case. Panic swelled inside me at the pain. My heart was thundering in my chest and I could barely breathe, waiting for him to answer.

He dabbed his watery eyes again. He looked fragile, exhausted – had I pushed him too far? I could feel it inside, he was on the brink of telling me, I knew he wanted to tell me.

'What's going on?' I asked wearily. I was tired by this whole situation. 'Everything seems to be shrouded in secrecy and I think I'm the cause of it all.'

His eyes locked with mine, 'Dear Alice, you aren't the cause of anything. You have to believe me.'

I swallowed down a lump in my throat. 'I'm no detective, but I know that people fall out over either money or love. I know I asked the other day, but did your falling out have anything to do with my father?' It was the only thing that made any sense to me. 'Because I think I've found him.'

'You've found William?'

'On Facebook, Mum is friends with a William Hall. It may be a coincidence ... but ...'

'And what have you done about it?'

'Nothing ... as yet.' But it was on my list of things to discuss with Mum sometime in the next twenty-four hours.

'This situation had nothing to do with William. If only he'd been around, things may have been a lot different for your mum.'

I took the plunge, 'Grandie, she's coming back.' There – the words were out in the open.

Connie must have been listening, as she appeared at the door with a pot of tea which she placed on the table before slipping on to the settee next to me.

'Rose ... she's coming home?'

'Yes.'

His eyes lifted towards mine, 'When?'

'Today,' I said, my entire body shaking.

For a second there was silence in the room until Grandie began to weep.

'Here, have some tea,' said Connie, pouring a mug.

'Whiskey, I want whiskey,' he said, dabbing his eyes with his hanky.

Even though it was only just nine o'clock in the morning Connie didn't argue and hurried over to the decanter on the other side of the room.

Grandie took the glass from her, he didn't look at either of us but swirled the amber liquid in the glass and sniffed it, before taking a huge swig. Then he closed his eyes and rested his head on the back of the chair.

'Grandie, talk to me, I don't know what to do.' I felt helpless, the same feeling I'd felt as a little girl watching them argue. 'Shall we leave you alone?' I asked. It was breaking my heart watching him weep, and it was all my doing. Maybe I should have left well alone.

'Stay,' he'd lowered his voice to a whisper, 'both of you stay.' He slowly opened his eyes and gestured for Connie to sit back down.

'It's time,' he said, 'it's time you knew the truth – or my version of events, at least.'

As soon as Grandie said those words my throat became tight and I blinked back the tears. My lips trembled, and my hands were visibly shaking.

The adrenalin pumped through my body as I held my breath.

Chapter 35

As Grandie took a breath, I felt the reassuring touch of Connie's hand on my knee. Grandie drained the whisky from his glass and looked at us both.

I'd no idea what I was about to hear but my heart was pounding so fast I pressed a hand to my chest.

'I didn't want you to leave, you've got to believe me when I say that.'

Anxiety ran though my body. 'I know.' That was never in doubt.

'Florrie was my life, we were a close family unit. The day she died was the day my heart broke and it never mended. Of course, the pain eases in time but no one ever came close to what we had. The dance school was our passion, and our doors were well and truly open to everyone. Some great long-lasting friendships were made on that dance floor.' He took a fleeting glance towards Grandma's photograph on the sideboard before continuing.

341

'The night of Florrie's death,' he took a breath, 'we were attending the theatre. Florrie had been teaching over in the city that day and we'd arranged to meet outside the theatre with Rose and Connie.'

He dabbed his eyes once more as he cast his mind back.

'Rose was late and Connie and I decided to wait another five minutes in the foyer. It was the time before all this gadget lark, and we didn't know what was keeping either of them.'

Connie nodded in agreement. She knew what was coming next and plucked a tissue from her pocket.

'It was then we heard a screech,' Grandie said in a trance-like state, staring towards the window. 'And the bang.' He shuddered, 'People were screaming, and Connie and I rushed outside along with everyone else who'd been standing in the foyer.'

He was shaking, the tears freely flowing as he tried to mop them away with his hanky. 'She died, my wonderful Florrie died in my arms.' He was clearly distraught.

'You don't need to go on,' I said softly, feeling troubled by his pain.

'I do,' he took a moment to compose himself.

We all sat in silence for a minute before he spoke again. 'Connie, I think we all need a drink.' He tipped his head towards his empty whisky glass. Connie stood and placed a hand on his shoulder before carrying the decanter over to the coffee table. I watched as she poured out three drinks and I swigged mine back in record time, feeling the brown liquid burn the back of my throat. He'd clearly never ever got over my grandmother's death, but it still didn't explain the argument between him and my mum and why we'd had to leave.

'Florrie was killed by a stolen car. A man was arrested at the scene.'

'Oscar Bennett? The man in the newspaper.'

'That's right ... Oscar Bennett,' Grandie struggled to say his name. 'They say time is a good healer, but it's never ever healed where Florrie is concerned.'

Grandie looked pained and I felt my heart sink. I felt guilty and saddened that I was putting him through this, but I wanted to uncover the whole picture, for my own selfish reasons, and wasn't it time this situation was sorted out anyway?

'After Florrie, I didn't think I could go through any more hurt or pain. But then you came along and brought love and hope back into this family at the point when I was at my lowest. You came into this world on Florrie's birthday and I took that as a sign from Florrie. I know that sounds daft,' he smiled weakly. 'I can remember holding you for the very first time, you lay in my arms gurgling away and you looked just like her, the resemblance was so strong. I can remember breaking down and sobbing, knowing that she'd never set her eyes on something so precious ...' he caught his breath, 'and that's when I made you a promise that I would look after you forever, love you with all my heart and make sure no one ever hurt you.'

'So why, ten years later, was I whisked off to New York?' I probed.

He bent his head low. I knew I was pushing him, but I couldn't stop myself. I needed to know.

'I heard the argument, I was hiding behind the curtain in the room. You and Mum were shouting at each other. She'd let you down in some way and you said you were disappointed in her. What did she do that was so bad that you never wanted to see her again?'

The tears flowed fast and Connie took his hand and began to rub it gently. I could feel a terrible sadness bleeding through the room.

'Grandie, tell me. Why did we leave Brook Bridge?' I pushed some more, I wasn't giving up.

'Because ...'

My heart was pounding.

'Because ... I was driving the car that killed your Grandma.'

We all swung round to see Mum standing in the doorway.

A bolt of fear shot through me as the words registered, and my eyes widened with dread. 'No!' I gasped, my throat tight, and heaviness surged through my body. I didn't believe her, I didn't want to believe her.

'I'm so sorry, but it's true.' Mum looked defeated and slumped into the chair. Grandie was distraught.

In that split second my heart snapped in two. It had broken, just like Grandie's had when he'd lost Florrie.

The room fell silent.

All of us were now hurting for different reasons.

The truth was finally out and Mum was home. The two things I'd wanted most of all. But I knew nothing would ever be the same again.

Chapter 36

Mum was trembling, her face pained and her eyes blurred with tears.

'You've got to believe me, Alice, when I tell you I didn't mean for any of this to happen. The whole thing spiralled out of control that night.' Her voice was earnest.

I'd never felt so sick to my stomach in my life. I couldn't look at her and stared at the floor.

'What night?' I managed to say, my voice barely a whisper.

She took a second, then drew a breath. 'You've got to believe me when I say it was an accident,' she pleaded.

I'd no idea what to think, but remembering the newspaper article, I knew what she was saying couldn't be true ... could it?

'Why are you saying this? That man Oscar Bennett ... he killed Grandma. He went to prison, served time. You couldn't have killed her.' I dared to glance towards Grandie for understanding, but he didn't say a word and simply pressed a hanky to his eyes.

'Because he took the blame for me.'

I was confused and flicked a glance towards Connie, and the look on her face showed that she knew absolutely nothing about this.

'Why would anyone take the blame and allow themselves to go to prison for a crime they didn't commit? No one in their right mind would do that.' I said.

Mum was crying, her hands visibly shaking. 'I'd been dating a man named William who was emigrating to Australia. He's your father, Alice.' She gave me a weak smile. 'A lovely man, from a great family,' she paused. 'I was frightened, being pregnant on my own and before I dated William, I'd had a few dates with Oscar. Shamefully, I'd convinced Oscar he was the father of my baby, but it simply wasn't true. Looking back, I don't even know why I'd said such a thing, but I was young and pregnant and frightened, and once it was out there I couldn't take it back. Oscar and his brothers were a bad sort, had fallen into the wrong crowd, and his petty crimes were already beginning to escalate out of control. Once he knew I was pregnant he promised me he would give up all his criminal activity for me and the baby's sake, but of course his promises were empty. I'd got in way too deep, over my head, and I even began to feel frightened of him and his friends.'

I couldn't take my eyes off my mum as she spoke, this was all so surreal.

'The night in question, I was walking to the theatre when

Oscar pulled up alongside me in a stolen car. He'd that menacing look in his eyes, one I'd become frightened of. I'd decided that was it, I wanted out. I remember screaming at him to leave me alone, that it was over between us, but he just laughed at me. The next thing I knew, he'd jumped into the passenger seat and tossed me the keys through the open window and ordered me to climb in. I'd begun to walk away, but then he was suddenly out of the car. He grabbed me, pushing me into the driver's seat. I was petrified, pregnant, and knew if I fought back there was a risk you'd get hurt … or worse.

'It was at that very moment I knew I'd made a huge mistake pretending the baby was his. Why had I been so stupid? I knew that with Mum and Dad's support I could bring up the baby myself. It wasn't as though I even liked him that much. I knew I loved William but there was nothing I could do, he was gone. Hooking back up with Oscar had been a kneejerk rebound action and the biggest mistake of my life.'

Mum paused and swigged back a glass of whisky from the table. 'He told me I had to drive to meet his friends who were waiting for the stolen car in a lay-by. I did begin to drive but had no intention of driving anywhere near the lay-by. Five minutes later Oscar realised I was heading in the wrong direction.

'He demanded to know where I was going and when I told him I was heading for the police station he began shouting at me and grabbed the wheel. I told him to let go, but he wouldn't. So, I tried to scare him and pushed my foot harder on the accelerator and the car sped faster. He was shouting so loudly at me, screaming in fact, and I was about to blurt out that the baby wasn't his when I lost control of the vehicle and it mounted the pavement outside the theatre. And that's when I knew I'd ... I'd hit something ... someone.

'You have to believe me when I say I didn't mean to, it was an accident. My whole world came crashing down the second I saw Mum lying on the ground. I was in shock, I screamed and screamed.'

Mum buried her head in her hands and sobbed.

My whole world plunged into despair and reality hit me. I couldn't believe what I was hearing. Listening with absolute horror, I felt battered, bruised and physically sick. My whole body was shaking. 'But why didn't you get arrested? Why did he go to prison?'

'He went to prison because of you.'

'Me, why me?' I looked between all of them and waited for her to speak.

'Because he thought I was carrying his baby. I didn't tell him you weren't his. He didn't want me having a baby in prison. No one saw us get out of the car. Everyone was trying to help Mum, and when the police arrived he held up his hands and said it was him driving.'

'Why didn't you own up to it there and then?' I asked, my stomach churning.

'I was too scared. I panicked and just went along with it.'

I turned towards Grandie. 'Did you know she was driving the car?'

The colour had drained from his face, he looked exhausted. 'Not until Oscar had served ten years in prison and was released.'

I gasped and turned back towards Mum. 'You kept this all to yourself for all that time? How the hell did the truth finally come out?'

Connie cupped her hand around mine and Grandie picked up the story: 'When Oscar was released from prison he came here, to this house, demanding to see you. It was the first I knew that Rose had spun him a story. I knew William was your father, but Oscar tried to take you, wanted to claim custody of you. He thought he'd missed out on ten years of your life.'

'And you never thought to tell him, in all those years when he was serving time in prison, that I wasn't his.'

Mum took a deep breath, 'I never went near him in all that time. I didn't even visit. I wanted it all to go away. I couldn't live with what I'd done. Every day was a struggle. I was hoping he would forget.'

'He was hardly going to forget, was he? He served time for a crime he didn't commit.'

'He wasn't entirely innocent. He'd stolen the car in the first place, he forced me into it.' She took another breath, 'I know it doesn't excuse any of my behaviour ... but when he turned up here after all those years, I had to come clean. I couldn't risk him taking you. When I did tell him the truth he was angry, vile and threatening. He made it clear I was going to pay for what I'd done to him, and that's when I got scared, because he knew people ... people that you wouldn't want to meet down a dark alley.'

'And when Grandie discovered you were actually driving the car that killed Grandma, that's when you argued. He told you to get out,' I added.

'I knew I had to run and far away. I didn't want Oscar tracking me down, hurting me or you. I put a pin in the map and that's when we started a new life in New York. I was praying he couldn't find us there.'

Mum held my gaze through her tears. 'I thought New York would be the answer. I was hopeful we would set up a similar business out there ... a dance and drama school. I never realised it would be such a struggle or that we'd be so unhappy. Karma. I'm not proud of what I did, it haunts me every day. My careless actions lost me the mum I loved so dearly, and then I ended up losing my dad after devastating his life too. I spent the next few years looking over my shoulder and never letting you out of my sight, until I learnt Oscar Bennett had died a few years ago – a car accident on the M6.'

Mum turned towards Grandie. 'Please, Dad, I've no idea how I can ever put any of this right. I've hurt you so much and "sorry" doesn't even come close, but I am sorry, I really am.'

He looked between us both, his eyes were blurred with tears. He'd lost everything through no fault of his own and here we all were, sitting in the same room, finally with no more secrets to uncover.

'I've missed you so much, Dad and ... and I want to come

home, I want to come home to Honeysuckle Farm. If you'll have me ...'

Silence hung in the air.

Both of us were looking towards Grandie. Inside I was praying he would find it in his heart to allow Mum to come home, but I knew this was extremely difficult for both of them to come to terms with.

Finally, he spoke: 'I'm not saying any of this is going to be easy ...' He looked straight into Mum's eyes, 'I can never forget what happened that night or what happened ten years later, but I can learn to forgive.'

I exhaled, but Mum remained silent.

'Does this mean ...?' I whispered.

'You're my daughter, Rose, and I've missed you.'

Mum gasped, the tears were free-falling down all our faces and a sense of relief flooded the room.

'I am truly sorry, Dad, really I am.'

'I know,' he said, 'you've held on to all these secrets for all of these years, and the pain it's caused has torn this family apart. The lies and the deceit must have haunted you as much as they did me, but then to take Alice away from me too ...'

She nodded regretfully, 'I was scared, so scared. I'm sorry Alice, I really am.' She turned towards me, 'I hope over time you find it in your heart to forgive me. I know none of this is easy.'

Looking at the despair and hurt in her eyes, I knew everyone had suffered.

'I hope so too.'

Grandie mopped his brow with his hanky, profound sadness and tiredness engraved on his worn face. It was only now I understood the depth of pain that had been sitting below their skin for the last thirteen years. As the nausea swirled in my empty stomach and my heart struggled to keep a steady beat, I knew the black cloud that hung over us had lifted slightly, but we all had a long way to go to make peace with the past.

Chapter 37

Sam opened his front door, raked his fingers through his unruly hair and gasped.

'Alice ... you look ...'

'Dreadful,' I interrupted, knowing my eyes were swollen from crying and my face was blotchy. 'Here, open this,' I thrust a bottle of red wine into Sam's hand.

'I know it's still early but it's been a hell of a morning. I know ... and when I say I know, I mean I know everything. Mum's back from New York and everything is out in the open.'

'Come on in,' Sam said without hesitation, opening the door wide.

I'd left Mum up at the farmhouse with Grandie. They needed some time together to talk things through, and I needed to see Sam. He'd been treated unfairly in all this and after speaking some more with Mum and Grandie, I'd told them about my friendship with Sam and how some of the villagers had been treating him. It wasn't only our own family that had been affected by the secrets.

'What's happened?' he asked, taking my coat from me and hanging it up on the hook.

'There's more to this story than meets the eye. Go and pour us both a glass of wine, I think we are going to need it.' Sam looked intrigued and without saying a word took the bottle into the kitchen.

A few moments later, we both settled on the sofa. 'So,' he said, entwining his fingers around mine and looking deep into my eyes, 'what's happened?'

'The stolen car that killed my grandma – Oscar wasn't driving it.'

Instantly, Sam's jaw dropped. 'You must have got that wrong.'

I shook my head.

'I don't understand, Oscar went to prison, he confessed. If he wasn't driving the car, then who was?'

I blew out a breath, 'My mum.'

Sam gasped, his eyes widened. 'I wasn't expecting that.'

'Me neither. Drink your wine, let me tell you the whole story.'

For the next ten minutes, I told Sam everything. He listened in silence and when I'd finished he let out a low whistle.

'The heartbreak and secrets that have been kept hidden for years ...' he said. 'How are you feeling about it all?'

'Battered, bruised, exhausted but relieved it's finally out in the open. Even though Grandie and Mum have a long way to go, bridges to build et cetera ... I'm sure they'll get there.'

He nodded, 'In time.'

'I'm so sorry you've been hurt by this.'

'Me?' Sam sipped his wine.

'The way some of the villagers have treated you because of my family's lies and secrets.'

'Come here,' he pulled me in close, 'I'm just glad you've finally got the answers you need.'

'I always thought they'd fallen out over money or because my father was a crook or something. But, out of all this I've discovered my dad was actually a pretty good man and goes by the name of William Hall.'

'Is she still in touch with him?'

'Bizarrely, she'd discovered him on Facebook only a matter of weeks ago and had been deliberating what to do about it. So, before I came round here, I sat with Mum and Grandie and we decided the best way forward was to have no more secrets, get everything out in the open, and we composed a message to him. Mum has finally been able to tell him he has another daughter.'

'And?'

'And as yet, there's been no reply. I'm hoping that's down to the time difference. We'll just have to wait and see.'

'How are you feeling about that?'

'If I'm truly honest, I've no idea what to expect. I suppose a mixture of excitement and trepidation. I'll take each day as it comes. It's all I can do.'

He gave me a sheepish grin, 'So does this change how you feel about staying in England now?'

'We talked about it and the dance school ...'

'C'mon, the suspense is killing me.'

'I'm definitely staying in England,' I answered, my heart swelling with happiness as I noticed the beam hurtle across Sam's face.

Sam squeezed my hand, 'I've kind of been hiding a little secret of my own,' he confessed.

My eyes were now firmly fixed on him.

'Which is?' Every nerve in my body tingled.

He looked at me with the most kissable smile. 'Recently, there's been this woman, with a funny American accent who likes dressing in her PJs to buy bottles of milk ...'

'Loungewear,' I corrected with a goofy grin.

'I believe you, thousands wouldn't ... as I was saying ... she came into my life when I was least expecting it. She's warm, and definitely funny in her loungewear ... and I'm glad she's decided to stay in England, in Brook Bridge ...'

'Any particular reason why?' I teased.

He stretched his arms out towards me and I snuggled into his embrace.

'You're beautiful, Alice Parker. I think it's safe to say you've danced your way into my life, straight to my heart.'

I gave him a playful swipe, 'No cheesy chat-up lines, please.'

'I was being serious,' he said, cocking an eyebrow and laughing heartily before dipping his head and brushing his lips against mine.

Sam slowly stood up and, holding my hand, he led me slowly up the stairs and into his bedroom. I couldn't wait a moment longer to be wrapped up in his arms. It felt so right being with him. The moment he lay me on the bed we began kissing, slowly and softly at first but then with urgency. His kisses left me wanting more. Pressing my body against his, I ran my hands over his smooth warm skin and basked in the pleasure of his touch as he gently removed my blouse. I could feel his hardness against my thigh as I wriggled out of my jeans, my lips never leaving his.

'You are beautiful,' he whispered, kissing my neck and making me gasp.

'Sam Reid, you are perfect, now stop talking.'

'You don't have to tell me twice.'

Two hours later, I stirred, taking a moment to realise where I was. The bright-red lights from the clock said it was just past 4 p.m. Sam's strong arms were tightly wrapped around my body and I smiled to myself. An overwhelming feeling of happiness gushed through my body as I nestled in deeper while kissing him lightly on his chest.

'Mmm, are you awake?'

'Maybe,' I whispered, stroking his chiselled chin gently.

'You've worn me out,' he hitched a smile, lacing his hands through my hair then tilting my lips towards his.

As the kiss ended, he cradled my face in his hands. 'I'm falling for you, Alice Parker.'

'That's good to know,' I kissed him softly back.

I was the happiest girl alive.

Chapter 38

I didn't mind waking up to an empty bed, especially when the aroma of sizzling sausages greeted me. Throwing back the duvet and pulling Sam's faithful sloppy sweater over my head, I padded downstairs and slipped my hands around his waist.

The table was set, and he was standing at the cooker preparing breakfast, looking utterly gorgeous as usual.

'I could get used to this,' I smiled, squeezing him tight.

'It's a big day today, how are you feeling?'

I smiled, the last two weeks had been bedlam but there was no denying I'd enjoyed every second of it. Not only had I put the WI ladies through their paces but I'd chosen new colour schemes for the dance school, ordered a new sign to be erected outside, and next week there was a brand-spanking-new computer system about to be installed. It had been over a week since Mum's arrival and she'd now moved into

Honeysuckle Farm and everything seemed to be going from strength to strength. The past couldn't be changed but we all had the future to look forward to.

In such a short time, I couldn't wish for anything more. Since arriving in England my life felt complete, once more I had a purpose, something to focus on and work towards. I was going into the family business with Mum and both of us couldn't be happier about that. Things were about to change for the pair of us. I'd permanently moved in with Grace, renting her spare room at the cottage, but was spending more and more time at Sam's. I was truly happy.

'I just need to decide what to wear,' I answered with a smile, mentally flicking through a number of options. 'I can't make my mind up.'

The ladies of the WI were all meeting at the dance school around three, with the grand finale beginning on the main stage on the village green at 4 p.m. Their dresses hung ready on the clothes rail with their shoes neatly stacked underneath. They'd worked so hard in the last fortnight. No one had missed a practice and their feet hadn't touched the ground – literally. Connie had undertaken a magnificent job sourcing all the costumes from the charity shops and the local haberdashery had provided all the sparkle and sequins to transform the outfits into utter gorgeousness. Everyone in the community had pulled together.

Yesterday, I'd spent time with Bert, perfecting his dance routine and putting him through his paces one last time before he twirled his beloved Dorothy of fifty years around that stage in front of all their friends and family. We'd even managed to sneak in a quick shopping trip to purchase a suit. Bert looked distinguished and handsome in his tuxedo and bow tie. His face beamed as he swung his carrier bag with pride and he couldn't thank me enough.

Bert's secret was still safe. Dorothy had no idea that she would be opening the show.

As I sat down at the table, Sam handed me a cuppa while I flicked on to my iPad. I noticed that Molly had uploaded some new photos from a radio-station bash. I'd feared the moment I'd FaceTimed her to share the news that I was staying in England. I'd miss her dreadfully, but as good friends do, she'd said all the right things to me. She was happy if I was happy but we had both been tearful. I'd ended the call with an overwhelming feeling of sadness, knowing it was unlikely I'd ever return to New York permanently. We'd promised to keep in touch and she'd hinted that next time she took a vacation, she would consider England.

Sam took the plates out of the oven and placed them on the table. 'Here, eat up, you're going to need your strength today.'

'This all looks very impressive, maybe I should come for breakfast more often,' I smiled.

'Maybe you should.'

My stomach exploded into a hundred fireflies at the very thought of spending more time with Sam. In such a short time we'd become inseparable, spending every spare minute together.

We tucked into a hearty breakfast accompanied by Bucks Fizz. Sam had really gone to town, spoiling me. And just as we'd finished and begun to clear the dishes away, the front doorbell rang out, taking me by surprise.

'You get that,' he smiled, throwing a bunch of keys towards me. Opening the door, I was greeted by a delivery man who was hiding behind an enormous bouquet of blooms and a huge parcel.

'A delivery for Alice Parker,' he announced chirpily.

'Thank you,' I answered, surprised by the gorgeous scented flowers, yet puzzled by the cardboard box which wasn't particularly heavy. Who would send me flowers and gifts here, when I lived next door, I thought, mystified.

Closing the door in wonderment, I stared at the parcel. There was a printed label on the front but no return address on the back. Laying the blooms down on the bottom stair, I eagerly began to open the box. Inside, the contents were hidden beneath delicate ivory tissue paper and on top was a card which I turned over, my heart skipping a beat.

'Wow, someone loves you,' Sam grinned, standing in the doorway of the kitchen.

I read the card out loud: *'Good luck for today, you are simply the best, Sam xx'*

Clutching the card to my chest, I said, 'This is so beautiful and thoughtful.' Swelling with happiness then trembling with excitement, I unfolded the tissue paper and lifted the most exquisite dress out of the box. My eyes were brimming with happy tears. It was a simple dress, made from a shimmery violet satin, gathered at the waist with a satin band that floated to my ankles elegantly. The soft scoop neckline, sewn with sparkles and sequins, shimmered in the light.

'I don't know what to say, it's stunning.'

Sam took the dress from my hands and held it up against me. I twisted my hair, scooping it up on top of my head before letting it fall back to my shoulders. 'What do you think?'

'Absolutely perfect. You've worked so hard for today.' He pressed a light kiss on my forehead. 'You deserve to look like a million dollars.'

Even though I wasn't wearing the dress yet, I already felt like a million dollars.

'Everyone is excited for the finale and that's all down to you. You've co-ordinated the event, taught the WI to dance, organised the troops, the backdrop and the costumes.' He laid the dress back in the box and pulled me in close.

'And saved the village from Mr Cross's ukulele!' I added, and we both laughed.

'There is that, which I'm sure the village is eternally grateful for.'

Wrapped in Sam's arms, he whispered to me softly, 'I adore you and I'm glad you boarded that plane from the Big Apple and came into my life.'

'I'm glad I did too.' I snuggled in close, feeling safe and content in his arms.

Tilting my face upwards, Sam gazed into my eyes then kissed me so tenderly, sending shivers down my spine.

'You've made me the happiest man ever.'

My heart burst with happiness.

'Have we got time for ...?' he tipped me a cheeky wink.

'Er, no! It's a busy day!' I needed to check on the staging, make sure the backdrop was in place and transport the chairs from the dance school to the village green. 'As much as I'd love to climb back into bed with you, there's no time! There's so much to do.'

'Spoilsport!' He gave me that lopsided smile and his eyes sparkled as he tugged at my sleeve.

'Don't give me that look, you know I can't resist that look.'

'That was my plan.'

Sam was gorgeous. I pulled him back up the stairs, another fifteen minutes wouldn't hurt ...

All along the High Street the triangular coloured bunting weaved between the lamp-posts and flapped in the light breeze. The weather was perfect, the sun was shining and only a few clouds were dotted sporadically in the cobalt sky.

Mum and I followed the arrows on the makeshift cardboard signs hammered in the front gardens of the residents that pointed towards the village green. Sam was going to follow us down later on this afternoon. My dress was hanging alongside all the others in the dance school. We'd decided it was best if we hot-footed it over there at the last minute to get changed.

The village green was unrecognisable. Small huts bursting with colour lined the streets all the way around the green, selling items of necessity as well as luxury. We paused to look at the jewellery, the trinkets and then a little further up I spotted Bert. The Old Teashop's stall was abundant with the most delicious cakes, pasties and sausage rolls laid out on a red-dotted tablecloth. He was shovelling cup-cakes inside paper bags and handing them out to the excited children, who were eagerly waiting for a taste. He glanced up over the crowd and caught my eye, giving us a wave above his head.

'Where's Dorothy? Is she with you both?'

'Currently having her hair done,' I shouted over. Bert tipped his cap in acknowledgement and we carried on walking.

'It's good to be back. I've missed this,' she admitted.

'Me too,' I said, linking my arm through hers and finally feeling a part of a community once more.

We weaved our way through the hustle and bustle towards the far end of the green where a small crowd was gathered. I couldn't help but chuckle when I noticed Mr Cross standing there, dressed in gaudy clothes with a small group of excited toddlers jumping and squealing at his feet to the sound of his ukulele.

There were jugglers, stilt walkers and bouncy castles. Families were sprawled out on picnic rugs, eating sandwiches and enjoying a small tipple in the afternoon sunshine.

I was beginning to feel a little anxious about the grand finale as we ambled towards the main stage but all fears were soon eradicated when I noticed Grandie standing next to Jim admiring their own handiwork.

'Grandie,' I shouted and he spun round. 'Just look at this.' I couldn't believe my eyes, the sparkly backdrop was magnificent. '*Brook Bridge Goes Strictly*,' I read, '*Presented by Alice Parker.*' There was my name up in lights, something I'd always hoped for.

'I'm so proud of you, Alice,' Grandie hugged me and then gestured towards the judging table. 'What do you think?' The long trestle table was covered in a crisp white tablecloth and the seats were covered with shimmering violet sashes, the same colour as my dress. Feeling all warm and fuzzy inside, I knew Sam had thought of that special touch.

'Oooh, look,' exclaimed Mum, holding up a number paddle. 'I feel all important!'

'We need to set up the sound system, then if you're free for coffee and cake ...?' asked Grandie.

'Sounds perfect, see you back here in half an hour,' I said, glancing at my watch.

Mum and I carried on walking, enjoying the jovial atmosphere.

'Candy-floss, it's been years since I've had candy-floss.' She delved into her pocket and handed the loose change over to the man in exchange for two bags.

'That was your phone,' I said, already stuffing the pink fluffy mixture into my mouth. 'It just beeped.'

Mum's eyes were fixed on the screen.

'Facebook message.' At first her face was one of blind panic, then the corners of her mouth began to lift and she blew out a breath.

'Is everything okay?' I asked.

'I think so. I hope so,' she turned the phone towards me.

'Take a look. We have a word from William,' she spoke softly.

'We do? And ...?' I asked, lifting an eyebrow.

'Like I said, take a look.'

Shielding the phone screen from the sun, we stopped walking. My heart raced as I scanned the message. 'He wants to see me, he actually wants to come and see me.'

William's message was long. After receiving the news about my existence, he'd been shocked but also saddened that he'd missed out on twenty-three years of my life. He was married with two daughters and immediately he'd shared the news with them.

'They all want to meet me.' The relief was immense.

'I know, it's marvellous news. How are you feeling?' Mum held me at arm's length to gauge my reaction.

'Stunned and amazed. I'm happy, happy we are all back together and excited that I'm going to meet my dad. I don't think I could ever wish for a more perfect day.'

Mum pulled me in close, 'I'm sorry about the past. If I could change it, you know I would.'

'Mum, you don't have to say anything. The future is what we have to look forward to. The opening of the school, working together in our own business and enjoying Grandie's company.'

'Happy ending,' Mum breathed.

'Happy ending.' I fell into her arms and we held each other tight.

Chapter 39

We were all gathered at the side of the stage. The WI ladies looked stunning, their dresses were extravagant, their make-up perfect and their hair styled. We'd Lisa to thank for that from the local salon, who volunteered her services free of charge. All the ladies were thrilled when they'd been partnered up with the handsome men from the cast of *Mamma Mia*. The boys had been fantastic and for the last forty-eight hours had been at the girls' disposal.

'I feel like I'm floating on air,' exclaimed Dorothy, 'look at this dress ... but where is my Bert? He's going to miss me dance if he doesn't get a move on.'

'He'll be here,' I reassured her with a smile, knowing he was hiding out in the craft stall, waiting for his cue to appear on stage.

Then over the tannoy Jim's voice boomed: 'Ladies and gentlemen, boys and girls, please take your seats for the grand finale. The show will begin in five minutes.'

Immediately the footsteps of the crowd began thundering towards the rows of chairs in front of the stage. In a matter of seconds they were filled, virtually everyone from Brook Bridge was here.

Jim gave me the thumbs up and my heart was beating in double time.

We were ready to start.

'Live from the green, please put your hands together and welcome your host ... Miss Alice Parker! This is *Brook Bridge Goes Strictly*!' Jim's voice boomed from the microphone, followed by the *Strictly Come Dancing* theme tune playing out through the speakers over the audience. Everyone in their seats clapped along to the beat and when Jim handed me the microphone I skipped up the steps and on to the stage to the sound of enthusiastic applause.

There wasn't a spare seat to be seen, but where was Sam? I couldn't spot him anywhere.

Feeling a million dollars and like a celebrity, I brought the microphone up to my mouth: 'I'm Alice Parker and welcome to *Brook Bridge Goes Strictly*!' I opened my arms wide and everyone cheered. The atmosphere was electrifying and goose-bumps prickled my skin.

'Please welcome your judges for the evening, Grace Anderson! Connie Anderson! Rose Parker and, last but not least, Ted Parker!'

Everyone was out of their seats cheering all four of them as they appeared on the stage, giving everyone a wave before taking their seats on the judging panel.

The crowd were one hundred per cent behind us and it was an amazing feeling to be standing up there in front of them all.

'Our ladies of the WI have been locked away in the dance school for the last two weeks and now it's time for them to come out of the shadows and into the *Strictly* spotlight.' I took a breath, 'But first, we open the show with a very special dance ...' I could hear hushed whispers from the ladies at the side of the stage; they had no idea what was going on.

'We all know Dorothy and Bert Jones. They've been part of this community for a lifetime, serving us on a daily basis at The Old Teashop. Today they are celebrating their golden wedding anniversary and Dorothy thought she would be twirled around the stage by one of our professional dancers tonight. But in fact we have a very special surprise for her. Please come up on to the stage, Dorothy.'

All the WI ladies gently shoved a surprised Dorothy towards me. She'd no idea what was going on. 'And please welcome Bert on to the stage.' The crowd erupted in applause.

Dorothy gasped as she set eyes on Bert, who was making his way towards us clutching a bouquet of flowers, looking extremely handsome in his tux and bow tie, with his hair swept to the side.

He kissed Dorothy on the lips and handed her the flowers.

'I can't speak, I'm all emotional.' She flapped her face with her hand.

Bert hugged her.

'Mind my dress, I don't want it creased.'

The crowd laughed.

'We have another surprise for Dorothy. Her dream was to dance the foxtrot in front of you all, but little does she know, for the past two weeks, Bert has been a student of mine and tonight he's going to dance on stage with his beautiful wife! Please put your hands together for Bert and Dorothy dancing the foxtrot!'

The shock on Dorothy's face said it all as she handed me the flowers.

'I can't thank you enough, Alice. You've made my wish come true.'

Nervously, they took their positions centre stage and the music filtered across the green. Bert began to twirl Dorothy around the stage, every step perfection, elegance at its finest. Not once did they take their eyes off each other, the admiration and love they had for each other clear to everyone watching. When the music came to an end they fell into each other's arms as the applause rippled across the green.

Walking back on to the stage, I was brimming with emotion, there wasn't a dry eye in the crowd. Dorothy and Bert were still wrapped in each other's arms, tears of happiness rolling down their cheeks.

'Happy anniversary,' Bert whispered, 'I love you.'

'Listen to that crowd!' I exclaimed.

Both of them turned and gasped.

'How are you feeling?' I held the microphone towards Dorothy.

'I'm speechless, absolutely speechless.'

'For the first time in fifty years!' Bert chipped in with a loving smile.

She swiped him playfully, 'Where did you learn to dance like that?'

Bert wiped away his own emotional tears with a hanky and took the microphone from my hand. 'Can I just say how beautiful my Dorothy looks tonight?'

Once more the crowd cheered. 'I've been married to this wonderful woman for fifty years and I wouldn't change it for the world. Her wish was to dance on this very stage and thanks to Alice ...' his eyes twinkled towards me, 'thanks to Alice, that dream has come true. Alice put me through my paces, taught me to dance and I ... we can't thank you enough.'

With such a heartfelt thank-you I was overwhelmed and had to do everything in my power not to let my own happy tears cascade down my face. I was touched by Bert's words, they meant an awful lot to me.

Grandie caught my attention from the judging table and I shushed the crowd. Dorothy and Bert were still standing centre stage. 'We've just had word ... the scores are in!'

Everyone switched their gaze towards the judging panel.

'Let's go to Grace Anderson first,' I announced.

Grace beamed back at us. 'That was incredible! The crowd are going mental! Firstly, can I begin by saying your sparkly dress, Dorothy ... stunning! And secondly, you two smoulder when you dance. Happy golden wedding anniversary to you both!'

We moved along to Connie. 'You really came into your own ... watching you dance was an absolute treat. There was tension in the arms, a beautiful oval shape on the basic step ... Loved it!' chirped Connie.

Mum's opinion was next. 'For me ... exact timing, you hit that beat in sync. Excellent performance – you were here to dance!' added Mum.

Dorothy and Bert beamed, enjoying every moment.

'Now over to you, Ted!' I said, with a huge smile.

Once more the crowd hushed, waiting for Grandie to speak.

I noticed the wicked glint in his eye.

'The footwork was sloppy, you needed more rotation in the hips ...'

The crowd booed.

'I'm only playing the pantomime villain ... You were both A-M-A-Z-I-N-G!'

The crowd went wild.

'Let's see your scores,' I laughed.

'Ten!'

'Ten!'

'Ten!'

'Ten!'

All four judges held up their paddles and the crowd were on their feet.

'We've got a standing ovation!' Dorothy's face glistened with tears. 'I love you, Bert ...' They both stepped down from the stage, truly happy.

* * *

Forty minutes later, the rest of the WI danced their way through their own routines and by the look on everyone's faces, no one wanted the night to end. Everyone was having a fantastic time and after the last dance, I stood on the stage and was feeling immensely proud of what everyone had achieved. Two weeks ago, the ladies of the WI had struggled to put one foot in front of the other, and here they all were now, dancing like professionals around the stage on Village Day. Over the course of the evening I'd kept scanning the crowd but couldn't spot Sam anywhere and I was beginning to feel a little anxious, wanting to share this successful night with him.

It was time to close the show and, taking a deep breath, I brought the microphone to my mouth one last time: 'I want to thank everyone for coming this evening, and what a splendid night it's been. I've thoroughly enjoyed myself and I hope you have too.'

I was taken by surprise as the crowd began to chant, 'Dance, dance, dance, dance.'

I stared out over the sea of faces and then towards the table of judges who were all on their feet. Nerves shimmered in the pit of my stomach.

Stay focused, stay professional, the words whirled around in my head. Dance with who? What was going on?' Mystified, I looked towards Grandie, who grinned back at me. Suddenly I was aware of a man walking on to the stage. His suit was exquisitely cut and well fitted. I gawped at him, his black satin lapels were perfection alongside his black bow tie. I wondered where he'd parked his Aston Martin. Sam looked like a movie star. The raw chemistry that ignited every time I was in his presence took my breath away.

Hold it together, Alice.

When he reached me, he stretched out his hands and took mine. My heart was thumping so fast, there was no way I could dance in front of these people.

'You look gorgeous,' he whispered, kissing me on both cheeks. 'You can do this, I've got you.'

All eyes were on us.

Taking a deep breath, I glanced towards the judging table, and their smiles of encouragement meant the world to me. I swallowed as Sam tipped a wink towards Jim, who cued the music.

'Did you know about this?' I whispered.

But Sam didn't answer. He stood next to me elegantly, squeezed my hand and focused his gaze over the top of the crowd. His presence made every hair on my body tingle with anticipation.

'Ready?'

I nodded and the whole crowd was watching us intently.

'At least give me a clue what we are dancing to.'

The next thing I knew, Sam whispered in my ear, 'Bolero'. The heat of his breath tickled my ear and my whole body throbbed with desire for him.

We stood in our starting position and his lips were millimetres away from mine. I had to tell myself to breathe calmly. I wanted to reach out, and run my fingers along his strong jawline. His skin was smooth, his cheekbones were chiselled and he was utterly gorgeous.

The music began and all eyes were on us.

He held my gaze and slid his hands around my waist. His touch alone sent electricity flying through every nerve in my body. Enjoying the sheer pleasure of his touch, I had to force myself not to gasp out loud.

We began to dance, my nerves disappearing almost instantly as we glided together across the stage. I felt safe in his arms, savouring his every touch. I noticed his pulse in the side of his neck and I took a sharp intake of breath as his finger traced down my spine. Lust glittered from his hazel eyes, still locked on mine. I knew from that look in his eyes that he wanted me as much as I wanted him at that very moment in time. His eyes never left mine, his strong arms held me tightly. We moved slowly and gracefully around the stage and he made me feel like I was the only girl in the world. I lost myself in the music and his arms and I knew I'd fallen for Sam Reid hook, line and sinker. It was like no one else was there and I never wanted this dance to end. As he brought me in close I could feel his breath on my face, the attraction was on fire. All I actually wanted to do was lead him straight off that stage into the bedroom.

As the song drew to its end, temptation hovered between us, his lips so close. The music faded out.

I could barely stand, I was trembling so much. I'd never felt attraction like it in my life. Surely he'd felt that too?

I stood back in the spotlight and waited.

Time slowed.

Within seconds the crowd were on their feet, the applause was deafening. Sam bowed and I curtseyed in grateful recognition.

The beam spread across my face and I flung my arms around Sam's neck, and he lifted me off the floor and spun me around.

'You, Alice Parker, are amazing. I'm proud of you, putting all this together.'

Looking back over the crowd, the feeling of triumph was overwhelming.

A standing ovation – I couldn't quite believe it.

We stood hand and hand in the middle of the stage and I didn't know what was going to happen next.

Sam squeezed my hand and looked adoringly towards me. 'Just in case I forget to tell you later, today is going to be one of the best days of my life.'

'How do you know, it's not over yet?'

'Trust me, I know.' He leaned forward and whispered in my ear, 'I love you, Alice Parker.'

My heart thumped with excitement and I took in a breath.

Things like this never happened to me.

Suddenly the crowd fell silent and we both noticed that Grandie had walked on to the stage and taken the microphone. He extended his hand towards Sam and gave him a hearty handshake.

'Good lad,' said Grandie, 'good lad,' giving Sam a look of admiration before kissing me on the cheek.

Dorothy and all the gang were huddled at the side of the stage watching our every move.

He held the microphone up to his mouth and looked out over the green. 'Tearfully proud, I stand here.'

Again, the green erupted in cheers and we needed to wait for them to calm.

Grandie tried again, the crowd fell silent once more and all eyes were on us. 'Firstly, I want to thank you all for coming here, to Village Day today. Brook Bridge Village has always been my home and I couldn't imagine life without it. When tragedy struck ... my heart was broken in two. Florrie Parker was a huge part of this community and she'll never be forgotten. But ... but for the first time in thirteen years, I've felt that life can move on ... and that's down to Alice and Rose. Welcome home, welcome back to Brook Bridge.' His voice wobbled and I grasped his hand.

'For a long time there has been unrest in this village, unnecessary rivalry that should have been left in the past.'

Grandie continued, 'I want to thank Sam Reid for providing the male dancers for the show and for being by my Alice's side today.'

My heart soared with gratitude to him. He didn't have to say what he did, but I was truly thankful.

'Now for one last time ... after such an eloquent dance, it's time to go over to the judges ... the scores are in!' he bellowed.

Sam and I grinned as we spun towards Mum, Grace and Connie.

'Rose Parker,' prompted Grandie, 'over to you first.'

'You both look the part, played the part and ARE the part!' squealed Mum, hardly able to contain herself.

'Connie Anderson!'

The whole crowd waited in anticipation.

'You two smoulder when you dance! Such intensity!' exclaimed Connie.

'Grace Anderson!'

All eyes were on Grace.

'The footwork was sloppy, more rotation needed in those hips,' she gave Sam a warning look, 'way too many mistakes.'

The crowd booed.

'Only kidding!' she grinned. 'That performance was spine-tingling. There are some dances you just don't want to stop and that was one of those ... and can I just say, Alice Parker ... it's great to have you home!'

The crowd erupted once more as all three judges held up their number-ten paddles.

It took a few minutes for the excitement to settle and I took the microphone from Grandie.

'Speech, speech,' the crowd chanted once more before finally falling silent. All eyes were on me.

'Today has been amazing. There are so many people I want to thank. C'mon ...' I gestured, 'come up on to the stage.'

The whole team streamed on to centre stage, everyone was

hugging and patting each other on the back. This evening had truly been a success.

'Please put your hands together one last time for Dorothy and Bert, who are truly amazing ... for all the ladies from the WI, who have worked so hard to learn their dance routines ... for the boys from *Mamma Mia* for taking part at such short notice ... for Jim and Connie, who have worked so hard sourcing the costumes and working on the staging ... for Grace, for being my best friend ... for Sam, for being there from the second he met me ... for my grandfather and my Mum, for both loving me unconditionally ... and finally, *Brook Bridge Goes Strictly* couldn't have happened without you guys ... the backing of the community. Thank you!'

Everyone cheered and clapped.

'And finally ... and finally ... I've enjoyed every second of teaching the WI ladies to dance. So much so, I'm absolutely delighted to announce that the Florrie Rose School of Dance will be reopening its doors in September. Everyone is welcome!'

Mum was now next to me, handing me a huge bouquet of flowers. She moved the microphone towards her mouth.

'Today Alice has brought this community back together ... three cheers for Alice.'

The crowd responded: *'Hip hip hooray ... hip hip hooray ... hip hip hooray!'*

'There is only one thing left to say,' I announced, encouraging everyone to join in ...

'Just keep dancing!' we all shrieked happily in unison.

As the evening came to an end, Sam took me in his arms

and kissed me tenderly on the lips. I was overcome with emotion and even though tears welled up in my eyes, they were happy ones.

Today was the first day of my future, and everything was now exactly how it was meant to be.

Acknowledgements

Squeal! It's been quite a journey and I really can't believe my seventh book is being published! There is a long list of truly fabulous folk I need to thank who have been instrumental in supporting me and crafting this novel into one I'm truly proud of.

Mum, Dad, Chris, Emily, Jack, Ruby and Tilly, my mad gorgeous family, who inspire me every day. I couldn't do the job I love so much without the support of you all, thank you.

Woody, my mad, crazy cocker spaniel, who is by my side and unquestionably the best company ever.

The clever team at HarperImpulse, Charlotte Ledger and Kimberley Young. Both of course who are utterly fabulous. They have helped, encouraged and believed in me right from the start. My editor, the wickedly smart and simply hilarious Emily Ruston who, in the most awesome way made this book the best it could possibly be.

Thank you to my agent Kate Nash, for your energy, vision, continuous support and faith in me.

Big love to Anita Redfern, my BMITWE. Just remember if

we ever caught, you're deaf and I don't speak English! Thank you for being my one true friend.

Team Barlow! High fives to my merry band of supporters, Catherine Snook, Louise Speight, Suzanne Toner, Sarah Lees, Suzanne Golding, Alison Smithies, Ann Blears, Sue Stevens, Susan Miller, Bhasker Patel, Jason Moreland, Bella Osborne, Lisa Hall, Jenny Berry and Kathy Ford.

A special mention to all the staff at Tamworth Library and especially Debbie Smith who shouts and shares my books at every opportunity. Thank you.

Much thanks to some very special people, all the wonderful readers, book bloggers and followers for reading my books, reviewing my books, tweets, Facebook messages and all the lovely emails too – you rock!

Finally this book wouldn't have been written if it wasn't for Dawn Denman, Shannon and Peter Parker who provided that little spark of inspiration for this story over breakfast. Thank you.

I without a doubt enjoyed writing every second of this book and I really hope you enjoy hanging out with Alice Parker and Sam Reid. Please do let me know!

Warm wishes,

Christie xx

A Letter from Christie

Dear all,

Firstly, if you are reading this letter, thank you so much for choosing to read *A Home at Honeysuckle Farm*.

I sincerely hope you enjoyed reading this book. If you did, I would be forever grateful if you'd write a review. Your recommendations can always help other readers to discover my books.

I can't believe this is my seventh book to be published in the last four years; writing for a living is truly the best job in the world.

I am particularly proud of this novel, the characters of Alice Parker and Sam Reid have been a huge part of my life in the last five months, and I will be sorry to leave them behind. Alice's story is one of self-discovery, love, secrets and learning to be happy in life. I have, without a doubt, enjoyed writing every second of this book.

I want to say a heartfelt thank you to everyone who has been involved in this project. I truly value each and every one of you and it's an absolute joy to hear from all my readers via Twitter and Facebook.

Please do keep in touch!

Warm wishes,

Christie x

Read on for an exclusive look at Christie's novel,

The
COSY CANAL
BOAT DREAM

Chapter 1

Two years later...

Nell heard the creak of the door and looked up, startled, 'Hey, I can't believe you're up so early. I noticed the light on.'

Bea was standing in the doorway of the Nollie, her breath misting. She was wrapped up tightly in her duffel coat, sporting a warm smile and clasping a white paper bag.

'Come on in and shut the door, it's freezing out there.' Nell smiled up at her best friend.

Bea unbuttoned her coat and scooted over to the seat next to her.

'I couldn't sleep, I've had a bit of a restless night,' admitted Nell.

Bea touched her hand affectionately, 'Ollie's birthday?' Her voice was suddenly wobbly.

Nell met her gaze and they shared a sad smile.

'Yes, Ollie's birthday. The first of February.'

For a moment, they sat in silence, 'Cuppa?' Nell asked. 'I think I can squeeze a couple more cups out of the tank and have a shower before the water needs filling up this morning.'

'Yes please, and in there is a couple of warm croissants,' Bea slid the paper bag over the table towards her.

'Have you already been to the deli?'

She nodded, 'I couldn't sleep much either. I'm way ahead of schedule today.'

Bea owned the delicatessen in the hub of the marina called The Melting Pot, which was famous for its hot chocolate, savouries and scrumptious homemade cakes. Nell used to work for her part time, taking care of the accounts, but since Ollie had passed away Bea had taken her under her wing and she now worked for her full time behind the counter of the deli, serving customers, which was a welcomed distraction.

From the first day of high school Nell and Bea's friendship had been cemented over a pair of laddered tights. Bea had saved Nell with a spare pair she'd whipped out of her bag and from that moment they'd become best friends. They'd sat next to each other for the next five years, then from the age of eighteen frequented the local pubs together. Bea had attended catering college and spent most of time testing out new recipes on Nell. Her work ethic was faultless and she'd soon landed a job alongside a well-known chef in the city of Lichfield. This had been Bea's ticket to freedom, and she had escaped her suffocating parents, flown the nest and rented a flat above the delicatessen at the marina.

When the owners of The Melting Pot had decided to sell the business, Bea had immediately snapped it up for herself, whipping it into shape with counter array of cakes, speciality cheeses and flapjacks to die for.

Nell had beamed with such pride for her friend on her first day of opening – the deli was a dream come true for Bea.

Bea was married to Nathan and they had one five-year-old son called Jacob, who was the cutest thing Nell had ever set eyes on. But as his godmother, Nell knew she was biased.

When Ollie had been alive, the four of them had been firm friends and had enjoyed most weekends in each other's company, rambling around the marina and eating Sunday lunches at The Waterfront. Life had been perfect.

'What are you doing after work today?' asked Bea, 'Would you like to come over to the cottage for your tea? Jacob would love to see you.'

'I'd love to see him too, but I'm having tea with Mum, after we've visited the lake.'

Bea nodded, 'How is Gilly? I've not seen her for a couple of weeks.'

Gilly lived down the lane from Bea in Bluebell Cottage, the same property in which Nell had lived for the whole of her life. Gilly was the proud owner of a vintage bicycle with a basket and a bell and could often be seen cycling around the marina.

Nell rolled her eyes and smiled, 'She has her hands full at the moment!'

'Intriguing. What's she up to this time?'

Gilly, who was in her mid-fifties, but appeared much younger than her age, had been drowning in her own grief. Her husband, Nell's father, Benny, had unexpectedly passed away from pneumonia five years ago – an event that had rocked their world. Since then Gilly had thrown herself wholeheartedly into every local crafty organisation in the village, from basket weaving, painting antique furniture and had even joined the pottery club.

'Last week she was ferreting around in the greenhouse at the bottom of the garden when she found a tabby cat curled up in an old blanket on top of a bag of compost. She took it into the cottage and made it up a bed in front of the Aga. She thought it seemed a little unwell and a little plump and decided to make it an appointment at the vets for the following morning. There was no collar or tag. She didn't even know its name, but by the time next morning arrived Mum found three extra bundles of fluff curled up next to the mother.'

'Kittens?'

Nell nodded.

'How wonderful!'

'The little mews made my heart melt; utterly gorgeous to say the least.'

'What's Gilly going to do with them?'

'She's placed a notice in the vets and the local post office, but as yet no one has come forward to claim her. At the moment she's named her Rosie, because she was lying on the bag of compost she uses to plant her roses, and knowing Mum I think she would be quite happy to keep them all!'

'Maybe I could talk Nathan into homing one. I just need to make him think it's his idea and we'd be on to a winner,' she grinned. 'Jacob would love a kitten.'

Nell smiled at Bea. She pictured her curled up in front of the fire after a long hard day at the deli with a kitten snoozing on her lap.

They both finished their tea, then Bea glanced at her watch, 'The scones are due out any minute; I'd best nip back to the shop.'

'What time is it? I feel like I've been up for hours.'

'Just gone 6.45.'

'I have been up for hours.'

'I can easily sort out some cover if you don't feel up to coming in.'

Nell shook her head, 'Thanks, but I need to keep busy. I'll be along as soon as I'm ready.'

Bea gave her a quick hug before flicking the latch and stooping down to climb through the door. Her footsteps echoed on the plank that connected the towpath to the boat as she ambled across towards the deli.

'Right, Nell Andrews, it's time to paint a smile on your face, life must go on,' she murmured to herself, unconvinced, standing up and running her hand over Ollie's photograph while she blinked away the tears. Birthdays and anniversaries always hit her hard.

Five minutes later, she stared at her reflection in the bathroom mirror. 'Jeez, Andrews,' she said out loud, smoothing down her wild hair and washing away the smudged eyeliner.

'I really need to learn to take my mascara off before climbing into bed,' she muttered, reaching for her wash bag. Then, just like every morning, she took out her pack of contraceptive pills. She stared down at Tuesday's pill in the palm of her hand and suddenly had no idea why she was still taking these little pills after all this time. Everything had carried on in the same routine for the last two years. Her life had been on auto-pilot and she'd never wanted to completely let go of it, up until now. Even though Ollie wasn't coming back, she felt strong enough to look towards the future. Nell switched on the tap and made the decision to swill the pill down the sink.

After a quick shower, she twisted her blonde hair up into a bun, threw on her favourite jumper and dabbed on a smidgen of lipgloss. She was ready to face the world. Once outside, the cool morning breeze whispered around her ears as Nell stood on the deck of the 'Nollie' and breathed in the early morning fresh air.

She glanced across towards the blue and gold lettering of a neighbouring boat, 'The Old Geezer'. Fred Bramley had been their neighbour since they'd moved on to the 'Nollie'. Nell found him an interesting character with his grey bushy eyebrows and matching beard. He always wore a flat cap and a nattily kempt white cable knit that resembled a cricket jumper. He was retired and spent most of his days sitting on the deck of the boat fishing, even though in all these years she'd never actually seen him catch anything. For a brief moment the doors of the flagship opened and Fred appeared on the deck clutching a mug of tea.

'Good morning,' chirped Nell, catching his eye.

He tipped his cap in acknowledgement. He was a man of few words but always gave a nod and a smile.